Touching Shadows

By

Peter Williams

© 2018 Peter Williams. All rights preserved

No part of this book may be reproduced, stored in a retrieval system, or transmitted by any means without the written permission of the author.

First published by Amazon 08/01/2018

ISBN: 9781718011137

Dedicated to Alfred and Sidney Williams

Brothers in arms – 1939 to 1945

And to my best friend and wife Heather

together with our wonderful children Daniel, Kelly, Kit and Alexandra

Contents

Cover

Title Page

Dedication

Acknowledgments

Prologue

Chapter One 1940

An Army Nurse

A Phony War

Retreat to Dunkirk

Chapter Two 1940

British Kill French, French Kill British

A Black Woman Called Miriam

The Plymouth Blitz

Chapter Three 1941

A Cornish Haven

The Sea Rescue

A New Love

Chapter Four 1942

Back From The Dead

A Family At War

Goodbye to Cornwall

Chapter Five 1943

The Tide of War Turns

Invasion of Britain

Whites Only – No Blacks

Chapter Six 1944

A Silent Fear

Return to France

Chapter Seven 1945

White Rose of Munich

Return to Cornwall

Epilogue

Acknowledgements:

Many thanks to JC, JG, Capt. J. Madeley, Dan Williams and Kit Williams for many positive ideas and input, together with the ever helpful librarians and volunteers at the following: The St Ives Archive Trust, The British Library, The Imperial War Museum – Reading Room and Audible Centre, BBC Peoples War, The National Archives Kew, The Redruth Cornish Studies Library, Plymouth City Library, Truro Library, Falmouth Library, the RNLI Stations at Ilfracombe, St Ives and Plymouth.

Cover picture – Andrew Ray Photography Cornwall

Prologue

Towednack Church, Cornwall. 20th September 1945

  Despite every effort to drop the metal latch quietly, the heavy oak door seemed designed to punish latecomers as it closed noisily and echoes from her entrance bounced around the unlit shadowy interior of the ancient church.

 Anna Jack stood still before saying 'Good evening church, I'm ever so pleased your door is always open. Well now, as you can see I am back again! Yes, I survived the war, and I am pleased about that now, even though in some ways I feel guilty because I did'

 'Six years is a long time you know to be at war. I was twenty-three when it started and next year I will be thirty, and so much has happened that at times I can hardly believe it'………….

CHAPTER ONE 1940

An Army Nurse

******

A Phoney War

******

Retreat to Dunkirk

An Army Nurse

Cherbourg, 5th January 1940

   Anna Jack was the last to struggle through the narrow entrance onto the open deck and stand in the darkness; the collar of her army greatcoat turned up, shielding most of her face from a cutting Easterly wind as the troop ship rolled slowly in a long heaving swell.

  Holding the top of a kit bag with one hand she held on to a steel cable with the other as the ship left the naval escorts a mile from shore, slowed its speed to a twisting crawl and was guided through the anti-submarine defences of the old sea port into the inner harbour.

  Overnight the troop ship had carried Anna, five other nurses and sisters and over a thousand men of the British Expeditionary Force across the channel from Portsmouth to Cherbourg, the vessel, its two escorting destroyers hidden for most of the uncomfortable zigzagging journey by freezing sleet and driving rain. Quick shafts of yellow light began to dart across the deck and barked orders followed as the soldiers started to assemble on deck, black silhouettes except for the red ends of cigarettes cupped in clenched fists, the murmurs of laughter and chatter, the clanging of rifles and equipment replacing the noise of the engines as the vessel idled and two tug boats started to push and pull the troop ship towards the dock.

  Grey hints of dawn began to reveal the shapes of cranes and the uneven rooflines of warehouses and dockside buildings with the outlines of the young soldiers and nurses starting to form individual faces, most smiling, some looking nervous. There was also a sudden sense of shared excitement, of anticipation mixed with unease as the ships engines were silenced and the metal hull bumped against the quayside. The excitement doubled as soldiers and nurses started to scrabble their way slowly across a slippery, icy deck, eager to disembark and set foot in France.

For the first part of their journey to Rouen they were part of one continuous coil of army lorries, some pulling guns, most full of soldiers, sat like Anna under the thin canvas that covered the sides and roof of each vehicle, while pinched faces looked out of the open backs, numb and perishing with the bitter cold as they passed through Bayeux and Caen.

Ten miles from Caen their lorry veered away from the column of army vehicles onto quieter country roads. Stopping at a village Anna took her turn to sit in the driver's cab and the only source of heat that came from the engine housing and let the freezing numbness of the journey ease away from her feet upwards. Pointing to her watch Anna shouted to the driver of the army lorry above the din of the engine noise 'How much longer do you think?'

The young soldier fed the metal steering wheel quickly through his hands following a tight corner and leaned the top half of his body towards her as he shouted back 'Shouldn't be more than an hour now ma'am.' Lulled by the swaying rhythm of the lorry winding along the country roads and her newly found source of warmth, Anna began to think back over the past four months; four momentous months that had turned her life completely upside down.

She thought back to the day that war had been declared and back to a year before that, when several thousand nurses, doctors and surgeons throughout the country had been asked if they would volunteer to put their names forward for call up in the event of another war starting. Vivid memories came to her of Sunday the 3rd of September, two miles from the Houses of Parliament, and the red bricked Victorian buildings of St Mary's hospital, which were hidden from the warmth of the hot morning sun by the shadow of the ornately arched railway viaduct that towered above it, taking clattering trains across the river Thames, into the heart of London.

Inside the cheerless building Anna sat with hospital colleagues in a small staff room, the walls painted in two shades of bleached green to the cigarette yellowed ceiling. The wall opposite the half glass door of the room was dominated by a hand tinted print of the King and Queen, the wan colours giving some vigour to a backdrop of limp imperial flags and closed mouthed lions.

Each person in the room sat silently staring at the wood fretwork rising sun, cut from the walnut case of an *'Echo'* wireless set, the silence broken by the monotone voice of a BBC announcer until Ellen Smith, a dark-haired nursing orderly, spoke out nervously 'Well, well if there is a war it will all be over in months,' before adding in a quieter voice, 'least ways, that's what my Andy says.'

No one in the room commented but Anna Jack noticed Bill Munro, a porter at the hospital, massaging his right leg and the scars that hid metal fragments of a mortar shell from a Flanders battlefield in 1917.

At eleven fifteen in a solemn and grave voice Neville Chamberlain told the people of the Britain and the World, the grim news that finally ended the years of political appeasement and the forlorn hope for a lasting peace in Europe. Anna sat listening to the dispirited politician as he spoke the chilling words "As a consequence this country is now at war with Germany". She sat still and quiet in her chair until a shiver ran from her neck the length of her spine.

A war had started and there was a heavy silence in the small dull room as each of them absorbed the news and for a few moments they were bound by a common sadness and quiet personal numbness. Throughout Europe many believed that a war was inevitable, but most hoped it was not, and for the majority of ordinary people in Berlin and Paris that hot Sunday morning they shared the same stunned moments of silence and disbelief as their neighbours in London.

As the Prime Minister's announcement finished the national anthem was played and Anna watched as Bill Munro eased himself up awkwardly and stood to a painful attention, while he mouthed unheard words. He was quickly joined by the others in the claustrophobic room, all giving silent homage, except Ellen Smith who sang loudly and boldly as if speaking directly to the couple in front of her and their protective lions.

The music finished, the hospital porter reached the wireless and turned the black Bakelite dial until it clicked and the set was switched off. As the glass radio valves inside the wood case grew cold the slowly fading voices of the BBC were replaced by a new sound that reached the room as the grave and sombre wailing of air raid sirens started drifting over London and the solo singer slumped back heavily onto her chair, covered her face with her hands and began to sob in deep shuddering breaths.

Anna Jack stood above her, gently squeezed her right shoulder with one hand and remained silent. Listening to the young woman weeping and to the stomach-churning sound of the air raid sirens she realised with sad, deep clarity that her life had changed, and it would never be the same again.

Minutes after listening to the dispirited voice of Neville Chamberlain she was asked to report to her Matron. On her desk was a large buff coloured envelope, hand written at the top of it was Anna's name while further down the page, printed in bold black letters she read "Only to be opened in the event of War". Inside were instructions for her to report to a military hospital at Aldershot.

Anna remembered the reactions from her parents as she sat at the kitchen table of their home in north London. The hug from Mary, her mother, the solemn look on her father's face as he waited until his wife left the room before he put a hand over his daughter's and said 'Anna, you have to be especially careful. The legacy of my religion goes with you and the country we are now at war with has a special hatred for me and my kind. There's madness in the land where I was born and it's a madness that is very, very cruel,' the doctor stood up slowly, still holding Anna's hand and kissed the top of her head before finishing 'be careful, be safe Anna, and please, please do not forget what I said.'

'Up ahead, ma'am, that's the hospital'

Anna blinked and shook her head in an effort to clear her mind as she shouted back at the driver 'Sorry, what was that you said?'

'The hospital is right ahead of us, ma'am.'

On ground that sloped gently upwards she saw in the distance a large château with cone shaped turrets at each corner of a long roof covered in dark grey slates.

'It looks very grand from here, not a bit like a hospital to me!' she shouted.

As they got closer she could see rippling Red Cross banners hanging below the roof at each corner and in the centre of the châteaux. The driver laughed before replying 'Yes ma'am, I had the same thoughts when I saw it first. Châteaux Musar was a very posh hotel before the war, and a long time before that it was a royal residence for one of the French King's.'

Châteaux Musar, 6th January, 1940

A richly painted ceiling depicting bold Knights and soldiers being slain on a bloody battlefield claimed the attention of the grey-haired officer as he leaned against the corner of an ornate antique desk, looking up as the newly arrived nursing sisters filed into the library and stood behind carved oak chairs.

The commanding officer blinked several times and he sighed heavily before he looked towards the group and walked behind the desk, remaining standing and placing his hands on the leather top as he said 'Good morning ladies, please sit down and welcome to Chateaux Musar, or No 4 British General Hospital to give this beautiful building its very unbeautiful war time name'

'You will know by now that my name is Colonel Derek Wilson, and that the lady behind me is Mary Atkins, your Matron. What you would not know is that apart from years and years in the medical profession, Matron and I have another thing in common, and that is that we both served in the last war on the battlefields of France and Belgium', glancing up at the ceiling before continuing he said 'Ladies, if man's determination to kill and wound each other has not changed very much over the past years I am very pleased to tell you that the level of help and medical care we are now able to provide has advanced out of all recognition, and that is why we are all here.'

The sombre demeanour of the officer lifted as he continued 'Over the next weeks we are going to create four independent, mobile casualty clearing stations, or CCS's in short'

'Each of our CCS units will consist of two surgeons, anaesthetists, sisters and nursing orderlies, plus drivers and cooks, and be able to carry out emergency surgical field operations on the spot, and close to any battle front'

'What we will be creating was pioneered during the last war, and we firmly believe that our CCS's will provide battlefield care never seen or available in any other conflict. Ladies we now have an opportunity to work together as a team and be ready for the so called "Phoney War" to end and the real battles to start, so be prepared for hard work and a lot of excitement when the balloon does go up!'

He finished by saying 'One last thing. France is a fascinating country with surprises at every corner, so take my advice and in between all the hard work, take time to look around you, and take every opportunity to get to know the country, and of course, its people. And finally, good luck to you all!'

Paris, 16th January, 1940

The promise of hard work from their commanding officer was delivered in full as long days rolled at times into long nights with few periods of rest except when the pace was cut by the army's bureaucracy that would send officers and quartermasters into bellowing rages as materials failed to materialise and exercises would grind to a stop.

By mid-morning work had ground to an edgy halt and in the mess tent at lunch time John McCloud, one of the two surgeons with Anna's unit, announced to the nursing sisters 'Right ladies, I am pleased to tell you that my fellow surgeon, and soon to be Lord of the Realm, Major Peter Adnans, using his future title and a secret handshake, has got us a pass to travel in a supply vehicle to a railway station which is an hour from one of the most beautiful capital cities in the World, Paris!'

'Those that can, and of course would like too, we have to leave in half an hour, so please get your skates on, and them that want to stay in this depressing monastery, well you must be plain daft!'

Anna, Alison Forbes, Jan Mitchell and Margaret Doyle were ready in twenty minutes. Removing their white headdresses, blue and grey uniforms they replaced them with the compulsory grab of an itchy khaki shirt, tie, trousers and battledress top, before putting on a khaki beret, and their long army greatcoats.

The steam engine hissed and jerked into Gare du Nord station, joining four other panting and vibrating passenger trains resting at platforms, and in the wake of John McCloud and Peter Adnans they walked the short distance to the metro which brought them into the heart of Paris.

Following the north countryman like a party of boisterous school children the group hurried through manicured gardens, past statues, spouting fountains and under the shadow of the Eiffel tower before they reached a busy road where Major McCloud secured two tables on the pavement outside the Café Marque in time to catch the last of the winter sun.

Peter Adnans ordered a bottle of champagne and after the

waiter had eased away the cork the surgeon filled their glasses and raised his glass to John McCloud and the nurses before saying 'Ladies and gentleman, here's to us. To us and our few hours of freedom from the army when we can speak to each other by name and not rank and of course to the sincere hope that the war will be over soon and we can all pack up and jolly well go home!'

The chill of the last of the day was forgotten as they drank their champagne and looked at the Paris of January from under the café's awning of opaque frosted panes, each line of glass separated by inch wide black metal struts, the whole roof supported by elaborate cast iron arms.

Café Marque stood on a bustling, noisy avenue, shoulder to shoulder with other restaurants and bars where tables and chairs advanced onto the pavement, while across the uneven square cobbles of the road that separated them, a similar assortment of venues stood behind tall horse chestnut trees spaced along the cobbled walk way, each one protected by a metal cage at their base.

Anna and John McCloud sat next to each other. Without looking at her he said 'I spent three glorious months in Paris in 1937 trying to organise a medical mission to go back to Spain. I had a grand time here, absolutely wonderful.'

'Go back to Spain?' Anna asked.

Nodding he replied 'Aye, well we got thrown out by the very side we went to help, and, well it got very confused, very messy, too many different factions pulling in different directions, much to the delight of General Franco and his butchers.'

'Where did you live?'

'Montparnasse, of course! Ah, a great place Anna. Now our Lord Peter over there, bless him, would hate it, too messy and dirty for him, but I loved it. It was a special moment in my life after the civil war in Spain. If we get another opportunity Anna, I'll take you there if you like?'

Raising her glass Anna smiled and gave him a gentle nod in silent agreement before asking 'Is Mr Adnans really going to be a Lord?'

Tilting his head towards her his eyes held hers for several

moments before he shook his head and said 'I'm sorry, I didn't mean to stare, but you have the most beautiful, beautiful eyes!' Not waiting for any kind of reply or reaction he carried on by adding quickly 'Yes, now then, Major Peter with lots of silly middle names Adnans, aged twenty-eight, first son of Lord and Lady Roxenton, the unrepentant recipient of a classical public-school education and of the wealth that provided it, single, and before the outbreak of war widely thought of as one of the country's most gifted surgeons.'

Topping up both of their glasses from the new bottle of champagne that had arrived, he added 'That is our Peter......Oh, and I forgot to mention that he is a really nice bloke, one of the richest people in the country and more importantly, he is certainly the best surgeon I have ever worked with.'

Quickly studying the man she sat beside, she thought 'You really are handsome.' He was only slightly taller than she was, but broad shouldered, stocky even. His black hair was longer than the army liked and the shadow of a beard was not far from his angular face. 'Yes, I do like you!' she thought.

Leaving the café the Paris Anna saw and heard seemed much more relaxed than the London she had recently left, despite the badly enforced blackout attempts. Walking beside John McCloud she asked 'Is there really a war on? Just look around, beautiful, elegant women arm in arm with dashing men, laughing and joking with each other, everything seems so peaceful.'

Breathing deeply he tutted twice before answering 'Afraid so Anna. Aye, afraid so,' turning towards her he added loudly 'but not here tonight young lady, so come on, let's enjoy ourselves!'

Shouting over his shoulder he said 'Come on you lot, I really am starving, and I'm going to take you to a great place I used to eat in all the time when I was living here before the war.'

Walking quickly across several roads and streets in the gathering dusk they suddenly turned down a narrow lane towards the muffled sound of people and music. Stopping outside the boarded-up front of what could have been a grocery shop, a bakery or a butchers he gently guided Anna into a black void before saying 'In you go mademoiselle!'

The outside door closed behind her she pulled back the thick blackout curtain and stepped into Bistro Corsaire. After the near darkness of the Paris evening the restaurant, and its mixture of bright lights, loud music, louder voices and drifting cigarette smoke made her shake her head and blink her eyes before she looked back towards the entrance and at the two men and three women she had arrived with and watched as John McCloud shouted 'Tino, Tino mon amie!' loudly above the mayhem around them.

Looking up from the young girl and older woman he was talking to, Tino Sablon frowned and squinted before he broke into a broad grin and came striding towards them. The man hugged the officer who had shouted to him before kissing him on both cheeks and patting him hard on his back with his closed fists as he shouted instructions to busy waiters who hurriedly pushed and pulled two tables noisily together before he hurried away.

The bright red oil cloths that covered each table were given a wipe before chairs appeared and they sat down, adding to the noise of the bistro as their chairs scraped over ceramic floor tiles, the noise amplified by the tiled walls and high ceilings of the long room.

Glasses, bottles of wine and food started to magically appear on the tables and the new diners melted into the fabric of the restaurant as they ate, drank and added their voices and loud laughter to the ebb and flow of the evening.

Anna eased her chair next to John McCloud who had been greeted by the Frenchman, saying 'You seem very much at home here, what a great place, I really love it, it's got a very exciting feel to it. How did you get to know Tino?'

Nodding and looking towards the owner of the restaurant the skin around his eyes formed deep laughter lines as he shook his head slowly while at the same time he said 'Tino is some character Anna, some wild character. He was one of the first to join the International Brigade and fight in the civil war in Spain. I met him in Barcelona, where sadly we left many good friends; far too many to be honest.'

In the middle of talking to each other they were suddenly

split up by the arrival of the owner who ploughed a chair between them and straddled the seat before letting his huge frame lower itself slowly onto it.

Taking Anna's right hand, he kissed the back of it before saying 'Welcome to my restaurant mademoiselle, welcome,' turning quickly to John McCloud, he put his arm around his shoulders saying 'John, my dear friend, it's so good to see you again. I've missed you, damn it! Missed you, and missed the others as if the lights had been turned off.'

Moving his head slowly side to side Tino said 'We were right comrade, eh, sadly right. Franco's pigs win and now we have Hitler to deal with, but of course you know our government will do a deal with the bastards, don't you?'

Not waiting for a reply, he banged a bottle of brandy he had been holding on the table and motioned for a waiter to bring glasses for all of them before saying 'I fear the worst, my friend. Rumours are already going around that anyone tinged with any links to the communist, socialist or trade unions are being watched by the police,' tapping the side of his large nose he whispered into John's ear 'if things become difficult and the government cave in to the German fascists I will go to Russia and fight the bastards from there, fuck them, fuck each and every one of them!'

Slapping the table top loudly with the flat of one hand he looked around the group before saying 'A toast comrades. A toast to my good friend John McCloud and to you, his friends!'

Peter Adnans responded to the good wishes of the Frenchman before dancing with each of the nursing sisters in turn as an accordion player was joined by a guitarist and a trio was formed with the arrival of a young girl and her violin.

It was John McCloud that held Anna for the last dance and said 'Thank you Miss Jack, for just a few hours you made me forgot about the army, the war, and all the nonsense that goes with it! But sadly, its time to make a move back to the hospital.'

Tino followed them through the blackout curtain and double doors into the narrow lane outside his restaurant and embraced each of them as he wished them 'Bon Voyage'.

Turning to Anna he said quietly 'Be brave young lady, dark and sinister shadows are gathering and sadly I think death is on the way. Be brave, and good luck! Ah, also, please take care of my friend John, he is a good man, one of the very best!'

Retracing their footsteps to the metro and then the railway station they climbed into the back of the army lorry for the last part of their journey through the night.

Sat in the back of the vehicle with only the canvas cover between her and the cold night Anna sank deeply into her khaki greatcoat looking at the road in the silver moonlight as it disappeared like a swirling river.

The noise of the vehicle with its open back made conversation impossible but Anna was pleased; it gave her the opportunity to turn over in her mind the events of the evening.

The voice was distant and not welcome. Anna was happy in her dream as she danced with John McCloud, happy as she brushed past other couples with him. 'I really do like you!' was her last thought as a hand pressed her shoulder and the lorry came to a halt at the entrance to Chateaux Musar.

Chateaux Musar, 17th January, 1940

'Did yesterday really happen?' Alison Forbes asked as the nurses walked together like a chattering knot of sparrows towards the mess tent for breakfast.

Jan Mitchel was first to answer 'Oh yes, and I'll tell what girls, I loved it, really loved every naughty minute of it. And why are you so sullen Marg? You certainly weren't when you were dancing with your French sailor!'

Margaret Doyle blushed deeply before saying 'I'll tell you this now, four months ago the furthest I'd ever travelled was to Cork where I did my nursing training, and now here I am gallivanting around bars and restaurants in Paris of all places, and all I have to say is that I agree with you Jan, I loved it! I feel mightily guilty, but I really loved every exciting moment of last night, God forgive me!'

Alison then glanced at Anna 'Sister Jack, you should be

sullen but seem to have a rather permanent smile on your face. Is there any reason for that?'

She was about to answer when they all stopped and turned around as they heard John McCloud shout 'Good morning ladies, wonderful sunny day. Sister Jack, could I have a word please.' She waited for him as the other nursing sisters carried on towards the mess tent with heads nodding and the hushed sounds of suppressed giggles going with them.

Stepping into line next to her as they set off in the same direction he said 'I had a great day out yesterday Anna, and thank you for your company.'

Deciding it was best not to look directly at him she starred ahead and said 'It was a special treat Major, and thank you. Perhaps we could repeat it sometime?'

'Yes, well. Well the thing is you see, I've managed to wrangle a three day leave pass at the end of the month to visit a friend I qualified with who is stationed at Rennes. Well, well I was wondering, if we kept it quiet of course, and you would have to tell a little white lie to Matron, well I was wondering whether perhaps you may want to come with me? Although you probably can't of course, which is absolutely no problem, and I will certainly understand.'

A Phoney War

Rennes, 2nd February 1940

   Mary Atkins gave Anna a leave pass to visit a friend and worked extra shifts in order to earn the favour. Arriving early for the train to Rennes she lifted the collar of her khaki greatcoat to eyebrow level to keep out the morning cold until the engine arrived in front of the packed platform, shuddered its metal body, belched white smoke that scattered pigeons from iron roof trusses and hissed clouds of steam from under the front bogey wheels that engulfed passengers waiting at the edge of the concourse.

   Major McCloud merged with the throng of other passengers and was squeezed into a first-class compartment, one carriage along from Anna. The train, almost an hour late, wheezed away from the station leaving it in a fog of steam and smoke.

   Reaching Rennes Anna was carried along by the exiting travellers through the station barrier until she felt an arm under hers and a voice saying 'Phew, Anna, I'm glad we're off that blooming train. Got to grab a Taxi, hold on.'

   Arriving at the Hotel du Parc he looked at his watch 'I'm really hungry, lets leave the luggage at the reception and go into the restaurant before they stop serving lunch, and I must ring Neil as soon as we've ordered.'

   Their table was next to a window overlooking a formal municipal park gripped by winter and studded with idle fountains and ornamental ponds, the one in front of them shaded by the hotel and still covered by a thin layer of ice.

   Camellia bushes were dotted around the park, the red and pink blossoms at odds with the bare winter landscape; the fallen mush of petals marking bright splodges of colour on the ground beneath them.

   Finishing lunch John sat back and studied Anna before speaking 'Ah, well the truth is when I phoned Neil he offered me his motorbike for a couple of days, I won't mind if you don't want to, but do you fancy a trip to the coast tomorrow, on the back of it?'

She was a bit surprised to hear herself saying 'Why should I mind, I think it's a splendid idea! And where are you going to take me?'

Exhaling his breath loudly he started with a 'Phew!', before continuing 'That's grand Anna, I just wasn't sure about the bike, whether you like them and so on, but I do know you will like where we will go, it's a place called Pont-Aven on the Brittany coast.'

When John spoke next, he haltingly said 'Ah, another thing we have to decide is whether you want your own room or not.' Without looking at her he quickly added 'Excuse me Anna, I just need to go to the little boys room a second.'

Amused and also touched by his awkwardness when he returned she gave him a stern, disapproving look, while he nervously scratched his chin until she leaned across the table touching his hand and saying 'John, it would make me very happy if we could spend the next couple of days together' quickly putting a finger to her lips she added 'No, please don't!'

Puzzled he asked, 'What do you mean?'

Smiling she said, 'Please don't say 'Phew' again!'
The manager took details of their identity cards before they went to their room and opening the French windows he stepped onto a small balcony that overlooked the same park they saw from the dining room when he heard Anna shout from the bathroom 'My God, the bath is enormous, oh, please can I use it first John?'

Stepping back into the room he kissed her before saying 'Of course you can, but Anna, I just want to tell you, or to say thank you for, for....'

She touched his lips with her fingers before saying 'Please relax John. I really am so happy to be here with you, the two of us away from the army for a short while, so thank you for inviting me.'

Anna lit the five candles that were in the bathroom before turning off the electric light and watching the hot gushing water tumbling into the white metal bath, dispersing the honey scented bath salts she had poured from a topaz coloured

Lalique bottle, breathing deeply on the billowing swirls of fragrant steam while she lazily took off her uniform.

Stepping into the water and holding the rim of the bath on each side she eased herself down, her eyes closing very slowly as the hot water rushed around her, stopping under her chin, leaving Anna with a gentle floating sensation in the shadowy darkness and tepid heat of the room.

Wrapped in a towel Anna walked slowly and silently back into the soft light of the bedroom and towards John who was standing with his back to her looking out of the French windows. She put her arms around him and turned him gently around while looking up into his face and kissed him.

It was dark outside their bedroom window when they were woken up by the sound of the telephone ringing loudly besides the bed. John answered quickly, but still sleepily, 'Neil, I am sorry, I fell asleep, but I'll be down in a moment.'

She joined the two friends in the bar of the hotel where John introduced him 'Anna, this is Neil Bell. Neil, I'd like you to meet Anna Jack.'

Shaking her hand Neil Bell smiled as he said 'Hello Anna, I've been told so much about you I feel we've known each other for years! Now come on you two, I've booked a table at my favourite restaurant in town.'

The gossip, banter and laughter between the two single friends went back and forth across the dining table throughout their meal, with Anna included in each story of unknown events and past history. Reaching across the white table cloth John put a hand on top of hers, and squeezed it gently before saying 'Neil has recently returned from the Maginot Line Anna. So what is it like Neil?'

The tall, fair-haired doctor sighed deeply before beginning 'Well now, the engineering of the fortifications is very impressive indeed, but my goodness the poor state of the men and equipment is more than a bit depressing'

'John and I have talked about this before, but do you know the history of the Line Anna?'

'Only what I've seen in the Pathe newsreels in the cinema and my father's view that it is a waste of men and money!'

Nodding in approval Neil looked at Anna before saying

'Sadly, your father is probably right on both counts. The most glaring fact for me is that the fortifications stop at the Belgian border, leaving a gap of over two hundred miles to the coast which is completely mad!'

Interrupting his friend John asked 'Is it true that there is a lot of animosity and general argy-bargy between the French and British soldiers?'

'Afraid it is true John' Chuckling, he added 'The only thing Jerry lobs over at the moment are words. Pure propaganda most of it but some nights, just before dark, they start to broadcast on their loud speakers, poking fun at the French all the time.'

'What do they say?' Anna asked.

The surgeon continued 'They keep saying that while they are stuck in dug outs and pill boxes, the British are going off with their wives and girlfriends and because we get three times more money than the French, we are supposed to be having a right old time, bit of a holiday, sort of.'

'Puzzled, Anna said 'Is any of it true?'

Guiltily he answered 'Sadly, I have to say, yes, it is!'

Pont-Aven, 3rd February 1940

A narrow shaft of sunshine had woken Anna as it streamed through the window and a chink in the curtains of their bedroom five minutes before a gentle knock on the door was followed by a voice that announced the arrival of a breakfast tray.

After placing the tray of fresh croissants, rolls, jams and coffee on a table close to the bed the young girl who had delivered it gave Anna a description of the weather outside before leaving.

Twenty minutes later an excited John McCloud burst into the room. 'Anna, you won't believe what's outside, it's fabulous and Neil even lent me his camera, look.' John's articulated excitement surrounded the Norton 350cc motorcycle that Neil Bell had bought over from England on his last leave.

'John' she replied, 'You look very windswept, cold and in no condition to have your photograph taken, would you like a cup of hot coffee instead?'

Holding the cup in his hand he looked into a mirror. Smiling, he quickly agreed about the dishevelled way he looked as he sat on the edge of the bed sipping the hot drink and looking mischievously at Anna who was sat propped by every pillow on it, a cup of coffee in one hand the other holding the white cotton bed sheet in place under her chin.

Her thick jet-black hair, normally tied up into a tight formal bun and hidden under a white head dress or khaki beret, rested on the olive skin of both shoulders, framing a long neck, slender face and deepest of dark brown eyes, arched by thicker than usual eyebrows.

'You look like a Modigliani painting Anna.'

Placing the empty coffee cup back on the breakfast tray Anna said, 'Mr McCloud, it is my considered opinion as a nurse that you are dangerously close to catching pneumonia and that without access to any form of medication I can only suggest that you allow me to warm you up by placing your cold body next to my warm one, before we start our epic journey across La Belle France!'

Anna was an immediate convert to the motor cycle. After two hours on the road travelling south west towards the coast, under grey clouds that had replaced the early sunshine, John brought the machine to a halt outside a roadside café in the centre of an unnamed village, the signpost put into storage to deny invading troops its identity.

'What do you think Anna, bloody cold I know but this Norton is a super piece of engineering, eh?'

Grabbing his outstretched hand Anna lifted herself off the pillion seat putting both feet on the ground only to find her legs unable to support the rest of her body unaided. Expecting her reaction John supported both of her elbows whilst at the same time scooping her into his army greatcoat and laughing.

'Wobbly knees Anna, and it certainly isn't because of me!' Looking at her with an inquisitive frown he added 'Now tell me the truth young lady, was that the first time you've been on a motorbike?'

Linking an arm through his they walked towards the café as

she said 'I'm bloody hopeless at lying! My mother always catches me out and, well yes it was!'

Tugging at his coat sleeve she added 'But I loved it John, really loved it! Will you let me drive the beast later?'

Shaking his head slowly from side to side he answered with a smile 'I suspect I will have little or no option ma'am,' before adding 'at home in North Wales my mum and dad look after my pride and joy, a 1935 Ariel Red Hunter; which after you is the most beautiful object I have ever seen!'

Leaving the small village the Norton headed towards the coast where a wrong turn took them close to the shoreline and with it the sudden appearance of the military build-up and of coastal defences, sights both wanted to avoid.

Turning inland they came to a stop at a fork in the road and John shouted above the engine noise 'Here we are, Pont-Aven. I've been here before Anna, once with my parents when I was a child and then with Neil after we had graduated and we passed through the village on our motorbikes, you'll love it!'

They took a room above the Café du Baron, in the centre of the village. Eager to explore, the visitors were quick to leave it, staying on the same side of the cobbled square as they walked towards the Gothic spire of a church, the lower part of the building hidden by the roof tops of houses in front of it, the River Aven on their right.

Low grey clouds made the February afternoon dank and dull. Many of the shops had their wooden shutters closed to business with other shop windows left in the dim light of winter, their products covered by check or plain coloured squares of fabric.

'At least the cafes' and bars are still very open, fancy a coffee and cognac?' John said steering Anna towards a glass door, where a curtain of faintly yellowed lace prevented a clear view of the inside and matched others hanging from the only long window of the cafe, to the right of the entrance.

Thick tobacco smoke and a burning peat fire, set in a granite surround, welcomed them and an equally warm welcome came from an elegant looking middle-aged woman standing behind the wood panelled bar. 'Good afternoon' she said in English, rapidly followed by 'Do you speak French?' and thankfully accepting Anna's response she continued in her own language 'Thank goodness, my total English has just been exhausted! What would you like?'

They sat at a table close to the fire, acknowledging the nods and hellos from other customers, all the same age group, or older than the proprietress who had introduced herself as Marie.

Two cognacs arrived followed shortly after by the coffee which Marie placed on the table before saying 'You almost have the village to yourselves! Are you staying long?'

'Only for a couple of days' Anna answered, adding 'But you are right, it is very, very quiet!'

Nodding, the café owner said 'It will liven up a little at the weekend, but most of our young people have gone to be soldiers, and the village has lost its heart for the moment, so we are very pleased to see you!'

John McCloud asked, 'Are any of the galleries open today?'

'Oh, certainly' she said and the café owner looked across to the other customers saying, 'Who do you think will be open this afternoon?'

With instructions not to cross the Aven but walk fifty yards past the bridge on the same side of the road, the couple thanked Marie, nodded a goodbye to her cliental, opened the door and began to stroll along the uneven grey cobbles, turned to a dense black colour by a steady drizzle.

Looking into the darkened windows of closed galleries John could not stop talking: 'You know, this place has been famous for over a hundred years Anna, with painters like Gauguin, Emile Bernard, Van Gogh and lots of other artists, who flocked here, inspired by the Breton coastline, the richness of light, and perhaps a certain sense of freedom from Paris.'

John pulled at her sleeve, saying 'Look Anna, this must be the one. It seems to be open and the owner of the studio is working at the back of it, let's go in.'

Walking into the cold studio the painter introduced himself as Georges Viseup before adding 'So, good afternoon. Come on in, come on in. I need to stretch my back and take a holiday from my easel. Now tell me, will you both share a glass of wine with me?' and without waiting for a reply the painter continued 'Yes, good!'

Anna was the first to speak after they had introduced themselves 'Monsieur Viseup, your English is very good, but I must practice my French! And we would love to share your wine, thank you.'

The French artist, in his sixties or perhaps early seventies, had long silver hair that ran into a matching curling beard. His black smock had the same look as his pallet, with bright smudges and blobs of paint running down the front of it, while the blue trousers he wore finished as they disappeared into the tops of calf length black leather boots.

'Thank you for the compliment Anna, but ah you English, always so formal, Georges please! But yes, during the last war I was a liaison officer with an American army regiment and the visitors, and also painters, in peacetime from Britain and Ireland have given me the opportunity to keep my skill. So, tell me, what brings you here to my little village in the middle of a bleak winter, the war or the peace?'

John McCloud spoke for them, this time in English, as he said 'Both. We are escaping the war to get some peace! But alas monsieur only for a couple of days.'

After handing a glass to each of his visitors the painter, in a melancholy way, raised his glass to them 'Let us hope for a return to peace, return to sanity and away from this madness. My God, so soon after the last terrible war how could anyone endure another?'

In a lighter mood the painter showed them his work and talked about his years in the village, and after refilling their glasses he said 'I love it here at this time of year, no crowds, even the wind and rain are my friends in winter' the Frenchman paused while he thought for a moment and continued 'but you have a village in Cornwall, no, no, in fact two, St Ives and Newlyn, where the light, countryside and coastline are similar to my Brittany. I went over the channel on a fishing boat and stayed in St Ives for over a month in the early thirties. I had a wonderful time of things I must say.'

With the light fading Georges rubbed both of his eyes before saying 'My old eyes have had enough for today, and my feet are blocks of ice. Will you please join me at my local bar for a drink and I can then tell you the history of Brittany and of our struggle to keep our own cultural identity and language from the interfering bureaucrats of Paris over the centuries!'

Standing at the polished zinc bar of Café Aven were two painters about the same indeterminable age as Georges Viseup, together with a baker and retired business man. Accepting more wine the visitors talked to the regulars of the small bar as the light outside faded completely and a thin drizzle of rain began to obscure the windows that looked out over the main square of the old mill town.

Topping up their glasses the baker said 'The one thing we all have in common is the fact that we all fought in the last war. This country lost a million of its young people, the Germans lost many more,' the baker shook his head several times before he continued 'no, my belief is that Hitler has what he wants and the politicians will find a way for peace.' Each one of the veterans shared the same optimistic view.

The couple ate with Georges Viseup and outside the café after their meal he said 'What a pleasant and unexpected pleasure to meet you both. You have made a winter's day warmer, now I want you to promise you will come back as soon as a peace has been declared!' It was an easy promise for the couple to make and they talked about their return as they walked through the quiet, dark village in the steady drizzle and chilly wind.

Pont-Aven, 4th February 1940

'Now, my sweet, lovely girl, we have one day of freedom left. Andre, the proprietor's son, has told me about a favourite spot that all young lovers visit, and it is not an ugly tangle of barbed wire fences and machine gun emplacements, so one more top up of coffee, and off we go!'

John had been taking pictures since they arrived but it was Anna that asked if they could have one taken of the two of them in front of the main stone bridge that spanned the river in the centre of the village and an enthusiastic village postman was eager to fulfil their request and snapped away while he spoke of the terrible state of the world in which they lived.

Approaching the coast, the landscape began to change. The hedge rows disappeared and dense gorse and thick brown ferns took over from grass and pasture land.

Road turned to track, the track to bare earth and rock until John stopped the motorbike, and pulled it back onto its metal stand. The last two hundred yards was on foot. It was easy walking, and arm in arm they simply followed the well warn path trodden by countless couples over countless centuries.

They stopped to look at twelve weather-worn, irregular shaped stones, each about four feet high and forming a perfect circle. At the centre was one granite pillar that was much taller than the others, its top shaped to a stunted point by the wind and rain.

'I wonder what primitive tribe or religion put them up, Anna?' John asked.

Anna held on to his arm tightly, saying 'Feels a bit odd here, I feel almost drawn towards the centre, really odd! Come on, let's go into the middle John, come on, I can't help myself!'

She led a reluctant John McCloud into the circle of ancient stones. He frowned before saying 'I'm not sure I want too Anna.'

Laughing she said, 'Don't be daft John, come on!'

Reaching the centre stone Anna put her arms around it and took both of his hands in hers, saying 'I think this has been done for many centuries, perhaps thousands of years John by many pairs of lovers, probably completely naked, but it's a bit cold for that.'

Teasing the eternal doubter and man of science she tightened her grip on his hands and added 'John, who knows what strange evocations will take place when we break the circle!'

'You can be bloody scary at times Anna, wouldn't surprise me if you were a witch in another life; when these stones were put up!'

Breaking the circle, they kissed each other several times between laughing and heading towards the cliffs and the sea.

Approaching the barren granite headland, the wind became stronger, blowing in long fierce gusts, buffeting the couple as they held on to each other.

Water became visible on both sides of the cape as they neared it, the snow-white caps of the surging waves breaking up the deep blue colour of the sea.

A path led them under the point of the headland to a sheltered half circle of rock where the wind eased the further they went in. Cold, but now able to talk without shouting they sat down on granite seats carved over centuries by the wind and rain that swept the headland.

The view that had opened up was both beautiful and spectacular. The rugged Breton coast stretched for mile after mile in front of them, while waves crashed loudly against rocks, sending sheets of spray a hundred feet or more into the air that then drifted over the shoreline to filter the winter sun and make dazzling arches of two bright rainbows.

Anna and John watched two fishing boats as they gouged their way forward through the troughs of the waves, spilling splodges of white onto the darkest of indigo blue canvas as they inched their way slowly out to sea.

They sat close together with their arms linked and gazed at the scene of wild beauty saying nothing. Sitting until they grew cold a gentle squeeze of hands signalled the time to go back.

Within sight of the motorbike they stopped and turned around for one last look.

Anna kissed John's cheek saying, 'This year or next, I would like to come back here in the spring time and make love to you'

'Is that a promise?'

'Anna pressed herself into his army greatcoat saying, 'It's a promise, and I only hope it can be this year.'

Rennes, 5th February 1940

Rain followed them back to Rennes. Pestered incessantly by Anna, John pulled off the main road onto a track and let Anna drive the Norton. She ranted and raved saying 'That was fantastic John! Please, please let me have a little longer.'

His next problem was getting her off the driver's seat which she did only on the promise of another lesson before reaching their destination.

They met Neil Bell in the Hotel du Parc café and reluctantly handed back the motorbike and waterproofs he had loaned them. Neil said he would get the photographs developed and keep them until the next visit.

Steering Anna away from John he said, 'There is no doubt in my mind we are going to see each other often, crikey Anna, I've never seen John so happy!'

******

It took almost three more weeks for the team to pull together all the resources, and to practice the procedures to travel to and erect their mobile medical facilities to the satisfaction of themselves and their commanding officer.

Derek Wilson stood smiling in front them before saying 'Right then, all of you. First of all, I have to say that I am absolutely delighted by the efficiency and energy that you have displayed over the past weeks'

'I know it's been hard work, and in difficult circumstances, but I am pleased to be able to tell you that at 08.00 tomorrow morning we will start our journey across France towards the Maginot Line and the border with Germany'.

An unsuppressed murmur went through the tent before he continued 'I have also been told we have a new duty to perform. Due to the mobilisation of most of the doctors throughout France this has led to a severe shortage of medical help to the local population, and in particular to those in the rural areas'

'Our orders are to criss-cross the country en-route to the border with Germany. The exercise will give us a unique and valuable opportunity to practice our abilities and at the same time provide an urgently needed service to many people'

'Finally,' he added 'I don't need to tell you that many French people regard us with a degree of suspicion and some with outright animosity and hostility!'

'I believe we can help in our own way to redress this attitude by being both professional and disciplined in the area we are good at, which is providing medical care and help to people in need of it, so the best of luck to you, in fact to all of us, over the coming months, and once again, well done, all of you.'

Fremontiers, 20th February 1940

After a final inspection and breakfast, the members of the CCS units were on the road with Anna Jack's unit travelling the sixty-five miles to Fremontiers, a rural village between Amiens and Grandvilliers. The rest of the day was spent setting up a surgery in the village school.

The medical team spent four days treating the ailments any country doctors' practice would expect, with the more serious being referred to larger French hospitals in the cities, until they were instructed to proceed to Vouziers next, with the surgeons and anaesthetist given separate orders to go back to Base Hospitals in Abbeville and Rouen, leaving the Colonel Wilson to be the resident doctor.

Anna started to walk across the village square at five o'clock to meet John McCloud at *"Le Forestier"*, one of two village cafés, before he and the other doctors left at eight.

The February evening was cold, bright and dry. Anna saw several men playing boule in the last hour of daylight, and listened to the thankful echoes of shouts, screams and laughter coming from young boys and girls who rode their absent father's bicycles in make believe races from the square, out of the village into a flat countryside and back again.

Dressed in his khaki uniform, partly covered by a greatcoat, unbuttoned at the front, John sat at the end of a long wooden bench. She shook hands with two elderly men at the other end of the seat before sitting next to surgeon and resting her back against a powdery stone wall while he poured her a glass of white wine from a bottle that shared a space on the bench.

Handing her the glass he said 'Anna, the two gentlemen here were just telling me that our visit has been a great success and very much appreciated by people in the village and the farming community around it.'

Leaning over the surgeon Anna began speaking to the two

men when their attention was taken by a sudden hush around the boule court. Three men in the same age group as those on her seat stood erect and silent as a fourth, of the same generation, bent his knees with some effort while he extended his right arm until his whole body flowed quickly upwards and a dull coloured metal boule was launched high into the still evening air before returning to earth and landing an inch from the cochonnet, knocking away the boule of his nearest rival and breaking the silence with hoops of praise from the followers of the victors and sour jibes from the losers.

Looking at John she smiled and said, 'It most certainly is not England!'

Nodding in agreement he replied 'No, but I do like it here. Like it in a different way to home, but I do like it.'

'So, Mr McCloud, another place we must come back to!'

Other members of the medical unit were now milling around the square, some making their way towards them. Her left hand was clenched in a tight fist as it slid slowly across the bench seat until it met his, bunched in the same fashion. Both hands touched, and stayed touching until he said quietly 'Come on Anna, I don't want to move, but I think we ought to go inside and eat.'

Inside the café they both ordered a speciality of the area, 'Flemish Carbonade'. The beef and onions gently simmered in Flanders beer and herbs, with diced gingerbread added towards the end of cooking.

It was only the most casual of embraces outside that the couple were able to seize before he left, and that night, tucked up in bed, she admitted to herself it was not so easy to goodbye to John McCloud.

Vouziers, 29th February 1940

Travelling a hundred and forty miles south east another school building provided the medical unit with facilities to see and treat the inhabitants of Vouziers and the surrounding country area. The routine of packing and storing the casualty clearing station was being refined and the team were pleased by the efficiency and speed with which they were able to get on the road.

On the last night in the village Mary Coombe sat with three other nurses in the local *estaminet* and casually stated 'Do you know what, it's the 29th of February, a leap year!' Looking at Anna she continued 'Now then, do you have any one in mind you intend to ask to marry, Sister Jack?'

Crimsoned faced she blurted out 'Mary! Don't look at me, without any doubts whatsoever, I can assure you I have no intention of asking anyone to marry me in the coming year!'

Rozerieulles, 23rd March, 1940

'No.10 British General Hospital' was located in the village of Rozerieulles to the west of Metz and the river Moselle and only twenty miles from the Maginot Line and the border with Germany. It was here that the surgical and other supplies would to be restocked and the vehicles were turned over to the army for servicing, in preparation for the next schedule of visits.

Matron Mary Atkins addressed the nursing team 'I have just been told that it is unlikely that we will be here more than four or five days, and the C.O. has told me that there will be no duties for any of us, so make the best of the time'

'Unfortunately,' she continued 'Colonel Wilson is unable to issue train warrants and if you decide to visit anywhere locally, you must be able to be contacted. Metz is a nice little town, or at least it was when I was last there,' pausing for thought, she continued 'let me see now, over twenty years ago!'

Looking directly at Anna she said 'The officers mess is situated in the Café Auberge, across from the main entrance, and has a good reputation, or so I was reliable informed by Doctor Adnans and Doctor McCloud, who I met coming out of the hospital.'

It had been a long time since Anna Jack had blushed and it was Matrons knowing look that had suddenly caused her an acute attack of the condition.

Suppressing a grin, Alison Forbes's stony face looked into the distance, and, saying to no one in particular, muttered 'Anyone feel like a trip to the Café Auberge?'

The total compliment of nursing sisters from the unit descended on the officers' mess a little before seven, and a delighted Peter Adnans greeted the women with a sincere welcome and two quickly ordered bottles of wine.

It was twenty minutes before Anna caught a glimpse through the cafe window of the familiar gait of John McCloud, hurriedly striding towards them. Peter Adnans was quick to hand John a glass of wine as he entered the café which he raised, saying 'Well, it's good to see you all.'

Turning to Anna he took her gaze while walking up to her and kissing her on her left cheek before saying quietly, 'I've missed you Anna.' For the second time that day Anna felt a blush of red creep up her neck and into her face.

Leaving together Anna and John walked arm in arm out of the village through the darkened roads that joined the large detached houses of the prosperous families of the area to where the buildings ended and the countryside started.

In the chill of the late March night their walk was lit by a carpet of brilliant stars and a full moon. Sitting on a low stone wall and looking across rolling countryside towards the dark outline of hills that marked the German border John said softly 'Anna, I've found a really nice little hotel in the centre of Metz, do you fancy staying there tomorrow night?'

Talking a bigger than usual breath of air before she replied Anna said 'John, this is really difficult for me. Of course, I want nothing more than to wake up with you, and I hope you know that, but I think we are making a big mistake by being so open about our relationship; the last thing I want is for some army busy-body to notice us and make sure we are sent in very different directions.'

He was silent for a moment until he began shaking his head slowly from side to side and saying 'No, no Anna, I don't believe we've made any mistakes. There's a war on, and I saw in Spain the havoc and dreadful cruelty it brings. That havoc, that cruelty could be here tonight, tomorrow, I don't know when, but it will arrive, it will happen'

'I've had the happiest moments of my life with you Anna and I will never forget them, no matter what happens in the future.'

Anna stood up and with her back to the German frontier she put her arms around his neck and kissed the top of his head before putting her hands under his chin and lifting his face upwards.

The soft moon light reflected in the tears on his face as he said, 'What I remember most about the civil war in Spain was the very sudden confusion of everything, the terrible noise, cruelty and chaos of it all'

'It was like a river that's suddenly burst its banks, no one had any control over what was happening, no control at all. Intelligent, educated, religious men suddenly started acting like wild beasts, like bloody mad men. It was all so terrifying, and so utterly, utterly disgusting, I felt ashamed of myself for being part of it'

'Eventually, the madness calmed down, compassion and even some human dignity did return, but the numbness and guilt inside me carried on much longer, it's still there Anna, perhaps it carries on forever?'

He stood up and put his head on her shoulder, saying quietly 'You are right Anna, I'm sorry if I've embarrassed you.'

Anna's fingers slid across the nape of hair on John's neck several times before she kissed him and said 'John, I've never said this to any one before in my life, but I really love you. You haven't embarrassed me, but I'm so afraid that other people may think it best that we are sent to separate units, and that would hurt me, you see I don't want to lose you.'

Reluctantly, Anna and John agreed to play the Army's game. A hundred yards from the main gate of the hospital, with its sentries on guard outside, the couple kissed goodbye and Anna was the first to walk through, into their tented city.

Saint-Remy-du-Nord, 2nd May 1940

Arriving at dusk Anna was pleased to find herself billeted in a comfortable family house with her own room, across the landing from Matron's in the small village of Saint-Remy-du-Nord, close to the French and Belgian border, two hundred miles to the north east of Metz.

The house was owned by Louise Bridoux and her husband who was away serving with the army. The rambling old house echoed with the sound of the owners' three young children and their friends, sounds that brought back happy memories to Anna of growing up in London with her parents.

The weather was getting warmer and with it the hopes of most of the population of France that an accord would soon be struck with the Germans.

The medical team were quickly busy. It had been a long time since the villagers and the residents in the surrounding countryside had had such easy access to treatment and a steady stream arrived each day for the next week.

Saint-Remy-du-Nord, 10th May, 1940

Early in the morning on the 9th of May in London the head of the British Secret Service (MI5) reliable informed Rab Butler, head of the Foreign Office, that after examining all accessible intelligence from their agents overseas, the conclusion of MI5 was that there was "no chance" of an invasion of Belgium or Holland by the Germans in the near future as they were about to invade Hungary.

****

The banging on the door of the house where Anna shared lodgings with her Matron woke her instantly. A quick glance at her watch showed her it was just after six thirty in the morning.

Opening the window of the bedroom she leaned out to see the beaming face of their batman looking up 'What is it?' Anna asked.

A jubilant Private Jeffries shouted to Anna 'Balloon's gone up ma'am, right and proper, it has'. A quick pause for breath and he added, 'The C.O. would like to see you and Matron immediately, ma'am.'

Anna had a queasy feeling in her stomach as she quickly rushed across the landing to where Matron had her bedroom. She knocked hard on her door before going in and saying 'Matron, the C.O. wants to see us immediately, and Private Jeffries is very excited about whatever it is that has happened.'

Sitting bolt upright in bed she stared at Anna and sighed deeply before saying 'Well, my dear, here we go again. Quickly get dressed and wait for me downstairs.'

Louise Bridoux sleepily appeared along the corridor 'What is the problem, Anna' she asked.

'Oh, probably just another exercise to get us all jumping around, Louise, but we have to report quickly, and I will let you know later what is happening.'

Louise Bridoux was now wide awake. 'Anna, I have a bad feeling, but I hope you are right and my feeling wrong.'

The two women hurried across the village square to the open fields and orchard where the mobile group were situated. Tents were being taken down and wood boxes loaded onto lorries as they approached.

'I think this is it Anna,' Matron said 'the 10th of May, 1940. You will remember today for the rest of your life.'

The Matron was guided into a tent and Anna went to the vehicles to find the drivers and orderlies busy loading the medical gear into them.

The other sisters were arriving almost as one from their various billets in the village. 'What's going on Anna' Jan Mitchell and Margaret Doyle asked in unison, arriving out of breath and still adjusting buttons to their uniform.

Rising her shoulders in puzzlement she could only say 'Apart from the summons and obvious delight from Private Jeffries, I honestly don't know'.

'What do you think will happen next?' Margaret asked. Before any answers could be offered the Quartermaster told them to hurry to the briefing tent.

A grim-faced Colonel Wilson spoke to an excited audience in the bulging tent, 'I have some very serious news to pass onto you. In the early hours of this morning a large number of German troops, tanks and aircraft, attacked Belgium and Holland'

'We have been ordered to proceed at once towards the Belgian border and to liaise with members of the British Expeditionary Force that have been dispatched together with French forces, to halt the German advance'

Pausing for a moment he continued 'We must leave here as soon as all the lorries have been loaded, which will be in less than thirty minutes time. Those of you who are in local billets quickly collect all your equipment and personal belongings'

After a pause he added, 'At this stage we do not want to cause panic among the local population, so I must remind you that you are not to pass on anything you have been told at this briefing, and remember, you only have thirty minutes, dismiss.'

Matron called to Anna 'Take Private Jeffries with you and collect my belongings together with yours, while I supervise the final packing here.'

Anna packed and bundled all of her matron's possessions with the help of the smiling soldier who kept telling her he couldn't wait to have a go at 'Jerry', and after sending him back to the vehicles she started to empty her own room.

Louise held Anna's gaze as she came down the stairs under the full weight of her baggage. The young French woman hugged the nursing sister she had become friendly with, after she had put down the bags held in her hands. Tears were in both women's eyes as Louise said 'So, my feelings were right I think?'

No words, just a silent nod from Anna, followed by 'Au revoir, Louise I know your husband will return home to you and the children safe, I just feel it.'

Estinnes-au-Mont, 10th May, 1940

Before mid-day the vehicles of the medical convoy passed through the frontier post that took them from France into Belgium. Anna sat in the passenger seat of the lorry with a puzzled look on her face.

The gates of the border crossing were a twisted, blackened tangle of metal scattered on both sides of the road, and armed British Military Policemen were directing traffic while infantry men had erected machine gun emplacements on the approaches to both sides of the border.

Above the engine noise the driver shouted, 'That's odd ma'am, almost looks like the Germans bombed the place, or something nasty happened' Anna nodded in agreement.

Driving into the village square of Estinnes-au-Mont, a few miles into Belgium, the convoy was greeted by local people, some throwing flowers, some waving, all smiling.

Outside the village a regimental HQ had been set up and the commanding officer of the medical team stopped his convoy to liaise with his superiors and to refuel his vehicles.

At dinner in the headquarters mess tent the nursing sisters shared bench seats and a long communal table with John McCloud, Peter Adnans and the other members of the unit.

The men and women were hungry. They were hungry for food and hungry for news of what was actually happening. Peter Adnans was quick to ask an infantry officer that had sat beside him if he knew anything.

Captain Richard Pearce was animated in his descriptions as he told his story 'I was with the leading group of infantry this morning travelling in convoy by lorries, when we reached the Belgium frontier post, down the road from here, that was at about nine o'clock this morning'

'There were three Belgian customs officers standing guard, and the damned fool of a duty sergeant refused to lift the barrier when the convoy commander halted in front of it until he received permission from his senior officer who was not going to be around until 11.00 am, think about it!' he said in amazement.

'Close to eighty lorries full of troops, together with armoured cars all lined up, and sitting ducks to bomb and machine gun attack from the air.'

He finished the description of events by saying 'The convoy commanding officer had good French and after a brief parlay with the customs men he had them arrested and disarmed, after they again refused to open the border gates without permission'

'Within minutes one of the scout cars travelling as escort was instructed to open fire on each gate post and destroy them, which is what happened, so as to prevent any further hold-ups, and the local chaps were replaced by a few of our own bods.'

****

The incident at the border post on the first day of battle was the first of scores of misunderstandings and catastrophic errors that would happen throughout the coming weeks due to a complete breakdown of communications and forward planning between the French, British and Belgian commanders.

The British troops had spent all winter and spring building strong defensive positions along the French-Belgium border. At dawn on the 10th May, Plan D (named after the Dyle river, east of Brussels) was initiated, triggered by the German assault and the well-prepared positions were abandoned, a decision openly queried by several senior officers.

It was only Hitler and his generals who knew exactly what was happening on the 10th of May, 1940. The French and British armies began their drive 70 miles to the Dyle river to take up new defensive positions that would stem the expected German onslaught through Belgium. The same planning officers believed the main thrust of enemy tanks and infantry would be along the same route in the opposite direction, so the most experienced and best equipped of both the French and British Armies hurried through Belgium to meet the advancing invader.

The German army had a 65-mile drive to the Dyle River. On paper the generals of the French and British armies believed that the Belgium forces would provide enough resistance with their prepared defences to hold any advance to the river for at least two to three weeks.

In fact, the Germans would arrive at the banks of the river in just four days, driving through the Belgian army with only scattered pockets of stubborn resistance.

Hitler could not contain his delight that the French and British armies were falling headlong into such a well-planned and brilliant trap. The Nazi dictator and his generals had given the Luftwaffe strict instructions not to interfere with the Allied advance, not to bomb them, not machine gun them, but to let them advance unhindered into Belgium.

At this early stage of the campaign the Luftwaffe's targets were the French airfields where hundreds of Allied fighter aircraft were taken by surprise and destroyed on the ground. Next on their bombing lists were the oil installations, ammunition dumps, and command centres of both armies.

By the end of the first day of the attack Hitler and the German generals had cause to be delighted by the way events were going and they had another devastating surprise in store for the French and British generals.

Genappe, 11th May, 1940

The order to move came just before four in the morning. A mug of tea had been produced by Private Jeffries and the second day of the real war had started.

At midday the convoy pulled off the main road and through open wrought iron gates onto a tree lined drive which lead to the Chateaux du Mont, three miles from the small town of Genappe. A former hunting lodge it had been requisitioned for use as the casualty clearing station for the medical team.

Alison Forbes shared a tent with Anna and during a break, cup of tea in hand she said to her 'I am really a bit confused. We arrest Belgian border guards, yet people on the roads are smiling and throwing flowers and shouting welcome, what is going on Anna?'

Anna replied, 'I only wish I knew Ali, I do hate this feeling of not being told and being left in the dark, but perhaps things will be clearer tomorrow.'

Within an hour, three lorries and two ambulances were driving into spaces set aside for incoming wounded soldiers.

Both sisters had the role of examining new casualties and to prioritise them according to the severity of their wounds or injuries before seeing a doctor.

Any anxieties the girls had been feeling disappeared as they and their orderlies started to shift through the thirty stretchers. The injuries were what they had been trained to expect. All the serious casualties were bomb related, from shrapnel wounds to severe burns.

There was a mixture of nationalities, mostly French and British, a few Belgians. After a couple of hours there was a definite feeling throughout the unit that they had got it right. The first test of their skills under battle conditions were being applied, and they could sense the professionalism bringing order out of the chaos.

Nothing was said but everyone knew the weeks of preparation and hard work were now paying off.

An orderly had produced a welcome mug of tea to a grateful Anna and Alison when at the same time the Quartermaster's head appeared around the entrance to their tent saying 'Well, ladies I've just been told that yesterday Neville Chamberlain resigned and Winston Churchill is now Prime Minister!'

Genappe, 13th May, 1940

Matron gently shook Anna's shoulder. 'Anna, Anna' Matron spoke quietly to her in an effort not to disturb the tent's other occupant. 'Anna, I need you to come to the town with me, please wake up.'
The sleep barrier broken Anna sat up quickly 'Yes Matron, what is it?'
Mary Atkins put a finger to her own lips before saying quietly 'Anna, we are running out of several items in the dispensary and theatre. I need your French skills as well as your professional ones to come with me to the pharmacy at Genappe on a begging mission otherwise I can see us coming to a halt in a couple of days. Private Jeffries is on the way with some hot water and cup of tea; I'll see you in my office in fifteen minutes.'
With only one passenger seat in the driver's cab, Anna sat in the back of the 15cwt Bedford army lorry with the sides of the canvas hood covering the back of the lorry reefed half way up, allowing the cool air to race through the vehicle as it drove down the driveway of the old hunting lodge, before headed out of the gates and onto the road that led to the small Belgian town of Genappe.
The vehicle slowed to a crawl almost immediately. The road ahead was crammed with thousands of refugees.
As the army lorry inched its way forward the three occupants had no choice but watch as men, women and children played out their part in the miserable reality of war.
Families and individuals walked along the road carrying all that they could in suit cases, bundles strapped to prams, trolleys and bicycles, furniture in farm carts, cars with broken engines packed high with generations of possessions, being pulled by horses.
Elegant women in expensive clothes and high heeled shoes

lugged shiny leather cases and walked besides poor miners' wives wearing wooden clogs and carrying their possessions wrapped in blankets, balanced on their heads. Men in rough farm clothes, some in fine suits, women in ragged peasant dress, all thrown into the same melting pot, they walked with the same dazed look of hopelessness and fear on their faces, all trying to stay in front of the bombing, machine gunning and shelling of the armies fighting around them.

It was strangely quiet when they entered the small country town. Looking at her watch Anna said to Mary Atkins 'For a lunch time it really is eerily empty. There's a café across the square shall I go in to find out where the local pharmacy is, matron?'

'Good idea' she replied. 'In fact, let's both go and see what is going on, driver, could you stop over there on the pavement.' The women got out of the lorry and walked across the cobbled street to the Café Marquet.

Inside the café four men sat at one table with the rest empty. The men looked up and stared hard at the two khaki clad women. No welcome or smiles. The looks were sullen, angry even, and the owner, stood behind a polished metal bar top looked equally distant.

Anna managed a smile as she offered the owner of the café a 'Good afternoon', but that was as far as she got before the door at the entrance of the café burst open and they saw their driver framing the entrance shouting 'Ma'am, one of their policemen is having a right go at me, but I can't for the life of me understand what it is he wants.'

An agitated policeman was standing behind the driver and Anna asked him what the problem was. Turning to their driver she said, 'The policeman is afraid that if a German spotter plane sees your lorry in the square they will send in bombers or artillery will shell the town.'

Looking at the café owner again, and without the smiles she said 'Monsieur, we are here to buy medical supplies from your pharmacy. We will not leave until that is done, so is there somewhere the driver can get his lorry under cover?'

Speaking first to one of his regular customers and then to Anna he said, 'This man will take your driver and the lorry to his repair shop and he can stay there under cover, until the pharmacy opens in a half hour or so.'

'Thank you' she said, and then explained to the driver the concerns of the policeman and that he should follow the garage owner and stay with the lorry and they would fetch him when they had finished. The driver shared the same worries as the policeman and was quick to accept the offer of shelter for the lorry and himself.

In the café, the owner had become less defensive and asked if they would like coffee, which they accepted. Sitting down at a table Anna said, 'The town seems deserted?'

Bringing two coffees to the women and putting them on their table he replied, 'Most of the people are preparing to leave the town as quickly as possible, and many, most in fact, have already done so'

Behind his bar he pointed at the customers still sat around one table talking quietly and said 'My four friends and I are undecided what we are going to do. We have all taken our wives and children to a small village some six kilometres from here, and now we wait. Monsieur Penn, the pharmacist is like us, but I think he will be closed in a couple of days, if not sooner.'

Matron offered to pay for the coffees before getting directions to the pharmacy but the café owner waved her offer aside adding 'I apologise for our lack of humour and manners madam, but these are desperate times for us, we wish you luck, but most of us feel you will be back in England soon.'

The pharmacist had most of what the medical unit needed until supplies came through from the base hospital. Like the others at the café, the pharmacist was sombre but showed a willingness to help as much as he could, and was generous in not charging for some items while keeping to normal prices for others.

The Bedford army truck swept out of the town and back onto the road leading to the hunting lodge that was their temporary hospital. This time they were heading into the stream of humans and their cargo of bundles and bags. Sat looking out of the back of the army lorry Anna and the refugees were the first to see them.

Two Luftwaffe ME109's flying a hundred feet above the road were screaming towards the lorry one behind the other, firing bursts of cannon shells and machine gun bullets into the road and column of refugees, cars, and army trucks.

Like parting waves, the sea of humans ran, jumped, and slid. Some were pushed, some thrown, in a frenzied effort to scramble off of the road and out of the path of the approaching machines.

Their driver glanced into the large oblong mirror bolted onto the door of the Bedford and saw them. His quick thinking and reactions saved them. Instead of giving way to the natural instinct to stop and run, the driver accelerated forward, his foot flat to the floor on the metal plate that pushed down the accelerator arm.

He had seen the buildings ahead and knew it was their best possibility of escape. The lorry swerved violently off the road in a cloud of dust and gravel throwing Anna sideways and onto the floor of the truck in the back as he crashed the vehicle through a wooden farm gate bringing it for a moment, side on to the approaching aircraft.

Anna heard the smack and thud of bullets and cannon shells exploding, tearing the canvas tilt roof above her head to shreds and blasting through the wood and metal sides of the vehicle, sending fragments and splinters in all directions, missing her curled up body.

The lorry hit a flat stone slab that sent it for a second flying forward like the aircraft that were hunting them. That one second was all the driver wanted as the ammunition from the second aircraft smashed against the granite wall and tiled roof of the open fronted barn the driver had skilfully aimed his vehicle for.

The cannon shells caused several thick roof tiles to explode into small fragments that showered onto the cab metal roof and what remained of the rear canvas cover. Looking out of his window and through the door less side entrance of the building he saw the planes start to bank away. He shouted to the passengers 'They're coming back, for fuck's sake hold on.'

Wrenching the long floor mounted gear stick into reverse the lorry responded with the sound of the six-cylinder engine screaming at full revolutions before he released the brake handle and the Bedford screeched back over the stone slab as the driver wrestled the wheel through his hands giving him maximum lock before crunching the stick into a forward gear and plunging the lorry through farmyard dirt and dust to the other side of the building.

Shouting wildly at the women he said 'You've got to run like fuck and get whatever cover you can, away from the truck and this bloody building, quickly!'

He was out first shouting 'Follow me, follow me'. They quickly glanced up and caught sight of the two black shapes that were now racing towards them.

The driver found a hollow in the ground close to a stone boundary wall. First in he grabbed Anna's wrist pulling her roughly down and as the whine of bullets flashed over them he grabbed matron's arm throwing her on top of Anna. 'Keep low' he shouted, but neither lady needed to be reminded of this necessity, they kept low and still, hardly bearing to breath.

Laying on the ground looking up at the sky they knew that the second Messerschmitt had not fired on them but had banked over to give the three a clear view of the fighter that was no more than a hundred feet above them, the noise from the BMW aero engine screaming at them was deafening, but the sound of the driver shouting at them brought them back from the mesmeric sight as he shouted frantically 'I think the fucker's going to have another go, shit, come on'.

They raced around to the other side of the low wall. There was no hollow, but the wall would offer some protection and the driver shouted again 'I reckon the first one don't have any bombs or ammo left but that second one has, so bury your heads in the earth and cover your ears, an if you can pray, please say one for me'

Needing to know what was happening and looking above the wall, he saw that only one aircraft was returning.
The fighter was a bit higher this time and the driver smiled to himself, saying aloud 'I thought so you fucker, this is your last chance ain't it.'

The Messerschmitt screamed over them, the pilot throttled the engine to give him maximum power to speed away upwards, having dropped his last 300lb bomb.

There was an awesome swoosh followed by a deafening explosion that seemed to lift the three of them into the air.

The concussion waves blew the top layer of stones off the wall and fell mostly on the driver, there was a second of silence then showers of earth, stones and small rocks fell on all of them like a winter hail storm.

Stones pinged off of their steel helmets and made dull thuds on their tunics as they fell from the sky, and then came complete silence. The driver looked over the wall again and got up shouting at the disappearing aircraft and shaking his fist 'You missed, you bastard, you missed my fucking lorry!'

The bomb had exploded on the other side of the farm building missing the army truck. Most of the tiles from the roof were now in the back of the vehicle in small pieces, the canvas tilt had caved in under the weight, and from the shredding received from a mixture of cannon and bullet holes. Both women got up, brushing earth and dirt from their tunics with their hands. They went over to the lorry to find the driver throwing the broken tiles onto the ground from the back of it. When he saw them he said calmly 'Well Matron, looks like we can rescue just about everything.'

Matron broke into a smile before saying 'What's your name?' Stopping for a second he said, 'Lance Corporal Best, ma'am,' sheepishly he added 'sorry about my language back there ma'am, it's something I can't help like, but I am sorry.'

Shaking her head she said 'Lance Corporal Best bless your bad language, is all I can say. You behaved with incredible bravery, I think we both owe our lives to your quick thinking and expert driving, so from both of us, thank you!'

Anna stood looking down the road before saying 'Matron, I think there are some casualties on the road.' They got together a basic medical kit and headed in the direction of the screams and shouts they could hear.

As they got closer they saw that a boy of seven or eight had been almost cut in half by the cannon fire from one of the aircraft. One leg and most of his thigh had been blown off and lay in the ditch by the road side, complete with a pulled-up sock and dusty black patent leather shoe. The mother sat covered in the blood from her child sobbing uncontrollably and clutching the remains of her once handsome, now dead son. Three other elderly people were found huddled together, all dead. They treated several of the refugees for minor wounds before heading back to their vehicle, past the sobbing mother and dead child now surrounded by other refugees.

The sight of the returning lorry brought everyone not in the operating theatres and able to the parking area in front of the lodge. With most of the canvas covers flapping behind them, the splintered wood and metal frame hanging over the back wheels and a layer of ochre dust and tile remnants covering most of the vehicle it looked like a total wreck. On inspection the occupants of the lorry looked in similar shape and colour. Colonel Wilson was wide eyed when he said 'Matron, are any of you hurt? What on earth happened?'

It was only when they looked at each other that they realised the state they were in. Matron answered her senior officer, 'We are all fine, thank you sir, we were attacked by two aircraft on the road and despite how it looks we managed to get most of what we need, largely due to Lance Corporal Best here.'

Matron sent Private Jeffries to tell Anna that she could use the shower facility in the lodge. Grateful for the opportunity of the hot water to wash away the grime and dust of the day she suddenly felt cold under the hot water and realised she had started to shiver. 'I'll be alright in a moment', she thought. 'Just hang on to something.'

Anna knew she was in shock. The day had been a long one without much sleep during the past twenty-four hours and the effects of the attack by the Messerschmitt's were now taking effect.

Back in her tent Anna looked forward to a couple of hours rest before going back on duty, but sleep would not come. It was the little boy not the aircraft that she kept seeing, and could not get him out of her mind even when she drifted into a troubled, haunted slumber.

Genappe, 14th May, 1940

The French and British armies had taken the bait Nazi Germany had set for them, the trap was now closing.

A German army group had attacked Holland head on, and Belgium through Luxembourg at the start of the invasion on the 10th of May, and the French and British Allies had sent their best men and most modern equipment to the Dyle River to counter the attack.

The second part of the German attack had now started and the devastating effect would complete the rout of the defenders.

Unknown to the Allied generals or Intelligence Officers a second powerful German army group comprising of over a thousand tanks, with supporting infantry, artillery and massive air support had negotiated the rough terrain through the dense Ardennes forests, an area said by French military strategists to be impenetrable by tanks or large-scale troop movements.

For the first time since the First World War the German army was marching on French soil again.

The light defence force facing the Ardennes was an ill-equipped force of French units, consisting of few regular soldiers and mainly older conscripts with minimal training.

A small number of road blocks had been erected along the routes leading out of the hills and forest which were armed with an array of light machine guns, but with no effective anti-tank weapons. Some of these points were manned by detachments of mounted horse cavalry.

The German forces entered France 30 miles North of where the Maginot Line ended, around the town of Sedan. Concentrated air attacks by Stuka dive bombers and continuous artillery bombardment quickly demoralised the defending French forces.

The Blitzkrieg tactics practised in the Spanish civil war by Hitler's Condor Legion helped the fascist General Franco while at the same time providing a welcome platform for the development of new techniques of waging war, techniques used with devastating effect in Poland, Czechoslovakia, and now in France.

Having been 'softened up' by bombing and shelling, the defenders of the Sedan area crumpled quickly and scattered when the onslaught of tanks and fifty thousand infantry poured over the river Meuse on a twenty-mile front.

The armies of France and Britain to the north had no knowledge that their right flank had been breached less than a hundred miles to the south and that within four days the German army would reach Abbeville and the English Channel.

With the Allied armies now in Hitler's trap the Luftwaffe were issued with new orders. Bomb and machine gun every military and civilian target that presents itself. Soldiers and refugees alike were now a target for the invaders.

****

Anna could never explain to herself how the pressure of the operating theatre during surgery seemed to enable her to focus on her own personal problems, while at the same time keeping one step ahead of any surgeon she was supporting.

Her nursing skills assisting Peter Adnans came as second nature and allowed her the opportunity to take stock of her life. She was twenty-three years old, the same age as Louise Bridoux, and the events of yesterday had made her realise how fragile was the life she had.

'It's that poor broken child' Anna thought to herself. 'The mother, covered in the blood from her own baby, how would I feel, my own child, so full of life and laughter one moment and then dead, the blood the mother had given him now seeping from his small body'

'Could I ever survive such an ordeal? The pain I felt seeing the mother, and feel now, it's a pain that comes', she hesitated, wrestling with the words in her head as she thought of them, and speaking aloud when they finally came 'I think it comes from being a mother'

'Being a mother,' she thought, and saying it again 'being a mother' and knowing that for the first time in her life she felt a need for herself to be one, to have a child.

Anna felt better, less tired, she also knew that all her feelings and emotions where tied up with the madness going on around her. 'Madness' she said. 'Where have I heard that before?'

Of course, she thought, nodding to herself. John had said that about the war in Spain. She remembered some of his words 'Terrifying, disgusting, guilt, madness' Most of them she had felt on the road full of desperate refugees yesterday.

Anna wanted to see him, she was not sure of why, but certain she needed too. She asked Peter Adnans if John was on duty. He quizzically looked at her saying 'Anna, are you alright, you had a bit of a shock yesterday, I'm…'

She cut him off in mid-sentence saying, 'I was a bit shaken, but honestly, thank you I really am fine, but I would like to see John, just for a few minutes, please.'

'He's about to finish in No 2 theatre as far as I know. I must have a break and use the loo after we finish sowing up this young man. I'll pop in and see him then.'

As the surgeon left the operating theatre, the orderlies took advantage of his departure to carry out a quick clean up, and Anna to grab a cup of tea and a sit down. The surgeon returned speaking quietly to Anna 'He'll be by the entrance to the tennis court, in a couple of minutes, I'll cover for you for twenty, off you go.'

There were sentries around the parameter wall, but down by the tennis court at the back of the lodge building it was as quiet as the war allowed. The hills to the north east gave a spectacular display of bomb and artillery burst and bright lines of tracer shells would reach up to an unseen formation of planes. Anna saw the glow of John's cigarette followed by his shape as a silhouette of black.

'Over here Anna' she heard him say. When she got to him he said nothing but embraced her so hard she could not have spoken had she wanted too.

He relaxed his grip saying 'Anna, I was worried sick when Matron told me what happened yesterday. I broke our rules by putting my head into your tent as it was Matron that suggested you may just be still awake, but you were out for the count.'

Anna kissed him before she spoke 'John, I do miss you, I know it can't be different at the moment, and I am sorry, but I just had to see you.' She buried her face into his chest and sobbed.

They sat down on a garden bench in front of the tennis court and said nothing until he kissed her ear and said 'Anna, we haven't got long before we go back to theatre, but a few weeks ago you, well truth is, you stunned me by saying that you loved me,' pausing for a few seconds, he continued 'I hope you meant it because I'll be honest and tell you I've not thought about much else since.'

She started to talk but he said gently, 'Please let me finish Anna, the fact is I'm not very good with these things, but I know that I really do love you as well, and, well - Anna, would you.....would you marry me when we get back to England?'

'Oh John' Anna whispered, 'I don't know what to say, I love you, that I know that for certain, but marry, are you really certain?'

'Anna, I'm more certain I want to marry you than anything I have ever done or thought about in my whole life.'

They were silent for several moments before Anna kissed him and said 'Yes John. I would love to be your wife!'

There was a long silence before John took a deep breath and replied 'Phew! I was really worried about what your answer would be, but thank you Anna.'

A lull in the stream of injured and passing aircraft gave Anna and her tent mate Alison a full five hours rest. There were no ugly images, only a contented feeling as she fell quickly and deeply to sleep.

After their batman woke them with tea and hot water Alison commented 'You seem extra pleased with yourself today, how come?'

She would not be able to tell Alison, or any one she worked with that she was engaged to be married so she replied, 'I managed to get a very naughty cuddle from John by the tennis courts last night in between operations, followed by the longest sleep either you or I have had in days, so I do feel good today!'

She thought to herself 'Me, yes Anna Jack, me, engaged to be married. It just doesn't sound real somehow!'

Both girls had been told to report to Colonel Wilson in twenty minutes, and the sisters blinked at the bright sun beating down on the Flanders countryside on their short walk to where their C.O. had his office, and after knocking on his door went in.

Feeling so good it was hard for Anna to accept the serious mood of those already in the room. The C.O. looked grey with fatigue when he spoke 'Right, we are now all here. I've had an urgent request for this unit to provide assistance to a battalion close to the front, because their MO has been wounded'

'As you can see outside, the lull we had early this morning is over and the casualties are now stretching us to full capacity again. Later today we will be able to move a lot of our patients to the rail head at Genappe where a hospital train is arriving so I can spare one team and I would like Sisters Jack and Forbes to assist you Major Adnans'

'Two ambulance vehicles and crews will move out before dark, and I expect you to be back here within twenty-four hours'

Looking at the two sisters he said 'Major Adnans will let you know what he will require for the trip, and you have a few hours to get things together before evening, and good luck to you.'

Walking past the tent that John McCloud shared with Peter Adnans, Anna smiled as she noticed that he was sat outside using a card table from the lodge to write a letter on.

He jumped up immediately he saw her saying in an official way 'Sister, could you give me a hand in here for a second'

Looking around, Anna went through the tent opening and as the flap closed behind her he pulled her gently towards him and kissed her until neither could breathe before holding her by both arms and saying 'I've had a wabbly tum since I woke up Anna, I've got to ask again, do you still want to …..eh,' interrupting his hesitation she said 'Marry you Major McCloud' it was her turn to hesitate before saying 'Yes please!'

'Please Anna don't make fun of me, I still can't believe you said yes, but to tell you the truth, it seems more important to me now than when I asked you.'

Anna pulled her fiancé towards her and led him behind the screen that acted as a dividing line between the two camp beds in the tent.

With a mixture of fun and passion the newly engaged couple fell onto the rickety wood and canvas single cot and made love.

Anna dressed quickly, kissed her husband to be long and passionately, and was heading towards the tent entrance using her hands to flatten the creases in her uniform, while John lay lifeless on his back before he suddenly shouted out loud, 'Sister, quick, quick, I need help!'

Anna raced back to him putting one hand over his mouth, and laughing before becoming serious and saying, 'For God's sake John, please stop, you'll have us both court marshalled!'.

She then kissed him tenderly while at the same time running the tips of the fingers of one hand through the dark hair on his chest and stomach before teasingly stopping just below his naval and saying, 'Now be a good boy, and put your clothes on!'

Turning back at the curtain divider she looked over to John and blew him a kiss, smiling broadly, he returned it over the palm of his hand and Anna left.

Wavre, 15th May 1940

Lieutenant Williams spoke slowly, his breathing and movement restricted by the pain from his injuries 'Jolly pleased to see you Sir' he said in a quiet monotone voice 'I got rather caught out yesterday as I was running between some wounded men. A mortar shell landed behind me and several small splinters are lodged in my back and shoulder, nothing too serious, but very uncomfortable.'

Pointing to a map on a table he took a series of short breaths before saying, 'Here is Wavre, and we are here, about four hundred yards from the front line, Sir,' the ashen faced officer drank more water, took more short, painful breaths and was about to speak again when Peter Adnans interrupted him, 'Now then young man, before you carry on let's get you off your feet. Face down on the stretcher if you please, then you can continue while I have a prod around.'

Peter Adnans inspected the officer's wounds before saying 'Your nursing orderlies have done a good job of keeping the entry areas clean and tidy, but you have a lot of tiny pieces of German iron work in your it's back, so it's off to base and surgery for you as soon as I finish this, give you a shot of morphine and then you can tell us where everything is and what to expect next.'

His breathing became easier as the morphine injection took effect, and as the two nursing sisters put clean dressings on his wounds they all continued to listen to his account of what had happened over the past days.

'The town has been taken by the Germans once but our regiment and another, with help from a squadron of French Somua tanks, managed to push them out yesterday'

'Fighting for the town had been ferocious, absolutely dreadful to be honest. Both sides fought house to house, hand to hand for possession, it was all very bloody'

The doctor of twenty-five turned over to face the two nurses and the surgeon before finishing 'The injuries from bayonet and knife were extremely brutal, and I also have to tell you Sir that we are expecting a counter attack by the Germans to try and re-take the town during the night or at dawn.'

As the Lieutenant, together with other wounded soldiers were leaving the first aid post three parties of stretcher bearers arrived and reported to Peter Adnans before they left to get as close to the front line as they could, and then grab as much sleep as possible.

Speaking to the two drivers and his nursing assistants the surgeon said 'Right now, it's almost one o'clock, let's have a last clean–up and as soon as it's ticketyboo I suggest we copy the stretcher bearers example and climb into the back of the ambulances and sleep for as long as we can.'

Three hours later their sleep was shattered as enemy shells started to pound the British troops dug in ahead of them. The noise and concussions from the explosions rocked their ambulances as they jumped down from the back of them.

As soon as the artillery bombardment stopped they heard the shrill sound of whistles and the wild, harsh shouts of men somewhere in the darkness ahead of them.

'What's happening Sir?' Alison Forbes asked nervously, pulling her greatcoat collar as far as she could around her ears against a sudden chill.

'It's the signal for the soldiers to 'stand to' Alison in readiness for any attack that the Germans might launch as soon as the dawn appears and they have enough light to move their tanks and men about and attack the positions ahead.'

Staring into the last moments of night they could only imagine what the young men in front of them were going through as they drew their bayonets from scabbards, fixing them to the ends of their rifles, before pulling back a breech bolt to push a bullet into a barrel, release a safety catch and wait silently in the darkness for the enemy they knew were only yards in front of them.

The noise from the bombardment had given way to a strange eerie silence and looking east towards the town Anna watched in silence and shivered inside her coat as the sky began to lighten and a fine thin line of mist appeared, hovering above the ground like ranks of haunting ghosts.

The silence that surrounded them was heavy, numbing. It stopped movement, hushed voices, and produced shallow, silent breathing as they peered ahead into the now grey light of no-man's land and the battlefield in the distance.

On the branches of the trees the birds saw the same streaks of light and in contrast to their human neighbours seeking safety behind the last moments of darkness they began their shrill singing as they marked out their territory and called to their partners to share their space for the rituals of the day ahead.

Veterans would have known, reactions would have been instant. The surgeon, drivers and nurses heard the sound. It was a whining, whistling moan, but they did nothing. Suddenly, and violently they were blown backwards by the concussion waves of shells exploding ahead of them. It was a prelude to an intense and concentrated bombardment that lasted for the next five minutes. The longest five minutes Anna had ever experienced.

They lay on the grass and earth as salvo after salvo of artillery and mortar shells fell less than two hundred yards in front of them making the ground ripple and groan.

Anna heard the whiz and screech of shrapnel flying overhead, slicing through the branches of trees around them and caught the odious clogging smell of cordite in the air.

As suddenly as it had started, the avalanche of metal stopped. There was a total silence once more until the birds returned to the branches of the trees as if nothing had happened, their warbles and whistles now replacing the ear-piercing sounds of war.

Within minutes the first stretcher bearers came running to the regimental first aid post with their wounded young men. With their arrival came a new and terrifying sound that made Anna and Alison stop in their tracks to look upwards.

High in the morning sky five Ju87 Stuka dive bombers flew alongside each other while a sixth was spiralling towards them, the high-pitched sirens fixed to the landing wheels of the vulture shaped aircraft screaming wildly as it descended.

One after the other all of the aircraft dropped almost vertically towards the earth, the deafening blare of the sirens making Anna put both her hands over her ears as she watched them roar over the medical first aid post to deliver their payloads of bombs and machine gun bullets on the entrenched troops and anti-tank gun emplacements in front of them, leaving clouds of black swirling smoke erupting from the positions as they disappeared behind the dark curtain they had created.

More casualties arrived and the first of the ambulance vehicles was sent back to the regimental H.Q. Anna shouted to her two colleagues above the screaming of an injured soldier Peter Adnans was treating 'Eight more lads outside, two serious the rest manageable, and………'

Her conversation was abruptly cut short by an infantry officer with a blood-soaked field dressing covering the right side of his head barging through the door.

Looking at Major Adnans he shouted, 'Jerry is less than two minutes down the road, get everyone in your ambulance and go now, no questions, you have less than two minutes, if that, Go, Just Go!'

The officer turned, ran through the farm yard and jumped onto an open topped Bren Gun carrier where it's driver was frantically revving the engine, waiting for him, before it roared away.

The ambulance driver stood nervously at the door, saying 'Sir, I've loaded everyone aboard and we can see a bloody big German tank heading this way, Sir.'

There were ten wounded men in the back of the ambulance as it bounced out of the farmyard lane and raced towards the main road.

Anna and Peter Adnans looked out of the sliding metal visor cut into each of the back doors of the vehicle. A hundred feet away two German Panzer 1V medium tanks were grinding their way towards them with soldiers carrying rifles and machine guns walking in the wake of the sinister camouflaged shapes.

They waited for both tanks and soldiers to open fire on them. The ambulance had the familiar Red Cross markings on the sides as well on the rear doors, would the Germans recognise the tradition of not firing on medical non-combatants? Anna thought of the refugees and dead boy on the road from Genappe, and waited.

The ambulance swayed violently to one side as it rounded the final bend that took them out of sight and rifle range of the advancing enemy. Looking at each other Anna and Peter remained silent but breathed a collective sigh of relief, gathering saliva in their dry throats, before turning their attention to the injured men in the back and finding that one of the serious casualties had died.

The design of the ambulance allowed for four separate stretchers to be slotted and secured in racks, two each side of the vehicle during normal duty, but on this trip instead of one man on each stretcher there were two, with the other wounded propped up on the floor.

Major Adnans swapped places with Alison Forbes who had occupied the front passenger seat and Anna was sat on the lower stretcher rack looking through the open narrow doorway that separated the cab of the ambulance from the causalities in the back.

Alison, standing next to Anna shouted 'I've just looked at my watch and I just cannot believe that so much as happen in so short a time. I've been shot at, dive bombed, chased by tanks, knocked clean off my feet by shell blast, and it's only ten thirty in the morning!'

The sudden laughter in the cab stopped as abruptly as it had started as the Bedford K2 ambulance turned a sharp bend in the road and they caught sight of the Chateaux du Mont in the distance and the billowing black smoke and flames rising from the building.

Slowly, the ambulance went through the open main gates and up the drive to where the front entrance had been and stopped.

The roof of the old hunting lodge had collapsed into the building and several of the smaller outbuildings had suffered shell and shrapnel damage. There were deep craters in the drive way and where tents had stood. Deserted tents, guy ropes, broken tent poles and fragments of canvass, and clothes were littered everywhere.

Burnt out ambulance's, lorries and other vehicles were strewn across parking areas, one of the large Red Cross banners that had been secured to a lawn was intact but the breeze had carried red embers from the burning building across it and dark scorch marks and smouldering holes gave it an ugly pox-marked look.

Peter Adnans told the ambulance driver to go with Alison around one section of the building and he and Anna went in the other direction. Alison had not gone more than twenty yards when she called out, and the other two hurried to her and the driver.

In the shelter of a wall were four lines of bodies, each wrapped in a white sheet or grey blanket, each body with a small white label tied around a foot or ankle.

Their friends and colleagues were in the top row. Jan Mitchell, Margaret Doyle, Mary Coombe, the quartermaster David Murray, their batman Private Jeffries, the last white sheet covered the body of their commanding officer, Derek Wilson.

As the four of them stood silently looking at their dead colleagues a sudden breeze brought a shower of small red embers and sparks from the burning Chateaux sweeping towards them, making the labels tied to each of their dead friend's flutter in the hot air like tiny flags.

Anna and Alison held each other, until Peter Adnans spoke to them gently. 'We must get away from here quickly. Our driver was told that a Red Cross train is due at a station near Soignies, which is about twenty-five miles from here sometime today, so I've decided to head there but we will have to go back to Genappe for petrol at a fuel depot before setting off, unless we find any here.'

Before they left the lodge, the surgeon suggested that the soldier that had died earlier should be left with the other bodies they had found, and with as much dignity as possible in the time allowed, the nurses removed his personal possessions and ID, cleaned the blood away from his face and wrapped him in a blanket.

A tag was attached to his foot like the others, giving his name, rank and service number details for a burial unit, German or British, which would at some stage arrive and bury their comrades.

During the search for petrol the driver had found some tinned army rations and had filled their water cans before the sisters climbed into the back of the ambulance. Alison Forbes put a hand on Anna's before saying quietly 'Well Anna, at least

John wasn't amongst them.'

Nodding, Anna could only manage a soft 'Umm, you're right, and I feel a bit guilty about what went through my mind back there, not pleased it was their bodies covered up, just pleased one of them wasn't John.'

The ambulance picked its way slowly through Genappe. The town centre was deserted, as though waiting. Anna was looking out of the rear door window visor as the ambulance went through the town square where only two days ago she and Matron had stopped for coffee.

Talking quietly to herself she said 'No, surely not, it can't be only two days ago, it must be more, surely?' Thinking back, she quickly added 'It was only two days ago' shaking her head she added 'Goodness, so much has happened.'

On one side of the cobbled square of the town most of the shops and houses had been destroyed by bombing and shelling, some were still burning fiercely, some smouldering, giving off the acrid smells of war.

She smiled when she caught sight of the Café Marquet, it was still completely intact. The windows had been deliberately boarded up but the canopy that gave cover to the tables outside was untouched; the red, yellow and black striped material that lead into the scalloped shaped fringe stood bright and defiant.

Propped up between the door and stretcher racks Anna joined Alison in an exhausted sleep. The women did not notice the vehicle stop at the army fuel depot, nor did they hear distant machine gun fire but Major Adnans and the driver did.

There were four soldiers on motor bikes parked next to a camouflaged area where a stock pile of ten-gallon cans of fuel were stacked. A Corporal got off one of the motorbikes and ran over to the lorry.

He said they should quickly take as much as they wanted as they were about to blow the lot up, before adding 'Sir, the Germans are about a mile and a bit to our left and there is a regiment of French infantry between us and them. We've had orders to head for Tournai at the double, Sir.'

The station for the hospital train was in a direct line with Tournai and the ambulance and occupants set off once again.

It was nearing six in the evening when they reached the assembly point and found over a hundred other ambulance vehicles and other army lorries stretched out around the concrete railway platform and recently erected medical tents.

The driver was marshalled to a parking area the exhausted man parked where instructed and was asleep sat behind the wheel of the vehicle by the time the piston rods in the engine had stopped.

Speaking to the two sisters Peter Adnans said 'The boys inside seem comfortable enough so I am going to see if any of the others from the lodge made it here.'

Alison was first to say 'Can we join you, Sir?'

'Of course,' he replied 'There seems to a command tent close to the railway siding, let's start there.'

The girls waited anxiously outside while he stepped into the tent. Ten minutes crawled past and the solemn look on Peter Adnans face as he emerged from the tent spoke volumes. Looking at Anna he said, 'Could I have a word, please.'

There was frantic activity inside but Peter Adnan guided Anna to a box of supplies that served as a seat, and motioned her to sit down. Sitting opposite her on an identical box he took her hands in his saying 'Anna, John is here' he continued quickly, hardly without pause, 'Anna, I have to tell you he has been very badly injured.'

'How bad?' She said.

'I've spoken to the duty medical officer. John is in the tent next to this one' he paused now, knowing he had to continue, knowing he had to tell her the truth, and not wanting to, 'Several pieces of shrapnel entered his tummy and lower half, they amputated his left leg this morning, he's lost part of his colon and most of his liver'

'Anna', he hesitated before finishing 'Anna, the M.O. doesn't expect John to live through the night. I'm so very sorry.'

Her hands gripped his tightly before she said, 'Can we see him, please?'

'I'll have a word now with the M.O., you wait here a second.' He went outside to look for the medical officer and told Alison what had happened.

He also told her that several members of their casualty clearing station were a hundred yards away, and suggested she checked out the soldiers in the ambulance and then try to find them.

The surgeon saw the duty medical officer in charge coming out of the administration tent and asked if it was possible to see John, 'Yes, of course' he replied.

Peter collected Anna and together they entered a large tent with several rows of camp beds in it. John was easy to find amongst the sea of occupied beds because they quickly made out the familiar shape of their Matron, with her distinctive style of head dress. She was sitting next to John wiping away beads of sweat on his forehead with her left hand, her right arm held in a sling.

She greeted both of them with a shake of her head, saying 'Thank God, you've made it out, is Alison with you?' she added quietly.

She accepted Peter Adnans 'Yes, Matron.' with just a nod of her head as she stood up and motioned Anna to take her place whilst giving Anna's arm a reassuring squeeze.

Matron and Peter Adnans walked out of the tent, leaving John and Anna together.

He was unconscious and it was obvious that he was suffering badly. A duty nurse gave him an injection of morphine on the instructions of a doctor, and Anna continued to sit and mop his brow and hold his hand.

The morphine eased his pain quickly and although still unconscious his expression was less strained, the perspiration on his forehead eased and his breathing became more regular.

A nurse brought Anna a tin mug of tea and twenty minutes went by before Peter Adnans reappeared beside them. He looked down on John and whispered to Anna that he wanted to see her outside.

It was dark now and the soft rain that was falling felt refreshing to Anna as the surgeon spoke to her 'The M.O. has told me that the Red Cross train should be here in a couple of hours,' he hesitated for a moment, leaving the sentence hanging, thinking before restarting 'now, Anna, we both know John is too ill to be moved. There are another nine or ten patients in the same condition as him in the tent and I have volunteered to stay here with them and John after the train is loaded and leaves'

'Tomorrow some of them may be a little stronger and able to endure the travel, and there should be another hospital train coming through here or if not the MO will organise transport to take us to another station nearby.'

Before starting his next sentence he was interrupted by Anna who said 'I want to stay with you, please. I can't leave John, you know that, and you also know that my attention to the other patients will be as dedicated as always.'

Frowning, he looked hard at her before saying 'The problem Anna is that no one really knows how far the Germans have advanced. Communications are practically non-existent and the feeling is that things are pretty bad. Just how bad is the problem,' pausing, he frowned again, and again looked squarely into her eyes 'the horrible fact is this could be the last train that is able to get away to the coast, so be in no doubt Anna, if you stay we could both end up as prisoners of war, in Germany.'

Anna had to admit to herself that she had never thought about the possibility of being taken prisoner by the nation of people her father had rejected and was so openly opposed to, and remembering the words her father said about a special hatred of Jews by the Nazi's, the prospect of being made a captive under them made her stomach churn.

She gulped hard before saying 'I don't want to leave, orders or not, I have every intention of staying and I hope you will let me do so, because I will be a great help to you and your patients, and you know that.'

He knew what her decision would be and in truth was pleased that she would be staying as he repeated his warning 'I know you will do everything for John and the other casualties, but I have to tell you again, the threat of becoming a prisoner of war is real, so are you sure?'

She nodded a yes, and the 1st in Line to the Earl of Roxendon smiled before adding 'Anna, let's go and make John and his fellow campers as comfortable as possible, I know that Matron is anxious to have a chat with you before she leaves, and as I still don't know what actually happened at the lodge I will join you for a second.'

Matron was waiting for both of them in the intensive care tent. Mary Atkins was grateful for the opportunity to talk to both of them and started by saying 'Well doctor, the girls and I have begged, borrowed and even stolen what we think you will need'. Pausing and looking into the boxes and at the list of items inside each box that was pinned to the side, she continued 'Apart from a measure of good luck, I think you have everything.'

The surgeon had a quick look in the boxes and replied 'Thank you Matron, everything we will need and more by the look of things' and adding 'Matron, what happen at the Lodge? When we got there the whole main building was a smoking ruin and the grounds looked like a battlefield.'

Shaking her head as she spoke, she said 'I really believe we were the wrong target. You know that we were constantly being over flown by the Luftwaffe for days on end without any problems but well before dawn, a few hours after you left, several artillery shells fell about a hundred yards away, a few minutes later, a salvo hit the perimeter wall, it all happened so quick after that, four, maybe five salvos came onto the building and grounds. It only lasted five minutes, but the devastation was dreadful'

'Poor Colonel Wilson and Sergeant Murray were killed instantly as were Margaret Doyle and Jan Mitchell. I thought Mary Coombe would make it, she was in the theatre assisting Major McCloud at the time, and the shell burst was away from them, but she died a couple of hours after the attack, and as you saw, several drivers and patients were caught in the blasts in various ways, and were killed, I was lucky.'

'It must have been quite horrible Matron' he said and finished by saying 'I'm going to get my final orders from the officer in charge before the train arrives, as I have a feeling chaos will be the order of the day when it does.'

The Matron asked Anna to take the place of the surgeon and sit opposite her before saying 'Anna, if my arm was not in a sling I would be the one staying here. Now I know you have a personal reason for staying as well as a professional one, but are you sure?'

'Yes Matron, very sure indeed.'

Mary Akins continued 'Anna, you know that John has no chance of surviving, his injuries are appalling.'

'I know,' Anna said quietly, 'I can see the distress he's in, and that he probably doesn't even know I'm here, but Matron I do want to be here, for him, and for the other wounded.'

'You know' Matron continued 'I seem to have known all of you much longer than I actually have, I can't believe it was only five months ago we all met. I can tell you now I am very proud of each of you. You've all been a credit to your profession, yourselves, and also to me.'

Pausing as if searching her memory, she said 'I was your age Anna when I came to Flanders in 1918. It was the last months of the First World War and I nursed a young infantry officer who had been wounded in battle back to recovery, he was such a handsome, pleasant man'

'We saw a lot of each other and the day before he went back to his regiment he asked me to marry him when the war was over. I said yes, and we became engaged. Sadly, he was killed going over the top attacking the Hindenburg Line'

'The anger and bitterness raged in me for years. It seemed so unfair that he had been killed when the end of the war was in sight. After it happened I put every moment of my life into nursing and it wasn't until several years after my John had been killed that I realised I was angry with me, angry and sad for not being with him when he needed me.'

Matron stopped talking and looked at Anna, her eyes full of the tears she had shed on so many solitary moments in her life since her only love had been taken from her. 'I hope we meet again Anna, but if we don't you should at least be thankful that you were with the one you love when he needed you.'

The two women walked to the tent where John and the other critically wounded soldiers had been placed. The flap of the tent closed behind them as Matron and Anna approached the nurses she was about to take over from, after first going to John's bed. He was starting to sweat again but seemed stable and as the nurses started to talk to each other the shrill sound of a steam engine's whistle blowing several times and the hissing of steam announced the arrival of the hospital train.

The tent flap opened again and the medical officer and Peter Adnans hurried in. The surgeon's prophecy of chaos as soon as the Red Cross train arrived was accurate. It took less than an hour to load over four hundred patients and medical staff.

Everything happened so quickly that Anna and Peter Adnans were unaware that the train was leaving. They were busy doing their first rounds together of the final seven critical patients they were charged with, so there were no goodbyes or waves, just the sound of a departing steam train as it hissed and bellowed away into the night.

Before the sound of the train began to grow silent in the distance the noise from the ambulances revving their engines outside took over. The surgeon and nurse stood by the tent entrance and watched the dark square shapes of the vehicles move away, the narrow shafts of yellow light from blackout headlamps probing a short way ahead as they scattered in different directions. It was suddenly very quiet.

Soignies, 16th May, 1940

 Hitler's army had advanced so rapidly that, against the wishes of his generals in the field of battle, the German dictator gave a direct order to halt the advance while the supply lines caught up with the panzers and infantry men.
 At the same time that Hitler was berating his generals at the Berghof, his home in the Bavarian Alps, in Paris the French Prime Minister, Paul Reynaud, telephoned Winston Churchill and shouted, 'We have been defeated, we are beaten.'
 The British Prime Minister flew to the French capital immediately where he found the situation much worse than he had imagined. He witnessed piles of government documents and papers being burnt on the palace lawns while any plans for the defence of the city seemed non-existent.
 The British premier requested the War Cabinet in London to amass all the aircraft in the country and send them to France in order to give a boost to moral and prevent an immediate collapse of the army and government. His request was rejected by the War Cabinet but amended to sending a quarter of the aircraft available, leaving the rest to defend Britain.
 The Allied retreat began during that night from the Dyle River to the new defence line, the river Escaut, it was less than a week since the same forces had so triumphantly raced to the rescue of Belgium. It was now in a fast and furious retreat.

****

 Pushing the tiny priming pump up and down with her thumb and fore finger several times Anna lit the second Tilley lamp in the tent, turning the wick down to give her the gentle yellowish light she needed without disturbing the sleeping patients and surgeon.
 She liked the petrol smell of the lamps that helped to hide the hospital odours of the tent and the hissing sound from them that eased the gentle sighs, sobs and cries that came from the men lying on their wood and canvass cot beds.
 Checking the pulse of a soldier Anna knew it was time to

carry out the surgeon's instruction and administer a dose of morphine. The young Belgian soldier had been in agonised delirium for several hours and she and the doctor had watched the pain roll through his shattered body for many of them. As she injected the sedative drug into a vein his contorting figure settled almost instantly.

A pallid look had come back to John's face and beads of sweat were forming on his forehead when she went back to him. Mopping his brow with a cold flannel she gently wiped his face and neck saying at the same time 'You have a very handsome face, and I do love you very much.'

Hearing a rasping, gurgling sound come from the Belgian soldier Anna went quickly to his cot. As she put her right hand around his and felt the clammy skin of his wrist he took a gentle intake of air that made his broken chest rise a fraction and stay suspended as life left him. 'No more pain, no more suffering' she said quietly before laying his arms across his chest and covering his young body with the bed sheet.

After Anna woke Peter Adnans they changed John's dressings, with neither saying a word. He was such a dreadful mess it was hard to look at his wounds and to think it was their friend they were treating. Finally, Peter said 'His pulse is steadier, but I don't like the sound of his breathing, we'll have to see how he is later.'

Anna told the surgeon that the Belgium soldier had died and after they had completed the rounds of the remaining patients they went outside the tent and were suddenly aware of the silence. It was a noiseless hush that took both by surprise and had an unnerving effect rather than the peaceful one they would normally feel when the sounds of battle stopped.

Standing still they were both looking up at the stars through a clear sky until he said, 'I'm grateful you're here Anna, I don't think I've ever felt quite so alone, and to be honest, I'm scared.'

Anna had no answers, she knew they were in a very dangerous predicament but her duty was clear which made the dangers seem somehow acceptable, slightly less daunting.

'I'm a little tired, I think I'll go in' she said. The surgeon followed her inside, looked at John and told Anna he would wake her in a few hours, or before if John needed her, adding 'Sleep for you madam!'

The drone of aircraft flying close entered her tired head several times soon after she fell asleep but it was almost eight o'clock when she woke, feeling a lot better. She looked at John before throwing cold water over her face. Peter Adnans had put him on a drip to replace the fluids he was losing and he looked peaceful with some colour in his face.

She noticed that another white sheet had been pulled over the cot of one of the patients but was surprised by another soldier asking for water. He seemed to have improved over the last few hours and Anna saw it was in order to give him a small amount of liquid for which the young man even managed a smile and thank you.

Anna found the surgeon outside the tent, the hush of the night had gone and the familiar sound of distant gunfire was now audible, mingled with the incessant humming of aircraft. In daylight their isolation seemed even more complete.

The station platform was the type used once or twice a week to collect farm animals and vegetables. With no buildings or shelters, and metal pens to hold the cattle and sheep. The flat countryside of Flanders lay either side of the concrete slab and railway line, while in the distance two rows of tall poplar trees, throwing long black shadows, followed the straight line of a road until they gave way to rolling green hills and thick woods.

The timeless rural scene was tarnished by ugly columns of black or grey smoke rising vertically beyond the distant horizon and by aeroplane vapour trails hanging listlessly in the hot cloudless sky.

Shielding his eyes with one hand he stood looking at the criss-crossing lines in the sky and said, 'John seems comfortable this morning, but as you saw, the sergeant died a couple of hours ago, but the other sergeant is a lot better.'

'I think we should bring the two lads that died out of the main tent and put them in the shade of the other tent. Afterwards, coffee, which I have found in the command tent and some rather stale bread for breakfast, but I'm starving!'

They laid out the two dead soldiers in the shade, wrapped in sheets. In the main tent Anna lifted and tied up part of one side of the canvass wall to let the air circulate through. She was just finishing and heading towards John when Peter Adnans arrived with the promised coffee and bread and they sat either side of John's camp bed talking quietly; eating their breakfast.

Another of the soldiers was giving the surgeon concern. Although the young man was not in obvious pain, his pulse and breathing were erratic, and laboured. After looking at John and satisfying herself that his condition had not changed Anna joined Peter Adnans.

The soldier that he was concerned about died as they were discussing the next treatment for him. 'Damn it Anna' the surgeon cursed. 'I know he never had any chance whatsoever, but it's such a waste of a young life.'

'You did what you could Peter, and at least he went peacefully, now please try and get some sleep.' Nodding wearily in agreement he occupied a spare camp bed and fell asleep instantly as Anna walked back to John McCloud's bedside.

Lifting his sheet she adjusted one of his dressings before she began to wipe away the small beads of sweat that covered his lined brow with a damp flannel.

It startled her when suddenly his eyes flickered several times and then slowly opened. He was trying to say something, but the sound was so soft, so quiet, his words were lost.

'John darling it's me. It's me, Anna. Now please save your strength, please don't try to speak, darling.'

He was still trying to speak so she knelt on the floor of the tent besides his bed so that she could lean over him and put an ear close to his mouth while one of her hands gently held his shoulder and the other found his hand.

She heard the soft, but unmistakable sound of his voice say 'Anna? Anna my love'

'Yes darling, it's me, John I'm here with you.'

Anna looked into his eyes, saw a sparkle of life and warmth in them and a faint smile appear on his face before he drew a short breath and blinked his eyes twice before they closed forever and he died.

Anna kissed his lips and tenderly brushed his hair with her hand, feeling the contours of his head with her finger tips and reaching the fine downy hairs on the nape of his neck 'I know you like me doing this, it makes you purr like a cat' she said, smiling.

With her mouth close to his ear she whispered 'You would have liked my mother and father John, and I'm sure I would have liked yours. I've thought several times that you and my dad would have argued through the night and I was looking forward to that'

'I was looking forward to so many things that we would do together, meeting friends, walking near your home in Wales, going back to Pont Aven on your motorbike, and I so wanted us to have children'

'Darling, I never had the time to tell you that love was something that had never reached me before we met, and truthfully, it took some time for me to realise how much I wanted to be with you because of you, being you'

'Your funny ways, your funny words, the slightly unsure ways you had, I loved them, all of them'

'I so wanted to be your wife, but most of all, I was looking forward to being your friend, and now you're gone, you silly boy. And John, I really don't want to go on without you on my own.' Anna stopped talking as she laid her head on his bare shoulder putting her arms around his still body and wept.

Peter Adnans had been awake for ten minutes. He knew what had happened and left Anna and his friend together as he went outside. It was three in the afternoon, and very hot.

Smoke was coming from the direction of Soignies and formations of aircraft were visible in the distance, but the gunfire they had heard earlier had stopped. He made coffee in the command tent and opened a tin of army bully beef before stepping outside and sitting down on a wooden box, shaded by the tent's awning.

'I really am going to miss you John' he said softly 'I'm going to miss you making me laugh, and even miss you talking your impossible and quite mad politics.'

He was apprehensive as he straightened his back and headed towards the tent where his friend lay. Pulling back the flaps at the entrance he saw Anna standing over John's still body. She had removed all the apparatus that had helped keep him alive and had bathed him before laying out a sheet to cover him, leaving his face free.

The surgeon said 'Anna, I am so terribly sorry.'

Not taking her eyes away from John she smiled before she replied 'I know you are, he told me that he thought you were a true friend,' shaking her head she added 'I'm just so angry Peter. Angry because, well I think we all deserved a lot more time together.'

Anna looked back at the now tranquil face of her fiancé before saying 'Do you think can we leave John here for a while, please, before we take him to the other tent?'

'Of course, Anna, let's put a screen up and you can sit with him whenever you want. I'm just going for a stroll outside Anna.'

Walking towards the grey concrete railway platform he noticed that to one side of it a wall had collapsed leaving a line of lose stones, he made a mental note of them knowing that very soon they would have to make temporary graves for the men that had died, including John.

Peter made his way to the command tent. He found the last of the bread, enough for the two of them, and opening two tins of stew from the army compo rations, he placed them in a metal mess tin and put it onto a 'Beatrice' paraffin stove.

Rummaging around the tent looking for water the surgeon let out a loud cry when he found two cases of Belgian beer and three bottles of red wine, his face brightened as he said 'Bloody hell, Mouton Rothschild, 1929. Bloody hell, Daddy would be quite envious.'

At the entrance to the tent he waved to Anna. She joined him and under gentle pressure from her commanding officer, she ate a little of the stew and a small piece of bread.

Peter handed Anna a tin mug with some Mouton Rothschild in it before saying 'Excellent year this, not really ready for drinking yet, should be left for a few years, can't get this for love nor money in Blighty you know, anyhow Anna, here's to our good friend John McCloud.'

Mug in hand the surgeon said 'Anna, you know we have to

move on. I can only think that the railway line has been bombed as it's close to twenty-four hours now without seeing another train and goodness only knows what has happened to our promised transport. If nothing happens before daybreak we shall have to leave John and the others here.'

'I know' Anna agreed before he carried on 'At first light I will walk in the direction of Soignies and try to link up with our own forces, I just cannot believe we have been forgotten, but it would seem that we have been.'

Putting his arm around her shoulder he guided her back to the medical tent in the fading light saying 'You know, John and I used to laugh like babies at times, I really am going to miss him.'

They were only a yard from the tent when they both stopped, hearing the sound of an approaching vehicle they turned around quickly.

In the distance, something was kicking up clouds of dust on the track, heading towards them. They said nothing, and strangely neither felt afraid. The bright setting sun caused the dark silhouettes racing towards them to take amorphous shapes until they were less than a hundred yards away.

With relief they recognized the familiar and definite shape of the British Army's tin hats on top of two motorcycle drivers and their machines.

As the motorcycles came to a halt and their engines were turned off the two medical people smiled as they heard a soldier with two stripes on his arm say 'Blimey, Sir, what on earth are you still doing here?'

Peter Adnans started to explain to the corporal why they were stranded while Anna went into the tent and came out with a jug of water and two mugs for the men.

The two soldiers told the surgeon they were starving hungry and he was more than happy to take them to the command tent where he opened two more tins of stew for the men, then opened two bottles of beer and sat with them before saying 'So where are you chaps heading then?'

The corporal replied between spooning his stew into his mouth 'We're both dispatch riders Sir, attached to a mechanised cavalry unit. Our armoured cars have been acting as a rear guard to the retreating troops.'

Talking to the doctor, the men told him that on all fronts over the last twenty-four hours the Germans had called a halt. Some artillery action had continued, but the main thrust forward by German troops had stopped. The lull in fighting had been a welcome surprise and the Allies had used the breathing space to good effect they said.

The men ate quickly and said that they were anxious to get back to their regiment. They also said that they would tell their C.O. that the medical unit was stranded here, and that they would come back with more news. With still a glimmer of light available, the two motorcyclist drove away, the dust they created hanging in the still evening air.

In the treatment tent Anna had spent several minutes with the remaining patients. She felt that two of them could be given solids, but the condition of the male nursing orderly who had been injured at the Lodge, had deteriorated badly.

It was now cool outside the tent with the early evening stars beginning to show themselves in an almost cloudless sky. Peter told Anna that the soldiers were going to report their situation, and that he was confident some form of help would arrive tomorrow.

Soignies, 17th May, 1940

Anna's last vigil beside John went quickly, his hands were cold now when she touched them and said 'Just one last thing I want to do darling before I wake Peter.'

Picking up a pair of scissors Anna cut off a small lock of her own hair which she pressed between John's tightly closed right hand and then cut off three locks of his black hair which she wrapped in a small piece of clean field dressing binding and grafted the thin fold onto the chain of her identity tags that she then placed back around her neck.

Anna finally pulled the white sheet covering his body over his head, kissing him one last time on his brow before the white cotton material took the shape of the face she would in the future see only in her memory.

The surgeon woke her before five o'clock with a cup of tea. During the night he had managed to slide John's body onto a trolley without disturbing Anna, and had wheeled him to where the other bodies were laid out. He told Anna that as they both expected, the nursing orderly had died a couple of hours ago, but that their remaining two British patients were doing exceptionally well, and were both asleep.

During the first hour of daylight Peter Adnans carved out five separate sallow graves, placing each body into them. He had found a shovel in the command tent and the ground he had choosen had been mercifully easy to dig. With a thin layer of earth over each of the men he then carefully placed the stones that he had found yesterday on top of the graves to form small mounds on each before placing a wooden stake at the head of their temporary resting places with the men's Army details written on it and the date of their deaths.

It was ten o'clock in the morning by the time his thankless task was complete. It was also very hot as he entered the treatment tent and wearily flopped on a cot. It was Anna's turn to make and bring him a mug of coffee and three slices of tinned Spam and dried biscuits for breakfast.

They both moved outside the tent and sat on empty boxes facing each other. 'Thank you Peter, that must have been pretty unpleasant for you.'

A glug of coffee stopped an instant reply from him but after he had finished he said 'To be honest, I'm jolly pleased we were able to do it, Anna. When transport does arrive, I have a feeling we shall be away from here *tout suite,* and I really did not like the thought of just leaving John, so to speak'

After a lot of munching he added 'Do you know, I love Spam for breakfast Anna, hate the biscuits, but I do love the Spam'

'Now look Anna, I was thinking that after breakie I'm going to use the tin bath they have in the command tent and clean myself up after my stint of hard labour. I would then like to put the cleanest uniform on that I can muster, and after that I thought I would say a few words over the resting places of John and the other lads, before we leave, do you think that's a good idea?'

'I can't think of anything nicer or more fitting Lord

Roxenton' she replied, and continued, saying 'I've been so absorbed I have only just taken a look at where we are. We seem to be out of the way of everything, which is good in one way but you don't think we've been by-passed and forgotten do you?'

'Truth is I don't know' Peter replied, shaking his head and hunching his shoulders 'I do know that the rest of the team would not let us be forgotten, but I think it's likely that it may have become impossible to get help to us.' Looking around he continued 'I find the silence ominous rather than comforting. What has happened? One minute all hell going off and then near silence, the two lads on motorbikes were as puzzled as we are.'

'I am super confident that help will come from the regiment that the dispatch riders were heading back to, and that sometime today contact will be made, but other than that, I simply do not know, but if nothing happens by the end of the day, as I said yesterday, I will head for Soignies, and hope for the best.'

Getting up, Anna said 'I'll go and get some food for our patients before you start to carry out your ablutions. I would like to swap tents with you after you've finished so that I can clean myself up and look as smart as my commanding officer.'

After Anna and Peter had taken advantage of their first bath in many days and found a miss-matched change of uniform they took a quick look at their patients and walked slowly to the spot that Peter Adnans had chosen to put their friend and the other patients.

Looking at the graves that had the shade of several Oleander bushes, Anna said 'What a peaceful spot you found for them.'

Deep in thought he replied after a moment 'Yes, it's rather like the corner of an English garden. At home, I suppose I would be called religious because we all go to church, in fact on the estate in Scotland, we have our own church, but I confess Anna I'm not sure what to say, but I will have a go'

They both clasped their hands in front of themselves in an attempt to look as reverent as they could before Peter started by saying 'God, I know you are frightfully busy at the moment, but we would be grateful if you could look after these brave soldiers and our close friend, John McCloud.'

Pausing, Peter blinked a few times searching for more words before continuing 'They were all very young people God, and frankly they should have had many more years to enjoy the beautiful things you have created with such care. John would have loved the Mouton Rothschild we tasted last night, but of course he wasn't able too, which is a great shame, really'

Listening to his words Anna found herself smiling, knowing John would have done likewise, while at the same time dabbing away her rolling tears with her handkerchief she listened as the surgeon continued.

'I don't pretend to understand what this is all about if I'm totally honest, but God, Anna and I would be very pleased if you would look after John, as he was a very special person to us, and we are going to miss him dreadfully. So, thank you and umm, well Amen.'

Anna put her arm through Peter's saying 'That was perfect, very sweet, very honest, and I'm sure that God will know exactly what you meant.'

Peter went back to the treatment tent, leaving Anna alone. She wondered around the country railway siding and gathered five separate bunches of wild flowers and placed a bunch of the brightly coloured blossoms on each grave leaving John's until the last. She knelt down on the ground beside him and put the flowers close to the head of the stone mound.

A little after seven they both left the treatment tent when they heard the distinctive sound of a motorbike approaching. It was the same corporal from yesterday, this time on his own. He steered the motorbike so that it blended in with the frame of the abandoned ambulance. With the engine turned off he pulled the machine back onto its stand, before walking over to them saying 'I'm ever so sorry, Sir, I tried every trick in the book to get back before now, but I had to go in the opposite direction first, then double back here.'

Major Adnans had gone to the command tent when he first spotted the driver approaching and was able to point to another box to sit on before offering a bottle of Belgium beer to the parched soldier.

'Thank you, Sir, very welcome. Major Tomkins, our C.O., sends his regards Sir. He's been in touch with H.Q. and it seems they were surprised to hear you were still here, they thought all forward casualty clearing stations and their patients had been evacuated on the last train a couple of days ago'

Peter and Anna exchanged knowing looks before giving their full attention to the new arrival. 'We've been told that our next move is to re-deploy the whole battalion to the South of Lille, back into France, Sir, which is why I've been driving around to all the forward positions all day to give them the C.O.'s orders. We slip out under Jerry's nose soon as it gets dark tonight, otherwise their artillery and aircraft gives us a right bashing'

After taking another long swig of the beer, he continued 'Most of the battalion will keep to the main roads because of our heavy equipment but I'll lead the lorry the C.O. has provided for you and the patients here and we can go across the country lanes I know and re-join the main group later.'

'Now, how many bottles of this beer can you get into your pannier bags, I don't intend to leave any for the Germans, so come with me and help yourself, just one last thing, what approximate time do you imaging you will get here.'

The corporal looked at his watch before saying 'Between twelve and one o'clock, I should think, Sir, we really want to be away from the main roads before it gets light, the rumour is that the quiet of the last couple of days is about to come to an end.'

With bulging pannier bags and a borrowed knapsack on his back full of bottles of beer the motorcyclist left them. Peter returned to the treatment tent where he found Anna in the process of selecting the medical supplies she thought they might need for their trip.

Standing between the camp beds of the wounded British men the surgeon said 'Well gentlemen, in a couple of hours transport will arrive and we will start our trek back into France and a decent hospital. Now then, do you have any questions?'

The second lieutenant with the head wound spoke first 'Sir, why are we all retreating back towards France?'

The surgeon stared at the man, while he searched for words before saying 'Lieutenant, I only wish I could answer your question, but in honest truth I do not know why, but I have to say that it seems that the Allies have suffered a major reverse, and we are all retreating.'

Retreat to Dunkirk

Soignies, 18th May 1940

Picking up a torch Anna walked the short distance to John's temporary grave. In a hushed voice she said 'It's almost time for us to go darling, I promise I will come back to see you when all this madness stops and as you told me, some human dignity returns'

She added 'I also promise that I will be in touch with your parents and tell them that you are at least resting in a pretty place. Bye, bye darling.' She blew him a kiss over her hand before walking back.

At half past one in the morning they heard the sound of approaching vehicles and as a lorry and motorcycle came to a halt a thunderous explosion erupted from the direction of Soigines which sent brilliant flashes of pyrotechnics high into the night sky sending shock waves that rustled the canvas of the tents behind them.

The driver of the motorcycle looked back at the town and said, 'The last blokes out had to blow up the battalion ammunition dump, the fact that it's so soon after we left means that Jerry is close behind them Sir'

'Right then Sir' said the corporal, 'We ought to load up and get under way as soon as poss, if you don't mind Sir.' The lorry they had been given was one Anna was familiar with, a Bedford 15cwt, similar to the one she and Matron had gone to Genappe in when the Messerschmitts had attacked them.

In twenty minutes they were loaded and with Peter Adnans sitting in the front cab with the driver while Anna took the

only space available in the back next to the tailgate.
The lorry had a canvass tilt cover to keep the rain off and the back was open. Anna, was sat with one arm resting on the tailgate the other gripping the slatted wooden seat beneath her as the motorcycle and lorry started to move away. She looked towards the area were they had buried John, and quietly said 'Bye, bye my love.'

Armentieres, 20th May 1940

Sat crouched over a wireless set he started to get up before Peter Adnans motioned him to stay where he was, saying 'Lieutenant, I need to get to the No 8 'G' hospital, north of Lille, what's the present situation that way?'

Rubbing bleary eyes, he said 'Sir, I've been told that enemy formations have been engaged around Roubaix, here,' the lieutenant said and pointed at the town on a large-scale map 'My orders are to steer all the traffic I can around the South of Lille towards Armentieres and any of the northern channel ports. I do know that a sizable hospital near Armentieries was taking casualties in yesterday Sir.'

A salute from the dispatch rider who had led them from the railway platform in Belgium back into France was returned with a wave from Anna as he headed away towards Arras to find his regiment and the Bedford 15 cwt crawled back into the stream of vehicles, refugees and soldiers on the road heading towards Armentieres.

The Red Cross signs were clear well before they reached them, hanging down the front of the châteaux, from the bedroom windows to the top of the front door and ground floor windows.

Anna could hear, but not see the three Dornier bombers that made the vehicle stop while Peter Adnans and their driver watched their progress as they passed in front of them at tree top level before each man breathed a sigh of relief as the machines continued until they were lost to view.

The small army lorry had no Red Cross signs to identify it as an ambulance, and so far they had been luckier than the hundreds, and hundreds of burnt out wrecks that smouldered or lay black and twisted on the roadside; epitaph's to the British and French collapse.

Driving past the open gates onto a drive that led to the front of the building they saw bright yellow squares of dead grass on the green lawns leading to the entrance of the châteaux where tents and marques had recently stood.

The tent poles and guide ropes to some were still in place, the skeleton frames missing their khaki canvass coverings, while supplies and clothing were littered over the ground in all directions.

There were two army lorries and three ambulances parked to the side of the building but no signs of life. Their lorry came to a standstill at the bottom of a flight of stone steps that led to the closed wooden front doors of the former residence and joining Peter Adnans as he walked slowly up the steps it was Anna who spoke first

'Two days of dodging aircraft, what a dreadful journey. Peter, I think you should have a look at both of our patients, I'm not too happy with either of them.'

Reaching for the handle of the front door he turned his head towards the sister to answer her as the door opened inwards and they faced a ruddy faced medical lieutenant on crutches who spluttered 'Good God, or rather Thank God, I'm sorry Sir, I'm Michael Sterling' in a strong Scottish accent.

Returning the man's awkward salute Peter Adnans asked 'Are you attached to this hospital?'

'No Sir, we got here half an hour ago, I've got several badly injured men in the vehicles you would have passed on the way in Sir but this place is like the Marie Celeste, no one about at all and it looks like they took off in a tearing rush, it's eerie, a lot of beds inside are made up, and there are a few medical supplies, but absolutely no people'

'Sir, I'm so pleased you are here, I'm in a bit of a pickle since I twisted my ankle and tore some ligaments and wonder if you could take a look at my patients. I'm very worried about two in particular, but find it impossible to move around the inside of the ambulance where they are.'

Peter remained silent for a moment before he said 'Yes, right then Michael, let's all have a quick look around inside the building and then sister and I will see to your men'

Coming out of the abandoned hospital he faced both of them with a deep frown on his face before saying 'I am very clear in my own mind that despite the Germans breathing down our necks we have a clear duty to the men in our charge. I want all of them brought in here so that we can assess them individually, and then decide on our next move.'

Over the next three days most of the casualties were treated and sent towards the coast when the surgeon gave the nod including the two men they had arrived with, until finally he said to Anna 'We have to go this morning. Could you arrange to cut down the Red Cross signs and tell everyone to be ready to leave in an hour.'

The two remaining ambulances drove past the two mounds of earth in a flower garden that marked the temporary resting places of the men that had died in their care before they pulled out of the grounds of the châteaux and slotted into the heavy streams of people and traffic heading remorselessly towards the sea.

Progress was slow and difficult. It was pitch black and almost ten thirty at night when the ambulance with Lieutenant Sterling in it came to a stuttering clanking halt, and both drivers confirmed the bad news to the senior officer that the drive shaft of the vehicle had broken and could not be repaired on the shoulder of the road.

Peter Adnans rapped his fingers loudly on one of the metal mudguards that arched over the front wheels for several moments before calling Anna.

Occupying the passenger seat of the broken ambulance Michael Sterling sat and listened to the surgeon who was stood outside, beside his door 'Now then, this is a dammed difficult situation, and unless either of you have a better suggestion then I propose to cram all our injured into one ambulance with just one nurse, the spare driver and you Michael to take care of them'

'We can't be more than twenty odd miles from Dunkirk which is in a straight line and those of us left will simply walk the rest of the way.'

The final words came from Lieutenant Sterling after the wounded men had been placed in the single vehicle and his head pushed open the canvass and plastic passenger window and he shouted 'Good luck Sir, ma'am. See you all back in England!'

Three nursing orderlies, one nursing sister and the surgeon were left on the road side as they each watched the ambulance inch its way back into the mass of vehicles and people heading slowly to the coast.

Last in the line led by Peter Adnans Anna felt a strange sense of panic, a sense of claustrophobia brought on by the shifting throng of faceless marchers that tightly surrounded them in the near total darkness. She thought to herself 'So this is what it's like to be a refugee, being bumped along, not knowing where or what is coming next, completely unable to change events, totally helpless. What a horrible feeling.'

Godewaerseide, 25th May 1940

Peter Adnans had been leading the nurses along the road for an hour when he stumbled into the back of the man ahead of him. At the end of the line Anna heard the major apologise to the dark shape of the refugee and then heard a string of insults and abuse from the stranger being hurled at the surgeon.

Within seconds several other refugees had gathered around him, one pushing him in the back, making him stumble and fall onto one knee. Anna saw his silhouette stand up, retaliating with more words of apology which the hastily gathered crowd drowned by their angry baying.

Shouting in French Anna pleaded 'Please calm down, we are not soldiers, we are a medical unit, please leave the doctor alone, we mean no harm.'

In the darkness individuals seemed to lose their outline, congealing into a single swarming black cloud of rage and anger like one seething animal. More pushing, more frenzied shouts and screams started and Anna felt scared by the ugly, violent way the dark mass was reacting.

The man who had started the fracas shone a torch on the

surgeon as he tried again to stand upright. She saw that the protagonist had been joined by another and both were now jostling Peter Adnans backwards with hard pushes in his chest and face.

The sister and nurses had been isolated from the surgeon by the group whose voices screamed at them. Trying to break through the crowd she felt hands grab her hair from behind and more tearing at her tunic.

She lashed out at the unseen attackers with her hands until she felt a sudden stab of pain to the side of her head. Stumbling to the ground she felt more blows to her body and a sharp kick in her ribs that made her double up in on the ground and shout out in pain before she grabbed the leg that had kicked her and used it as a lever to straighten herself up.

The hand of the person pulled her hair viscously but Anna quickly turned her head around, at the same time sinking her teeth deep into the thumb of her attacker. As he yelled she hit him with every seething oz of bottled up anger in her body before charging him in the chest with her shoulder and stepping on his face as he crashed to the ground.

In a blind fury she hit out wildly at every part of the black monster in front of her until suddenly she saw flashes of torch light and then heard the sound of several loud gun shots rip through the darkness. Like Anna the mob stopped shouting and clawing, turning as one towards the noises.

She could now make out the shape of three soldiers standing around Peter Adnans and four, maybe five others behind them. She watched as one of them brutally punched one of Peter's attackers in the face and stomach, while the other was clubbed to the ground with blows on his head from a pistol barrel. The crowd scattered after two more shots were fired into the air and several at the ground followed by harsh, loud orders to keep away. The tail of the black monster rose defiantly as more shouts and threats crossed the night.

Without hesitation soldiers rushed forward and clubbed a man and a woman who continued to ignore the instructions with their weapons, leaving them heaped on the road, gasping, groaning and bleeding.

Peter, Anna and the nurses found themselves being pulled

willingly away from the scene leaving the battered, bleeding people on the road side and after ten minutes they came to a cross roads with heavy defensive positions dug in around it, manned by British troops.

The incident had shaken all of them. At this stage of the war, they were well used to the brutalities initiated around them; well able to help those directly affected by the conflict, but until moments ago they were all innocents in the savage game of war.

None of them had been part of the madness that makes normal people act like beasts and each member of the medical team knew they had been tainted by the cruelness and meanness of war, and that their slightly smug innocence was now a thing of the past, for Anna and the others realised that the moment they had stepped over the injured people lying in the road, covered in blood, they were as guilty and as frail as those around them.

The soldiers at the cross roads were part of an infantry regiment, acting as rear guards while the bulk of their regiment started their retreat to the coast and evacuation.

The sergeant who had fired the first shots into the air told the officer in charge what had happened, and why the doctor and nurses were with him.

'Second lieutenant Gerald Davies, Sir. Had a spot of bother I hear, well it's very likely that the two men that started the trouble were French or Belgium army deserters, they seem to stir up the civilian refugees by blaming us for all that has happened, but when we arrested a couple of similar types yesterday, we found they had stolen money, jewellery, identity cards and all sorts on them, just petty thieves really, but pretty unpleasant ones without any mistake.'

Peter Adnans did not want to know the fate of the men the officer talked of, instead thanking him and the sergeant for his timely appearance as he asked 'Where exactly are we?'

Shown into a make-shift tent where a radio operator was sat besides his machine, a map of the area was laid out on top of a box and the second lieutenant pointed to the village of Godewaerseide, which he said was 25 miles from the coast.

Outside the wireless tent the group gladly accepted the mugs of sweet, strong tea, and with the nurses once again gathered around him, Peter Adnans said to them 'Right now, I can hardly see any of you but ladies, thank you for trying to come to my rescue after my rather feeble attempt at calming the situation down. I think I have a few new bruises but nothing to worry about, but are any of you injured?'

Anna had already asked the three nursing orderlies if they were alright and answered for them by saying 'A few bruises like you Sir, and a slight case of shock for all of us, but nothing that will keep us off the road to the coast and home, Sir.'

Invited to share their food by the infantry officer, the Major told the nurses that they would eat and rest for a while before setting off again. Drawing Anna aside he added quietly 'My God Anna, that was loathsome, quite brutish and frightening, are you sure you are unhurt?' He accepted her 'Yes' before he began shaking his head from side to side and adding 'Those poor people who were clubbed down, shocking, just shocking.'

Touching his arm before speaking Anna said 'Peter, we were very lucky, and at least none of us are hurt.'

The infantry officer told them that he had been engaged in heavy fighting since the 12th of May, losing more than half of the regiment, killed or captured in the process. He explained with some bitterness that every engagement had ended with them withdrawing, even though they had in turn stopped the German advance on many occasions, he said 'The problem has been that we could never build on any advance we made, without aircraft and few tanks to support us, it was hopeless, and each time we were overwhelmed by counter attacks'

'On two occasions along the river Escault the Belgian troops supporting our flank simply disappeared, leaving their positions undefended. I found some of the same men drinking beers in the village bars behind the main defence line, some jeering and taunting my chaps, but not for long, I can assure you, Sir.'

'What we all find difficult to understand is exactly why we have so obviously failed the Belgium people, nothing seems to make much sense Sir, we all of us feel such failures, and when you see the fields next to us, in daylight, full of modern, but now destroyed equipment, it makes one almost cry, it wasn't what I joined the army for Sir.'

Neither Peter nor Anna had any answers but could only continue to listen to the out pouring of anguish and disappointment of the young man 'At times we have had outstanding support from the Allied troops, and especially the French. We have a French liaison officer, an infantry captain, Charles Lamont, who joined us when we arrived in January and trained with us all through the winter months, a great chap'

'He was on leave when the balloon went up but actually travelled from Paris to Brussels in a taxi so that he could be with us and eventually found us south of Louvain, and has fought bravely with us throughout the campaign. Sir, he has been as puzzled and even more humiliated than us at the collapse of our armies'

'At first the lines of communication seemed good, but as soon as we moved into Belgium on the 10th of May, everything started to go wrong. Maybe I shouldn't be talking like this Sir, please say if I should stop, but it is true.'

Peter and Anna saw the seething frustration of a young man, aged twenty-one, perhaps twenty-two, mature in many ways but still needing to seek answers to questions that were shaking his belief in himself. There was a craving to find the truth of what had, and what was happening to him and his friends around him.

The senior officer replied 'No, Gerald, please carry on.'

The lieutenant continued, saying 'Well Sir, two days ago, our regiment was making a move to support another infantry battalion who were defending a bridge over a canal near Tournai against some savage German attacks'

'Captain Lamont had to negotiate with a sergeant of his own army because the man refused an order to pull his teams of horses towing artillery guns to the side of the road to allow our lorries to get past. Sir, in the end, after a lot of bitter arguing and threats, the Captain drew his revolver and shot his own countryman dead in front of us. It was quite extraordinary'

'We got to the bridge and were able to support the troops that were dug in but by the next day, after Jerry brought in his panzers and had blasted us from the air, we had to blow it up, and then Sir, on the way to our new positions we went through a small Belgian town and hanging out of almost every window were white sheets, towels, anything white to signal surrender.'

Hardly pausing for breath, he continued what seemed like an act of confession before communion 'Sir, less than two weeks ago we had a problem getting through Brussels because of the crowds of people trying to shake our hands, pat us on the back and give us flowers, food, wine. Two days ago, I saw people shouting insults, shaking their fits and spitting on the ground in front of me. I'll be honest Sir, I felt ashamed.'

Anna and Peter were saved from offering the wise counselling they thought the young officer sought, and which both knew they were utterly unable to give, by the appearance of the signalman who told his officer he was wanted on the field telephone.

After five minutes he returned saying 'That was my C.O., I've had orders to destroy our wireless and every other piece of equipment except our small arms, and retreat to Dunkirk immediately, so there we are, we are finally finished it seems. But would your group care to join us on the road, Sir?'

They walked three abreast, the direction being very easy to follow, as an orange glow simmered in front of them, which was Dunkirk. It was still pitch black when they started, with showers of light drizzle keeping the first tones of dawn at bay.

After less than an hour it was very obvious that the medical team were holding up the progress of the infantry men and a puffing Major Adnans struggled to keep up with the striding lieutenant while at the same time telling him that as it was now close to daylight and that in his opinion it was important that he and his men should 'push on' and that they would proceed at their own pace.

Tactfully thankful for the senior officer's suggestion he halted his men by the roadside for a short break, during which the medical team wished them well, looking forward to seeing them at the coast. Anna was the last in line of the group headed by the surgeon as they set off again towards the glow of Dunkirk in the distance.

A clinging misty rain turned the first strains of daylight that fell onto the flat open countryside of the Pas de Calais to a dull grey as Anna and the others saw for the first time the scenes of utter chaos and confusion that surrounded them as the Allied armies fled towards the coast in full retreat just ahead of the advancing German army whose guns they could hear clearly.

Many of the British, French and Belgian soldiers around them were hopelessly drunk, some unable to stand, many wondering around the roads, with bottles of Champagne, wine or brandy in their hands.

Discipline had broken down completely for many of the retreating troops with hundreds of the leaderless soldiers wondering around without orders or instructions, following the person in front towards the columns of smoke in the distance.

They had re-joined the road heading towards Herzeele, which was less than a mile away. It was crammed with troops, refugees, military vehicles and motorbikes.
Hundreds of army lorries, cars, motorbikes all abandoned, all disabled or totally destroyed were dumped in fields and on the wide grass verges each side of the road as far as the eye could see.

The major dropped back and began to walk beside Anna, slowly shaking his head from side to side he said 'My goodness, who would have thought it possible, acres and acres of equipment destroyed by our own troops. The young officer was right Anna, it does make one feel rather ashamed, humiliated even.'

They walked in the drizzle that was now constant, wrapped in their army ground sheets that doubled as a waterproof 'poncho'. Dunkirk was now only ten miles away, and the low cloud base reflected an orange glow from the fires that were raging there.

By five o'clock the rain that had given them cover from German aircraft stopped and each had a clear view of the spiralling columns of smoke coming from Dunkirk as they trudged slowly along the straight open road shoulder to shoulder with their fellow escapees.'

As dusk began to fall they reached the outer perimeter defence line of Dunkirk, at Bergues, which was manned by British and French troops. The area they had entered was to be the last line of defence to hold back the Germans while British and French troops were evacuated back to England.

Stretching from the sea below Mardyck to Bergues, Furnes, Nieuport and ending back in the sea at Neiuport Bains, the crescent shaped shield measured 37 miles.

Bergues, 26th May, 1940

The loud, shrill sound of whistles being blown repeatedly woke Anna and the others when it was still dark. Men were shouting, some running, some walking outside the abandoned army lorry that Anna and the others had made their sleeping quarters.

'I'm going to wonder over to the field kitchen to see what's going on' Anna shouted as she jumped down from the back of the army lorry.
Twenty minutes later she reappeared bringing back a jug of tea and said 'I'm sorry to start the day with bad news but I was told by one of the army cooks that the Belgian King surrendered unconditionally during the night and their troops have stopped fighting on all fronts.'

Peter Adnans finished his mug of tea and went quickly to the command tent of the military police to find out more news. When he returned he said despondently 'Absolute chaos everywhere, truth is no one has a clue were anything or anybody is except that all personnel are 'Commanded' to proceed to the beach areas to the east of the town immediately. So ladies as soon as we can we should set off, I'm sure we will come across a medical post on the way and get a better view of what is happening.'

Walking past by three abandoned ambulances the nursing orderly who was walking besides Anna stopped before saying 'Sister, I'm not sure, but I thought I heard someone shout from inside.'

Opening the doors, they found seven wounded soldiers. The nurses and surgeon quickly brought the men out of the fetid air of the ambulance and laid them on the ground in the open. There were three more men in the next vehicle and the last one was empty.

Of the ten soldiers five were dead, with the remaining men suffering from dehydration and various types of battle injury and only one of the wounded men was able to speak. He had no idea how long they had been left abandoned in the ambulance he told them.

Angrily the surgeon almost shouted 'I'm going to go on alone and try to locate a first aid post and return for them as soon as I can.' Starting to walk along the road Anna saw him stop, hesitate for a moment and come back. She watched as he climbed into the driver's cab of the first ambulance.

The vehicle sprang to life almost immediately, and kept going. He switched the engine off and climbed down before coming back to them saying 'I would like to get my hands on the people who simply deserted these men, it's nothing short of murder. Come on, we will have to leave the lads that died but we can put the others into the front vehicle and we'll try and find a CCS or something similar.'

Anna sat in the passenger seat next to Peter Adnans as he fumbled with the ignition switch before the Bedford sprang noisily into life. 'Do you think you can handle the ambulance?' she asked.

'O ye of little faith, Sister Jack, of course I can handle the beast, that is once I get the hang of things. Actually, it's a bit like one of daddy's farm trucks that I drive when we go to the estate in Scotland on holidays, rather fun really!'

Unable to suppress her smile Anna shook her head at the same time of saying 'Estate in Scotland! I honest to God don't know how my father would handle you Peter, I really don't!'

Her words distorted by the noise in the lorry cab the surgeon shouted back 'Easter in Scotland, no, no Anna, huge mistake. You must get up for Hogmanay, bring your parents, do your mother and father hunt?'

'Of course they do Peter all over North London!'

'What was that? Oh, excellent!'

With Peter Adnans driving the Bedford ambulance they crept forward in a series of jerks and jolts until they saw another ambulance parked up with a driver and nursing orderly in the cab. Anna jumped out of their vehicle and walked to its twin and realised quickly that both occupants were in a deep sleep.

The orderly was twisted awkwardly with his head laying on his chest while the driver sat slumped over the steering wheel. He woke with a startled jerk 'Shit, shit. What time is it? What happened?'

'Don't worry driver' Anna said quickly and added 'My goodness you both look exhausted, I just want to know if you can direct me to a hospital or first aid post, I have some badly injured men on board my ambulance.'

Rubbing his eyes with both palms of his hands he answered in a way all too familiar to the nursing sister well used to the fatigue of long hours 'Sorry ma'am, Mick an me 'av bin ferrying injured lads all night to the docks trying to get as many away as possible before the bombers come back. I'm on the way back to a temporary hospital if you want to follow me, I'll lead the way.'

They shadowed the ambulance through the streets of the ancient sea port of Dunkirk at little more than a walking pace. Dense smoke from burning buildings and oil storage tanks on the docks drifted back inland in blinding clouds and enveloped them completely at intervals, bringing the two ambulances to sudden halts until the choking fog passed.

Most of the buildings on either side of their route had been hit by bombs or shelling. Tall grand homes of traders and merchants had been reduced to teetering blackened frameworks of scorched red brick and stone and others turned to piles of smouldering rubble that at times reached across the road in front of the slow-moving vehicles.

They drove past fountains of gushing water cascading from fractured mains pipes in the road and flooding into bomb craters and the basements of buildings.

In the door ways of houses and shops were clusters of soldiers and civilians, some with children, some standing alone or huddled in groups, they would scatter and dive for cover as bombs and shells were heard whistling downwards from the sky above.

With both hands gripping the metal rail welded onto the bulk head that held the windscreen in place Anna turned in her seat looked at Peter Adnans and shouted 'It's like a picture of Dante's hell, the poor people, just look at them, it's terrifying, just horrible.'

'Hang on dear girl, hang on, we seem to be heading away from the town and docks area towards a sort of sea front.'

They followed the ambulance in front for another mile before it came to a halt outside a small hotel set in a terrace of similar tall buildings. A large Red Cross banner hung over several windows and ambulances were lined up in the road outside the building.

The surgeon went into the hospital while Anna opened the back doors to the ambulance. She paused and looked up as two formations of Luftwaffe bombers flew loudly overhead towards the town and the docks that were two miles away.

The wounded men were carried from the ambulance and placed on the pavement. Anna looked at each of them more closely, changing dressings where necessary and giving what help that could be given. One of the orderlies who was helping her turned saying 'Sister, isn't it nice to be by the sea side, even if half of it is covered in thick black smoke!'

Anna had not noticed the changes around her. Looking across the road from where they had parked and in between the mass of abandoned and burnt out vehicles that lined that side of the road she could make out a long sandy beach, a blue sky that met a bluer sea.

The hotel that was now a hospital was one of dozens of small hotels in Malo-les-Bains, a popular holiday destination in peace time. Sitting on the pavement in front of the stretchers with their backs against a wall, the nursing sister and orderlies fell asleep.

It took the surgeon a while to gently wake her. With a start Anna found herself coming out of a dream in which she was being chased by hounds and men on horse in scarlet jackets across an English countryside before rubbing her eyes and focusing on the unshaven face of Peter Adnans.

They walked away from those still sleeping and sat down on

the steps that led to the former hotel. She shared a tin mug of hot tea Peter had been given while he explained what was happening by saying 'They have about four hundred wounded outside and inside waiting to be…..' he stopped and looked at her before continuing 'I know I'm stating the obvious by saying you look tired, as I know you are, but is everything else alright?'

Anna replied, 'Apart from being chased by huntsmen on horses and their pack of hounds, and feeling like death, yes, everything is fine!'

'Good,' he replied, but stared vacantly for a second before continuing 'Actually I can't wait to go hunting in November when the season starts, simply can't wait. Now, as I was saying, the four hundred or so wounded that are going home on ships in two batches, one this evening the next in the early hours of tomorrow'

'Conditions are absolutely dreadful in there,' he said wearily at the same time stifling a loud yawn 'they have stopped operating completely and are now concentrating on keeping the wounded alive long enough to get them on board any ship that will take them.'

Focusing his attention on a cloud he finished by saying 'I've been told to set up a field dressing station on a beach called Bray-Dunes, six miles up the coast, I will need one person to come with me as a nurse and those left are to go with the ambulances to the embarkation areas and help get them onto ships, and also get on board if the opportunity arises, now Anna, I want you to go with the ambulances this evening,' without giving her the opportunity to speak he said 'I owe it to John to make sure that you take this chance to get away Anna, so please do not argue with me.'

Five violent explosions followed in rapid succession the sound coming from the town and making speech impossible as they instinctively crouched below the wall that led up the steps to the hotel and watched the concussion waves rattle and bend the window panes facing the sea.

Without looking at her commanding officer she said 'I believe I owe it to John to stay, and Peter, apart from my parents I have no one to go back to, but the girls do, so I would ask you to please reconsider your order, as I want to stay. Please!'

Knowing defeat he mouthed 'Drat, right then, now look Anna, well you, you just organise things, would you, I'm going to get my head down for an hour and then we will leave.'

The explosions had woken the nursing team and Anna told them the good news that with luck they may be on their way home tonight or tomorrow.

The order for the wounded to be to taken out of the hospital came earlier than expected and by five in the afternoon the first batch of ambulances moved away towards Dunkirk, leaving Peter Adnans and Anna to gather up a pitifully small amount of medical supplies for the new first aid post at Bray-Dunes.

The six-mile journey took over two hours, driving through the chaos of abandoned tanks, lorries, cars and avoiding deep bomb craters they arrived at Bray-Dunes beach with barely an hour of daylight left and Peter Adnans decided to make the ambulance the aid post until daylight the following morning.

****

The German air force had been bombing Dunkirk and the docks in particular for several days, dropping thousands of tons of high explosives turning most of the targeted area into a blazing inferno. There were two exceptions.

These were the two long structures that acted as breakwaters and piers to the main shipping entrance of the sea port.

Each concrete pier was over a mile in length and looked like a pair of arms stretching out into the sea, and they were to prove the most welcoming of arms to the British and French troops waiting on the beaches.

The Royal Naval officer in overall command of all the Allied troops and their evacuation had spotted the oversight by the Germans and the Eastern and Western moles, as the breakwaters were known locally, would help thousands of troops to get away.

He quickly moved men and ships to take advantage of the situation and for a while even the weather had turned in the Allies favour, as low cloud and rain came rushing in and the Luftwaffe was unable to take off from the captured airfields of Holland, Belgium and France that they now occupied.

Bray-Dunes, 27th May 1940

The weather in the morning was dull and cloudy, the Luftwaffe grounded. Anna stepped out of the lorry cab into the soft sinking sand of the high dunes that stretched for miles in both directions and walked to the edge of them before looking down to a flat sandy beach with the sea at low tide, a couple of hundred yards away, in front of Anna.

At first she thought that thousands of birds were swarming in dark clusters on the sand and at the water's edge, she rubbed the sleep from her eyes and looked again, saying out loud, 'Bloody Hell, they're soldiers, thousands and thousands of them!'

Rushing back to the ambulance she saw one of the rear doors was wide open, Peter Adnans was sat leaning back awkwardly against the stretcher rack sound asleep, a cup in his hand, the contents long ago deposited on his trousers and the floor.

She left him sleeping and found Private Young, their driver, heating up a pot of hot water 'For a brew up, ma'am, also thought the major might like to use the water for a shave perhaps.'

Nodding she said, 'Well done George, he's definitely in need of one, any going spare I will take it to wash my bleary eyes, have you seen the numbers of troops on the beach?'

Without a word he poured out enough water for Anna to rinse her face and hands before saying 'Yes Sister, and I've been talking to another driver mate of mine and he says they have the same number at La Penne beach, a couple of miles up from here. He heard there are more than twenty thousand men on each beach.'

Placing her aluminium mess tin with the hot water in it on the bonnet of the ambulance she left it there to find a dip in the dunes to go to the toilet in peace.

'Peace and quiet' she said softly 'for the first time in days, it really is, but I wonder for how long?'

Walking back Peter Adnans head appeared around the back of the ambulance asking 'Sister, do you need me immediately, if not I will have a quick wash and tidy-up?'

'Sir, I think you ought to come to edge of the sand dune before you do.'

They walked the few yards through the sand and tuffs of green spider grass to the edge of the dune and looked down on the beach in front of them. Anna studied his face while he surveyed the scene without uttering a word until he broke the silence, saying 'Criky Anna, they told me to expect no more than a steady trickle of at most a few hundred, and not a few thousand.'

Looking at the same scene she replied 'Yes, twenty thousand or more according to our driver, with the same number on the next beach up from us, I think we are going to be rather busy.'

Turning back towards the ambulance the surgeon said 'We had better get down there quick and have a look.'

'Can I suggest that if I organise a bag for us, you take advantage of the hot water Private Young has provided for you?'

Leaving the driver to look after the ambulance the surgeon and Anna went through the dunes and scrambled down onto the beach. Now they could see that off-shore a dozen or so ships lifeboats were lifting soldiers who were chest deep in the water onto them and then ferrying them out to larger vessels waiting a mile or so from the beach.

As they got closer they saw that there was no order to the queues only a frantic scrambling and panic to get out of the water as boats approached. They witnessed one lifeboat swamped by men trying get on board which then capsized, throwing everyone back into the sea. The boat was quickly righted and the same frantic scramble started all over again.

Peter and Anna watched as a figure dressed in a heavy dark

blue naval greatcoat onboard another lifeboat went along side and drew his service revolver, firing several shots into the sea just in front of the scrambling men.

They could not hear what was said but a semblance of order was restored, and under the continuing eye of the naval man the troops got into the lifeboat until it was full before it made its way out to sea through the mild line of surf.

More men dressed in the blue of the navy were now visible on the beach in front of them. One of the naval party pointed to a lorry at the base of the sand dunes and they both walked towards it.

On the beach side of the army lorry eight naval officers and senior ratings were gathered around the naval commander who was in charge of getting the troops away from the Bray-Dunes beach. He and his party had arrived late last night and the officer was clearly unhappy by what he saw this morning.

Peter Adnans introduced himself to the beach commander Derek Dunbar a wiry, tall New Zealander from Auckland. Looking at the surgeon he nodded in the direction of the beach before saying 'Welcome to the party Major. It's all a bit of a cock-up as it stands but give us a few hours and I guarantee that we will instil a sense of order down there, now then, how can we help you?'

The offer of setting up a medical post in the sand dunes away from the naval HQ was gladly accepted and Private Young quickly enlisted the help of a number of borrowed soldiers to erect the two tents they had brought before staking out the large Red Cross banner in the sand in front of them.

From on top of a dune Anna watched the scene in front of her while the medical post was being set up. She could see loose bands of men and individuals roaming aimlessly around in all directions, with hundreds more arriving as she watched.

She could also see that the naval men were bringing a sense of order to the beach. Lines of rope were being laid from the dunes to the sea, coloured signal flags had been erected between the rope corridors and the way the soldiers responded to the instructions and orders of the officers and naval ratings conveyed to Anna a sense of relief on the part of the men who were waiting.

The sound of explosions from incoming artillery shells could now be heard further up the coast at La Panne beach, but the calm continued around Bray-Dunes.

The field dressing station was ready for use well before the cloud had started to be blown away by a shift in the wind direction. By mid-afternoon the leaded sky gave way to periods of blue and Peter and Anna were not surprised when the first formations of bombers were spotted high in the sky above them.

The thrust of the German air attacks was concentrated on the harbour at Dunkirk. Wave after wave of bombers and dive bombers took advantage of the clearing sky trying to breach the Eastern mole pier and sink the ships that were alongside and evacuating soldiers.

Bray-Dunes, 28th May 1940

The shelling that had battered the soldiers and sailors at La Penne beach had arrived at Bray-Dunes during the night as the German army crept towards the French coast bringing their large artillery guns within range. There was now the constant sound of explosions on the beach, in the sea and around the sand dunes as German artillery shells landed in front of the first aid post in a random and haphazard fashion.

The soft sand was good protection from shrapnel as most of the blast was cushioned on impact but men caught close to the immediate explosions were coming in with injuries the surgeon was unable to treat without an operating theatre and the best he could offer was morphine, for the critically injured before they were taken to the temporary hospital at Malo-les Bains.

At dawn the surgeon and nursing sister walked to the top of the sand dune that gave the first aid post some protection and looked at the scene the stretched for miles on both sides.

The evacuation of troops from the east and west moles at Dunkirk was going well but the vast numbers of men to move meant that the beaches had to used and since the arrival of Peter Adnans and Anna thirty thousand more troops had descended on Bray-Dunes, British and French.

The organized zig-zag lines of soldiers' six to ten abreast ran from the dunes to the sea where the men stood waist deep in the incoming surf waiting for the small boats to pick them up and transport them to the larger vessels offshore.

Watching the evacuation from the dunes in front of their medical post Anna looked down on the soldiers as she said to Peter Adnans 'They look like lines of swarming bees.'

He was about to answer when a salvo of shells whistled over their heads falling one after the other in a straight line that covered a distance of fifty yards from the shore line into the sea, exploding amongst the waiting men. From their high vantage point they watched as the water turned crimson with the blood of the men who had been standing in the sea seconds before.

'Anna, I'll grab my bag and get down to the beach while you get Private Young to bring down the stretchers and men to carry the wounded back.'

The closer Anna got to the tidal line between the beach and the sea the more disturbing and gruesome the scene became, with the shredded bodies and limbs of the men who had been killed floating in the sea, or held on the beach by the outgoing tide, bits of red pulp looking like driftwood or someone's discarded junk.

Dazed men stood motionless, waist deep in water, staring out to sea or up at the sky, like stone statues. One broke his trance and ran screaming past Anna his eyes and mouth wide open, blood covering the front of his uniform. Two soldiers carried a blood covered comrade towards Peter Adnans, another walked slowly along the tide line towards him carrying the top part of a man's torso on his back, like a grotesque haversack.

Anna felt dizzy and sick as she sank to her knees in the wet sand, took in long shuddering gulps of air, lent forward and vomited violently. She put one hand to her forehead, covered her eyes with it and cried out 'No more please, please no more, I just want to go home.'

She heard voices, loud voices. One said, 'The madness will end, it will end Anna, truly it will end, come on lass.' another said 'Anna, have you been hit Anna. Are you alright?'

Opening her eyes she reached out to a familiar shadow on the wet sand, a shadow that faded as she blinked her eyes again and saw Peter Adnans and two stretcher bearers kneeling in the sand around her 'No, no, John...Peter, I'm alright, I just felt suddenly sick and faint, you just go on.'

Bray-Dunes, 30th May 1940

It was six in the morning when Anna finally fell onto the stretcher that she and the surgeon took in turn to use for a rest and two hours later she was woken by Private Young saying 'Brought you some hot water, a cuppa and a spam sandwich Sister.'
Making her way back to the surgical tent Anna almost walked into a Naval Lieutenant who was part of the New Zealander's team and they stopped to talk, the conversation pausing when they both heard loud explosions and he explained 'La Penne beach is within easy range of all the German guns and getting a bit of a pasting, but they are still getting a lot of men away,' he told her 'We've had a really good twenty four hours here, but recovery is still difficult and slow, so fingers crossed for a cloudy day and no bombers!'
Looking towards the beach Anna said 'At least you and your men have brought a order to the beach which must be a bonus for you?'
Nodding he replied 'It has made things a lot easier, and has helped us get many more of the men home to England, but as you can see the numbers of men waiting to get away is growing and growing as more arrive each hour. We need more boats. More boats, more cloud and perhaps even a miracle!' Unable to suppress a loud yawn he laughed and apologised 'Excuse me, I'm exhausted and off for a kip for a while!'
Watching him go she thought to herself 'Home to England. Home. I will make it; but it just seems a very long way away at the moment.'
Towards the middle of the morning when Anna was on a break for some fresh air and an hour's sleep she noticed a lot

of activity along two of the roped off areas that went from the beach and into the sea.

  Fascinated, she watched and counted over fifty lorries being driven down the beach towards the sea. Torn between being wretchedly tired yet curious about what was happening, she stayed and looked on.

  While she was standing there Peter Adnans came out of the tent and walked over to her saying 'Anna, is everything alright, I thought you were getting some sleep?'

  She motioned him to come closer, saying 'Peter, look, I don't know what's going on, but something very strange is happening.'

  The surgeon looked at the beach through tired red rimmed eyes and said 'Hell, it looks like they are jolly well going to forget the boats and drive home! Anna, I must get back, but as your Commanding Officer I hereby order you to go over to the Naval HQ tent nose around and find out what is happening, it's all very strange and I cannot stand the mystery.'

  She was saved the journey when the same naval officer she had spoken to earlier that morning came walking towards both of them.

  'Young man' the Major said 'What on earth is going on?' He walked over the sand to them with a warm smile on his face and explained 'Well, Sir, it seems that an officer at La Penne beach has come up with the brilliant and very simple idea of driving twenty or thirty army lorries down the beach and into the sea at low tide and then linking them together so that the smaller lifeboats can come along side and the men can jump in rather than go through the tricky game of swimming out. They moved almost a third more men yesterday then we were able to.'

  Over the next day two lines of army vehicles stretched into the sea at Bray Dunne and ten more lorry jetties were made on the beaches from Dunkirk to La Penne, helping many thousands to escape.

  Peter Adnans and Anna had just finished putting a splint on a wounded soldier's leg when a sailor popped his head into the tent saying 'Compliments of the beach commander Sir, but he thought you would both like to see what has appeared out to sea.'

Walking across the sand dune in front of the first aid post the weary surgeon and nurse looked towards the horizon. They both stood still and blinked in disbelief at what they saw in front of them.

A ten mile stretch of sea from Dunkirk to La Penne beach was a bobbing mass of hundreds of boats of every size and shape imaginable.

They could see small motor boats, large motor boats, gleaming white motor yachts, village club yachts, sailing boats, fishing trawlers, lifeboats, Thames Barges, seaside pleasure boats, fire tender boats, coal boats, familiar looking RNLI lifeboats.

Most of the crews onboard these little ships had been working at their normal jobs only days ago as postmen, accountants, carpenters, bank managers, pensioners, tailors, dentist.

They had all answered the call to help rescue their fellow countrymen and Allies and had crossed the English Channel guided by the Royal Navy.

Anna and Peter stood still, both speechless. Swallowing hard before being able to speak Peter Adnans, said 'What an extraordinary sight. I am truly humbled Anna, truly humbled.'

Glancing at Peter Adnans before looking back out to sea at the bobbing armada Anna said, 'The navy man did ask for a miracle Peter, and I really think he's got one!'

Bray-Dunes, 31st May 1940

Commander Dunbar came into the tent and asked Peter Adnans if he could have a word with him outside. The naval man said gravely 'Well Major, I have to tell you that it is highly probable that La Penne will be in German hands by this evening, Bray-Dunes by tomorrow morning'

'An hour ago, I sent a message to one of our destroyers off the beach that at a given signal from me or my second-in command one of two lifeboats will be made available to my party of men within an hour, that's how critical the situation really is. I've been instructed to pass on orders for you to pack up and take your wounded men to Dunkirk and make your way to the eastern mole pier immediately. I have three vehicles for you, plus whatever you have at the moment, but please do not hesitate, the battle here is lost, go now.'

Slowly, the convoy of four vehicles arrived back into the town of Dunkirk, then headed to the docks area. Anna's vision of Dante's harrowing paintings was renewed when she saw the devastation of a further two days of unabated bombing and shelling of the town and docks by the German air force and the artillery men who were closing in on the perimeter defence line, inch by inch, minute by minute.

A solid line of thousands of men five or six abreast snaked ahead of them. They had been stationary for ten minutes when four Military Policemen approached the vehicles and Peter Adnans popped his head out of the open window when he saw one of them wanted to speak to him.

The soldier said 'Sorry Sir, but we have orders that no more vehicles can go beyond this point. All casualties have to be taken to the pier on foot or on stretchers, and the other thing is that you have to ditch the vehicles and put them out of action, Sir'.

Looking at the soldier the major said 'How far are we from the pier, corporal?' Hesitating to think, he replied 'Bout a mile, maybe mile and half, Sir, but it's not easy and Jerry is shelling the hell out of everything.'

Pausing a moment, he said 'Corporal, do you have any idea if there are any stretcher bearers in the area, or chaps to help us carry our wounded?' the corporal nodded in the direction of the waiting soldiers and said, 'If you want Sir I'll get as many as you want from that lot, especially if I tell them they might just get ahead of the queue!'

The major got the men he wanted in no time after the military policeman told a sergeant of his request.

Peter Adnans instructed the other drivers to pull onto the site of a hotel, now consisting of several piles of collapsed and smouldering rubble. There they proceeded to smash the radiators and leave the engines running so that the engines would eventually seize, tyres were punctured, windows smashed, and earth slipped into the fuel nozzle.

After checking their patients, the surgeon led the line of those able to walk and those on stretchers away from their wrecked army lorries and ambulances towards the loading pier.

It took two hours of stop and start before they turned a corner and moved away from the cover of the buildings and saw the two long arms of the western mole and the eastern mole piers arcing towards each other in the distance, like giant electrodes expecting the bridging flash of an electrical charge.

Their destination was the Eastern mole where a thick twisting line of khaki uniforms and glinting steel helmets pressed towards the vessels berthed either side of the wooden and concrete structure.

They watched, helpless, as Stuka dive bombers swooped on the close knots of men and ships, and held their breath as smoke and water bellowed high into the air after a stick of bombs reached a destroyer loaded with men on its deck, and breathed again after the breeze carried away the smoke and spay and they saw the vessel was still intact.

A frigate, it's decks and superstructure teeming with uniformed men, reached the entrance of the port between the two piers to start its journey to Dover when it was hit by two bombs on the bow and one below the waterline.

It quickly started to list onto its side throwing many of the men on the upper deck into water. With strict orders to avoid blocking the entrance to the port and jeopardising the entire rescue mission, the captain of the ship was forced to ignore the cries for help and the screams of the injured and take his vessel into deep water where she turned over and sank, taking hundreds of troops and sailors with her.

The raw efficiency was chilling to watch. When a ship was fully loaded and moved away from the pier its place was quickly taken by another, and another after that. Under the constant rain of bombing and shelling, and the killing of friends and comrades that came with it, the men in the vessels of all sizes continued the rescue mission without interruption.

There was no let-up in the pace of the evacuation, at times there were twelve or more ships leaving, crammed with

British and French soldiers below decks and on every inch of space on the decks above them.

The air was a choking mixture of noxious cordite fumes mixed together with the stench of burning oil and rubber. The noise was an ear shattering cacophony of exploding bombs, machine guns and anti-aircraft guns firing from the land, soldiers firing their own rifles at the black shapes in the sky. The ear piercing, nerve crumbling noise was impossible to get away from.

She watched the theatre of madness with a calmness and numbness that was shared by thousands of others around her. Men would look out to sea, cower or dive for safety when they heard a shell whining its way towards them, or a bomb whistling down, the danger passed all eyes were back on the ships that were their lifeline away from the death and suffering surrounding them.

There was a lull in the bombing and shelling when Anna followed the last of their stretcher bearers onto a wide concrete apron that marked the start of the eastern mole pier. Four coils of barbed wire had been placed at the start of the apron separating it from three small huts, which were surrounded by a high wall of sandbags, and manned by armed naval personnel with sub-machine guns all pointing in their direction.

Anna saw another smaller barbed wire emplacement pulled across the only entrance to the pier. In front and behind the barbed wire stood more armed sailors.

Out of one of the huts came a very tall, big framed naval officer with a megaphone in his hand. He stood facing the waiting crowd and bringing the loudspeaker to his mouth he said in a Canadian accent 'I am the commander in charge of all the vessels and men leaving from this embarkation point. I want you to understand that under no circumstances whatever will any officer or any soldier be allowed to proceed beyond the barbed wire coils in front of you without my permission.'

Pausing briefly the Canadian naval officer cleared his throat to emphasize his next message 'I want you all to clearly understand that any officer or soldier attempting to jump the queue will be immediately shot by myself or one of the naval party behind me. Officers and soldiers of all ranks will be called forward when ships are available, and not before.'

Within half an hour the Canadian addressed them again 'The first barbed wire barrier will be pulled across shortly to allow the next batch of you onto the pier, I will repeat my warning that any officer or soldier that tries to force his way through will be shot without further warning' looking now at Peter Adnans he added 'No stretcher born casualties can be allowed through at the moment, only walking wounded.'

A naval officer with two heavily armed sailors made their way through the wire and approached the surgeon. Anna could not hear what was being said but could see by the body language and hand gestures it was not good.

She was tired, very tired, but knew she had to breathe deep and carry on. Going to Peter Adnans who was away from the wounded soldiers she said, 'Bad news, Peter?'

'Yes, Anna, I have just been categorically told that we will not be able to take any stretchers along the pier, only those that can stand and walk will be allowed to go at this time, because the stretchers are taking up too much room on the rescue ships and we will have to wait for a proper hospital ship to arrive.'

He paused for a moment before looking at her again and saying 'Anna, now, now I really do need to speak to you. Anna, with a bit of luck there are six or seven of the men that we could patch up to get them away on the boats, and, well, you know it really is time for you to go Anna.'

Softly she replied, 'I know it is Peter, and thank you for letting me get away with so much, I do know that John would have been very grateful to you.'

It was dark by the time Anna and the surgeon had selected a final eight wounded men to walk the mile along the Eastern mole to the ships waiting for them. The patchy orange light from burning buildings and lorries on the dockside was not enough to see what was happening at the evacuation command centre and they could only hear and not see the man behind the distorted Canadian accent speaking through a loudspeaker, as he said 'The barriers will be pulled back to allow the next batch forward in a moment. I will remind all of you that we will not allow a stampede of any type to develop. We have direct orders to shoot any one of you that contravenes my orders, and we shall do so immediately, if required, without further warning.'

The effects of exhaustion and lack of sleep made Anna feel that she was taking part in a strange dream. She saw Peter Adnans face her and say 'Goodbye Anna, now please be careful, and I will see you back in England.'

Without thought for army authority or custom she threw her arms around him saying 'Peter, thank you, thank you from John and me, you've been a true friend.' She kissed him on both cheeks and hugged him tightly before turning around and start to lead the line of eight wounded men into the surge of pressing soldiers.

They passed through the first barbed wire barrier and waited while it was pulled across to prevent more than the allotted number of troops across. She could only hear the angry shouts of the men excluded and the lost sound of orders shouted through the loudspeaker.

She looked back and saw the dark silhouettes of men waving their arms, some holding rifles, and the darker shapes of the navy men. The shouting grew louder until she saw the officer in charge fire three shots from his revolver into the air. More sailors had quickly formed another line behind the officer and the press of bodies against the barrier eased.

Anna heard the sound of several muffled explosions in the sky overhead which was followed by the pin pricks of bright white light which grew in intensity as the parachute flares floated down from the sky.

The light from the flares gave Anna the opportunity to look at each of the men she led. As she did so she thought 'These are brave blokes, I just hope they can manage to stay brave, some of them look really bad.'

The pier had a solid wooden rail each side and the men rested against the one on their side to gather their strength for another move forward. Anna acted as a buffer to fend off the tide of soldiers from her patients. She pushed at the moving mass to give the group just an inch of space as they were overtaken, but slowly like a shepherdess she guided them forward towards the waiting ships and home.

A heavy artillery bombardment was going on and loud explosions were heard and felt though the pier as shells hit the line of soldiers two hundred yards ahead. She raced to the front of the group as she heard a number of soldiers fall twenty feet into the water through a gap made in the rail from an earlier bombardment. She could see the white phosphorous outline of water being thrashed by the struggling men.

Knowing that she would have to move each man from one side of the walkway to the other she told them to rest on the rail while she took the first of the wounded men across the advancing line of men.

Some of the weary soldiers helped her, some cursed her, and when she was leading the last of her patients across a soldier deliberately pushed her in the back causing her to bump into the wounded man who cried out in pain.

Anna swung around and faced the man and in a blind and furious rage she hit him twice in the face, shouting at the top of her voice in 'You cowardly bastard, he's a wounded man, you pig!'

In her anger and contempt, she spat out the same words in French before turning her back on the dazed man who by now was being kicked and punched repeatedly by several men in the inching crowd.

All the time she kept moving up and down the line of injured men, talking to them, encouraging them, telling them 'Hang on boys, please hang on, it won't be long now, another inch forward and closer to home. Just hang on.'

The shells that had hit the pier over an hour ago had demolished part of the wooden floor as well as the railing that was on their side. This time the move across the flow of troops went smoothly.

Several men had been killed by the earlier blast, their bodies pushed off the pier, some dangling from the concrete cross members of the structure below. They inched by the gristly sight without a thought.

One of the wounded men said quietly 'Sister, it ain't no good, I'm sorry, I just cannot go on'. Anna went to the man saying 'Hold on for a few seconds, please don't give up.'

Squarely addressing the men passing by she pleaded in English as well as French 'Would you please, please give me a hand for the last hundred yards, please, I am desperate, and so are my patients.'

Six soldiers, English and French stopped and gave her the help she wanted over the last few yards by supporting the wounded men in her charge.

The shelling had intensified but the mole led a charmed life as salvo after salvo exploded on both sides with few actually hitting the intended target. Anna could see a destroyer loading troops on their side of the pier, would they make it, she thought, and again to herself she said 'Please let us get on board, these lads cannot go much further, please let there be room for them.'

A big English soldier helping one of the wounded bellowed at the top of his loud voice to the two sailors manning the gangway to the ship 'We've got badly wounded men here, mate, can you help us?'

Two more sailors appeared and cleared a path for the last few yards helping the soldiers with the wounded men. What Anna saw next made her freeze. The big destroyer was tied loosely to the pier and was at least fifteen feet away from it.

Running from the ship to the mole was a single wood plank no more ten inches wide and at least twenty feet from the water below, with the ship rising and sinking slowly with the tidal movement.

She could see that the most able of soldiers were not finding it easy to cross and that the sailors were literally pushing them and shouting to get a move on, or get off.

Without hesitation the first of the wounded men went across helped and guided by a soldier, none looked down, and the final yard was helped by the firm hands of the sailors onboard the ship.

A mad, utterly ridiculous thought came vividly into Anna's head as she started walking along the narrow wood plank. Suddenly she was stood with John McCloud in the centre of a stone circle holding hands and laughing out loud. Her head was spinning, she felt sick and light headed as she cried out 'I can't make it. I'm not going home John, I just can't get there.'

Dover, 1st June 1940

Anna was aware of a gentle rocking motion, a steady humming noise and of a wonderful floating feeling. 'I must be dead' she thought 'I wonder what will happen next.'

She was afraid to open her eyes, in fact she wasn't sure that she could open them until she felt a warm feeling on her face, the gentle soothing warmth of water and it reminded her of bathing John McCloud's face before he opened his eyes, and died. Not afraid of being dead or of dying she opened hers.

A smiling face said 'Good morning Sister, I'm nurse Thomas, how are you feeling?'

After swallowing hard to bring moisture into her mouth she said, 'To be honest nurse I'm not sure; where am I?'

Propping Anna up with a cushion the nurse offered her a glass of water before replying 'Well ma'am, this is HMS Brent, a destroyer, and we're docked in Dover harbour, and have been for about an hour.'

Anna touched the side of her head which had now started to ache and the nurse continued 'You took a bit of a bang to the side of your head when you were coming onboard, doctor thinks you may have a bit of concussion, but the skin wasn't broken or anything. If you don't mind Sister I had better go and tell him you're up, and I am sorry that we had to leave you in your khaki, but we have no gowns or anything else really.'

When the nurse left Anna slowly sat up, she still wore the coarse army shirt that she had worn for the past three days and the same underwear. Her trousers and battle dress top had been laid out at the end of the bunk she had been asleep on. The bunk was in a small cabin, and obviously the home of one of the ships officers, with family pictures fixed to flat surfaces and bulkheads.

With aching, tired limbs, she dressed, putting on her dirty, stained clothes, when a knock on the cabin door announced the arrival of Surgeon Commander Kemp a moment later and saying, 'Morning Sister, how's the head, bit achy?'

Anna answered as perkily as she could, 'Good morning Sir, yes I am a bit groggy, but better for a bit of sleep, thank you. Sir, did all my patients get on board, I don't really remember what happened, come the end'

Looking into each eye with a pencil light and talking at the same time he said 'Yes, Sister, one of them was in a serious condition but improved the closer we got to home, the others will definitely be okay. They were the first to be taken off and put on a hospital train, as soon as we docked'

'I think that if you have family waiting for you, home would be a better place for you to rest up, you do have signs of some concussion, but your main problem is one of extreme exhaustion, which is understandable, given what you have all been through, Sister. If you go out on deck and wait for me I will take you down to the officers' reception area, where you can check in and we can also get some breakfast.'

Following the naval doctor through a heavy metal door she winched, quickly bringing her hand to her eyes as a shade against the bright sunshine that was reflected off the still water and buildings of Dover harbour, she had a problem keeping her balance and steadied herself by holding onto the hand rail on the after deck below the bridge of the vessel while she stared in amazement at the scenes below and around her.

HMS Brent had been tied up alongside the jetty, and she could see a cross channel ferry berthed next to them and another big warship next to that. Tied up to these three vessels were attached other ships so that hundreds of troops were walking across all of them to reach the gangplanks that led down to the main dock and for most their homeland, and for many a safe refuge in a foreign country.

In both directions from where she stood she could see thousands of troops of all nationalities slowly edged forward along the docks and there to greet them was another army of hundreds of volunteers handing out mugs of tea, sandwiches, and cigarettes.

A military band was playing and the troops responded with hoops of laughter and cheers, large banners hung from rooftops, windows, walls with slogans roughly painted on them that read 'Welcome to the heroes of Dunkirk' or a simple 'Welcome Home' message.

She watched the men rejoice in the realisation that for them they were at last safe after the weeks of being hounded and hunted across the fields and plains of Belgium and France to the coast and now Dover.

As if in a dream she went to the reception building and gave an army captain her service details of name, regiment, rank and army number. Breakfast with tea, 'Now I know I am back home!' Anna said to herself, and when the doctor asked what her plans were now, she answered 'The good captain at the reception tent has given me a rail warrant to take me to Victoria Station, five pounds, ten shillings and six pence and told me stay on leave until I get my next orders'

'He also gave me a chit for a gas mask and box, plus tin hat and hinted that I may be lucky to find a clean uniform to travel in from the same building along the dock, and by the way he said it I must look a bit of a state!'

Thinking before replying he tactfully said, 'You certainly look well-travelled Sister, but the truth is you have been, and few would blame you for how you look now' he got up to leave adding 'Did you leave everything over there? I mean all your personal possessions?'

It had never occurred to her to think about it before but she had lost everything. What she had was what she was standing up in as she shook hands with the doctor and said, 'Well Sir, I can replace everything that has been left in France, except of course for my friends and colleagues.'

The army quartermaster had a surplus of gas masks and tin helmets and found her a khaki cap, but no change of uniform to travel in. Her drowsy, giddy feeling had returned in the army lorry that had been provided to take her and other officers to the railway station that was a mass of soldiers' eager to get away.

She got onto the train and inched her way sideways along the narrow corridor of the carriage past men in a mixture of khaki, some asleep on the floor, some asleep standing, all sharing the same ragged look of the defeated before sliding open the door to a compartment reserved for officers and let gravity find her a space in a corner of one of the two rows of seats that faced each other.

Clouds of white steam hid the platform as the passenger train started to ease slowly out of the station and Anna looked around. Most of the occupants of the compartment were already asleep, with heads angled in awkward positions and bodies slumped heavily against unknown neighbours.

An infantry lieutenant sat opposite acted as a bookend to the five other passengers on his side. A colonel's head rested casually on his shoulder, a padre with his mouth wide open showing a set of hovering yellow false teeth on the shoulder of the colonel and three others, with heads buried deep into their chests, all six men slumped in crippled exhaustion.

Anna was soon aware that her own tattered uniform was not out of place when she looked at the colonel who wore a mixture of British and French army clothing with a tartan weave to the bedroom slippers on his feet.

Each person in the compartment had travelled a long way each was utterly burnt out by their own experiences and battles of the past weeks.

The quickening rhythm of the train tic tacking over metal rails began to show her the countryside as it rushed past. The lush greens of fields and pastures, the yellows of wheat and corn the reddish browns of ploughed acres seemed unreal to Anna.

She wanted so desperately to share her new neighbours prize of sleep but her troubled mind was racing out of control. Only a few miles from the coast the train passed through a small village, dominated by the square Norman church and graveyard. Next to it she watched four ladies dressed in smart whites playing tennis in the warm sunshine.

She meant to think it but muttered softly instead 'How? Why? What went so very wrong? I simply don't understand. I don't understand why everything here is so peaceful, so normal'

'Only hours ago I left a scarred, tortured country, its towns and cities in flames, with roads choked by troops, refugees, rotting animals, burnt out lorries, and the dead bodies of men, women and children on the road sides'

As Anna shook her head slowly she repeated the same word

over, and over out loud 'How? How?'

For several moments Anna tried to work out who was calling to her, she was aware of a soft Irish voice saying 'Now then young lady, time to wake up' and in her own head she remembered the same words spoken by her father when she was a child, she heard them again, together with a press to her shoulder 'Time to wake up, we've arrived safely in London!'

Slowly, her eyes opened and she saw the army padre beaming at her, teeth now firmly in place. The compartment had emptied and she tried quickly to get up from her seat only to lose her balance.

The padre caught her elbow, saying 'Not so fast young lady, we have plenty of time on our hands now, and no need to rush any of it. Just sit down for a second and we can then help each other down the platform to the barriers, I'm Father Donald, by the way'

'Do you have anyone to meet you?' the priest asked as they passed through the barriers towards the main road outside. 'No. Uh, no. I never had time to telephone my parents' she replied.

Nodding, he said 'Now look, I think you should get a taxi, to be on the safe side, is that alright with you?'

Before she could answer, the priest made a special effort at making his not so white dog collar and not so black vest as visible as possible before striding into the busy road and waving down a black London cab.

Helping Anna into the taxi he then sat next to her and said, 'I'm going about a mile down the road, now where do your parents live?' He gave the cab driver the two addresses before sitting back into the worn red leather upholstery of the taxi and saying, 'What's your first name?' when she told him he continued 'Well Anna, we have been through an ordeal, haven't we, but with God's help we made it home, and we will go back again of that I'm sure, when the time is right'

'Now, I will try and say a prayer for you tonight Anna, but to be honest, after I have a bath, it's more than likely that first thing I will do is to raise my glass of Irish whiskey to you, and wish you well!'

Anna shook his hand warmly as he left the taxi, and after

speaking to the driver he waved to her as they drove away. Driving past streets with names she had known since childhood the taxi stopped outside Anna's home.

Without moving from his seat, the taxi driver put his hand out of his window and turned the chromium handle of the black passenger door downwards to open it.

Getting out she asked the driver how much she owed him, and he looked at her saying 'The Padre paid for it Miss.'

'Oh.' It was all she could say.

The driver added quickly 'And welcome home Miss, we're all right proud of you!'

As the cab drove away her gaze followed it for a moment while she muttered the word that had puzzled her 'Proud?' and adding 'Proud of what?' before turning to face her home from the pavement.

She sighed deeply twice, and tried to smile, but couldn't. She looked up to the bedroom windows and then into the sitting room before returning to look at the borders of brightly coloured anomies that lined the short gravel path from the red gate to a dark green front door.

Her keys were somewhere in France, so she rattled the door knocker that was part of the brass letter box. Through the circle of different coloured and plain leaded glass sections in the top half of the door she saw the diffused outline of her mother take shape as she approached, and as she opened it they both spoke at the same time, the words from her mother of 'Anna, Oh, Anna, thank God, come here' were lost as they fused with her 'Mummy, I'm home!'

Mother and daughter embraced and hugged each other, tears of emotion and relief mixing and when Anna opened her eyes through her tears she saw her father standing behind her mother smiling broadly, waiting patiently for his turn to be reunited.

With his arms around his only child he said, 'My little baby, we've been so worried about you, so very worried.'

He led her through the hallway into the familiar surroundings of the kitchen. With Anna at the top of the oak table and her mother and father each side of her she held the hand of each with hers, and rested her brow on the clenched fist. Anna could not speak, she sat silently and closed her eyes, falling into a deep, exhausted sleep.

Her mother and father lifted her to her feet and guided her up the stairs to her old room. They pulled the khaki battle dress top and trousers off and her mother peeled away the shirt and underwear, replacing them with clean pyjamas. They both knew she needed rest more than a bath which would come later. Her father looked at the swelling to her head, going through the same procedure as the naval doctor earlier that day. She would mend, he told her mother. It was only rest she needed now.

London, 2nd June 1940

Anna slept for thirty hours without waking. Her parents took turns by her bedside and saw the physical signs of the trauma she had gone through as her mind relived many of the episodes of the last weeks.

She laughed, cried, thrashed her arms and legs about, and shouted out loud things neither parent understood. It was a sharp pain that finally woke her around six in the evening the next day.

She gripped her mother's arms and screamed loudly. As her father reached the bed and removed the bedding from on top of her they saw a large red stain appear as she began haemorrhaging.

Anna suffered two more spasms of acute pain followed by more loss of blood. The doctor in her father and nurse in her mother took over.

The bleeding stopped and Anna fell back into a deep sleep. David Jack took her temperature and examined her before saying 'I don't think we should send her to hospital, Mary. No, let's keep her here, besides which, she will have a very good nurse at hand!'

Mary looked at her husband of many years for a moment before saying 'And?'

'And, what?' he said.

'And, because you are stood there tapping your teeth with

your thrum nail, something else is on your mind!'

'Ah, well, yes. To be on the safe side I'd like Jim Morris to have a quick look at her, and I do hate it when you read my mind!'

Jim Morris worked with David and was a close friend of the family. He arrived within the hour, and confirmed the father's thoughts. The mother washed her daughter and put fresh bedding under her before replacing the soiled nightclothes. Every hour they would bathe her forehead to wake her, and get her to take liquid, and with each hour she improved.

London, 3rd June 1940

When Anna woke the next morning she felt better, she knew something bad had happened, but she felt better. Sat up in bed she talked to her parents, telling them everything about the past weeks, and of John's death.

Early in the evening, and still in bed, she said to her mother and father 'Did I have a miscarriage yesterday?'

Her father took her hand saying, 'Yes you did Anna, it was very early, I don't think you were more than six weeks pregnant, but you did have a miscarriage.'

Anna thought of the refugee clinging to the remains of her baby boy. She told her parents about her, told them how much the little boy's death had affected her.

Anna's thoughts drifted for several moments, she just stared ahead, and then nodding her head gently, she took hold of both her father's and mother's hand and squeezed them saying 'What's happened is not fair, I wanted John's baby but the war killed both of them. I refuse to let them kill me, I will not let John, our baby or the others down, I want to get better quickly. I have a lot to do.'

She kissed both of them, and for the first time since arriving home she smiled broadly, adding 'I think I must smell like uncle Ben's old dog used to when we went to his house, I would love a bath!'

London, 4th June 1940

The next morning Anna was up before her parents, she put on a dressing gown and crept steadily and silently downstairs into the kitchen. She registered the familiar things in the house that she had grown up with, they all made her feel better, safer. Making a pot of tea she took it to her parents' bedroom. After a muffled knock at the door she said, 'Good morning!' David and Mary Jack knew that it was a "good" morning, their daughter had finally returned.

Anna had agreed to meet with her father later in the day at the hospital for an x-ray to satisfy himself that the bruise to her head did not hide any fractures. She sipped her tea propped up on cushions next to her mother, and listened happily to her telling her the latest news and gossip of relations, friends and neighbours while her father used the bathroom and got ready to go to work.

An hour later she joined Mary Jack at the breakfast table with the comment 'Mum, just look at me, this is the first time in months that I've had a dress on, and nylons, I feel quite naked!'

Mary smiled at her daughter, saying 'Darling you look beautiful, and so much like your old self.'

Mary Jack and her daughter walked arm in arm down the terrace of tall regency buildings towards the main road, where they would be able to catch a bus to the hospital. The welcome from neighbours was genuine and warm, people crossed the road to shake her hand and say hello. Even the bus driver was pleased to see one of his old customers again. Anna loved every minute of her outing with her mother.

In the evening, after dinner, they went into the sitting room of the house. It was Anna's least favourite room, it was to formal, to orderly. But like most homes throughout the country it was the only one in the house with a wireless set which rested on a small table next to the fireplace. She and her mother sat on the floral brocade cover of the settee, her father in a matching winged arm chair listening to the news.

The sound of the telephone ringing in the hall way brought them out of there fixed stares. 'It must be for you darling'

Mary Jack said looking at her husband.

Leaving the room, the ringing stopped as David Jack picked up the telephone
and he reappeared in the frame of the sitting room door saying 'Anna, it's a Major Neil Bell on the telephone, do you feel up to talking to him?'

Anna got up quickly, too quickly, as a stab of pain in her stomach reminded her. 'Ouch' she mouthed as she steadied herself on the arm of the chair, but smiling she said 'Daddy, I'd love to talk to Neil, can you ask him to hold on a moment, please'.

Anna took a couple of deep breaths and her mother said, 'Just go more slowly, dear, you have plenty of time!'

'I know mummy, I know' Anna replied, and added, laughing at the same time 'Can there ever be any worse patient than a nurse?'

Shaking her head slowly her mother answered, 'Probably not dear, probably not!'

Picking up the black Bakelite telephone she said 'Neil, it's so good to speak to you.'

Neil Bell's voice was a tonic in itself for Anna when she heard him say 'Anna, how wonderful it is to hear you, a chum of mine at the ministry managed to find out that you got away safely from France and were at home, and how are you, when did you get back?'

A thought raced through her mind, does he know about John, 'Well Neil, it's all been a bit of a blur really, but I got back on the 1st of June, from France,' hesitating she continued, saying 'Neil, Neil have you heard about John?'

Pausing briefly, he replied 'Yes Anna, I have been told. In fact, I've just got back from spending the day with John's parents and they gave me your father's telephone number, so I hope you don't mind my contacting you?'

The warmth in her voice drifted into the sitting room where her mother heard Anna say, 'Listening to your voice Neil is like being back in the restaurant in Rennes, with you, me and John, and I've thought many times that was one of happiest evenings of my life, so of course, I am over the moon that you rang.'

Laughing he said 'It was a good night, you are absolutely right! Anna, if it's possible I would like to pop in and see you before I go off leave?'

Hardly giving him time to finish his sentence she said, 'Of course Neil, anytime you like, we would all love to see you, and look forward to it.'

Mary and David Jack wanted to know everything about John McCloud, the man that should have been their son-in-law, and the life that their daughter had been leading since she left home. They knew it would all come out in time, Anna's time, and so, bit by bit, at odd hours of the day and night, it did.

They learnt about the man coming tomorrow. In her letters to her parents she had written about Peter Adnans and her friends among the other sisters, and at length about John McCloud.

They both sensed a growing strength in their daughter, they also sensed something else, something new, she had become purposeful, decisive, stronger. Before she went away she no interest other than her vocation as a nurse, now there was something else, what it was the parents were unsure of, again they knew that she would tell them, in her own time.

London, 5th June 1940

The first conversation of the day contained a kindly rebuke for Anna from her father who had been woken up much earlier than planned by a bouncy grown up child carrying a tray of tea and biscuits. 'Anna, you are supposed to be resting and not playing nurse to your mother and me!'

Sat next to her still dozing mother she replied 'Daddy, please do not be grumpy, I am looking after myself honestly, and I am feeling so much better. And, I can't tell you how I'm so looking forward to seeing Neil, later today, I just know you will like him, Daddy!'.

Her father said sleepily 'Has mum told you that we have a meeting at lunch time, but we should be back later in the afternoon, is that alright?'

'Try to get back as quick as you can, please' she said in reply.

Rationing books had been introduced throughout the country at the beginning of the year. The purchase of all dairy products, meat, sugar, tea and a host of everyday items, including clothing was now strictly controlled.

Like most people Mary Jack balanced her coupons well, and was able to leave her daughter a beef casserole to be watched over during the day, that would be eaten at dinner, with their guest.

The four o'clock BBC news had finished on the wireless set when Anna heard a knock at the front door. Neil Bell stood on the short path leading from the gate to the entrance of the house.

He offered his hand and at the same time kissed Anna on each cheek before being led into the hallway and through to the kitchen. 'He looks older than when I last saw him' she thought, 'Well now, perhaps I do as well!' was the next thing that went through her mind.

Neil unconsciously ran his fingers through his tangled head of hair and placed a pair of motorcycle goggles on the table, before taking off a khaki haversack looped over his shoulder and a brown leather jacket which he hung on the back of a kitchen chair. Sitting down he accepted the offer of a cup of tea. 'You came up by bike, did you have a good trip, Neil' Anna asked.

'Really nice, thank you Anna, I'm staying with my folks in Oxford, until I go back to duty, in three days' time.'

Balancing two cups on saucers she sat down opposite her guest. There was a quick moment of silence, an awkwardness while he shifted around on his seat, before Neil spoke again 'Anna, I've got a couple of bottles of red wine in my haversack, would you rather have a glass of that than the tea?'

Without any hesitation she smiled before saying with meaning 'Absolutely right I would!'. The cups and saucers were stacked on the grooved wooden draining board to be washed later, and Anna returned to the table with two wine glasses and a bottle opener.

Filling half of their glasses with the wine he raised his while tapping Anna's in a toast, saying 'Anna, here is to our best friend, John McCloud.'

'Yes Neil, to our best friend John McCloud.'

Putting his glass on the table he looked at her and said 'I rang John's parents in Wales as soon as I got back, and went to see them two days ago. They told me that he had been killed Anna, I am so sorry, I know how much he meant to you, in fact how much you meant to each other.' pausing to take another sip of wine he added 'He wrote me a very excited letter telling me that he had asked you to marry him, that you had accepted, and that he wanted me to be his Best Man at your wedding. His parents had also received a similar letter telling them and his sister of his engagement to you'

'Anna, you must know that his parents' and his sister are heartbroken, but honestly, if anything has helped then it's been the true knowledge that he was happier than they had ever known him just before he was killed.'

Anna had sat listening while looking at her glass, the table, the corkscrew, unable to make eye contact with Neil, knowing that her wretchedness would be uncontrollable if she did. When he stopped she put her right hand to the brow of her head, and was softly rubbing her eyes with her thumb and finger when she started to speak 'Neil, I find it so hard to believe he's gone. He died while I was by his side, his very last breath rushed over my face, I will never ever forget it, never want to forget it, but I so want him here, I'm so bloody angry, he should be sat with you and me, drinking your wine......'

She couldn't carry on. He put his hand on hers and Anna cried for several minutes.

'Anna' Neil said, 'Can I show you the pictures you and John took when you both came to Rennes and went on to Pont-Aven?'

Through her misty eyes came the sight of John McCloud, sat proudly on Neil's motorbike in the middle of the French village.

Crisp images in black and white showed both of them sat on the Norton motorcycle and Anna said to Neil 'I remember the postman taking this one of us, and Neil look at this one of the three of us outside the hotel in Rennes, these are just wonderful, truly wonderful, I'd forgotten all about them, and I haven't any photos of John at all, nothing to show anyone.'

'Anna, I had our local chap process three sets, one for you, one for John's parents and one for me, and the negatives are yours.'

Anna leaned over the table and kissed him twice on his head, saying 'Two kisses, one from me the other from John, thank you so much from both of us.'

Here was the link Anna needed, that stepping stone from dream to reality. Here was a picture of her fiancé; this was him, not just a description but here, a reflection of their brief but total happiness together.

There were no more tears, there was no more a need for them, for the next hour Anna told Neil about her journey across Belgium and France to Dunkirk. The help and support from Peter Adnans, his friendship with John, and of her concern for Peter after leaving him at Dunkirk.

He told her of his relatively easy trip back from Cherbourg after he was ordered to go back to England to take up a new staff appointment in Whitehall, and of the promotion that went with the new position.

'Did you have to leave your beautiful motorbike behind, Neil?' Anna asked. Nodding sadly, he said 'Yes, Monsieur Henry, the owner of La Tuffiere, you remember? the restaurant we all ate in, has promised to look after it for me.' Knowing he had arrived on a motorbike she added 'And you've bought yourself another already!'

With the last gulp of his wine he caught Anna's eyes with his, saying 'Well now, that brings me in a very timely way to something else we have to discuss Anna. In one of the letters John wrote to his parents he effused about your new-found love of motorcycles, and admitted to his parents that you were a good driver.'

Reaching into the haversack Neil pulled out an envelope addressed to her, saying 'Anna, this letter is from John's parents.'

Neil made an excuse of needing to use the bathroom to give her an opportunity to look at the letter, which read 'My Dear Anna, I am sure you will forgive this brief note, written in some haste, before Neil Bell departs. We are delighted by the news Neil brought us today that you got back to your parents safely. We shall be writing to you over the next few days but would like to tell you that you are very welcome to come and stay with us at any time, when you are fit and well, as we would love to meet you. This note is about John's motorbike. It would please us very much if you would accept it as a gift from us, knowing you and John had such jolly times motoring around France together. We look forward to hearing from you when you are well, Our very best wishes, Jim and Judith McCloud.'

Neil Bell sat down at the kitchen table trying to gauge her reaction, it was unusual to say the least for young women to ride motorcycles, more unusual still for one to own one. Anna's face was still looking at the note and expressionless. It was when she looked up that Neil understood exactly why his good friend John had fallen so helplessly in love with this woman.

Her smile bought a feeling to his stomach that was a mixture of guilt and pleasure. Anna spoke quickly and was animated with her hands as well as her voice, saying 'Neil, this is the most fabulous present, I really cannot believe it, are you sure Neil that John's parents really want me to have his treasured motorcycle? it's just too much.'

His answer was easy 'Anna when you meet his parent's you will instantly recognise that John's trait of being decisive was inherited rather than cultivated! If these good people say something, then it's because they mean it, in fact I think it would hurt them a little if you didn't accept it.'

David and Mary Jack arrived back at six thirty, walking into the kitchen David greeted Neil saying, 'It's very good to meet you, but first I must apologise for my daughter's bad manners in not offering you a gin and tonic, as it's well past the hour, will you join us?'

'Yes please Sir, that would be good' Neil replied.

With all four of them sat around the long kitchen table it was only Anna that held centre stage as she showed them the photographs Neil had given her, one by one, and each with a full and in-depth description.

When Mary Jack got up to check the casserole Anna was

close behind her carrying the picture of John on his motorcycle in Pont Aven. She squeezed her mother's waist with her right arm while holding the photograph in the other and said, 'What do you think of him, mum?'

Returning the squeeze, she said 'Anna, he's a very handsome, kind looking man, you must be very proud of him?'

Anna thought for a moment before replying 'I never thought about that before, but your right, I am very proud of him.' She kissed her mother on the cheek before returning to the table.

'You'll stay the night Neil, I hope?' David Jack asked.

'Sorry Sir, but I must catch the last train back to Oxford, about ten, if that's alright?' Slightly puzzled David added 'Ah, I thought the shiny bike outside was yours?'.

Hesitating he said, 'Well Sir, if I could use the bathroom, I think Anna has something else to tell you.'

Neil should not have been concerned by Anna's parents' reaction to her being the proud new owner of a gleaming motorbike, they were delighted.

Both parents stood at the front door as Neil showed Anna the layout and controls of the motorbike, and both parents held their breath as they watched their daughter sit in the driving position and kick start the machine before revving it up and weaving away onto the main road.

Turning to her husband and shaking her head gently from side to side Mary Jack said 'I do think she should have put suitable trousers on and a warm top rather than wear that frock to go gallivanting around the neighbourhood, but I'm sure she knows best, what do you think of it all, David?'

Putting his arm around his wife as he led her back to the kitchen, he said 'Darling, all I know is that we had our little girl back in the house when we came back this evening, and I think it was good to see it. No need to fret Mary, Anna's been through more than we will ever know, but we've watched her get her physical strength back over the past few days, tonight I believe she got most of her mental strength back'

Neil's taxi arrived before ten to take him to the station. It had been a good evening and the invitation for Neil to return at any time was said with sincerity by David Jack. Outside, Anna thanked Neil for his kindness. They both knew that their bond would be one of friendship and trust, and that both would be important to them in the future. She kissed him as a friend and waved as he started his journey back to Oxford and the next stage of his war.

For Anna the next few days went quickly. The next morning in the post she received orders to report back to her headquarters hospital in seven days. Her first visit was to the centre of London to the tailors to be measured for another cape and dress uniform to replace the ones left somewhere in France, after that Anna went to Lillywhites to buy suitable clothes for a girl to tear around the countryside on a motorcycle. Relations and friends were visited and after making a phone call, Anna got onto her red and chrome 500cc 1935 Ariel Red Hunter, and headed off in the direction of Wales.

****

'Dynamo' the code name for the operation to rescue the Allied armies, came to an end at 3.20 am on the 4th of June, 1940 when the last British destroyer HMS Shikari steamed out of Dunkirk harbour, past the two helping arms of the eastern and western moles, bound for England.

Surrendering their liberty to the advancing German army over two thousand French troops stood to attention four deep, on the western mole, the flames of the town glinting on their steel helmets, while their commander and his staff stood on the deck of the British destroyer as it headed towards the sea.

Each group bravely saluted each other in a final act of comradeship before the vessel was lost to view.

A total of 224,686 British and 102,570 French had been evacuated to the safety of England. The 'miracle' of Dunkirk would live on. Those rescued would be the ones who would regroup and form the corps of experienced members of the navy, army and air forces that would sweep back to France in future years.

CHAPTER TWO 1940

British Kill French, French Kill British

******

A Black Woman Called Miriam

******

The Plymouth Blitz

British Kill French, French Kill British

Paris, 14th June 1940

Desperation and disbelieve swept through the people of France following the German army's entry into Paris, and the city's capitulation on the 14th of June 1940. Two days before the surrender of the city the government of the country had fled to Bordeaux.

The next day France's Prime Minister, Paul Reynaud, sought Churchill's approval to break the agreement between the two countries and to seek a separate surrender, an approval which Churchill refused.

In London, frantic efforts were being made to keep France in the war and an idea was conceived that the top echelons of both countries fervently believed would stop the surrender, and would also arrest the defeatist pressure the French Prime Minister was surrounded by.

A bold proposal was put before Reynaud that France and Britain should become one integrated country with each citizen of the two nations having equal status in law and life.

The 'Declaration of Union' between France and Britain was sized upon by Reynaud as being the vice that would hold the two great democracies of the World together and ensure that France would fight on.

An enthusiastic Charles de Gaulle gave full approval and begged his premier to embrace the plan fully and continue the struggle both in his country and in its colonies around the world, assured that a victory would be theirs in time and that the shame of their country capitulating would cast dark shadows over its history for decades.

The British War Cabinet agreed the historic declaration and Churchill set a time to meet Reynaud and his ministers in Bordeaux the next day, June the 17th to augment the proposal and bind the two nations inexorably together.

Later that night a telegram was received from France to cancel the meeting, and during that evening Paul Reynaud was forced to resign and Field Marshal Philippe Petain, at the age of 84, a hero of the first war, took over as the Prime Minister of France, and ordered all French forces to lay down their arms immediately, pending an armistice.

On the 18th of June, the BBC gave the man many thought of as the new Napoleon his first opportunity to address his fellow French citizens. In a call to arms General Charles de Gaulle denounced Marshall Petain and urged every man and woman in France to fight on.

The General's rallying speeches were to give a nation in shock and turmoil a spark of wild hope that made Marshall Petain convene a court martial that condemned de Gaulle to death, in absentia.

High on the list of the British Premier's worries and concerns about a French surrender was what would happen to its large and modern naval fleet, the fourth largest in the world.

Sensing an easy victory an opportunistic Benito Mussolini and his fascist party had taken Italy into the war on June the 10th on the side of the Germans and with it had come Italy's navy.

The British could see that their one and only military advantage of having the largest naval force in Europe was being quickly eroded and that the incorporation of the French fleet into the Axis war machine would cause havoc, cost many thousands of lives and prolong the war by a long time.

Adolf Hitler had personally set the agenda for the final humiliation of France which came at 3.30 in the afternoon on June the 21st, when the French military and political delegation was led into the very same railway carriage in the Forest of Compiegne, north of Paris, where the First World War Armistice was signed and Germany had been forced into a total and unconditional surrender.

Hitler sat grim faced and rigidly upright at the head of the table in the ornately decorated carriage which had been placed like a monument in a wooded area on a short piece of railway line.

The German dictator looked on silently while his entourage dictated his only terms which included that the French fleet would stay under nominal French control, but would not be allowed to leave French territorial waters.

Once outside the railway carriage and alone with his generals a laughing Hitler danced a jig of sheer glee and delight in front of them. For the former Austrian army corporal who had fought in the trenches of the first war this was a crowning moment of personal and national revenge.

In the following months the railway carriage was taken back to Berlin where the symbol of German humiliation was publicly burnt.

London, 2nd July 1940

The knock on the door of her office was gentle, but it caught Anna off guard and she jerked her whole body around from her seat as the junior nurse entered and said, 'Sister Jack, I'm sorry to disturb you, but Matron would like to see you urgently in her office, please.'

'Thank you nurse, that's alright, I'll go right over now' Anna replied.

After the door closed she stood in front of a mirror to adjust her head dress and noticed her hands were shaking slightly.

Speaking at the reflection she said, 'Steady girl, steady now, no jitters, calm down, deep breaths.'

She felt good but an unexpected noise, the sudden shout of a patient sometimes caught her out, laid bare the defences, and at these times she knew she was still edgy, as if on a brink between coping and… 'and what?' she said aloud while still looking into the mirror 'no, Anna Jack, you are doing well, and you have a lot to do, so go on and do it!'

The posting to the regimental hospital had been what she

needed and the last weeks had been enjoyable. Anna had arrived and was put charge of a team of theatre nurses. Many of the patients had been injured in France and she had lots to talk about when the men were recovering and she found the act of talking others through their ordeals a way of coming to terms with her own.

Her Matron was of the 'old school' and Anna found her permanent state of grumpiness both unhelpful and irritating, but she was very happy in the job she had been assigned too, and what little contact she had with her senior officer was easily dealt with.

Through the half-frosted glass door of the office the outlines of two figures were visible when she tapped on the pane and heard 'Come' in the recognizable and, like the office door, frosted voice of her Matron.

Anna went into the office and stood to attention facing the lady behind the desk. Aware of another figure sat with her back to her Anna could hardly suppress a shout of surprise as the figure turned around and Mary Atkins stood up.

'At ease, sister, and please take a seat' Mary Atkins said, motioning her to the chair opposite her.

Matron got up stiffly from behind her desk and stood to attention in the direction of Anna's former matron before saying 'I have many things to attend too, so I will be around the hospital if you need me Matron-in-Chief.'

Anna stood up as the Matron left the room and broke into broad smile as the door closed and she took her seat again, facing the woman she had last seen in Belgium.
Mary Atkins had written to Anna at her parents' home when the regimental headquarters had told her of her safe evacuation from Dunkirk and that John McCloud had died. She had replied telling her everything that had happened on the long journey back to England.

'Well, Anna' she said warmly, 'as you can see I have two arms to throw about again and with a bit more brass on my shoulder I can make life really difficult for certain men in high places! Now, how are you?'

She found it easy to say 'I really am very well Matr…ah!, I mean Matron-in-Chief! But do you have any news of Major

Adnans?'

The warm smile left as she replied 'Nothing Anna. I checked again this morning, knowing you would ask. The Red Cross have no record and sadly, his parents have been informed officially by telegram that he is 'missing, and presumed dead'. We must just keep our fingers crossed Anna that somewhere he is a prisoner of war.'

Still without a smile, she continued 'Now Anna, I'm chasing time and I have to hurry along, but the reason I'm here is that I have a special job I want you to be part of. I want you to go the Royal Naval Hospital in Plymouth and report to a Commander Morris before nine this evening.'

Bewildered Anna replied 'Can I ask what I am going there for?'

Shaking her head she replied 'No Anna, all I can tell you is that your nursing and French skills will be called for and that a military action is about to start, the consequences of it at the moment are unknown but it will be of the utmost importance to the war effort.'

Hardly pausing for breath, she continued 'Now, transport is the problem as time is pressing on, but go and collect your kit and I will arrange a train or car for you.'

Anna interrupted 'I do have my own motorbike which I could use and be in Plymouth by late this afternoon.'

The glint in the eyes of Mary Atkins returned as she said 'Really, I hope you know Sister Jack that your exploits on motorcycles in France had many a tongue wagging! But yes, that would solve a problem. I will arrange for your Matron to get the necessary travel documents and fuel docket organized within half an hour, so when you are ready, report back to her, and please do not forget Anna, no one, Matron or anyone else is to know why you are going to Plymouth. Do you have any questions?'

Looking puzzled and with the mention of motorcycles and France the red of a blush creeping up her neck Anna could only say 'Well Ma'am, as I don't know myself why I am going to the West Country it will be very easy not to give any secrets away, and you can rely on me totally!'

Standing up Mary Atkins said 'Anna, I know that I can rely

on you, that's why I'm here, but things might happen that seem crazy to you at this point in time, but believe me as events unfold through the war they will start to make sense, now off you go, and the best of luck!'

Anna came to attention and saluted before turning around and leaving the office.

The frost surrounding Anna's matron had turned to ice by the time she reported back to her office twenty minutes later. Following her knock on the office door the 'Come' had risen two octaves to just below a shout and a crimson faced nursing Matron could only splutter 'Well I certainly don't know what all the fuss and hurry is about, but I suppose you do Sister?'

In honesty Anna could look the ruffled women in the face and say 'No Matron, I really don't, I'm sorry.'

As the travel documents were laid down with a thump on the oak desk the Matron added 'Have you known the Matron-in-Chief long, Sister?'

As innocently as possible Anna replied, "She was my Matron in France before the evacuation, but not before then.'

Without looking at Anna her senior officer cynically added 'Do remember that there's more to nursing than fighting wars alongside men. Personally, I believe a women's place is here in England and not swanning around foreign parts Sister.' Nodding her head Anna replied 'I completely agree Matron.'

By twelve thirty Anna had reached the A303 road and was heading South West. The rolling countryside each side of the original Roman road was lush and green between acre after acre of wheat and barley, the timeless scenes of peace blotted and spoilt by squat brick or concrete pill boxes, recently constructed at cross roads, and the edges of flat plains, with machine gun or anti-tank gun muzzles poking out of dark slits - waiting.

The ancient villages that straddled the route had become anonymous to travellers, their names obliterated from all sign posts, the entrance of schools, church notice boards, the stone bases of First World War monuments. The familiar swinging pub signs lay hidden in sheds and lofts in order to deny a wondering invader a quick and definite map position.

The industry of farming continued until she reached a

crossroads that marked the beginning of Salisbury Plain when together with army lorries, buses, and two Austin seven motorcars she was made to wait for twenty minutes by military policemen wearing their peeked red topped caps.

The sight of these men made Anna think back to France and she was deep in these thoughts as a motorcade, headed by two military police motorcyclist in front of three large Humber motor cars and speeding army lorries roared past in front of her.

She noticed the policemen snap to attention and salute as the cavalcade flashed by, but her only clear thoughts were that she was impatient to get under way again.

****

Unknown to Anna, in the middle staff car that sped past sat Winston Churchill. Drawing on his cigar his thoughts at the time he was passing in front of her were also of France, for he knew that a decision he had made during the night would affect the thinking of generations of Frenchmen towards the British nation and its people.

The decision was also a gamble that if it went wrong would alienate many people around the world, and most importantly, America with its powerful lobby of people wanting to maintain the stance of strict neutrality.

****

Salisbury Plain was like a vast tented army camp as she began to pass mile after mile of fields and open stretches of land with rows of the canvass shelters and training grounds on both sides of her, and the road itself scarred at intervals by chicanes of concrete tank obstacles and barbed wire check points guarded by men armed with rifles or machine guns.

Purring to the top of a gentle hill, Anna blinked several times behind her thick goggles, pulled the Red Hunter to the side of the road, and let the engine idled as she put both feet on the ground to balance the machine before looking down and at the ancient ruins of Stonehenge a mile in the distance, the circles of stone slabs surrounded by fields of yellow wheat that rippled lazily, like shaken silk flags, as the shimmering heads of the crop were caught in drifting winds.

Without a moment's hesitation, she went back onto the A303 for half a mile and veered off onto a minor road that swept past the four-thousand-year-old monument before taking a track that led her to within twenty feet of the stone circles.

She switched off the engine, got off the motorbike and stretched her back and arms as she watched cows wondering freely through the arches made from the stone pillars and Anna did likewise, touching the weatherworn surfaces with her fingertips as the cows were touching them with their hides.

Smiling, she thought of how she had pulled a reluctant John McCloud into the smaller circle of stones on the cliff top in Brittany and addressing one of the cows who had stopped to inspect her she said 'You know these stone circles have a very strange feel about them, here and in France, I wish I could explain what it is, perhaps you know why they seem so powerful, so important? Anyway, I have to race off to the seaside; it was nice to meet you, good bye!'

To make up time she had lost she raced the Ariel on towards Devon and reached the outskirts of the city before five in the afternoon. Anna stopped the motorbike at the top of a hill that took the road on its gradual decent into Plymouth four miles in the distance.

Leaving the road, she stopped the machine and pulled it back onto its stand before climbing up onto the top of a low wall and looking towards her destination. Using her thick leather motorcycle glove to shield her eyes from the bright sun Anna could see sparkling diamonds of light dancing in a dark blue sea between two headlands, and above them eight large grey barrage balloons.

Plymouth was a 'restricted area', a military zone banned to all foreign aliens without a special permit and needing special clearance for those forces personal entering the city.

The Royal Naval Dockyard to the West of the city was going to be a principal target for German bombers. With a workforce of more than twenty thousand men and women repairing and building naval and merchant ships, it was one the world's largest naval bases.

Showing her pass and travel order to a plain clothes policeman at a check point as she entered the city Anna was directed to the Royal Naval Hospital where, after parking her motorcycle, she reported to the main gate office. An orderly made a telephone call before escorting her to a waiting Commander Morris.

The stern looking naval officer seemed irritated by Anna's arrival when she was shown into his office, greeting her with the words 'Sister Jack, well for the life of me I can't see why you are here. We have adequate staff available from within the hospital, so what are your marvellous and special talents?'

Anna was shocked by the commanders abrupt and unfriendly manner finding the question difficult to answer, and could only think of saying 'Sir, apart from nursing and being able to speak French and German fluently I can think of no extra special talents that I have that most sisters would not.'

With a cold stare he said 'Quite Sister, exactly what I thought. We have a good team here and I will not have that balance interrupted, do you understand?'

'Yes, Sir' Anna replied.

Standing up from his desk the commander moved to a window and looking out of it with his back to her he continued 'We both know that a special operation is planned for tonight. What that operation is has not been divulged to anyone in the hospital. All we know is that we are to expect and to be ready to receive an unspecified number of wounded men'

'These men are to be placed in total isolation in a separate part of the hospital, and under no circumstances are they to be allowed to mix with other patients....' a knock on the office door interrupted the flow of his cold diatribe and pausing he barked 'Enter'.

'You asked me to report to you at eighteen hundred hours Sir.' The voice belonged to a tall black woman who entered the office and stood stiffly to attention in front of the officer.

'Yes Sister Bonnard, thank you. This is the sister I was speaking to you about, be so kind as to show her the area we have set up for tonight, and I will remind both of you that this matter is to be treated with the utmost secrecy. As soon as whatever happens starts we will all of us be confined to the secure area until I get a direct order from the commander of the hospital to the effect that we can stand down and return to normal duties. That's all.'

Outside the office the two nursing sisters walked silently down a flight of wide lime stone stairs and into the evening sun. In a friendly, welcoming tone Sister Bonnard said, 'This way here, across the Quarterdeck'.

Anna stopped and looked around her, saying 'What a beautiful hospital, how long have you been here, Sister?'

'Now please, Miriam is my name. I've been here for five months now, and I presume that cold old fish gave you his usual hostile greeting, eh?'

'What a beastly bloke, do I take it he's normally like that? And by the way, my name is Anna.'

Miriam replied 'Ho, yes, yes Anna, and if he's had a disagreement with his snooty wife, well then, ho, he's a lot, lot worse and we all suffer!'

Chuckling she added 'And to be honest he's also been in a dreadful flap because his precious routine has been disturbed and the hospital commander has been hot on his heels all day, making sure everything is ready for whatever is going on! Do you know what is happening?'

'Honestly Miriam, I really don't, but I suspect that the good commander thought I did!' Shielding her eyes from the sun Anna said, 'How old is the hospital?'

Miriam told her that the naval hospital had been completed in 1762 and delighted in giving her a history lesson about the complex which consisted of sixteen detached two-story limestone buildings around a large square of grass three hundred yards by three hundred yards.

Linking each building to the other was a continuous glass colonnade that gave shelter of sorts to the patients and all medical staff. Two stone paths crossed the grassed area known as the Quarterdeck and at its centre was a stone sundial with bench seats and flower beds surrounding it. Outside the quadrangle of grass and hospital buildings were the ancillary structures of chapel, mortuary, isolation area and stores.

The two nursing sisters walked past the sundial at the centre of the hospital, Miriam acknowledging the 'Hellos' of other sisters and nurses who were sat talking to each other.

They passed outside the square of hospital buildings coming to three single story structures where Miriam stopped, saying to Anna 'These are the isolation houses. We had a few men in here which have now been transferred so that we can use them.' The three single story blocks had thirty beds in each and were ready for immediate use.

'You have a room next to mine Anna in the nurses' accommodation block; we can get something to eat if you like and perhaps a bit of sleep before we start again at midnight.'

Anna could not help looking at Miriam. She had the broad Negro features of the Africans Anna had seen in pictures and books, and she was so black her skin seemed almost as if it had a blue tinge to it.

After they had eaten they sat outside on a bench facing the sun and Anna asked awkwardly 'Is Plymouth your home town, Miriam?'

Slapping both palms of her hands on outstretched legs she answered 'Gracious me no! I'm the first black woman most people around here have ever seen. There are a few black chaps around that I've seen and because Plymouth is a sea port then I suppose they would be a familiar sight, but black women, no, I tell you I think I am one of the first! My home is sunny Jamaica Anna.'

The infectious laugh from Miriam made Anna smile before saying 'So what brought you here?'

Looking slightly surprised, as if the answer was so obvious she said 'The war, naturally Anna. I had been a nurse in Kingston for about a year when war broke out. My father is a solicitor in the town and has a practice there, and my mother has been a midwife for as long as I can remember, so as soon as war was declared, well, my brother Henry, he went off quickly and is now in Canada training to be a pilot, and I arrived in England in January leaving three younger brothers at home.'

Anna was embarrassed by her own ignorance and arrogance. It had never crossed her mind that coloured people on thousands of miles away would have the same passion to preserve a way of life that she had. She could only think of saying 'So you really are a long way from home, do you like it here?'

With a slightly sad look she said 'When I first arrived in Liverpool it was so cold I thought I was going to die Anna and that's the truth. I went to London and joined a hospital and for the first few weeks I was so home sick, it was terrible. But you know it got better, and I found a church close to the hospital where I was working and the people there were very helpful and supportive.'

'Did you ever think of going home?' Anna asked.

'Oh, many times, I can tell you, at first that is. But as I say things got better, and the thought of going home and facing my mother and father, well that kept me going, I can tell you!'

Anna felt silly, knowing she was handling the conversation badly, that her questions were fatuous; she knew she was unable to ask the questions she really wanted to.

The conversation went onto the professional level that both were at ease with before the young black woman showed Anna where her temporary room was, and they left each other to get some sleep.

Plymouth, 3rd July 1940

Miriam introduced the four nurses and four nursing orderlies they would be working with when the two sisters went back on duty at a little after midnight. The routine was a familiar one. Anna and Miriam would assess each casualty before Commander Morris saw them and if they needed surgery they would be taken to the operating theatres which were on standby, in one of the main hospital buildings.

The sisters divided the nursing team into two so each could take an hour's break and at two thirty in the morning Miriam's hand gently shook Anna's shoulder as she said, 'Anna, something seems to have started. Two ambulances have arrived outside and the lads are bringing the stretchers in.' Six casualties were laid down in the reception area and the two sisters went quickly to them.

The first wounded man Anna came to was a young officer. He was unconscious and in a grave condition with open wounds to his chest. Anna told an orderly to cut away his uniform while she went to the next stretcher where a sailor with deep cuts to his face and head and a single bullet wound to his shoulder. Next to him was another unconscious sailor.

Anna went back to the first casualty and was looking at his wounds when Commander Morris arrived 'Well Sister' he said quickly 'What do we have?'
With all thoughts of the previous meeting behind her she rapidly answered, 'Looks like two bullet entries, middle and lower stomach on this one Sir, a similar priority on the third stretcher along, and a bullet entry to the shoulder on the middle case with multiple lacerating.'

Looking quickly at each man he turned to Anna saying, 'Very good Sister, get the two over to theatre immediately while I look at the rest.' She had just finished giving the orderlies instructions when the commander shouted to her 'Sister, over here quickly.' Rushing over to where Miriam stood the commander continued 'This lad is refusing to let me or anyone else near him and is babbling away in French, find out what he wants.'

Speaking to the French naval officer who had been shot in

the chest she said 'Now please, you must calm down and let us help you.'

Shouting loudly, he replied 'You English are going to kill all of us, get away from me!'

In a more severe tone she said, 'If you don't let me help you, you will die from your wounds, I promise I will make sure you are well treated, now please let me help you.'

The Frenchman calmed down as Anna and an orderly cut away his tunic and the patient was put onto a gurney trolley and taken to an operating theatre.

Two more ambulances arrived and from the eight casualties two more were classified as most urgent and taken to have surgery, one British, one French.

The nursing Sisters and Commander Morris now moved the rest of the wounded into the prepared wards. Six were French and the rest British. Speaking out loud the Commander said, 'What the hell is happening, all these lads are supposed to on the same side, damn it!'

With Sister Bonnard close to him the commander said to one of the British wounded 'What has been happening, young man?' The sailor replied 'We boarded all the French navy vessels in Plymouth, Sir, 'bout an hour or so back. The crew of the submarine I went on tried to scuttle the ship and fighting broke out when we tried to stop them, it was all so sudden, but a lot shots were fired in each direction, Sir.'

Anna was next to a French sailor whose arm and leg had been broken when he fell down an open hatchway. 'How did all this start?' She asked him in his own language.

'Sister, I am not sure, to be honest. It had been rumoured that the English might try to take over the ship but none of us thought it would happen like it did, first there was a lot of shouting and people running all over the ship, then shots were being fired at us, we could not believe it.'

As she was talking she noticed that several armed marines had entered the room and an officer was talking to Commander Morris. 'Sister' he called. When Anna reached him he said 'The captain here wants all the wounded French men to be put into the next building so that they are separated from our own lads, and I would like you to stay with them and let Sister Bonnard take care of our wounded.'

With the help of the nursing orderlies Anna took the wounded Frenchmen into their own ward and settled them down to wait for treatment. Three more patients were added to her charge, all with superficial wounds that required minor attention. As they were brought in she noticed the arrival of four armed marines who had positioned themselves at the entrances of the room.

Commander Morris worked quickly and efficiently in giving his help to the wounded men. Despite their unfortunate start Anna could not fault his ability as a doctor and when she stepped outside of the building and met Miriam lighting a cigarette she told her, adding 'Miriam, what a sad business this all is, I wish I understood what is going on.'

Offering Anna a cigarette which she said no to Miriam said 'I've just taken in a rather dishy sergeant Anna with a broken arm, and he told me that the other French ships were taken over without any serious problems, it has just been the men on the submarine, *'Sourcuofe'* it's called, that resisted, and listen to this, my dishy sergeant seems to think that we are now at war with the French as well as the Germans!'

Drawing deeply on her cigarette and exhaling before she spoke she added 'Oh dear, where will this all take us. Well, at least the flow of wounded seems to have stopped, if you want to take a break, I'll cover for you.'

Anna thought for a moment before answering 'I hope your sergeant is wrong, but sadly nothing is going to surprise me. Miriam, thanks for the offer, but to be honest I'm a bit nervous about the guards in my ward, I think I'll doze for a bit in the corner behind a screen in case there are any misunderstandings, everyone seems to be so on edge and nervous at the moment.

The third building of the isolation block was used by the nursing team to rest and eat the food that had been brought to them by another party of Royal Marines. Sat opposite Miriam at breakfast Anna said 'At last I know how it must feel to have a rare tropical disease that cannot be transmitted to the outside world! I just wonder how long and why we are being held here.'

'I know what you mean Anna', Miriam replied 'I find it quite disturbing, it's like being a prisoner.'

Like most nurses Anna had the gift of grabbing a 'cat nap' when the opportunity came and she was asleep behind a screen when the noise woke her. Pushing the screen aside she saw two of the guards shouting and one of them pointing his rifle at one of the French officers who was trying to get through the door to the outside. Several of the other Frenchmen that were able to stand had started to get off their beds and were going to the aid of their countryman.

Anna got in between the wounded men and the sentries and spoke to the French officer, 'Sir, what is the problem here?' Adjusting the sling his arm was in the naval submarine officer said 'Sister, I wish to return to my ship immediately and I want to speak to the commanding officer, but these men are threatening me and will not let me pass.'

'Sir, I will go and fetch the C.O. for you, but could you please stay here for a moment while I do so?' Nodding an agreement, he went back to his bed and began talking to the other wounded men. Anna let herself through the entrance guarded by the marines and found the marines senior officer talking to Commander Morris. 'Sir,' Anna said 'There seems to be a problem in my ward and one of the French officers is demanding to leave the building and would like to speak to someone in authority.'

'Right Sister' the doctor replied, 'As it happens Lieutenant Johnson and I were on our way to speak to them, so now you can do the translating.'

Inside the ward the marine officer spoke to the senior French man, with Anna translating she said 'Lieutenant Johnson has been instructed by his C.O. to tell you that all of you will be reunited with the rest of your ship's compliment at Stonehouse Barracks at seventeen hundred hours. Until then he points out that you are all required to stay here, inside the wards.'

From the edge of his bed the angry French officer replied, 'Why are we being kept prisoners until then?'

Speaking through Anna the British officer replied 'Lieutenant Johnson has no idea why you have to stay here, Sir, but he has very definite orders that you must all do so, and if I may add Sir, it is only a matter of a few more hours until you will all be allowed to go.'

Looking at the British marine officer with contempt but addressing Anna he said 'Please tell this officer that I will register my strongest possible protest at the way in which my men and myself have been kept prisoners here to the appropriate level, and one other thing I would like to know how our second engineer is after his operation?'

Commander Morris looked coldly at Anna before saying 'Tell the arrogant sod that both of the British casualties together with his own countryman died in the operating theatre of their wounds.'

Before five in the afternoon three lorries arrived and the wounded men boarded them and were driven away. With only the medical team left in the isolation buildings Commander Morris spoke to them 'I have been told by the surgeon captain that we can all stand down and return to normal duties after the wards have been cleaned up. One last thing, I have been instructed to tell all of you that we are to say nothing, and I do mean nothing, of what happened here to anyone outside of the hospital, that is all. Sister Jack, I would like a word with you,'

'Sister, Matron Atkins would like you to report direct to her at her headquarters tomorrow, in the p.m., that's all.' Standing to attention she said 'Thank you Sir' to his disappearing back.

As if reading her mind the voice of Miriam Bonnard said 'I know Anna, what a pompous white ass he is! Never mind girl, look, if we have some tea and get washed up and changed, how would you like me to show you the world-famous Union Street?'

A Black Woman Called Miriam

Plymouth, 3rd July, 1940

From the main hospital gate of naval hospital it was only a walk of two hundred yards to the start of a street that every British sailor knew, and each had a story to talk about. Stretching a quarter of a mile into the distance, although only seven in the evening Union Street was a jostling lively forest of sailors and soldiers, moving like blue and brown trees on both sides of the wide road.

Creeping around to the West, the golden light of the evening sun was shining down the whole of the arrow straight road, casting long shadows of Anna and Miriam as they stood looking at the scene in front of them.

There were no sophisticated trappings of London or Paris here, this had more of the Wild West frontier atmosphere from the cowboy books and films and Anna found it strangely exciting.

Stopping outside a pub called 'The Star' Miriam said, 'Anna love, I must have a fag, let's go in here, I know the owner's wife Dorothy from when she came to the hospital, it looks rough but it really is safe enough and she is a very kind woman, come on.'

The pub was crowded, noisy, smoky, the light minimum, and both women squinted as their eyes became accustomed to what light was available. Dorothy was serving behind the bar. A huge, formidable looking woman with bright ginger hair and a booming bass voice, she greeted Miriam like an old friend and shook Anna's hand with a vice like grip.

During the introductions, a young sailor rapped his empty glass loudly on the counter in an attempt to get the landlady's attention and more drinks for him and his fellow matelots. His reward was a cold stare from Dorothy followed by her booming voice saying 'Ee can wait yer bleddy turn or ee can all fuck off, reet now!'

Turning back to Miriam she continued quietly 'Err now, what can I get ee two maids, tis ever so good to see ee gain, Miriam.'

At this end of Union Street the pub was a 'local' to the people who lived in the hundreds of small terraced houses, tenements and flats, many in near slum conditions.

The 'Star' sold a selection of beers and cider poured direct from metal ringed wood barrels raised a foot from the saw dust covered floor behind the bar. At eye level stood rows of bottled beers and stouts separated by whiskey and gin optics, most of them victims of rationing and empty.

The two nurses ordered gin and tonics. Looking at the bottle of gin above the row of barrels Dorothy knowingly said to them 'I'll get ee two sommert nicer from the back, a drop of real Plymouth Gin' and disappeared.

After she had won the fight to pay for the drinks Miriam waited as the landlady put her money into an ornately decorated cash till, and returned with her change before saying 'Dorothy dear, I must take the weight off me tired aching feet and sit down!'

Taking the drinks from the bar the two women sat at a corner table in the smoke filled room. Lighting her cigarette Miriam inhaled deeply and shook her head from side to side before saying 'What a sad, strange couple of days. British men killing Frenchmen, Frenchmen killing British, it's all topsy turvy un no mistake, Anna.'

Nodding in agreement before she answered Anna then said 'Miriam, look over there, see, by the window, those sailors are French, and they're sat with a bunch of our sailors laughing and joking as if nothing had happened, you know I was told to expect to see things I would find difficult to understand, and it's turned out to be completely true, it's all mad.'

Thinking back over the past days Anna said, 'What makes a man like Commander Morris such a disagreeable person?'

Picking up the question her companion replied, 'He is a bit of a puzzle, and at first I thought it was the usual problem of me being black, but he now treats me better than a lot of the staffers that have been here donkey's years.'

Laughing out loud between having a drink and drag of her cigarette the sentence was finished with 'Mind you, I don't think the poor man has much luck in the bedroom, Anna, and that's the truth of it!'

In the thick fog of cigarette smoke and with the comfort of a couple of gin's both women sat back in their well-worn seats and felt relaxed as Anna said, 'You were right the 'Star' is a tough old pub with some rough, tough people in it, but there is an honesty about the place that makes it feel safe.'

Looking straight ahead Anna had to ask the question that she had wanted to ask since the two women had met 'Miriam, a minute ago you said something about the problem of being a black person I really need to ask you, and just hope you don't think I am being very rude, but is being black so much of a problem here in England?'

Sharing her forward gaze Miriam paused before she answered with a deep sigh, followed by 'Well yes Anna and it can be hurtful, I have to say. So hurtful that at times I've had to go away and cry. It hurts inside when people refuse to serve you in a shop or in a café or when you just know other nurses are sniggering behind your back, yes, it hurts.'

Turning to look Anna in the face she continued 'As a nursing sister, well at first it sort of eats away at your self confidence, you begin to believe you are not as good as white people, and sometimes you make silly mistakes, but then you meet someone who sees only how good and professional you are at your job, and I have to say Anna, Commander Morris is like that, I do my job well, damned well in fact, and that's all he sees, not the colour of my skin, simply me.'

The Jamaican woman lit up another cigarette before saying 'You know, I was thinking about what you said yesterday, about why I am here, and it certainly is for the reason I mentioned to you but there is one other thing that really sticks in my mind, and that was the reaction of my brother Henry when he read a book that our father gave him that had been written by Hitler while he was in prison, called *'Mein Kampf'*

'In it he wrote that all Jewish and black people are inferior beings, little better than animals, now Anna, that really got my gander up, my brother and me, I can tell you'

'Oh, that Henry, he was so, so mad he went down to the Colonial Office in Kingston to volunteer for the RAF the week after war was declared, only to be told that Britain did not want him because he was not of pure European blood!'

'Think about it Anna he has a degree in engineering from a British University, a pilot's license to fly aeroplanes, and he's not good enough!'

'I have never seen my father so angry. Real sparks. He got together the politicians and the other professionals in Jamaica and they gave the High Commissioner such a hard time I can tell you. Well, there are now hundreds of men coming over to fly in the RAF, our Henry was too impatient to wait, which is why he went to Canada and started training immediately'

'Both of my parents are very strict Church of England Anna, and they brought all of us to believe in 'fair play', English justice and the damned boring cricket. Now my mother and father, they are real King's people, as far as they are concerned they would follow the King and his family into the grave, and Great Britain can do no wrong in their eyes, but our generation see a different future, we are happy to fight and possibly be killed for freedom in Europe but only on the condition that we can have our own freedom at home sometime in the coming years'

'One thing is certain Anna, there is no going back to the old ways, the genie is out of the bottle and he's a real devil to get back!'

With one elbow on the small table in front of them Anna turned and glanced sideways at Miriam before saying 'My father gave me the same book to read, you see he's Jewish and the same sparks of rage came out of him as from you and your brother!'

There was a rather hard stare from Miriam towards Anna

before she said, 'And what about Anna Jack, were your sparks flying, girl?'

She found it difficult to return the eye contact, there was even a hint of her shuffling her bum on her seat and tapping her feet in that irritating giveaway set of signals that meant an awkward question had been posed and it needed an honest answer.

Draining her glass before locking onto Miriam's dark brown eyes Anna said 'It must have been 1936 or '37 when daddy circled mum and me as we sat around our kitchen table at home in a raging war dance with a copy of '*Mein Kampf*' in his hand'

'In honesty, I have to admit it meant little to me. I knew Hitler was a mad, cruel man, but I hadn't been touched by his madness or cruelty until that moment. You see, I had never thought of myself as anything other than an English girl, never, ever did I think of myself as a Jewess, or rather half a Jewess. I remember being so cross, so angry because suddenly one man's madness had made me feel so insecure, so vulnerable.'

Clearing her throat Anna said, 'Come on, one last gin before you show me the rest of this wicked Union Street!' As she was returning to the table a scuffle broke out between two of the several prostitutes that used the pub. Dorothy's loud voice and freckled hands separated them before she issued orders to the girls to stop. An order instantly obeyed.

Putting the drinks on the table Anna asked, 'Well Miss Bonnard, I do wonder what our respectable mothers and fathers would say if they could see the salubrious surroundings we are having our evening drinks in!'

Laughing out loud Miriam clapped her hands together, saying 'My father would be horrified, but I think my mother would like to be with us, she would enjoy the atmosphere, and your company Anna.'

The sun had gone when the two women walked out of the pub into the last hour of light. There seemed to be more sailors around now than earlier as they joined the boisterous throng. It was a fair ground atmosphere where young men felt this could be their last 'run ashore' before sailing away and they were going to make the most of it.

Union Street was a cauldron of temptation and good fun for the thousands of sailors that poured onto it from their ships of every size and from every corner of the World. The 'fleet' was in, and so were the girls to greet them.

Anna and Miriam walked past pubs and cider houses, some with narrow alley ways running along the side where tattoo parlours awaited the sailor that would forever be reminded of his trip to Plymouth by the name of a lover, a wife or a mother whose name curled around a red heart or dagger on his forearm or other parts of his body.

The same shadowy alley would allow the mariner with 'Joan Love for Ever' still tender from the needle of the tattoo artist on his arm, to wake up in the arms of Diane, a prostitute who had worked the 'Street' since she was fifteen.

On either side of Union Street there were fruit and vegetable shops, butchers, bakers for the local people. The shops were settled between bars, Billiard rooms, hotels, and the three Medici brass balls of the pawnbrokers' shops that would allow for one last pint, or one last embrace.

Posh shop fronts with imperial looking signs announcing that they were Naval tailors and outfitters, small café's where local fish and chips could be eaten, Union Street was a self-contained world of its own, where everything was on offer and available.

The blackout was starting to be enforced along the whole of the street and the pubs would soon be closing. Any drinking or dancing would now have to be done in the back rooms and clubs in the surrounding areas.

Both nurses were tired, it had been a long two days, and a lot had happened. They walked back along the darkening street where parties of Naval Provost policemen broke up groups of sailors, sending them back to their ships and air raid wardens shouted to occupants of the houses and flats to observe the blackout rules.

As they approached the main hospital gates Anna said, 'So it's just us now, Britain alone, against the Germans and the rest of them, I can't believe we can lose, but I get scared to death when I think we might do so Miriam.'

Squeezing Anna's arm gently Miriam whispered, 'Not just Britain alone Anna, there are millions of us across the world from my small island in the West Indies to Africa, Indian, Australia and New Zealand for Mr Hitler to defeat, and I ask you, who would want to tackle Dorothy in The Star!'

House of Commons, London, 4th July 1940

Before a packed House of Commons, Winston Churchill told his fellow members of parliament about his "hateful decision" to destroy the French fleet while it lay at anchor in the Moroccan ports of Mers-el-Kebir and Oran, and to commandeer all French vessels in British ports to serve under the Free French Flag, or be scuttled.

Members of parliament from all political parties were seen to be visibly shaken by the announcement and gasps of surprise were heard around parliament as the full details were given.

The House was told that at seven a.m. on the morning of the 3rd of July an ultimatum had been delivered to the commander of the French fleet lying at anchor by the commander of the British fleet that lay six miles offshore.

Four options had been offered to the Frenchman. To join forces with the Royal Navy and carry on fighting against the Germans; for the fleet to sail to a British port; for the fleet to sail to a French colonial port and be immobilized; or the last and final option of scuttling the entire fleet as it lay at anchor.

An answer was required by five p.m. that day, and if none were received the British Commander told his French counterpart that his ships would open fire on his.

The French Commander of the Fleet signalled his superiors in the Vichy government that the British had given him one option only, which was to scuttle his fleet within six hours.

Field Marshall Petain's government responded by telling the Fleet Commander that reinforcements were sailing from Toulon and Algiers and the only option he was to take was to engage the British naval fleet.

The message from the French government was intercepted by the Royal Navy and the action by the British Navy Force 'H', which had sailed from Gibraltar, started at five thirty in the afternoon, and lasted for only sixteen minutes.

Many of the ships were sunk or damaged and a total of 1,380 French sailors were killed with 370 wounded in the action.

In Plymouth the world's largest submarine, the 'Surcouf',

was the only French vessel of the several hundred that were boarded at the same time throughout the country to resist, with the loss three lives, two British and one Frenchman.

Camberley, 7*th* July 1940

Arriving at Mary Atkins home in Camberley, close to Aldershot, before lunch Anna parked her motorcycle and knocked on the front door of the semi-detached house in a quiet cul-de-sac and was welcomed into the hall before being taken out into the garden and the warmth of the July sun.

'Some habits from France die hard Anna!' Mary Atkins said as she poured her a glass of white wine and handed it to her before saying 'First of all, my apologises for not being able to keep to our arranged meeting last week, but thank you for your very thorough report about the seizure of the French vessels in Plymouth. So what did you think of the city?'

Smiling she said 'I think I'd like to go back and have a longer stay, my first impression was that I've never seen so many sailors from so many different countries. The atmosphere was quiet exciting.'

'Did you go down Union Street?'

Pausing she said 'Well, actually yes I did.'

With some amusement she said 'Oh, go on Anna, don't be embarrassed, everyone goes there at some time, I certainly did on more than one occasion, I can assure you!'

Topping up both glasses the Mary Atkins then said, 'I've booked lunch for both of us at a little hotel in the centre of the town that my family have used for decades, but before we go I'll tell you what I can about the operation we were involved in'

'Most of what I know has now been reported in the newspapers and on the wireless but what hasn't been reported is that the war department had to draw up contingency plans for a very serious clash with the French sailors and their marines, thankfully a serious clash that did not materialize'

'We knew very well that the Vichy Government was not going to upset their new masters in Berlin by agreeing to any proposal for their fleet to be scuttled, and we also knew that they wanted all their vessels to return to their home ports, because that is what the Germans had demanded!'

The pause for a drink of her wine let Anna ask 'We were told that the French had or were about to declared war on us, do you think that will happen?'

With hesitation the Colonel replied 'The big question mark Anna, most seem to think not.'

'What about General de Gaulle' Anna asked, 'Does anyone know what his reaction was?'

Mary Atkins brightened at the question saying, 'I've met the General Anna, and I like him' pausing while she laughed at her own statement before adding 'Well perhaps like is too strong a word! I just believe he is the only hope France has. But your question'

'Apparently, he very naturally flew into a rage at the loss of over thirteen hundred of his fellow countrymen but in private he has let it be known that he believed Churchill to be correct, and he has put the blame squarely on the shoulders of Marshal Petain and his puppets for not neutralizing the fleet.'

Anna looked at her mentor before saying 'The newspapers seem to think that public opinion in America was quietly in favourable to the operation.'

Nodding in agreement she said, 'I was told that Churchill breathed a huge sigh of relief when he spoke to President Roosevelt and got a good reaction and even tacit agreement for the engagement'

'But Anna, I have also been told that the action has done one very important thing, and that is to show Adolf Hitler that this country will not let anything stand in its way of continuing the war against him and that countries on the cusp of entering into the fighting on the side of Germany, like Spain and Ireland for instance, have received advance notice that this is just the beginning of a long and bloody struggle and that even standing alone, we intend to continue it.'

Leaning back on the wooden garden seat under the warm sun Anna talked about Louise Bridoux, the artist and his friends she had met in Pont-Aven before asking the question 'I wonder what those kind people we met in France will think of us as a nation after all this?'

Looking into the distance Mary Atkins thought for a moment before speaking

'The German and Vichy propaganda machine is hard at work as we speak Anna, but the people who helped us will see through the lies, but sadly I do believe a generation will only be able to blame us for the failure of their own generals and politicians and the collapse of their country, but I hope not, and what about a toast Anna, to those kind and brave people we met France!'

Falmouth, 28th March 1941

Yawning with stretched arms Gail Moore shouted 'God, Anna, your choice in men is an even bigger mystery to me than you are. What you see in Richard is beyond me.'

An unseen Anna replied, 'He's a very honest and pleasant person thank you with few complications, and unlike a certain lady I know who is having an outrageous affair with a married man, that is most certain to end in disaster, Richard is single!'

From her crumpled bed Gail moaned 'But he is so boring. Tell me, what's he like in bed? Don't bother, I don't want to know, and of course you're so bloody secretive, I know you won't tell me anyway!'

As an afterthought, she added 'One thing for sure, he won't last, he just suits your needs for the moment. My Jan on the other hand is tremendous fun, a great bang, and I know it will probably end in disaster, but frankly, I really do not care'

Pulling the candlewick bedspread around herself she said in a quieter voice 'Anna, did you know I had two of my patients die yesterday? Both very ordinary, hard working girls, married with children and husbands fighting away somewhere. Little wonder dear that I am finding it difficult to think of the disasters ahead when I am surrounded by other peoples' disasters on my doorstep right now.'

Anna came out of their shared bathroom pulling a towel around herself and cursing the coldness of the flat she shared with Gail who was a nursing sister in the same hospital where

Anna had worked since her posting to Falmouth in November the previous year.

Not for the first time Anna thought to herself that she envied the way Gail was able to wear her nakedness like any coat or frock she owned, as she slipped out of her bed and walked to her wardrobe before wrapping herself in a dressing gown.

The flat that the two nursing sisters occupied nestled in the eaves of a large imposing house built for a long dead sea captain and his family, one of many in the town that had had made fortunes from sailing fast three-masted clipper ships from England to all parts and corners of the globe in the 1800's.

Its grand days were past and as it was only two hundred yards from the hospital that cared for both civilian and military patients it had been requisitioned as living quarters for staff at the start of the war.

Anna sat on the edge of her own bed in the smaller of the two bedrooms that she had chosen because it had a tiny diamond shaped window that faced south and gave her a narrow view of Falmouth Bay from her bed.

She knew about the two women in Gail's ward. Both had died after the last bombing raid on Falmouth docks two days ago. Anna could not bring herself to tell her flatmate that as she was finishing her shift last night the relief sister told her that one of the children of the dead woman had also died from the injuries received after he and his mother were dug out of the rubble of their little terraced house in the small Cornish town.

From the tiny space called the lounge Gail shouted 'Oh, Anna, a whole day and a bit off, sheer luxury. We have the prospect of the 'Spitfire Fund Dance' this evening, which should be a bit of fun, and today I am going to do nothing other than sleep, and later on' she added 'I will wait for some warmish water to trickle into our wonderful bath and after that make myself totally beautiful and the envy of every other women in this horrid, mean little town which I do hate so much.'

Jan Thompson and Richard Bannister were civilian marine surveyors supervising the repair of ships in the small but sprawling dockyards and dry docks of Falmouth. The port had become very important with the onset of war as it was the first sea port with the facilities to handle a damaged vessel approaching the island from across the Atlantic and Mediterranean.

Anna had been introduced to Richard by Gail and although they been out together on several occasions and she did enjoy herself in his company she had made a point of telling him about John McCloud on their first meeting.

'Gail' Anna thought to herself 'You are right, but I could never admit it to you, I suppose I am using Richard, it is handy to be able to say, "Yes I have a boyfriend" it makes life so much less complicated, he is sweet, and I know it's a waste of time and breath trying to tell you that we have never slept together and never will.'

In the darkness of early evening the two couples walked arm in arm along the black streets to the town hall with only the red ends of cigarettes showing and occasionally the narrow beam from a small torch that belonged to Jan.

Once through the two sets of blackout curtains it took a moment to adjust to the glare of bright lights and smoky atmosphere.

'What are you drinking girls?' Richard asked. Both nurses ordered gin and tonics before the men headed towards the bar.

The big room was festooned with red, white and blue bunting together with groups of union jack flags like bouquets of flowers. Above the stage where the band was busy setting up its music stands and tuning their instruments hung a large painting of a Supermarine Spitfire Mk 11 and underneath it the image of a red thermometer the degree bars replaced by the amounts the town had collected towards their final goal of five thousand pounds. The town needed another eight hundred pounds before it could present the Royal Airforce with another fighter aircraft that would have the name of 'Falmouth' proudly painted on the fuselage.

The two girls found a table and were sat down when their drinks and escorts for the night came back and joined them as the master of ceremonies for the evening announced into a crackling microphone on the stage that the band would start by playing the music to dance a quick step.

  Both couples took to a crowded dance floor after a sip of their drinks and dodged and bumped their way through the mixture of civilians and service men and women in a variety of war time uniforms.

  As the evening wore on the heavy Cornish accent of the M.C. guided them through the popular dances of the day, and when the interval came Gail announced that a much-needed trip to the loo was in order and Anna joined her.

  As they headed for the 'ladies' together Anna said, 'Gail, who is that very dishy chap standing at the end of the bar. You see, he's with two other men and a very horsy looking girl?'

  To eager to be discreet or quiet, Gail tugged Anna's arm saying 'Simon Tremayne. Don't know who the horse is, but I suspect it's probably his fiancée. Sadly, both very local Cornish people and both equally boring. Did you say 'dishy' Gawed, Anna, now your eyesight is going.'

  Several dances later Gail sat down heavily with her drink in hand as she declared 'Gosh, I'm pooped, can we sit this one out Jan, please? Besides which, I can't stand these progressive dances, it means you have to meet the locals!'

  Grabbing Richard's hand Anna said, 'I find them quite fun!' as they shot off towards the dance floor.

  Towards the end of the evening the hundreds of small mirrors stuck to the rotating ball in the centre of the high ceiling sent flashes of coloured light revolving around the ballroom and as the lights dimmed the M.C. announced the last waltz.

  As the final dance came to a shaky musical end the two couples joined the rest of the crowd of dancers and stood rigidly to attention as the lights were switched on full and 'God save the King' was loudly sung by everyone in the hall.

  As the two girls waited to collect their coats from the cloakroom Gail said to Anna 'So, you managed to get your hands on Mr Tremayne then!'

  Smiling, Anna whispered back 'I have always loved the dances where the men have to change partners, it's such a good opportunity to meet new people!' Another smile and Anna added 'He smells nice.'

Too loud, Gail asked 'What else then, come on, tell me?' Squeezing Gail's arm Anna said 'He told me about a wonderful walk on the North coast from St Ives to a small village called Zennor.' With eyes towards the stars Gail said 'Nice walk! Bloody Hell, I told you he was boring!

The Plymouth Blitz

Falmouth, 21st April 1941

Alec Read, the officer in charge of the hospital, looked grim and anxious as he came through the ward doors and approached Anna who was behind her rostrum in the centre of the room.

'Good Evening Sister Jack' he said hurriedly 'Sister, I've just received a telephone call from the operations officer in Plymouth. The Luftwaffe is giving the city another terrible battering and they have asked me to send as many people up there to assist as I can spare. I would like you and all but one of the duty doctors and nursing staff on this shift to come with me,' after a glance at his watch he continued 'It's almost midnight, we will leave as soon as we can after we get a few essentials together.'

Travelling in four ambulances some of the medical party tried to sleep as the vehicles followed the narrow twisting main roads out of Cornwall towards Devon and sat in front of the second ambulance Anna's head kept bouncing off of the passenger door as she dozed uncomfortably in the swaying lorry, but her drifting stopped when she heard the driver say out loud 'Jesus Christ, what the hell is going on?'

'What's the problem' Anna asked.

'Oh, sorry ma'am, thought you were asleep, but look ahead, the whole sky is lit up over Plymouth, and were still over forty miles away.'

She looked upwards. The night sky over Cornwall was studded with bright stars and was cloudless, but as Anna's eyes turned towards Plymouth she could see that a dense halo of thick smoke hung above the city, and trapped beneath it was a bright orange and red glow.

As the convoy got closer the driver and nurse watched as

brilliant flashes of molten colour from exploding bombs bounced off the clouds of smoke that came from the fires that were raging throughout the city.

  Looking at her watch pinned to her uniform Anna said to the driver 'Just after one, what time do you think we will get there?'

  'Bout half two mam, if we're lucky.'

  Staring through the windscreen Anna said 'It looks as bad as London, poor people. I think we are in for a busy time.'

  It was past three in the morning when the small convoy of ambulances drove through the gates of Devonport Naval Hospital in the heart of a city where hundreds of homes had been turned into blazing torches, turning the black of night into an orange and red daylight.

  The German bombers had started their return journey across the channel to the captured airfields of France an hour before the ambulances had arrived, leaving behind them thousands of burning incendiary bombs that had been dropped on the city by the first wave of twenty Heinkel HE111 aircraft, acting as pathfinders for the main bomber group.

  With their blazing target now easy to identify another hundred aircraft flew unopposed over the city dropping tons of bombs and a further 30,000 incendiaries in a raid that went on for over three terrifying hours.

  The medical team from Cornwall worked all night assisting the hospital staff as relays of ambulances arrived with hundreds of casualties, both civilian and military.

A public air raid shelter had received a direct hit, the doctors and nurses helped those they could, but many were beyond help, men, women and children, a single bomb had killed seventy-two people.

  A stick of four bombs had fallen on a military barracks killing ninety-six sailors and marines. As the survivors were being brought in Anna saw Commander Morris, the officer that had given her so many problems last year racing frantically around.

  As she lost sight of him she felt a gentle squeeze on her shoulder and heard the voice of Miriam Bonnard, the Jamaican nurse, saying 'Good to see you Anna can't stop, I'm assisting one of the surgeons in theatre but I will find you when I finish.'

Later, Anna could not remember if she had replied to Miriam's welcome, even with a nod, because at the same time of seeing her a stretcher with a woman on it had been had been placed in front of her and her nursing orderly.

The male nurse made sad knowing eye contact with Anna before he looked down again at the person in front of them. Her age was impossible to determine as all her hair had gone and burns covered her head and face together with practically the whole of her body.

The nurse quickly but carefully started to cut away the woman's charred clothing while Anna checked her airways. The intense heat had burnt the inside of her throat, tongue and nasal passages and shrivelled the eye lids so that they were moulded to her blacked, scorched cheeks. She made dull, faint noises which were indefinable, her body convulsed and twitched in spasms of pain.

They both knew it was hopeless and while Anna set up a plasma drip she asked the nurse to fetch their C.O. Finishing his examination he said nothing but looked at Anna and gently shook his head from side to side before telling her to administer a dose of morphine and going to the next bomb victim.

Two hours later, the influx of casualties had eased. Anna took a break and sat in the corner of the ward beside the young woman holding the only two fingers of her left hand that were not burnt in hers.

For the first time she noticed the woman worn an engagement ring. The gold band with three small stones set into a neat cluster reflected the lights of the ward, its sparkling brightness out of place against the rest of her charred, shattered body.

The rasping noise of her breathing had become steady and her blackened body had stopped twitching in pain as the morphine took the teenager back to her old world and away from the terrible agony she had suffered as the intense heat from the bomb blast had enveloped her body. Now she was back in a world without pain again, a world where she was a beautiful girl aged nineteen with long black hair.

In a hard-backed chair the nursing sister fell asleep by her patient's bed, still holding her two fingers. In that space between sleep and consciousness Anna had also entered her own comfortable world, one where she was safe and happy, in it she could embraced John McCloud, walk along cliff tops, stare out onto a wild blue sea, drive motorbikes,....'

'Anna, Anna wake up, please'

She knew the voice and forced her eye lids open to see Miriam standing over her with her hand on her arm. 'Anna, the young lass has gone, so why not rest in the nurses' quarters, come on girl.'

It was almost noon when she woke up and saw the note Miriam had left, 'See you in the mess hall, M'. To get to the officers' mess she had to cross the 'Quarterdeck' with the sundial at its centre.

As she began walking she noticed that three of the main buildings around the square had been badly damaged and were boarded up and also that the hospital seemed almost deserted after the frantic efforts of a few hours ago.

From behind the high stone wall that ran twenty feet high around the whole hospital smoke still bellowed into the air from last night's raid and the acrid smell of burnt timber and cordite filled the quadrangle.

Miriam saw her push open the door to the mess and met her with an embrace before saying 'How are you Anna? Come and sit down'.

Taking a seat before replying Anna said 'I'm fine Miriam, but goodness, what has gone on here since last year? And why is it so quiet?'

Getting Anna a cup of tea and sitting down she said 'Well, you saw the buildings. They were bombed last month, sadly, we lost three patents and three nurses killed in those raids'

'As you know the naval dockyard is only just over the tree line, about a mile from here and a main target for the bombers so it was decided to disperse most of our patients to other hospitals further out from the centre of the city and we now act as a kind of casualty clearing station for civilians and servicemen injured during the bombing on the city, in fact it seems to be working well.'

It was only now that Anna noticed the difference in the nurse she had first met last summer. It came through the young black woman's eyes she thought. She was edgy, unable to hold eye contact, she was waiting. Waiting for what? The next bomb, aircraft noise? Anything, that was the answer. Ready for anything bad, anything unpleasant.

'What are you staring at Anna, are you alright?' Miriam asked.

'I'm sorry, I didn't mean too, but you do look a little grey, so things have been pretty bad here I take it?'

Laughing out loud she said 'So now I'm grey, when we first met you couldn't get over how black I was, so is it an improvement!'

'You need no improvement and you know it!'

Over lunch Miriam told Anna about the dozens of air raids the city had gone through and of the worst nights of last month when dozens of civilians had been killed by the bombing.

'Most evenings now thousands of people leave the city, and who can blame the poor souls, honestly, these people are real heroes. Anna, I'm on ambulance duty this evening, do you want to come along with me, if we can swing it?'

Her commanding officer gave Anna permission and after sleeping during the afternoon the two nurses met in the mess for dinner before going on duty at 8 p.m.

The nine ambulance drivers together with Miriam, Anna, two other sisters' and three nursing orderlies and stretcher bearers waited in a room next to the administration block of the hospital where the main telephone switch board was situated, and two operators sat waiting for instructions from the air raid warden headquarters in the middle of the city.

Above the hubbub of noise and chatter a driver, in his sixties said loudly 'Well lads, it's going to be a bloody bad one tonight, on my way here I saw a lot of the buildings still on fire from the last go and I think 'they' know we don't have enough fire engines or the water, to put out so much as a bloody bonfire, bloody disgrace, surrounded by water and no way of using it, bloody disgrace!'

'Shove it Arthur' said another of the drivers 'the fire brigade lads are doing as much as they can, and some have arrived from London to help, and we can do without you mouthing off about your bloody politics.'

Suddenly the room became as silent as the slow wailing of the air raid sirens started; bringing a knot of fear in the stomach of the most hardened of men and women. Death was on its mean way, and everyone knew it.

For fifteen minutes twenty planes circled the city and dropped over 10,000 incendiary bombs. The pattern of the attack was the same as the nights before.

Incendiary bombs were small, only eighteen inches long, three inches wide with a magnesium alloy outer case that was packed with red iron oxide and aluminium powder and triggered by a small explosive detonator that caused it to ignite on impact and burn at over a thousand degrees.

The anti-aircraft guns stopped firing and the droning noise of the bombers engines grew faint before another voice said, 'Any minute now, and off we go!' The voice had hardly finished the sentence when a military policeman pulled open the door of the room and shouted, 'Number one and two ambulances to the buildings next to Farley's factory.'

For twenty minutes Miriam and Anna waited before it was their turn to speed out of the entrance of the hospital, past its two twenty-foot-high limestone gate posts and onto the uneven road towards Union Street.

'My God!' Anna said aloud as the ambulance swung onto the long straight Union Street and memories flashed quickly through her mind as she remembered last summer when she and Miriam Bonnard had walked down the long street in the last warm hours of a balmy summer evening.

The sun of summer long gone, Union Street was now lit by fiercely burning buildings and vehicles on each side, and from the man-made light of war Anna could see some of the devastation the crippled city had suffered after a year of bombing.

Pulling the web strap through the metal buckle with her thumb and fore finger Anna tightened her steel helmet and put both hands on the cold steel rail that was welded onto the dash board in front of her while she looked at the raging infernos ahead and on both sides of the long road.

Her eyes widened and her mouth formed a grim smile has the vehicle came towards two buildings still totally intact. The 'Star' pub and the ornate Palace Theatre were surrounded by burning buildings while groups of firemen struggled with whipping hose pipes as they directed streams of gushing water onto fanning flames and showers of swirling orange cinders that erupted from blazing buildings into smouldering clouds, jumping from rooftop to rooftop as the wind caught them.

Many of the three and four-story properties with shops or businesses on the ground floor were beyond the help of water as long dragon tongues of flame shot out of windowless openings, the bellowing roar making Anna wince as the ambulance halted and the driver looked anxiously ahead before saying 'We'll have to turn around Sister, it looks very tricky up ahead, and...'

His sentence remained unfinished and their tin helmets clashed violently as each ducked below the level of the windscreen and the ambulance shook from the vibration of tons of masonry falling onto the road in front of them from a building as it collapsed.

Sitting back as the shock waves passed over they both watched as emerging like white ghosts from a swirling storm of debris and dense smoke came a party of firemen and air raid wardens who stopped in front of the ambulance, one sitting on the front bumper while the others gathered around him, shouting to each other as they scrapped their eyes clear of dust and shook their heads as their ear drums popped and their hearing returned.

Jumping down from the lorry Anna and the driver went to the front of it, getting there just ahead of Miriam Bonnard, before Anna shouted above the noise of the burning street 'Is anyone hurt, can we help?'

As another thunderous series of 'clumps' announced the landing of more bombs exploding towards the docks area, a fireman answered, 'No thanks Sister, none of us are hurt, and we're all here,' turning to their driver he added 'you'll be better off going back and skirting around this lot!'

The two ambulances turned around, driving over mounds of fallen bricks and shattered glass and past the burnt-out skeleton of a double decker bus, its rubber tyres the only thing left to burn.

They twisted towards Sutton Harbour where a tenement building had been set on fire, the medical teams arrived as firemen were pulling their ladders away from four windows on the first floor as thick black smoke and orange flames started to belch out of them, like four erupting volcanoes.

Four blankets covered two men and two elderly women, who had died in the inferno, a fifth blanket covered the still body of a man who had died after jumping from the top floor.

Miriam and Anna treated several casualties suffering from burns. Some had large blisters on their faces and bodies others had areas of weeping red flesh where the skin had been burned off. They were all in shock, some crying, some screaming.

Above the ferocious noise of the fire sucking oxygen into its core and the anti-aircraft guns firing came a loud shout 'Nurse, there's more injured on the other side of the building.' The voice belonging to a ARP warden.

A battery of unseen anti-aircraft guns started firing at a German bomber two searchlights had locked onto. The shafts of light held the aircraft in the almond shape of two merging circles and for a second or two Anna stared up at the bomber and saw flashes of red as shells exploded under it, above it, followed by arching dotted lines of tracer shells that that raced like sprinting fire flies towards the aircraft.

Above all the noise surrounding both women they heard the droning engine sounds of the next wave of bombers approaching and the steady thud of the explosions from their bombs getting nearer, sounding like a striding giant walking slowly towards them.

Miriam shouted to the ambulance drivers to take the fully loaded vehicles back to the hospital and then come back before the two nurses rushed past the fire engines and around a warehouse to get to the other side of the buildings.

They bumped into the ARP man who was running back towards them shouting 'I don't think they made it, part of the roof collapsed and they just vanished,' the elderly man looked nervously over his shoulder towards a line of warehouses, black shapes in front of the glow of fires burning behind them before finishing 'come with me over to the air raid shelter, the bombs are getting closer, come on!'

The explosions from the bombs were getting louder, and shock waves from a blast carried both women across the road towards the brick screen that sheltered the heavy reinforced steel door at the entrance to the newly constructed shelter.

Miriam seemed to fly through the door and Anna bounced off a pillar of sandbags that were on either side of the entrance, sending her tin hat rolling into the shadows until an unseen arm pulled her through the door and into the building. Another, this time familiar arm, guided Anna to a space along the wood planking that formed the seats for the people seeking sanctuary.

Three loud blasts shook the thick steel door and made the whole single story building shake. The two nursing sisters locked each other's arms and instinctively drew closer on the slatted wood bench seat, while others in the shelter gave a variety of sighs, shouts, screams and swear words.

The next explosions sounded further away and tense bodies relaxed as Anna looked around. There were about twenty five people in the building. A sailor in uniform with his wife and two children, one a baby the other a boy of two, maybe three in one corner. Two lone mothers with five children between them sat opposite, well prepared with bedding, books, food and water, these seasoned refuge seekers started to play games.

A group of older men had brought bottles of beer from a pub and they sat wordless, as they played rummy, while a mixture of men in uniforms mingled together as a group, with four young women the centre of their attention.

In the lull of bombing the door was opened slightly by the warden and Anna edged towards it and looked out. The brick wall in front of the shelter entrance was now a pile of rubble, and through the billowing smoke from the fires raging across the city the colour of the sky had turned to a mixture of blood red and bright orange, framed by a black halo.

As she watched the steel door opened fully and she could see five people making their way across the road, their progress hampered by two others they were supporting.

The party was led by a woman ARP warden dressed in a blue overall, wearing Wellington boots, her black tin hat glistened with water from the firemen's hoses.

The group brought in two women and the nurses sat one on a portion of the wooden seating while the other was laid on the floor, on top of a blanket.

Anna looked at the motionless woman on the wooden seat. She had a blue naval greatcoat wrapped around her shoulders and was naked under it except for the shoes she wore.

A chief petty officer spoke quietly to Anna, saying 'We found her and the other girl outside a burning building that I think were offices just down the road, it looks like the blast from a bomb whipped her clothes away, the other lass has cuts in her leg and is really upset, but this one hasn't said a dickie bird, just stares ahead like she is now.'

Miriam looked at the girl on the floor, also in deep shock, but also losing blood from her wounds. She kept repeating 'Oh goodness, poor people, poor people'. The sister tied a tourniquet at the top of her leg to stem the loss of blood before removing several pieces of glass from her leg and putting a field dressing over them.

One of the mother's of the five children came over to Anna and said 'I think these two maids work in the ministry office, don't know them names like, but us hav' both seen 'em round. Us hav this blouse and skirt, if tiz any help'.

'Thank you' Anna replied, adding 'That's very kind. She's in deep shock, but I think she will be alright.'

The noise from the ack ack gun batteries started to pound away again as the drone of aircraft returned and Anna slipped the heavy greatcoat from the woman's shoulders and dressed her.

Anna was handing his coat back to the naval man when the action turned into slow motion as they all heard the unmistakable whistling sound of falling bombs.

For the next seconds each person could only wait and hope. It was an agonising, stomach knotting wait while the noise came nearer, and each hoped, prayed, begged that these would not be their final, ugly moments on earth.

The first explosion rocked the shelter and the foundations trembled under the feet of the occupiers.

The second was closer and they felt and heard the rush of air hit the metal door and a swishing sound as though an express train was thundering past over the top of them, followed by a flickering of the lights and then total darkness.

The young woman Anna had just dressed started to scream as the next bomb exploded, her voice mingled with the deeper voice of a man shouting in a language unknown to Anna and with the cries of some of the children, hysterical with panic and fear.

Shouts to God, mothers, lovers, and husbands joined the cacophony of human fears when, from the darkness of the black tomb, a flash of bright light appeared as the steel door at the entrance smashed back against the concrete wall it was hinged to and a raging gust of hot air swept into the building like a brutal tidal wave into a cave.

Anna felt as though her insides were being pulled out through her mouth. She gasped for air but none came, she wanted to shout, scream, anything, but couldn't.

A vacuum had been created in the building for a second, and like a genie in a bottle it escaped back through the air raid shelter entrance, and disappeared, replaced by new air to drag desperately into gasping, empty lungs.

Light from the burning buildings around them crept through the open doorway into the dark room. It was followed by three air raid wardens and their torches.

'Miriam' Anna called 'Miriam, are you alright?'

A light from one of the torches of the air raid wardens found Miriam at the end of the shelter in a corner, sandwiched in between one of the mother's and five children.

Anna watched as the black woman got up, the automatic action of dusting down the front of her uniform with the flat of her hands was also like a quick self-examination which she completed before saying 'Yes, yes I am, and you?'

'Think so' Anna replied.

A wailing of anguish from the young mother with two children and plea for help from their sailor father made the nurses and wardens turn towards the sound.

The light of the torches found them in the corner opposite Miriam. Both nurses saw the broken body of the toddler laying in a pool of blood shared by a young Polish sailor and a British soldier.

All three were dead. They lay like broken dolls, their limbs twisted at odd angles as the full force of the blast had dashed them against the concrete wall.

The five children who been huddled together had escaped the blast completely, not a hair out of place.

Another shout from the entrance took the nurses to it. Behind the reinforced steel door was the body of the ARP warden who had led Anna and Miriam into the building. He had been crushed when the heavy door had been violently slammed back against the concrete, his life extinguished like the flame of a candle.

Across the road the nurses heard more cries for help. 'I'll see if I can do anything over there' Anna said, leaving Miriam to cover the body of the warden and comfort those inside.

The planes were still flying overhead but the explosions were now coming from the West of the city, towards the naval dockyard. Four firemen had been hit by shrapnel from a bomb. The same metal fragments had pierced holes in the hose pipes of the fire fighters and Anna stepped through small fountains of gushing water to reach them.

Two of the men were getting up as Anna approached, indicating to her that they were only slightly hurt, and with them she went to their colleagues. One had small fragments of bomb casing in both legs, and although suffering some shock and loss of blood Anna knew he would not be listed as a priority case at the hospital, after she had applied field dressings.

The remaining man had dragged himself onto his side, and although in obvious pain shouted, 'I'll be alright Miss, thank you, nothing to worry about!' as she got to him and knelt down beside him Anna said quietly 'Let me have a look and then you can both go to hospital.' She applied two dressings to stop his loss of blood and ambulances started to arrive as Miriam reached Anna and her patient.

They loaded the dead, wounded and distressed people of this single bombing raid into the waiting vehicles.

As they were finishing the air raid siren sounded again. Not the up and down wailing sound warning of approaching aircraft, but a long continuous note to announce the 'all clear' to the blitzed people of Plymouth.

Anna looked at her watch, and said aloud to her companion 'Four in the morning, six hours of bombing, what next?'

Guiding Anna to the last ambulance Miriam said 'For us, dear girl, a ride back to the hospital, a cup of tea and some sleep. For a lot of the people living around here, maybe the same, but after the sleep they will clear up as best as they can, salvage what they can, talk to their neighbours to find out who was killed or injured, and then wait for the next attack'

'The funny thing is Anna the more air raids and hardships they suffer, the stronger, and more determined they all seem!'

Later in the day Anna's commanding officer assembled his medical team and told them that fresh reserves of doctors and nurses had arrived and they would be travelling back to Cornwall early that evening.

Miriam hugged Anna before she left, saying 'Soon as I get some leave I'll come down to Cornwall and you can buy me one of those pasty's you keep talking about!'

Laughing, Anna replied 'I will even buy you a pint of Cornish cyder to go with it! Please take care Miriam, see you very soon.'

****

Two more nights of heavy bombing took place after Anna left Plymouth and on the night of the 29th of April, 1941, the German air force staged a ferocious five hour attack during which a stick of bombs fell on the Royal Naval Hospital killing Miriam Bonnard, another nurse and two patients.

CHAPTER THREE 1941

A Cornish Haven

******

The Sea Rescue

******

A New Love

A Cornish Haven

Falmouth, 15th May 1941

Gail Moore was irritated, and the object of her irritation was slumped quietly in a chair reading a book and continued reading as Gail shouted from the bathroom 'Oh do come on Anna, the boys will be here in twenty minutes, please change your mind and make up the four so we can all have a drink and a laugh, please, please!'

Turning the page of the book and without looking up Anna shouted back 'For God's sake Gail, I don't want to go out, I'm tired, and just now all I want is to be on my own, now please go out with the boys and enjoy yourself, I am perfectly alright.'

Raring to go, Gail breezed into the small lounge saying 'Anna, sweetness, I know the last few weeks have been a nightmarish hell but I think you would feel much better if you went out and forgot work and all the other nasty bits that have gone on, please do come on.'

Placing a book mark between the pages and closing the novel Anna turned to her flatmate 'Gail, you are very kind, and I know you mean well, but please leave me to sort myself out, I'm fine, just a bit, well it's hard to explain, but I just feel a little bit sad at the moment and the only way I know how to deal with my sadness is to throw myself into work or be on my own, it's just the way I am, now go and enjoy yourself!'

'Alright, I don't agree with you one small bit, but I'll leave you to your boring book. At least we have tomorrow off and we can go somewhere.'

Unable to look her flatmate in the face Anna sat with an elbow on the arm of the lounge chair while her right hand supported her forehead. With closed eyes Anna said quietly 'Gail, if the weather is good tomorrow I'm going off early on the bus to St Ives so that I can walk around the cliffs to Zennor.'

Before there was any reaction to her comment the head and

smiling face of Jan Thompson appeared around the open door of the flat saying 'You ready girls?'

With one last look in a mirror Gail said loudly 'Well I am, Anna is going to have a super time reading the bible or something similar and then tomorrow she's going on a bloody pilgrimage to the wilds of North Cornwall. Be warned Anna my dear, there are some bloody strange people up there, even more bloody strange than they are here, if that's humanly possible!'.

Falmouth, 16th May, 1941

Lifting the edge of the blackout curtain of her bedroom window Anna said to herself 'Fantastic, some bright sunshine at long last!'

After almost two weeks of continuous south westerly drizzle and rain a change of wind direction overnight had brought a clear day of early May sunshine.

Looking at the picture of her fiancé she said 'Getting to St Ives is the problem John. My Pass will let me go to most places but I've little or no petrol for the bike and absolutely no petrol coupons left this month to buy more, so train or bus? Emm, bus I think.'

The old Leyland bus spluttered and coughed its way out of Falmouth, as the driver, Mabel Trevellenion double declutched the gear box as she followed the steep hill out of the town.

Almost excitedly Anna said to the thin, pale woman she shared a seat with 'What a beautiful day after all the rain.'

Turning her small head towards her, her travelling companion said 'Aftur that cabby wethur tis a rite traat ta see they sun crakun tha edges lik. Sow, whare bay gwain?'

Anna found herself tilting closer to the woman whose strong Cornish dialect took seconds to understand before answering 'St. Ives for the day.'

'Sow, av ee bin fore?'

'Yes, I have, but today I want to walk along the coast and over the moor to Zennor, if I can. I work at the hospital as a nurse and need some fresh air on my day off.'

At the last bus stop out of the town four more women got onboard to the loud cheering and clapping of the rest of the passengers. A pretty young girl was the last in line and it was clear that the attention was centred on her as crimsoned faced she followed her elders to the back of the bus.

'Er did get mar-ried laas waak an tis er first daay baack aftur er hoheymoon, poor maid!'

Suddenly aware that the loud noises coming from the engine of the bus had been replaced by the loud banter between the passengers Anna looked around at her fellow travellers, realising for the first time that they were all women.

Anna's companion on the seat next to her explained that most worked the lathes and industrial machinery of all types making anything from engine parts for tanks and aircraft to cartridge belts or skim nets for camouflage under the cover of well disguised factories in St Ives and surrounding villages.

The war had brought similar changes to many quiet picturesque backwaters in all parts of the country, and it had also brought with it the necessity to replace the men who would have operated the machines in these small factories by women.

Reaching Carbis Bay Anna began to catch blue flashes of sea between hedges and buildings. An excited feeling in her tummy and a smile started as the bus turned the corner at the top of Trelyon Avenue that gave way to a view of the whole of St Ives Bay with the early sun reflecting off the shallow water and waves gently lapping the shoreline.

The bus made the long decent down the hill and through the narrow, winding town centre before finally spluttering to a halt opposite the Sloop Inn, just yards from the beach that collars the inside of the main harbour of the town, giving shelter to the fishing boats just returned or ones waiting for the tide to give enough water to start the day.

It was a little before eight when she started to walk up the cobbled street away from the harbour towards the gas works building and the beach to the West of the isthmus that divided the town.

As the beach came into view and the shelter of cottages gave way she felt a slight drop in temperature as a bite of cold reached her face from the wind coming off the sea.

In front of her lay Porthmoer Beach which was a sad tangle of barbed wire and concrete defences. Anna vividly remembered the directions Simon Tremayne had given her at the Spitfire fund raising dance at what seemed a lifetime ago in March and they were easy to follow. Skirting around the war scene of the beach she followed the coastal path which quickly became a picture of pre-war normality. Walking quickly Anna was determined not to turn around, happy to have the sun warming her back and the fresh sea breeze cooling her face, leaving tiny salt crystals along her top lip.

She stopped for a moment and studied the landscape ahead. Her eyes saw a patchwork mixture of green fields framed by stone hedges and moorland that swept down from rocky lunar peaks in the distance to high cliff tops that gazed out over the Atlantic.

Closer she could see giant slabs of granite that teetered crazily on top of one another with parcels of bright yellow flowers on prickly green gorse surrounding them, together with acres of tall swaying ferns.

The most important thing to Anna was that there were no people. It was people that today especially she wanted and needed so much to get away from.

Anna knew that the salty crystals were not from the sea, but from her own tears as they rolled slowly from her eyes to her top lip and onto the tip of her tongue. In a whisper she said 'I feel sad today, sad and very alone, or perhaps sad and very guilty?'

'Guilty more like. Why am I still alive, Miriam should be alive, she had so much she wanted to stay alive for, John should be alive, Peter should be alive but now they are all dead, all gone, and this place is too lovely, I should not be allowed this pleasure.'

She sat down on a rock and looked out to sea, still talking quietly out loud, 'One year ago today you died John, just one long and horrible, miserable year. You see, if you were alive I would have a reason to be here, if you were a prisoner, at least I could look forward to seeing you one day and know we would walk along this path together, sit on the same rock and feel the same sun on our backs, but I know that can never happen. I do miss you John'

'I miss you so bloody much it hurts inside all the time. I think losing our baby was the final hurt, I wonder if it was a boy or a girl? I've often thought about that, not that it would have been a problem, girl or boy………'

Her immediate thoughts trailed off as she narrowed her eyes and watched what she thought were people swimming to the right of a large out crop of rock three or four hundred yards out to sea.

As the shapes swam closer Anna realised they were seals. There were twenty or more swimming fast in a tight diamond formation, and she could see they were a mixture of adults and playful adolescents.

As the herd swam closer she saw them break their formation and dive deep into the clear water the adults followed by the youngsters, before returning close to the surface and turning over onto their backs to continue their glide through the sea.

In front of the seals a dark cloud seemed to be moving fast below the surface of the water towards them and Anna saw a school of fish swim over the white stomachs of the seals.

As one unit the whole herd of seals attacked the fish from underneath, turning the calm water into a frothing cauldron. It was over in seconds, hundreds of the fish decimated the rest scattered, the hunting party of seals, successful in their adventure returned to a loose formation and swam back out to the open sea, the young pups playing games of dodgems with each other as they swam along. The remaining fish regrouped back into their dense cloud, wisely swimming in the opposite direction.

Loudly Anna shouted 'That was fantastic, wonderful. Oh damm it, damm it, damm it! John, I need to go home and see mum and dad before I go completely mad, they are my last rock of sanity.'

As she finished the sentence Anna saw a movement out of the corner of an eye and a natural impulse made her turn around sharply on her rocky seat.

She found herself looking into the dark brown eyes of a

golden retriever dog, lying on a patch of grass with his head angle to one side returning her stare, as if confirming Anna's own prognosis of approaching madness.

She looked around for an owner while the solitary animal held its position on the grass. Seeing no one Anna looked back at the animal but he had turned his head away and now looked towards the retreating seals in the distance.

'Well then' she said 'What on earth are you doing here? Are you lost?'

The dog brought his head back to face her, giving Anna a look that that made her smile as she said to him 'Yes, I know, the only creature around here that is 'lost' is me, isn't it!'

Her new companion wagged his tail on the soft grass a few times as if in acknowledgment of her statement before getting up onto his four paws and began walking along the rocky path in the direction of Zennor. Or at least Anna hoped so.

'Alright then' Anna shouted to her guide 'I'll follow you, if that's in order?'

The animal stopped again and turned his head towards the sound of her voice before he wagged his tail and resumed walking.

Anna tried hard but could not help releasing a smile as the two of them followed the trail to the peak of a cliff that gave her the most breathtaking and spectacular view of the wild and dramatic coastline of North Cornwall as it stretched in front of her as far West as she could see.

Below them were isolated beaches where even in the calm of today's weather the surge of the sea threw white rollers into ravines and over rocks that lay half submerged in the blue green colours of the water.

She sat down on a ridge of rock, the sight was too good to leave quickly. Her new friend came back and sat close to her, he was also looking into the distance at the picture nature had been painting for many millions of years.

The high-pitched note of a bee made Anna turn her head. Below the peak of the cliff top, behind a protecting line of rock, was a small flat area of grass. Growing there was a group of deep purple flowers.

Walking over to the splash of colour she spoke to the cluster

'You are beautiful. Are you flowers or are you plants? And is this grass? It seems to thick, to coarse to be ordinary grass,' the golden retriever kept a fixed stare at the coast and sea as Anna said, 'It's very obvious that you know, do you?'

The oscillating tail and wise eyes gave her his answer.

Sitting down again Anna patted the dog gently on his head and smoothed the thick fur around his neck before saying 'We haven't been formally introduced have we, so my name is Anna Jack. Now as you have no dog tags or any means of identification, I will call you…..umm, what now,….I know, Star,'

'You don't mind being named after a pub in Plymouth, do you? Good, now Star, my problem is that basically, I am ignorant about the country side, but not by what pleases me, and when I look at those beautiful…..I will call them flowerplants, but please don't laugh at me will you, when I look at them it simply amazes me that anything so intricate and colourful can exist in a world alongside such ugliness and nastiness, what do you think?' another tail wag let her finish 'Quite so, I'm pleased you agree! Come on then let's see what else we can discover!'

The two new friends continued walking Westward. For Anna it seemed as if she had been given new eyes to see things with. 'Star, I didn't know there was more than one type of seagull, look over there, those have different markings around the eyes and an odd shaped noses.'

The track began to take them downwards and after twenty minutes the steep path led them onto a small rocky beach. In seconds Star was jumping into gentle surf, his bark echoing off the sheer cliffs surrounding them.

Anna unbuttoned her battledress top which she then took off together with the rest of her army tunic until she was naked. The small pebbles felt cold under her feet as she walked quickly into the cold water, her shrieks encouraging Star to bark more, and louder.

'My God, it's so cold!' she shrieked as she plunged into the sea and began swimming frantically. She felt the strong tug of the tide pulling her from the beach and saw that Star had joined her in her exercise, and shouted to him 'Not too far

Star, let's head for that rock'

The swimmers sat for several minutes on the flat wet surface, the early May sun warming them both. The water was so clear they both sat motionless and watched as small fishes chased each other darting around and under boulders and weed on the sea bed.

'I'm getting cold, we had better get back, come on!' Anna dived headfirst into the dazzling clear water, and swam for the beach.

Dressing she sat on another rock and looked out to sea, saying to her swimming companion 'I'll let you in on a secret, but don't tell anyone, in May last year, a whole year ago, I went swimming with my boyfriend in a lake in France, we were both completely naked and it was as cold, in fact colder than today and after our swim we had a picnic with some lovely wine and cheeses'

'My boyfriend, well in fact he wasn't just a boyfriend he was my fiancé, and we were engaged to be married, but I know John would have liked you because I think you have a free spirit in you, Mr Star.'

With fur heavy with sea water the dog edged closer to Anna and as she went to pat his wet back he decided to dry himself off by shaking his whole body with a fury that took her by complete surprise and showered her with spray.

'Thank you very much! Yes, I think I was right, there is a bit of the devil in you!'

At the top of the cliff Anna and Star followed a well-worn path that took them at times inland a hundred yards or so through small areas of heath land rich with dazzling carpets of flowers and plants most with vibrant bright coloured blossom.

Arcing back towards the cliff path the two walkers stopped and watched two birds larger than seagulls with long necks and jet-black feathers dive from a hundred feet or more vertically into the sea and pop up again after their dunking with a fish between their beaks before flying to unseen nests on the cliffs.

'What are they called? I want to know more!' she said loudly, and again 'I want to know everything about these cliffs and the land above them!' Her confederate wagged his tail and barked towards the sea as loudly as Anna shouted.

They had come to a fork in the path where Anna stopped. To the right she could see that the path would take them onwards following the coast and the left fork headed inland. With no sign post she was unsure of which to take.

Star seemed to have no doubts as he carried on walking inland until he stopped when Anna said, 'You seem very confident, but how do you know that's the way to Zennor?' Looking at her his head went to one side in the way that she had come to recognise as she said 'Alright, I won't be silly, I do trust you!'

The change in direction brought the sun onto her face as Anna followed the retriever until they reached a stone wall with a low stile cut from solid pieces of rock that the dog jumped over with ease while Anna negotiated them more cautiously.

They passed an official looking building that had sand bags at the gate which she thought was another coastguard station with its prominent position overlooking miles of sea and coastline.

After passing the lookout post there was an immediate change in the landscape as open moorland gave way to fields with granite wall boundaries. Cows occupied several of them, sheep others.

The path the woman and dog walked along had a gentle uphill pull and it quickly changed into a country lane with high stone wall hedges on either side that had bushes and plants growing out of them on the sides and on top.

Star came bouncing back from chasing an unknown enemy and walked panting beside Anna before she stopped to peer over a wooden five bar gate that broke the line of a hedge to let the livestock graze in the pasture.

Past the fields she could see several buildings and a church that made up a village in the distance. She patted the dogs head, saying 'Well Star, what a good guide you've been, civilisation at last'

'I just hope we can get a drink of something and some food, I'm starving! And what about you? I can't take you back to the hospital, and anyway, believe me you would not get on with my flatmate, Gail I can assure you!'

'I'll make some enquiries in the village to find out where or to whom you belong. To tell you the truth Star, I really have enjoyed your company, thank you!'

The farm yard smell came before the view of the cow sheds as the two walkers followed the lane around a corner before stopping again. On the left of the granite hedge Anna could see a large farm house and outbuildings. In the nearest of the sheds a boarded gate hid the lower halves of six light brown cows. The doleful eyes of the animals followed Anna as she walked past.

On the right-hand side of the lane directly in front of her several pine trees stood with their tops bent over towards the hills in the distance, fixed for their lifetime by the almost constant buffeting of the Westerly winds.

The odd collection of pine trees almost hid the buildings behind them, but dominating both, and everything else around it, was the forbidding grey granite stone of a square Norman church tower, over a hundred feet high.

The lane widened into what Anna thought was part of the entrance to the farm and walking through the hardened waste of the cow pats she rounded the dark pine trees and found a narrow cobbled road that separated the ramparts and graveyard of the church from two houses opposite.

Ahead of her a straight narrow road dipped down for a hundred yards before it started to rise upwards the same distance. Granite cottages stood on one side together with a larger detached building that looked like a chapel. A tractor was parked off the road, behind it a car, a trap without a horse between the shafts, two ancient lorries and one army truck.

Walking onto a small stone cobbled square, with buildings on three sides, she saw that stacked high against one wall were wood barrels and wooden crates holding empty beer bottles and tucked into a corner was a solid oak door under a pillar-less canopy and a sign on the ground that read 'open'.

'Well I think we have at least found a pub' Anna said aloud and at the same time looking around for Star, who was nowhere to be seen. 'Star, here boy' she shouted, retracing her steps past the church and into the farm yard she walked down the lane a short distance but found no trace of her new ally.

'Ah well, my new friend must live somewhere in the village' she thought as she made her way back to the entrance of the pub; a bit sad that he was gone.

She turned the handle and swung the heavy door inwards and stepped down into the one long room of the ancient public house.

Stepping from the bright sunshine of the day into the gloom of the bar Anna was still squinting from the change of light but instinctively she turned left and headed towards the sound of men's voices.

By the time Anna had reached the bar the barrel like figure of the man behind it had stopped serving his customer and cheerfully issued a good morning to her followed by his view of what a beautiful day it was before adding 'What can I get ee miss?'

The conversations of the men in the bar had gone quiet as they looked at the newcomer to their local. The 'Tinners Arms' was the focal point of Zennor village for most farmers, farm labourers, tin mining managers and miners, a few summer visitors and in more recent times members of the three armed services.

Dressed in her khaki uniform the men at the bar knew this pretty stranger was no early visitor from the city, and the noise from their conversations returned, there was even a couple of mumbled 'mornun'.

Before ordering she said 'Well, I've just walked along the coast from St Ives and I'm really thirsty, could I have a half of bitter shandy please.'

Producing a thick half pint dimple glass from a shelf he looked closely at Anna, saying 'You had a ansum day for it, sure enough. Beer shandy ee said.'

Turning around he stooped down to the wooden barrel of bitter that was placed a foot above the smooth stone flag stones of the bar floor, almost filling the glass before topping up the last half inch with lemonade from a stone jar.

He placed the drink in front of her and said, 'Can I get ee anything else?'

Taking a sip of her drink before she answered with a 'Umm,

that was wonderful, thank you, is it possible to get a sandwich or something to eat?'

Nodding he replied 'Yum in luck, the missus baked some bread this morning, so how would ee like some cheese from Trevessa Farm down the road a bit, an our own pickles to go with im?'

'That sounds wonderful, thank you.'

Pointing along the room he added 'There's an empty table under the window, now like as not you'll bay needing another shandy bay the time the wife gets the food to ee an her'll bring im over.'

From where she sat Anna could now see a group of men wearing working clothes and overalls sat on high stools by the bar counter talking to others standing near them, some in army uniform, hiding a resting fireplace.

At the end of the room where she was sat was a second fireplace, black with the soot of winter months, brass fire dogs supporting pokers, bellows and tongs. This fireplace was surrounded by men dressed in suits or sports jackets. Their talk was more subdued and had a serious edge to it, but from both ends of the room all the men took turns in glancing at the fresh pretty face of the stranger.

The May sun warmed the back of Anna's head and shoulders as it shone through the bay window with the excess rays filtering into the room and reflecting off of the heavy cloud of tobacco smoke that hovered under the low ceiling.

While she was deep in thought a tray appeared in front of Anna and the landlord's wife said 'Mornun, I ear ee av cum all tha way from St Ives bay tha rocks, do ee live un St Ives?'

Smiling, Anna answered 'No, I'm a nursing sister at the military hospital in Falmouth.'

Anna knew the problem. She was a stranger and the war had made everyone aware and nervous of spies, saboteurs, 'fifth columnist'. Her answer was exactly what they all needed to hear and it circulated the pub in seconds.

From the landlord's wife Anna found out that a bus went from the village in half an hour, back to her starting point and that the driver always tooted his horn before he left so she had no need to hurry.

She paid at the bar for her lunch and the landlord and landlady told her that they hoped she would come back again.

Anna answered with an honest 'Thank you, I had a lovely walk and lunch and on my next day off I will certainly be coming back again, and oh, there was one thing. I saw a wonderful.....well, I think it was a plant, but it could be a flower, along the cliff tops, it had a green stem and a clump of bright purple flowers at the tip, I just wanted to find out what it was called?'

'Twas a Purple Orchid' the landlady replied with a smile. 'Ef ee cums agan I got us a bok with lots ov pictures ov tha different types ov everythin growing up there along tha cliffs, I'll get in out fur ee.'

'Thank you very much, I would love to see your book, and I will be back again, I promise' Anna replied.

London, 19th May 1941

Muffled sounds came from the attic room of the three-storey terraced house in North London, home to the Jack family. Anna's voice shouted 'Mum, do you know what happened to those homework text books I had at school for my natural history exams?'

The time weary voice of Anna's father echoed along the passage from the small bedroom that he used as his office 'Remembering the siege like state you always kept your room in, they are probably still under a pile of your old gym clothes!'

Anna's mother answered for her, saying 'Thank you David, enough of that; our dear daughter is back on leave for three days and if she wants to look for books that she hated when she needed to look at them for her homework, so be it. And by the way, it is well past gin and tonic time and you are not on air raid duty this evening so you can relax and enjoy one. Two perhaps!'

Peering into Anna's bedroom Mary Jack frowned in puzzlement as the rear end of her daughter was the only visible sign of her as she searched the wardrobe that had been built into eaves of the roof and had become the depository for the whole family's discarded bits and pieces.

'Anna, darling, it really is such a treat to have you home on leave but since you arrived this afternoon all you've done is burrow into dusty drawers and cupboards, so what are you up too?'

A muffled shout of triumph came from the dark space followed the upper part of Anna becoming visible as she reversed into the room on all fours and said 'Got them, look there're all still together, and there are two more that I don't remember, and look they're all in really good condition. Let's go down stairs and I'll tell you all about my magical walk.'

David Jack was waiting in the kitchen for his wife and daughter with a full glass for both of them. Welcoming Anna home with a touch of their glasses he added 'The press and wireless censorship gave only a scant mention that a West Country city had been bombed so I spoke to one of the Labour members of the war cabinet I know who confirmed it was Plymouth,'

Looking at his wife he added 'I have to say we were selfishly relieved, thinking you were safe in Cornwall until you rang us to let us know you had been to the city during the raids'

'Anna, my friend told me that Winston Churchill had visited Plymouth a week after the bombing and that he had never seen the man, usually so optimistic, bombastic even, suddenly so melancholy and sad'

'My colleague also told me that thousands of homes had been destroyed and hundreds killed in just three days of bombing.'

Anna confirmed what her father had heard, and told her parents about her friendship with the young Jamaican woman, finishing by saying 'So poor Miriam was killed in one of the worst raids. She was a really nice person, brilliant nurse, and I tell you what, she would have made both of you laugh!'

Pausing for just a moment she went on 'Dad, does our government operate a colour bar? Are there really people out there fully qualified from our own universities and part of the Empire not able to come and help us because the colour of their skin is not white?'

David Jack began tapping his front teeth with his thumb nail before he spoke 'At the outbreak of war on paper the answer to your question is that there were no colour bar restrictions, but in reality, the answer is that a definite cruel and totally mad system was in place to keep out of the struggle very capable men and women because of the colour of their skin'

'I had a case of one of our constituents, who had a white father and coloured mother who had applied to enter the army as a doctor, I knew the man as a talented and hard working professional and the excuses for his rejection were utterly ridiculous. We put a lot of pressure on the ministry to reverse the decision, which eventually they did'

'Now of course the shortage of people has signalled a change in policy, but a lot of unnecessary hurt has been caused, there can be no doubt about that. A resentment has been created that will have many long-term implications'

'Winston and his Empire building was behind most it. Yes, even I have to admit he is the right man, no, I will correct myself, and say 'the best man' we have for the job of handling the war but I and a lot of my friends have grave reservations about what will happen afterwards.'

Putting his glass on the kitchen table he left the room to use the toilet. Before he was out of sight his wife placed a hand on her daughter's and said, 'You look happy enough, are you?'

Unable to look directly at her face she placed her hand on top of her mother's and rested the side of her face on it before she replied 'Yes mum, I think I am. I miss John like mad, and feel very lonely at times'

Sitting upright and looking into Mary's eyes she added with warmth 'But oddly, I'm only beginning to realise that I was lucky in some way. Lucky because I met John in the first place and because we did have that brief and wonderful time together, so yes, I am as happy as I should be without feeling guilty because there is a war on!'

Continuing her look she added 'Children are incredibly selfish at times and I always forget to ask how you are both coping, are you happy enough, mum?'

With a beaming self-satisfied grin Mary Jack said 'Strange that you should ask darling, but guess what, your mum has been asked to go back to nursing. Now how strange that suddenly I can be a woman, a wife and a mother and also a competent nurse! As the saying goes my dear 'needs must' and the country is so short of nurses, my time has come around again!'

Sitting heavily back on the wooden captain's chair at the table David Jack said 'Has your mother told you how indispensable she has become to nursing? Believe me Anna I have no doubts that the same change of direction in government policy that was taken to allow your mother back into the profession was the same change in thinking that has recognized the plain and simple fact, which is that just so long as people have the qualifications then having black, white or even green skin is of little importance to a man or woman who has just had his or her legs or arms blown off'

'Strictly between the three of us I can tell you that the casualty rates from the bombing have sent shivers through the war cabinet'

'They won't release the figures to the press or general public of course, but in April well over six thousand civilians were killed in air raids across the country. Six thousand ordinary people, and not including the military casualties!'

Frowning, Anna said 'So what is happening in America? Why haven't they come off the fence, it will be two years soon since war was declared, what are they waiting for?'

Putting a reassuring hand on his daughters he said 'Calm down, I know it is frustrating but they will declare war on Germany. Roosevelt has only recently won his term of office. Unlike Hitler's Germany, in this country and America we have governments that even in a state of war must report to the people, and don't forget the 'lend-lease' program is only just beginning to have a good effect in bringing ships, aircraft and munitions to us.'

Returning to the table Mary Jack said, 'No tonic, this time, lime juice is all we have', handing a glass to her husband she added 'I'm sure you are right David, but what piece of the family silver will we have to give up this time? We surrendered parts of the West Indies for some old destroyers, what on earth are we going to give next?'

With a resigned shrug of his shoulders he grunted 'Uummph, not much left as far as I can see, let's face it as a country we will be bankrupt when all this is finished but what choice? No tonic! It really is all too depressing at times, and I don't mean the sudden disappearance of tonic water, although it is funny what causes a drop in personal moral!'

'Come on you two' Mary Jack interjected 'Stop all this for the moment, I want to know Anna how it is that you have developed such an interest in the country side, and especially the Cornish coast line.'

Falmouth, 19th June 1941

'Reckon as not yew could bay lucky weth tha wethur Sistur'. Tom Gibbs was looking at the sky across the bay and talking to Anna on the steps of the hospital. He was a full decade beyond retirement, but like many other men and women in the same situation Tom did his bit for the war effort by working as a part time gardener and odd job man in the same hospital as Anna.

His life had been spent at sea, fishing the local waters around as far as the Lizard and catching the fish that were migrating with the seasons and swimming into the inshore fishing grounds to feed.

He still had his open wood dory but reserved his days at sea to when good weather was assured. Before the war he would tune in his wireless set to the BBC for the twice daily 'shipping forecast', a service that was withdrawn the day war was declared. Now he relied on his experience of as he looked at the sky as soon as he got out of bed.

Most days he and Anna would chat and several times he had given her a fish or two that he had caught the day before, wrapped in layers of the local newspaper. Still looking out to sea he said to Anna 'Ay, us sud both bay lucky tamorrow. Yew fer yer waalk, me fower ma fishun.'

Queuing for the bus with the ladies and girls going to work Anna recognized several faces from her first journey and one of them recognized her, saying 'Oall rite, yew gwain S'Ives gain, thaan?, ansum day for ee.'

Happy to be remembered she said 'Yes, and this time I'm better prepared, with a full flask of water with and a couple of sandwiches to eat on my way to Zennor.'

Shaking her head gently from side to side another young Cornishwoman said 'Sanweeges! If ee don't mind I sayun muss, you will be missing a right propur treat if you don't try one of Green's pastay's. Tiz a little bakery on Down Road, and you can go past im on the way to Porthmeor Beach' Shaking her head again she quickly added 'Fact is, the smell of them coming out of his oven is temptation himself!'

The noise of the engine and the raucous laughter and chatter of the women passengers all came to a halt with their arrival outside of the Sloop Inn on the quay side in St Ives.

With a final set of instructions and pointing hand signals to find the bakery from her fellow passengers Anna left the group of workers as they all emptied from the now silent bus and headed off in different directions.

The smell brought waves of saliva racing into her mouth and Anna smiled as she went into the shop like a fish to a lure. Mr Green had just pulled out a large hot metal tray, a yard square, of golden brown pasties from his oven, out of sight at the back of the shop, which he carried through and heaved onto the shop counter with the practice of decades.

All service people were required by regulation to carry a gas mask that fitted into its square case at all times, on or off duty. Today the case was empty of the cumbersome mask and its place was now taken by sandwiches, make-up and a large freshly baked Cornish pasty.

Her khaki haversack was heavy from the weight of two books rescued from her parent's attic and a sketch pad. One book depicted British birds and the other a natural history book listing flowers and plants belonging to the island.

Passing the ugly gas works that overlooked Porthmeor Beach Anna took the path that was strewn with fist sized boulders that she remembered would mark the route all the way to Zennor Churchtown.

The sun blazed down on her back and she was glad she had left her heavy battledress top behind and had adopted the regulation summer wear of khaki shirt, tie and trousers with the ever present steel helmet, gas mask case and haversack.

With a half smile Anna thought to herself 'Did Star exist, or did I invent him! Either way he was good company the last time I was here and I needed that bit of company desperately.'

She had brought a pad to make notes in and to sketch anything she found interesting and wanted to know more about. Walking no more than another fifty yards she reached the first granite chimney that signalled the abandoned workings of a tin mine that had stopped producing the ore over fifty years ago and started to draw it.

Time had turned the engine house into a sanctuary for nature. The thick slate roof had long ago disappeared with the rafters and joists now supporting farmers barns or fishermen's cottages elsewhere along the coast and the exposed walls were now covered in a tangled mass of ivy with the seeds of trees that had snatched shelter from the ferocious winter storms and now had strength in their roots to cling to the corners of walls and cracks in the stone work.

Anna finally gave in after finishing her sketching, saying aloud 'The smell of that pasty is just too much too bear, I have to eat!'

As she was taking the meal out of its brown paper bag she heard the distant sound of a dog barking and although she could not see any visible signs of the approaching noise she knew immediately that Star would share her late breakfast.

The golden retriever bounded the last twenty yards barking and waging his tail to greet his delighted friend. From her army water bottle Anna poured a drink for Star into her steel helmet and watched as the grateful dog lapped all that was available and lay down in front of her, his tongue lopping from side to side as he panted and continued to wag his feathery tail.

Breaking off a piece of the pasty she put it in front of the dog, saying 'I knew you would be around, not sure how, but I just knew it!'

Finishing the pasty Anna said 'Star, that was utterly delicious, full marks to the girl on the bus, now come on, we have work to do.'

She delighted in the flamboyant displays of flowers, plants and heathers that she could see all around her, and this time Anna was prepared for the beauty that lay to be discovered in hidden and almost secret patches and locations.

'Over here Star, look at these…ehh, whatever they are. I can't find them in the book I have so I'll do a rough drawing for now. See here, now I know this one, the whole patch that goes out onto that bluff is called Chamomile, the scent is just wonderful, isn't it.'

Following the same path as on the last walk they reached the cove that just over a month ago they had swum in the cold water of May. Then the sea had been calm but with a strong end of winter surge, today it was a mill pond and there was no hesitation on Anna's part to take off her uniform and reach the water a fraction of a second behind Star.

The water was cool rather than cold and fantastically refreshing. No screams this time just a sigh of delight as the cool salt water balanced the heat from the summer sun and the freedom from gravity seemed to regenerate her body as she breathed deeply from the air on the surface of the tranquil blue and green sea.

They swam around from the small beach to another inlet before turning and swimming to the rock they had both sat on in May. Both swimmers peered over the edge of their resting place into the clear water onto the bottom of the sea bed watching schools of tiny fish and this time a small detachment of spider crabs that were busy walking from hollows beneath rocks.

Pulling on her uniform they had hardly reached the top of the cliff before the sketch pad was quickly whisked out of her bag. She sat and watched as a flock of twenty or so birds, a little larger than crows, flew out over the sea from the cliff and back again where they landed and walked around in a lively and chattering group. Anna had no idea what type they were but was fascinated by their bright red legs.

When she got up it marked the signal for the flock to take to the sky. Watching them Anna returned her gaze to the ground in time to make a swift side step and to look at what she had almost crushed with her left foot. It was a small plant with a similar head of flowering petals that the Purple Orchid she had seen on her first walk.

This one was different, the flowers were smaller, packed tighter together and the one she had missed shared the grass with three others also in full bloom. She made a note of where it grew on her hand drawn map and a simple pencil outline of the flower as it grew on the stem.

Putting her pad back in the haversack she headed along the path that led her slightly inland across a narrow plateau topped with gorse and thick fern, stopping to call Star who had disappeared from view and gone mysteriously quiet. Several shouts of his name and more whistles produced nothing. She stopped and remained quiet, listening for any distant yelp or whimper.

What seemed like an explosion of sound made her reel backwards tripping and falling into the think gorse bushes. with their protective spines. 'Ouch, Bloody hell' Anna shouted before watching the biggest rabbit she had ever seen in her life dashing in front of her feet followed by Star in hot pursuit.

As if in slow motion she saw the creature jump over her feet and turn its head in her direction giving her time to see the enormous black eyes that seemed out of all proportion to the size of its body.

The creatures cold stare frightened Anna, stunned her into silence until it sped out of sight followed by the rushing sound of the golden retriever who also had time to glance her way before disappearing into the undergrowth.

Picking herself up Anna spent a moment to take out several thorns from her hands and ankle, while at the same time swearing in true army style under her breath, before looking in the direction her companion had propelled himself and shouting several times 'Star, good boy, come here!'

A minute later Star reappeared looking decidedly shame faced and also in some discomfort. He slumped down in front of Anna whimpering while trying to scrape several thorns out of his nose and ears.

Unable to keep a straight face she bent down and started to pick the needle sharp thorns from the dog's nose saying 'Well now, it very much seems to me that the rabbit has won the day here, old friend!'

Star winced as he was purged of the spikes and she poured water over the wounds. After she finished they set off again and a very quiet dog let Anna lead the way along a remembered path that at a fork in it put them both facing into the sun and the granite buildings of Zennor Churchtown in the distance.

They were only fifty feet from the stone stile that ended the landscape of natural moorland and the granite hedges, when Anna said to Star 'I was better that time, but I was still thankful for your company' looking directly him she added 'And now I suppose you will disappear just as soon as I reach the pub? If you do then please remember to stay away from monster rabbits in future!'

Expecting the change in light from bright sunshine to the dimness of 'The Tinners Arms' Anna remembered the step down and the cautious left turn towards the bar and the noise of the men drinking there together with the hearty voice of the landlord, Terry Nancekivell, as he said 'Goodday, Miss, tis good to see ee back again. Have ee had a nice walk?'

Nodding with pleasure she replied 'Wonderful again, and thirsty again as well, could I have a half pint of shandy please.'

Pausing for a second he said 'Course ee can. Funny thing is the missus said ee would be back soon, and here ee is.'

There was a general hubbub of voices from the group gathered around the bar and a collective laugh after one of the men said 'Tell ee what, she's a witch that missus of yours, still, truth is livin we you she needs to be able to read your mind to keep you out of trouble!'

With a friendly but hard stare in the direction of the voice that had made the joke the landlord of the Tinners said 'Nuff of that in front of customers lik, Jan, and ee can be sure missus will already know what ee have just said, so ee best go careful, lik!'

Returning to Anna he put her drink down on the bar in front of her and added 'Do ee want a ploughman's, same last time? Good, ee can sit by the window lik and I'll bring in over to ee.'

Sitting down she took a long drink from her glass and at the same time glanced out of the window her chair backed into. From this angle of the building which faced the sea rather than the Church, the window overlooked the back of the pub through the same buckled pine trees she had passed on her way around to the front entrance.

In front of the trees was the farm yard now almost full of light tan coloured cows and a man who was guiding the last of them into the enclosure with the able assistance of an excited barking golden retriever, Star.

She smiled broadly at the sight and was slightly startled by a voice that said 'Yew do luk appy miss, here's yewr ploughman's.' The voice belonged to the landlord's wife who now shared Anna's view of the herd going into the farm yard.

'Thank you' Anna said, and looking back out of the window she continued 'You see that lovely golden retriever, I met him on my first walk along the coast where he kept me company until I got to your pub and he did the same again today, does he belong to the farmer?'

'O yah thet's Sterenn, farmer Squires doug, or wun ov em. Yah, ees a rite roamer, tha un, mind yew, nevur misses milking times, lik ees got a pocket watch on em!'

'I'll leave ee to ate yer food' the landlord's wife said, but before leaving she added 'I got owt me bok weth tha pictures an all ov them plants an flew-wers upalong tha cliffs ef ee wood lik ta see eem?'

'Oh, yes please, I've got an awful lot to ask you!' Anna said.

As the woman went past the group of men by the bar she said 'An thank yew Jan, I dud ear whaat ee did saay, an remembur tis a gibbous moon at tha moment but twil bay full bey weekend, so luke owt ma boay!'

The laughter came from everyone, except Jan who added 'Twas only a joke missus'. Which brought more laughter and more hurt looks from Jan.

Anna was earlier than on her last visit to the Tinners and as she started to eat so both ends of the bar began to fill up with people. The group that was at the bar when she entered swelled by another five or six men followed by three young women wearing the uniform of the Women's Land Army.

The look on the women's faces when they saw Anna was of irritation, as though their secret hideaway had been discovered.

Anna knew what they were thinking and she waved one of the girls over saying quietly 'I think this place has to be neutral territory, don't you? After all, us girls don't have too many places we can go, so let's treat this one as one where we can all go and be at ease together, agreed?'

With a broad smile the attractive young girl replied 'Thank you ma'am, wonderful. We only work up the hill so sometimes it is nice to pop in for a treat.'

The atmosphere returned to normal as the enlarged gathering at the bar drifted towards where Anna sat. She had finished her snack and was looking at her sketch book, adding detail to the outlines of the plants, birds and the infamous rabbit when a leather bound book was placed in front of her followed by a voice saying 'Now me name bay Mabena, Mabena Nancekivell thet is, an im bind tha bar is me husband, Terry Nancekivell. Is it oall rite ef I show ee me bok?'

Almost excitedly, Anna was able to say 'Yes please, and by the way I'm Anna Jack. I really would like to look at your book and will quickly admit I am ignorant of so many of the things I've seen.'

Mabena was shown the sketch pad of the mornings work, including a very rough outline of the coast she had drawn.

The landlady of the pub turned to a blank page of Anna's pad and quickly drew an outline of the coastline from St Ives to Gurnard's Head. Mysterious names began to appear in coves and on jutting headlands.

The old mine engine house and breathing chimney she had drawn were close to Hor Point, next came Pen Eynes Point, Pagassick Cove, Carn Naum Point, Mussel Point.

Anna's swims were from Wicca Pool, and Zennor Head was where she and Star turned into the sun, with Horseback Zawn, Gurnard's Head to the west of their path.
Most of the names were meaningless except for the mystery each seemed to hold.

Anna only spoke when the short plumpish woman had

finished the drawing, saying 'Horseback Zawn, what does that mean?'

Still filling in the line of a stone wall she replied 'Ossbaak Zawn. Anna, next time ee walks up from tha ead down road, luk ta ee's rite, tis obvious than, an a dangerous spot tis.'

The drawing of a cluster of ground plants with red and brown foliage was confirmed as being Navelwort 'Cause ee looks lik a belly button!' Mabena said.

The two sea diving birds were Cormorants. 'Thay waas just hanging thay feathers out ta dry, maid. But tis a lovely sight, na mistaking thaat'

When showed the drawing of the red legged birds she shouted to her husband behind the bar 'Hay Terr, tha maid seen a flock ov Cornish Chuffs on cliffs, yew waas a bit lucky I tell ee, thems few an far tween'

'Now this orchid is a bit ov a mysterry, not in tha book, but I av sin em, now where did yew find em?'

Anna pointed to cliffs above Wicca Pool on the freshly drawn map. 'Ah!, I know, tis a pyramid orchid, he's gat tow scents that ee gives out, wun in tha day so tha bees an butterflies go ta im an towthur ah foxey smell at night fur them moths an flies.'

Turning over to the last drawing Anna said 'It was just after I saw the orchid that the monster rabbit flashed past me with Star, I mean Sterenn, in hot pursuit!'

Looking at Anna then directing another shout to her husband behind the bar Mabena said 'Terr, thaat evil ol witch is back up on the cliffs above Wicca'.

Turning back to Anna she continued 'T'was a Hare yew saw me dear, whaat makes tha eyes luk so big is tha line ov darker fir round um, sort ov makes em stan proud lik'

'Folk about eer is superstitious 'bout em. Sum thiks em is tha spirits ov sailors that drowned on tha rocks, or witches.'

Conspiratorially Mabena leaned towards Anna and whispered 'Least way's thaat's whaat they do tell tha holiday makers! Tis a load of twaddle if yew ask me, but I don tel tha boays lik, cause tween thee an me et suits me well thaat they aint too sure ov me an me magical powers, even iv I ain't got non maid!'

Both women were laughing as they got up from the table and Anna said 'Mabena, thank you very much for helping me understand and explain things to me, I really am a dunce about what is around me, but I enjoy learning, and the walks are a treat when the rest of the week I'm stuck in the hospital.'

Picking up her haversack, tin hat and gas mask case to leave, her last question was 'I've never heard of your name before, or Sterenn, are they both Cornish names?'

Putting her leather book under her arm she answered 'Propur Cornish. An Sterenn means Star un yewr language. Yew knaw Anna, I think us av met fore, strange, well, et must 'av bin un another life, but I reckons yew were ere a long, long time ago.'

Placing the book behind the bar counter she then went around collecting glasses and stopped to talk to other customers while Anna went to the bar and paid the landlord for her ploughman's lunch, saying 'That was really good, and thank you both very much. Oh, there was one thing I was going to ask your wife, but she's busy at the moment, can you tell me what is the meaning of the word Orchid?'

Terry Nancekivell went bright red with a flush of embarrassment and the two men he had been talking to seemed to choke on the beer they were drinking before he hurriedly said 'Well miss, the St Austell mild barrel needs changin quick lik, so yewd bettur ask the missus.' Before she could ask any further questions the burly landlord disappeared through a doorway.

Feeling embarrassed herself she went to the door of the pub and caught the eye of the landlady before leaving to catch the bus that had just pipped its horn in the lane to announce its imminent departure.

Mabena walked outside into the sunshine and listened to Anna as they walked towards the bus 'I think I've really embarrassed your husband, but for the life of me I don't know how, all I did was to ask him what Orchid meant.'

'O deary me Anna, whaat a shy old goat ee ken bay at times, deary me. I'll tell ee. Orchids get's them names cause tha tubers, thaat bay tha roots, looks lik men's balls, so Orchid means testicles!'

Anna climbed the two steps into the bus and sat down still clearly able to hear the loud raucous laughter of Mabena Nancekivell as the bus started the gruelling climb out of the village towards St Ives.

St Ives, 21ˢᵗ August 1941

With the third year of the war approaching there was a small degree of optimism about. Britain had air superiority over its own shores and the Royal Navy still had the upper hand at sea, with only the U-boats of the German navy able to wreck havoc amongst the convoys of merchant ships bringing supplies to the island fortress.

Each day the country's defences and also ability to strike back at the enemy increased. The production of aircraft, tanks, guns and munitions gathered pace throughout the length and breadth of the land, helped by the delivery of vital life saving supplies from America and the countries of the Empire and Dominions.

More and more men were being 'called up' for military service, the vacuum created by their departure being filled by women who worked at the machines to manufacture the armaments of war.

On June the 22ⁿᵈ 1941, Hitler ordered his generals to invade Russia. Winston Churchill was jubilant. He knew that this order would be the beginning of the end for the Nazi regime. Sooner or later the tide of war would turn but in the meantime Britain would stand alone, and stand firm.

During the week that Russia was invaded the BBC had announced for the first time in its news broadcasts over the wireless that active resistance teams were operating in France, attacking industrial and military targets.

****

Throughout the summer months of July and August on her days away from nursing duty Anna made the trip to the north coast by bus or on her motorcycle whenever her petrol coupons allowed. It was her one day of most weeks when the war, the routine of nursing and the hospital could be forgotten.

The war was with everyone all day, every day, a heavy weight on the shoulder, a shadow on the ground, but the gut wrenching fear of imminent invasion of a year ago had receded.

Anna, with her colleagues at the hospital, were well aware of the activities in France mentioned in recent BBC news broadcasts as they tended many of the wounded from these highly secret operations after they were carried ashore from boats that docked in Falmouth harbour.

Falmouth had become a focal point for covert operations by the newly formed Special Operations Executive, the SOE. In a call from the Prime Minister to 'set Europe ablaze by any means available' the operations were dangerous and always shrouded by the utmost secrecy and security.

Using French fishing vessels and crews who had sailed across the Channel when their country had been overrun; together with fast British motor boats they would land agents, weapons and equipment for sabotage operations throughout the country, sometimes returning with airmen and soldiers who had been smuggled through France by members of the resistance movement and ordinary families.

During the night, several casualties had been brought in after returning from France and Anna had been on duty until the early hours of the morning. Today was her day off and she was determined to get away. A few hours sleep made her too late for the bus and without enough petrol for her motor cycle she decided to take the train from Falmouth to St Ives.

With all day on her hands she walked in the sunshine to the small railway station where the branch line from Truro terminated in two sets of red painted buffers, yards from Falmouth Bay and the squawking seagulls that patrolled it. It was eerily quiet as Anna walked into the station with the cooing of pigeons in the rafters of the building being the primary sound except for a gentle swishing noise from an overweight man she thought in his late seventies wearing an ill-fitting railwayman's uniform, who was sweeping the platform.

'Good morning, could you give me some information of times of trains to St Ives, please' she asked.

Straitening himself up seemed to take a lot of effort and energy before the man said, 'Very difficult from here, young lady, you will have to go to the ticket window and ask there.'

Surprised by the abruptness of the well-spoken man she simply thanked him for his help, and after looking in the direction he had indicated she added 'All the windows seem to be closed at the moment.'

Muttering under his breath he said, 'I can't be in two places at the same time you know' before placing the wide broom against a wall and walking slowly and speechlessly past Anna until he was out of sight.

Now totally alone she turned around and was about to walk out of the station entrance when she heard the sound of bolts being slid back and a vertical roller shutter being raised at one of the two ticket windows.

Slowly the shutter went up to reveal the middle portion of the platform sweeper before it stopped below his chin. Anna heard the headless torso say, 'Can I help you?'

Holding a giggle and knowing that any hint of one would probably bring the partly open kiosk shutter crashing down like the portcullis of a castle under siege, she repeated her initial request and asked politely 'I wonder if you could tell me if there is a train that will take me to St Ives this morning, please?'

After a moment of silence the voice said 'You really are far too late for the best connection, simply far too late, that went an hour ago. However, the next train arriving here will take you to Truro. Change there for the Plymouth to Penzance train and get off at St Erth'

'The branch line train will take you from St Erth to St Ives, but be warned, the schedule is haphazard to say the least. I can assure you that if I had my way I would sack every man and woman working on that branch line immediately. Communists most of them, or arty types dodging war service. St Ives people have always been the same, pirates, smugglers and drunkards. That will be one shilling and two pennies return.'

Stunned by the torrent of verbal information followed by the robust damnation of all St Ives people from the headless form, Anna quickly put a half-crown piece into the brass cup-shaped receptacle that lay between her and the voice.

The immediate sound of her change being dropped back into the same cup followed by two tickets made her grab them quickly as she saw that the shutter had already started on its downward journey and snapped shut as she scooped out her purchase and change.

She wondered down the platform and sat on a bench seat that was positioned out of the protective reach of the overhead canopy with the traditional fascia of foot long scalloped wood planks, in the sunshine, and importantly, away from the station assistant.

Not bothering, or now daring to ask the time of the train's arrival she sat and mused over the morning's events, which despite being difficult to believe had an amusing side to them.

Over the next twenty minutes three steam engines puffed their way towards Anna only to veer to the left and into the sprawling docks area or to the right to a Goods Shed as the points shifted the direction of the trains fifty yards in front of her.

Small squat engines, they reminded her of farm sheep dogs, full of vital energy, and always keen to run to places rather than walk as they shunted their wagons around with great gasp of steam billowing from under them.

At ten thirty a larger train with three carriages began to approach her in the distance, its appearance was the signal for other passengers to materialise from nowhere.

Anna said softly 'Did they all hide outside, perhaps in the air raid shelter across the road, or the sand bagged wall outside the station? All of them too afraid to disturb the station emperor!'

Relieved when the train began to hiss and puff its way out of the station its first stop was Penryn, only two miles from the start of the journey. Her amusement of the morning faded as she thought back only two months to a dark night in May.

Then she had raced to the small town from Falmouth as part of a fleet of ambulances carrying doctors and nurses.

After a bombing raid on shipping anchored in Falmouth Bay and the docks area the attacking planes had dropped two parachute mines into the middle of Penryn, destroying the centre of the small town and turning it into a blazing inferno. The raid had killed eighteen civilians and had injured dozens more.

Anna had been told that Falmouth Docks was a difficult target to bomb. Lying under the high shadow of Pendennis Castle bombers found it hard to penetrate the bay for a clear run onto the targets at anchor or the dock installations. This made the indiscriminate and random bombing of areas surrounding the town a frequent and terrifying reality to the men, women and children living there.

She was pleased when the train doors slammed and the conductor gave three shrill blasts on his whistle, the final signal to the driver to start the next leg of the trip to Truro station.

Determined to push the bad memories aside for the moment she got off the branch line train when it arrived at the capital of Cornwall and had time for a cup of tea before crossing to the platform where she would get her connecting train to St Erth.

Arriving at St Erth Anna was surprised that the station house was not festooned in red flags bearing a yellow hammer and sickle in the corner. Nor did she have to wait longer than ten minutes for the train that was the same size as the one from Falmouth to Truro to arrive and the waiting crowd of holiday makers, solders and local people to opened the doors and begin to board.

A very sober station guard approached her as she stepped up into one of the three carriages and without a hint of beer or Cornish cyder on his breath said 'Miss, if this is your first time on the train, sit by the window if you can, the view is wonderful, especially on a sunny day like today, and even better, my advice would be to stand in the corridor by one of the doors so you can pull down the window and look out, you will not be disappointed, I can assure you!'

In a letter to her parents that evening she wrote:

'The distance is only four and a half miles, but my goodness what a wonderful engineering feat it is as the track clings to the estuary and coast, in fact I had a sense of being at sea in a boat for some stretches!'

'The train seems to glide down the track until it stops at a place called Lelant before setting off again at full steam ahead. Here the countryside that was on both sides of me gave way to land on one side and sand dunes that very quickly open up to the deep blues of the open sea'

'There are long beaches of golden sand that stretch for miles and miles to the right which end with a group of dangerous looking rocks jutting out into the sea which has a lighthouse perched on the end of them'

'Smaller beaches, equally as golden, lie within a step of the track that my train was puffing gaily along. Alas, as always these days, reminders that the war is never far away are stark as the beaches are heavily defended by coils of barbed wire, tank traps, land mines and sinister looking squat pill boxes on each promontory that keep a silent lookout for any invasion force. In peacetime this must be one of the most beautiful railway lines in the country'

'A local lady who lives in St Ives sat next to me and she told me in hushed tones, clearly suspecting me of spying, that she 'thought' the next stop was called Carbis Bay! It has its own small but sheltered sandy beach with nice hotels and guest houses set back from the railway track, whose car parks now seem full with as many army vehicles as visitors' cars'

'I could now imagine the fireman on the trains footplate shovelling like mad to get enough steam-up for the last leg of the journey which took us gently uphill, just feet above the rocks and sea below to give a spectacular view back in the direction from where the train had just travelled and across the bay to the long beach's where small clusters of people were visible playing in the sand dunes'

'Before leaving Carbis Bay I had decided to leave the other five passengers in the compartment and stood, as recommended by the railway guard at the start of my journey, by a door of the carriage and opened the sliding window *downwards'*

'Despite blinking from the smuts of soot that flew into my eyes from the smoke stack of the engine it was well worth it. The fresh smell of the sea came tumbling through the window and when suddenly my view was totally blocked by a stretch of steep embankment I was rewarded for the interruption as the train raced into the open and by the wonderful sight of St Ives bursting into my eyes with the tide very high and a thin line of white surf breaking gently onto the beaches, wonderful! I just wish we could all be here together and the war long forgotten'.

It was well past noon by the time she left the train and walked down the hill and through the narrow lanes of the town to the sea front. Too late in the day to complete a walk to Zennor Anna decided to explore the town instead. After a pint of bitter shandy at the Sloop Inn she bought a pasty from Mr Green, who greeted her like an old friend, before walking to Porthmeor Beach.

Towards the town end of the beach and the rocks that led to St Nicholas Chapel a band of holiday makers, locals and off duty servicemen had eased away the coils of rusty barbed wire and were enjoying a swim or dangling their feet in the sparkling calm water.

The loud peals of laughter from adults and the excited screams of children as they splashed and danced in the sea was a wonderful reminder to Anna of holidays with her parents and their friends before the war.

St Ives and the area surrounding it, together with most of the popular pre-war holiday resorts in Devon and Cornwall, was now the temporary home to thousands of service men and women from all parts of the world that were using the moors, beaches and surrounding cliffs for training and war games.

Khaki uniforms blended with the summer clothes of local people and holiday makers from factories in the midlands and other parts of the country.

War or not, it was summer time and life went on. Artists still painted, sculptors and potters still formed shapes from stone and clay. It seemed that more than ever many people wanted to see through the eyes of others the bright, vivid colours they had not forgotten, but were simply unable to let into their war time lives. It was as if the war itself had become a dull uniform everyone was forced to wear.

Walking to the end of the beach Anna sat on the rocks that marked the start of her walks to Zennor. Finding some shade from the sun she took off her army shoes and coaxed her heavy nylon stockings through trouser legs and sat on a rock while she dangled her feet in a tepid pool of trapped sea water. Breaking off a small portion of Mr Green's pasty she put what remained back into her gas mask box.

'What a mad sight 'she thought as she watched men and women in battledress shirts with their khaki trousers rolled up to the knees playing football on the sand, paddling in the water, while she could plainly hear the loud voice of an Australian or New Zealander busy organizing a game of cricket on the beach.

Toddlers splashed in the small waves and were inches away from coils of barbed wire that covered the beach, restrained by mothers holding their hands while teenagers in bathing suits jumped off rocks into the turquoise blue and emerald green sea, looked on by soldiers with rifles slung over their shoulders and others sat on a sand bagged wall that housed a machine gun.

On her way back up the hill and through the main street of the town towards the railway station Anna stopped and walked into a gleaming white dairy shop. Lured by a sign that rested against a double fronted shop window and proclaimed, 'Mr Clements Famous Cornish Ice Cream, made with fresh local clotted cream'.

The counter facing Anna was a ten foot long slab of white marble with blue veins trapped in the surface. It gave the inside of the shop a cool feel and the two bowls of clotted cream, the almost yellow crust on top of them gleaming like twin harvest moons, would have broken the resolve of the strongest person alive not to taste them.

Milk measures hung from hooks secured to the ceiling. Quart, pint and half pint brass jugs hung side by side. The long brass handles welded to the side of each ready for the hand that would lift the lid off the ten-gallon milk churn standing in the cold room at the back of the shop before ladling out the requested amount into bottles, basins or milk jugs of the people of the town.

The proprietor, Mr Clements, stood behind the counter wearing a crisp white apron over his clothes. A thin, delicate and pleasant mannered man, he suggested a middle sized wafer to Anna which she agreed to.

Placing an oblong wafer biscuit into a metal mould the same shape and size he then spooned the fresh ice cream into it, leaving just enough room for the final wafer biscuit to complete the process before pushing the bottom plate up and dropping the ice cream wafer onto a square of grease proofed paper on a white oval plate in front of Anna.

A single bell rang once as the shop owner pulled opened the wood tray of his till to place the money Anna had given him into the separate compartments for each coin. His nervousness evaporated only after she had completed the first lick of the ice cream before saying 'Umm, this is as delicious as your sign told me it would be, thank you.'

Walking slowly back to the railway station with the sun on her back the trappings of war and its cloak slipped as Anna remembered summer holidays as a young girl with her mother and father when ice cream cones and wafers lasted forever.

Zennor, 24th September 1941

Anna watched the season changing from summer to autumn with each walk along the coast. When the weather was bad and the gales from the Atlantic pounded the coastline she took the inland route along ancient paths, and over fields, divided by the irregular shaped granite hedges.

She walked through farm yards, stopping to talk to the women, children and elderly men, all of them involved in producing food of one sort or another from the fields or animals.

The last walk of the summer started as usual on the cobbles outside the Sloop Inn. She could sense as well as feel and see a definite change of season. Once on the cliffs she noticed that the sun was lower and it cast long shadows around the rocks and stone slabs that were scattered like a giant's toy marbles on the landscape in front of her, the sea air had a slight, hardly noticeable but cool bite to it whenever she stopped to look seaward.

   The thick carpets of colourful flowers from the summer months had retreated, replaced by the vivid richness of the purples of the heather that covered most of the land from the tops of the jagged hills to the edges of the cliff tops, broken up here and there by patches of green gorse with its second flowering of bright yellow flowers, and the once green and feathery ferns, now various shades of brown. Sterenn joined Anna later than normal and she had passed Wicca Cove before the echo of his barking reached her. She greeted his bouncing and wagging tail with pats on his head as she said 'Did you get up late today, or did you have to work longer? Not to worry, it's so good to see you!'

   Smoothing the fur on his back she said aloud 'Even your coat is getting thicker Star, winter is approaching, eh!'

   An unusual sound above made both of the walkers look up and out to sea. Coming towards them were three flights of Geese flying in the traditional formation of one leader with a chevron of followers trailing behind him.

   'My mum bought a set of three of those for the front sitting room wall, above the mantelpiece and do you know what Star, I don't actually know what they're called, ah well, another question for Mabena!'

   With the last hundred yards to go, Zennor Head behind and the Tinners Arms in front, Anna smiled to herself as she thought back to the early walks when at this stage she would have been exhausted in all body departments and the refuge of the pub seemed like a distant mirage. Now she walked with ease, her breathing steady, her stride steady.

   Mabena Nancekivell had became a teacher of botany and ornithology to Anna as well and as becoming a friend. She and her husband had three children, two boys and a girl with only the youngest daughter, Lowena still living at home. Enjoying hero status with the thirteen year old girl, Anna was looking forward to seeing her, together with her mother and father.

Today it would be only a fast drink, a quick chat and a seat on the bus back to St Ives. The afternoon had turned warm for late September with the front door of the pub open to collect the passing breeze.

Anna walked through the open door blinking the sunlight from her eyes and adjusting to the perpetual dimpsey conditions of the bar. Frowning from the change of light, she headed towards the sound of Terry Nancekivell's voice and the man he was talking to.

Anna reached the bar and gave her familiar 'Hello Terry, how are you and how is Lowina and Mabina?'

The landlord of the Tinners Arms enthusiastically replied, 'Hello Anna, them's both braave, propur braave, them ill both be down dreckly, so is ee oall rite? Us was only saying last night us hadn't seen ee for a couple weeks.'

Hanging her gas mask case on one of the brass hooks that was screwed into the wood below the bar line she looked at the landlord before saying 'I've had a lovely walk, Terry, there's a touch of autumn in the air but I think I've been lucky with the weather today, it was really hot out of the wind.'

Nodding in agreement he added 'Lucky tis Anna. If he carries on twil make winter a bit shorter, maid!'

Anna was pleased to have just a moment to laugh and also to quickly compose herself, the customer Terry had been talking to was Simon Tremayne.

Looking hard at the attractive woman who seemed to be so much at home in his local pub and knowing he knew her; but not sure from where, he said 'Hello, I know we've met before, can't just say where or when, but my name is Simon Tremayne.'

The few seconds were enough to adjust to the light and surprise of meeting him, before Anna replied, saying 'Hello, now then, I remember that we met at a dance in Falmouth, at the start of the summer, which seems like an age or maybe two ago!'

'Of course, I remember now. So, what brings you here', interrupting himself he quickly added 'I'm sorry, what would you like to drink?'

Anna replied 'Sadly, I only have ten minutes before my bus arrives, but thank you, I think a glass of lemonade would be really refreshing after my walk up the hill'.

'Terry' Anna said, leaning comfortably on one elbow on his wooden bar, Mr Tremayne here is the person I mentioned to you and Mabena in the early part of the summer as being responsible for my first expedition from St Ives and to your home,'

'Don't look puzzled,' Anna said amusingly, looking from the landlord to Simon 'it was late in the evening, but I do remember you saying that the most magical walk in Cornwall ended right here, or to be absolutely correct, I think you may have said in the village and not the pub!'

Simon most certainly did remember Anna. He wasn't lying when he said that, but the events of the evening had become blurred, so that all he had retained of their brief meeting on the dance floor was a detail of her striking face and jet black hair, characteristics seen occasionally in a few Cornish families.

Spanish sailors from before the Armada and Mediterranean miners during the Bronze Age had ensured that the genes of these men had remained ashore to offer the occasional raven hair colouring and dark skin to numbers of men and women of the county.

As well as her hair, it was the high cheek bones and deep-set brown eyes of Anna that gave her a bewitching quality, loved and hated in equal measure, but always noticed, she was not the sort of person that could ever hope to be anonymous or forgotten.

The beep on the horn gave the village a warning that in five minutes the last bus to St Ives would be departing.

Anna finished her drink and after a brief conversation with Lowina and Mabina who had just appeared, she said goodbye to Terry and gave a gentle handshake to Simon Tremayne.

As she touched Simon's hand Anna felt an unusual warmth in it. She realised that the moisture had gone from her mouth and that she had to make an effort to get the saliva back again to speak.

Even then her speech was just an octave higher, and slightly forced. Clearing her throat, she managed to say to him 'Weather and war permitting, I will be earlier next week, goodbye, and thanks again for the drink, and of course your advice, you were right, it is a lovely, lovely walk!'

For the first time Anna failed to look at the surroundings on either side of her as the bus climbed the hill away from the village. The rich mauves and purples from the acres of heather spread out on both sides of her went unnoticed.

Back at the Tinners Arms the front door had been locked and the only window with a view onto the bar had its blackout curtain put in place. An 'after hours' drink was by unspoken invitation. The regulars knew the rules, and nobody ever spoke about them.

When Terry looked at the old pendulum clock, set in an oak case behind his head and shouted the customary 'Time, Gentlemen' one of two events would start. If he put a bar towel over the best bitter hand pump, then doctors, farmers, solicitors, miners or clergy, everyone, without question, finished their drinks, and went home.
If no bar towel was visible immediately, the game began.

Strangers would be politely hurried along, ash trays would disappear from tables, to remove the most entrenched of the 'unknowns' the final plea of 'I dan't waant ta loose my license' would prise the most determined of drinkers away from the settles and chairs by the fires.

To the frequently asked question 'Where is the nearest place I can get a drink at this time of day?' Terry's stock answer was always the same 'Thaat theere France, me ansum.'

The 'locals', now down to the last half-inch of beer or cyder, would sense the last ritual, the removal of the till's cash box, which was replaced by a solid brown glazed bowl made at a nearby pottery. Should the forces of Methodist thinking ever insist on a police visit, the bowl would be seen close to the poster for the 'Spitfire Appeal Fund'.

That afternoon Simon Tremayne was thankful for the opportunity of a last drink.
The landlord was quick to make the observation, and quicker to pull Simon a pint.
Simon was also pleased not to be alone. The chatter of a group

of people with similar business and local interest was a welcome diversion to the unfamiliar feeling in the pit of his stomach and the strange excitement he felt towards the young nursing sister who had just left.

Over the next weeks Simon made a point of being in the Tinners on a Wednesday and Thursday lunch time whenever he could. Anna's visits were not so regular, the war saw to that, but there was no denying the feeling of disappointment both experienced when their visits did not manage to merge. The disappointment was never admitted or shown by either.

The first casual meetings between Anna and Simon at the Tinners Arms that had started in late September passed without any interest to the locals at both ends of the pub and to the villagers, but as autumn rolled into winter the brief but regular meetings were noticed.

It was difficult not to see a softening to a normally, not hard nor aloof, but certainly distant Simon Tremayne, during his openly amusing conversations with this pretty nursing Sister.

Gossip was a rare relief from the daily ingestion of war bulletins and news of more stringent rationing of basic food items. The gossip of this small rural community had heads nodding in the village and surrounding farms as the third Christmas of the war approached.

Simon Tremayne was the second of three sons and one sister. His father, Robert and mother, Patricia, lived in one of the merchant houses of the capital of the county, Truro. While still active in all his business ventures Robert Tremayne was content to leave the day to day management of both farm and mining businesses to his sons and managers.

Although on good terms with his two brothers, Simon had always been closest to his sister, Christine. His parents had channelled his education towards the family mining interest while the eldest brother, Henry, and the youngest son, David had been seen by their parents from the cradle, as the next farming generations.

'Howlsedhes', 27th November 1941

'Howlsedhes' is a granite faced lonely looking house, perched below the Logan Rock, a mile from Zennor village, back from the road to St Ives. Normally, as Westerly winds swept in from the sea towards his home Simon Tremayne would stand behind rattling windows while twists of cold air would blast through newly found and age-old gaps and smile. But not today.

The oak desk in his office was set to catch the setting sun, and sat behind it he knew the rain would not give up and the early night of winter would give only various shades of grey until darkness.

'Not to worry,' he thought 'the colours outside match my mood today. Time to pull the blackout curtains and finish my work.' It had never been a problem before but over the past weeks getting anything finished had become irksome and difficult.

The truth was Simon kept thinking of Anna. This girl, woman, certainly stranger, had rattled him. He was irritated, cross with himself but couldn't really think or understand why.

Aloud, and loudly, he shouted 'For Christ's sake get a grip of yourself.'

Christine Tremayne's voice startled him when she spoke 'A cup of tea, dear brother, and how are you? Still barking wildly to yourself I hear!' she said laughing.

Simon replied 'All the better for you bringing me back to reality. You okay sis?'

Frowning, she looked at him, saying 'Well, like most people I am just so fed up with this war, I could cry. But you know Simon, most of my trouble is that I'm frustrated because I don't think I'm doing enough to help, in fact anything to help, and that's the truth of it.'

Putting down her brother's favourite mug besides him she said 'Simon, I'm going to ask mummy and daddy if they would let me join one of the services. I met Charlotte Bennet at the weekend, she went into the WAAF's last year. She was very secretive about what she is doing in London, which was really annoying, but the fact is she had that sort of superior way with her that made me feel very insignificant.'

'You have no chance, Chrissie' Simon said as he put the finishing touches to the blackout curtains before switching on the angle poise lamp on his desk.

'You know how mum and dad see the matter. It's essential that the farms keep going to their maximum and that I keep producing as much ore as I can get the men to bring to the surface, and since Louise left us to work in the skim factory your role as general factotum has made you totally irreplaceable.'

'Factotum, just stick to general dogs' body, no fancy words are needed!' Christine mouthed, before adding 'Don't forget, I shall be 21 next year and I have every intention of doing something beyond these walls, I can assure you!'

'Did you know there was another attack on the ships in Falmouth harbour yesterday? The grapevine has it that two German aircraft were shot down, but another four people were killed in the raid on shore and one of the naval vessels was hit and badly damaged.'

Trying not to sound anxious Simon asked, 'Where were the people killed Chrissie, by the dock area, or further into the town?'

Christine replied casually 'I don't really know. All I do know is that when the grapevine, in the large shape of Eric Thrump told me, I just felt like going there to see if I could be of any real help to anyone.'

Pulling her seat under her at the small table that supported the ancient Underwood typewriter she used, she sipped her tea before winding the paper into the machine and said 'Anyway dear brother, enough of my moaning. I'm going to type out the report you need and afterwards, if the rain eases, I thought we might pop down for a drink at the Tinners?'

Simon nodded a quick agreement 'Good idea dear sister, I need a bit of uplift. I've got to go to Falmouth tomorrow, is there anything you need?'

Christine pondered the question before answering 'Emm, let me think now, I am very short on boyfriends at the moment, could you bring one back for me, please?'

Smiling, Simon glanced at her over his empty mug, saying 'After the last disastrous boyfriend it's little wonder that our parents would rather have you under observation here and not fighting the enemy. Besides which, it may not be fair to let you loose on the Germans, after all they're not all bad!'

Christine gave him a loud 'raspberry' before her fingers started their tapping at the typewriter keys.

'Not all bad' thought Simon. He was thinking back to only four years ago when a young German had arrived to work in a local pottery in St Ives together with a potter from Japan.

The three men had spent many hours in his home discussing art and politics. His favourite mugs had been made for him by the German under the direction of the talented potter from the orient. 'I wonder where they are now. Madness, all of it.'

The wind and rain had eased to a clinging drizzle when Simon and Christine started freewheeling their bicycles down the hill to the village and the Tinners Arms. The brother and sister stood talking with friends and neighbours until the offer of a lift back to Simon's house was made. Easing themselves out the cab of the farm lorry and taking their bicycles off the back they shouted a goodbye before putting their bikes away in the garage, and going into the house 'Chrissie, how do you fancy a whisky?'

Christine and Simon sat in front of the matt black Cornish slab cooking range that filled the whole fireplace in the kitchen. Two wrought iron doors had been opened to reveal the crackling nogs of wood burning inside.

Sat, cat like, in a large winged chair in front of the range Christine looked at her brother through the golden liquid in her glass, saying 'Well Simon, as I mentioned earlier, I shall be twenty one next February, and I certainly don't mind talking about it. But, dear brother the other big event of next year is the fact that you are supposed to be getting married, and it just seems as if you have maybe forgotten about it?'

Preferring to look and talk into the fire rather than at his sister Simon could only muster a 'Yes, umm' followed by a deep sigh, and another gulp of whisky.

'Simon,' Christine murmured quietly, 'is there a problem because you haven't mentioned either Clare, your fiancée of almost two years if you had forgotten, or getting 'spliced' as Terry at the Tinners would put it, for weeks.'

Still talking to the fire Simon said 'There isn't a problem Chrissie but you know getting married now with the war going on all around us, with people being bombed out of their homes and killed less than twenty miles away, it just seems…..well, frivolous, unimportant somehow at this particular point in time.'

Surer of his ground on his next subject he sat back and added 'And don't think I'm happy being here when my best friends are away in the forces being involved in the war in a definite way that is understood by everyone, and more especially, by themselves.'

Shifting around he said, 'I know that being a mining engineer what I do is important, but Chrissie it does irritate me when I catch the odd snide comment, and the fact that I've had to justify why I am not in uniform on more than one occasion. It does leave doubts about one's own value and importance.'

Back on unsure ground his voice lowered a little when he added 'I'm going to see Clare this weekend at her parent's house at Bodmin. She sort of agrees with me but I think her parents influence will get in the way of any meaningful change in plans. Strange how parents continue to manipulate their children long after they become grownups, sis, what do you think?'

Sharing her brothers view of the burning logs Christine looked up, and directly at him before speaking 'What I think is that this war has already changed the way a lot of people behave and think, and Simon, there really is no going back'

Looking back into fire she sighed as she said 'Our parents have been very generous to us, and I am thankful for that, but their way of thinking is over. When the war comes to an end, people, and especially women, will not go back to how things have been in the past. Things have changed for good, and I intend to be part of that change.'

Simon poured Christine another small measure saying, 'You always were the most radical of all of us, which is probably why dearest mother and father would not let you go to university in the first place' smiling now he continued 'I think they were convinced you would have come home with a member of the communist party!'

She laughed before saying 'Even worse, can you imagine the reaction of coming home with a Catholic!'

With a kink of their glasses Christine proposed a toast 'To us Simon, the future ''black sheep'' of our ancient family,' she paused to take a sip, and then looked squarely into her brother's eyes before adding 'and by the way dear brother, who is the girl you keep meeting at The Tinners?'

The Sea Rescue

St Ives, 3rd December 1941

Reg Barbary yawned as he stretched his right arm behind him, his thumb nail itching the small of his back as he looked out into the pitch black of night from his bedroom window. Loud, howling gusts of wind had woken him as they tried to prise away the heavy Delabole slate tiles on the roof above his head, and rattled the window frames in the weather worn sashes of the narrow-terraced house in Back Lane East, St Ives.

There was still more than two hours of darkness left, but Reg was restless, he had a bad feeling about the storm that was screeching its arrival outside his bedroom window.

Earlier, he had left the Castle Inn where he played for his team in the local euchre league. Walking back from the pub he had pulled up the collar of his pea jacket after taking a look out to sea and headed to the home where he had been born, and where his five children had also been born to Vi, his wife of forty-three years, before her death a year ago.

During the night the strong South Westerly gale Reg had looked at and listened to
a few hours before had veered to the North East. Looking at the luminous arms of his bedside clock he spoke to the empty room 'Vi, us haav a nasty bit ov wethur girl, bleedy nasty. Low tide waas a our baak an now us av a real black easterly that will drive next high tide rite unta tha haarbur. Tis no daay ta bay at sha, maid, but I've no mind ta stay a bed gnawin whaat's goin un outside.'

Seamen and their families along the coast respected and dealt with the range of Westerly and South Westerly gales that arrived throughout the year to buffet them. But all of them, and especially Reg, hated the savage North Easterlies that two or three times during a winter would bring a trail of destruction, hardship and grief to the small coastal towns and villages on the peninsular that jutted into the Atlantic.

A North Easterly had enveloped the Barbary family in grief less than two years before when a cousin and Violet's brother had been drowned, together with five other men in the town lifeboat. Setting out in a gale that turned into a hurricane, the rescue boat had been turned over three times by ferocious waves. Holding the kith an kin of the town's people inside the upturned hull, the shattered boat and one survivor was given up by the sea and tossed like a child's toy onto rocks.

At the cemetery of St Barnoon chapel, over looking Porthmeor Beach and the sea beyond, they said goodbye to a young man of twenty-two, and Vi's brother who had become coxswain of the lifeboat when he had taken over from Reg.

Tearful families said prayers for a father and son, and a cousin, all from the same family, and the grieving widows and children of two brothers-in-laws completed the tragic grave side scene.

The custom of RNLI lifeboat stations throughout Britain and both parts of Ireland was that the volunteer crews lived in the same town or small village. In peacetime, as soon as the maroon rockets were fired into the sky men and women would leave their beds or jobs and run towards the lifeboat house.

War had brought Reg Barbary out of retirement and at the age of seventy-two he was now back in his old job as coxswain of the town lifeboat. Apart from two teenagers, too young to join the services, the lifeboat crew were all around his age, most of them he had sailed with all his life, and four were related to him by birth or marriage.

He dressed quickly. The faded blue long johns were covered by thick weave cotton trousers, neatly stitched patches drawing together old tears. A collarless shirt was lost to view as he pulled a heavy dark blue jersey over his head, before tucking shirt and jersey into the trousers and drawing tight a two-inch-wide leather belt. Sitting on the bed he dragged on thick woollen socks before following the stairs down to the kitchen.

Jolting suddenly as the bell of the black Bakelite telephone started to ring as he walked past it he shouted 'Bleedy theng!' before he picked up the receiver, held it thee inches away from his ear and silently listened.

The familiar voice of the secretary of the lifeboat station, Arthur Wilky, was at the other end of the line. 'Reg' he shouted, 'Reg, just had Commander Simmonds on ta me, a big merchant ship has gone on the rocks at Veor Cove, just down along from Carnelloe Long Rock. There's hell of ov va sea running but I'll see you down the boat house, Oh, an ma missus as gone to knock up tha boays.'

The line went dead and his immediate thought was one of relief that he did not have to go through the torture of speaking at the black hand set, and knew that in truth he was actually afraid of the machine that been installed recently by the RNLI because war time regulations had banned the use of the traditional rockets to call the lifeboat volunteers to their rescue duties.

Stopping before he reached the front door of the house Reg sat down on a pine seaman's chest and pulled on each of his heavy black leather boots with both hands, wrapping the laces twice around the tops that covered his ankles and tying a final knot in each lace before standing upright and crashing each foot firmly onto the stone flag stones of the hallway.

The hundred or so steel hob nails and toe and heal rims that had been hammered into each boot by their owner sent loud echoes bouncing through the house before he struggled into his dark navy-blue jacket, adjusting a cap he had owned for over two decades and ventured out into the dark street.

Before he got to the end of the terrace Reg stopped and did up the top buttons of his coat, pulled his cap down and thrust his chin deep into the collar and listened for a second to the wind that was howling over the tops of the houses.

The next turn would bring him into Bethesta Hill. It would also bring him directly into the Easterly wind that was bringing the blast of the freezing weather from the Russia.

As he turned the corner the wind stopped him in his tracks

and took his breath away. Into his collar he muttered 'Bleedy 'ell Violet, tis a bad un. Badder than evur I reckoned maid.' before bending into the storm and heading towards the sea front.

The lifeboat coxswain saw two torch lights outside the boat house and heard the doors of the building being pushed back on the metal rollers that supported them.

'Tis a bugger ov a sha Reg, do ee think ee can get out into in?'

Good question the coxswain thought to himself, and one he had been contemplating as he had struggled through the wind and lashing rain towards the boat house, but to Dick Reynolds, who had asked the question and who was the driver of the tractor that would haul the four ton lifeboat into the sea he said, 'Reckon us av twenny minites Dick four I caan tell, let's get boat down ta tha beach furst; av ee sin Tom?'

Not waiting for an answer he knew would be lost on the wind Reg went past the tractor with its throbbing noisy diesel engine and into the boat house. The smell came to him instantly, the way he knew it would. It was a mixture of rope hemp, tar, dried sea water, damp clothes and oil skins.

Smiling for the first time that day he thought 'Tis always tha saam, thank God!' as he went underneath the stern of the boat towards the bow and the lockers where the men's oil skins, boots, hats and life belts were stored.

The boat house was suddenly a hubbub of activity and shouting as the eight crew members pulled up their yellow oil skin trousers and bibs, fought awkwardly into jackets that buttoned over thick knitted jumpers, stamped the last inches into long rubber sea boots and drew their oil skin hats down, before finally putting on the cumbersome life belts.

The coxswain breathed the familiar smells deep into his old lungs and felt at ease, he could hear but not see that the well drilled team of men were putting in place the procedure to launch the lifeboat.

He knew that outside the boat house Arthur Wilky, the secretary, and Dick Reynolds, the tractor driver and boat mechanic, would be organising the dozen or more local men and women who ran to the station as quickly as the crew following a knock on the door.

The crew felt and heard the weather bouncing off of their oilskins and hats as they instinctively turned their backs away from the direction of the storm as soon as they stepped outside of the shelter of the boat house. The mixture of rain and sleet felt like a barrage of small stones hitting them.

The noise of the wind took second place when the revs of the tractor's engine screamed upwards and a cloud of blue smoke exploded out of the exhaust pipe that was situated like the funnel of a ship, pointing to the sky and above the heads of the men, and of the sea when the tractor went onto the beach.

A loud shout and a clang told them it was hooked onto the lifeboat trailer and the lifeboat came out stern first.

As soon as the boat was clear of its shelter the crew, led by the coxswain, clambered into the cockpit and each member attended to the tasks each one of them was assigned to.

Reg Barbary stood upright in the open boat, with both hands raised in front of his eyes to shield him from the driving weather, he looked seaward and what he saw made him nervous.

Squalling blasts of cold rain and sleet hit the side of the lifeboat as the metal tank tracks of the tractor clanged and scraped along the narrow cobbled sea front road towards the ramp that had been built to launch the lifeboat onto the beach.

With double war time daylight saving in place it would be dark for another hour and the coxswain looked at his watch and out to sea again saying to himself 'Low tide waas fi-ve tweney, tis just paast sebben an tha wund is drivin tha sha straight inta tha mouth ov tha harbor. Vi, I wish ee waas ear maid, I waants ta talk ta ee, I'm propur nervus maid, an thaat bay tha truth.'

Reaching the ramp the tractor ground up hill a few yards heading away from the sea and into Downalong, the road that led through the town to the harbour. The lifeboat, perched four feet above the ground on its carriage was now at the top of the ramp with the bow facing the full force of the storm, where it stopped.

The Coxswain stood at the bow of the twenty seven foot long wooden boat looking at the mouth of the harbour and at the waves and surf that were now racing towards them. He knew that if he hesitated too long the tide would rise up and the waves pounding the beach would be to ferocious for the boat to launched at all.

His first responsibility was to his crew, and to Reg it was a heavy one. He knew that they would all follow his lead; based on his judgment. It was this judgment, and the memory of the seven seamen, including his own kin, who had drowned less than two years ago that made him hesitate.

With his words lost on the wind he said aloud 'Em al ov a biver Vi, high water at leven an weth this wind tha sha el bay over tha wall an in tha owses, sure nuff, Vi us ought ta go maid. Yah, us hav just got time, cum un!'

Leaning over the boats rail he gave the order to Dick Reynolds the tractor driver to push the lifeboat down the ramp and onto the sand of the inner harbour with the bow pointing at an angle from the ramp towards the blacked-out port light at the end of the stone pier.

When the driver saw that the lifeboat carriage was up to its axle's in the far reaches of the pounding waves he stopped and idled the engine ready to drag the boat and its crew to safety should the coxswain give the command, or provide the last push that may be needed to launch the boat.

Scanning the sea coming towards his boat Reg Barbary waited for the tide to raise a fraction with the engine of the lifeboat droning feverishly in the background, the propeller slowly slicing the salty air inches above the water.

His eyes never moved from the spot he had chosen. His nervousness had now gone completely and he was wise enough to realise that should he show the slightest sign of weakness or indecision his crew would know instantly.

Reg was now in charge, the elements determined to destroy him and his friends were the enemy and like all good commanders Reg knew his enemy well. Sixty-six years ago he went on his first fishing trip with his grandfather and father.

Eight gleaming mackerel came wriggling into the open boat from one trace as they passed through an August shoal. From that moment on the sea and the land became as one to him.

The first wave hit the boat head on, sending water and spray over the bow and making the boat shudder in the arms of the carriage beneath. The second wave broke before it hit the boat and the crew took the jolt to the boat with ease. As the next wave approached Reg shouted 'Ready!' above the din of the gale, followed by 'Full ead!' as the wave crashed over the bow.

The Coxswain pushed the throttle lever forward delivering a full burst of revolutions to drive the propeller. The timing was critical, to let the propeller spin in mid air at full revolutions could be fatal and cause the engine to stall or seize up, but Reg Barbary's timing was perfect, the wave thundered and foamed over the men and at the same time it lifted the four-ton lifeboat a foot from its carriage; the propeller bit into the water and the boat surged forward through the sea and into the next wave.

Behind the round wooden wheel the coxswain steered a course that would take them close to the end of the pier that protected the harbour and the town, knowing that he would gain some lee shelter from it before altering course again when they reached the wide-open expanse of the sea.

Going past the entrance and shelter of the harbour Reg and the crew felt the full might and fury of the gale as it screamed at them before hitting the lifeboat. He turned the wheel quickly, bringing the boat's head into the wind and felt the water drag his charge like a tiny cork into the trough a huge wave.

'Propur job!' he thought, pleased with himself, knowing the last manoeuvre was a very dangerous one. If they had been caught by a wave hitting them on the beam as they came out of the harbour it could have easily swamped the vessel and capsized it, but as long as he could hold a firm course straight into the wind and rushing waves, he would win.

All of his concentration was now on keeping a close eye on his course and on the direction of the wind and waves. An error of a few degrees, or one point, from his handling of the rudder could result in the vessel broaching and certain disaster. 'Luff an lic ma boay' he shouted into the wind 'luff an lic, hug tha wind lik fathur did wen ee ad a sail up un es fishun boat.'

Every muscle in his arms and legs were flexed in knotted bunches as he held onto the wheel and fought the power of the surging sea, using his legs to sway with the violent motion of the boat and act like car suspension springs as the boat rose to the top of a wave and would then crash into the trough that opened under it.

The noise was extraordinary as the wind, rain and driving sleet whistled through the rigging of the single mast and the safety rails and ropes around the boat.

Taking seconds to glance at the Binnacle in front of him the Cox was happy with his course and progress. The wind was blowing at sixty miles an hour and was still North by North East. A glimmer of light was now visible to the East, it was five past eight in the morning.

With his eyes fixed ahead he shouted to the deputy coxswain 'Is everyone ah rite Tom?' Hanging on to a safety rope Tom Jenkins shouted back into his ear 'Ay Cox, tha boays is good, ow far til us chan-ges course?'

Taking a quick glance at the compass he replied, "Bout ten minutes I reckon.'

The difference was hardly discernable with the overcast conditions of the sky, but for the Coxswain the feint hints of grey were a blessing. Now he could read the seas that were charging towards his boat and Reg knew that this knowledge would be a life saver.

He saw that the wind had increased to sixty-five miles an hour and was now bringing more freezing sleet than it was rain. The rim of his oil skin hat would dip as gusts of wind sent driving sleet at the eyes that never left the compass course the lifeboat was on, or the lines of now visible waves that thundered towards them.

The coxswain shouted 'Staady lads, a beg bugger cumming un!' The wave seemed to tower over the small boat, and for a few moments hover above it before hurling tons of sea water into the cockpit, sending a shudder from the bow to the stern. For a second it went quiet as the wind noise disappeared.

They were in the trough of the wave, at the very bottom, and now going up.

The twin 1000 hp diesel engines droned comfortably on,

pushing the small craft up the face of the wave, and through it. Shouting towards the open sea he said 'Tom, um goun ta altur course any minute, tell they boays ta ang un'

He had planned to leave the alteration in course for another five minutes, but after the last wave had hit the boat Reg brought the action forward.

The lifeboat had to be manoeuvred from its position of pushing into the teeth of the gale to turning around to be pushed along from behind so that it could follow the coast line to where the merchant vessel had sent up distress rockets. There would be one critical moment when the lives of the crew would hang in the balance and the survival of the lifeboat would hinge.

For the best part of a minute the lifeboat would be beam on to the raging sea and gale. Instead of the boat moving forward it would be vulnerable to a wave hitting the side of the boat and capsizing it.

Reg Barbary would have to make a judgment and his judgment would be based on the observations of his enemy. Observations made since leaving the harbour at St Ives.

There was now a huge sea running, huge by any seaman's experience, but it had a pattern to it and Reg believed he had read the pattern. His only anxiety, the one element that was unpredictable, was the violence of the gusting Easterly wind.

The small craft broke through the top of a wave giving the coxswain a view of the line of the next it would encounter. Talking to himself he said 'Rite Vi, thus is it, maid!' Turning the wheel hard to Port and cutting back to half speed he shouted at the same time, 'Cummin bout!'

In the lee of the trough of the wave the boat went side on to the crest of it before he pushed the lever into maximum forward revolutions. Seconds later the boat shuddered and shook until the propeller started to bite into the water and by the time the wind hit them again it was blowing onto the stern of the lifeboat, sending it racing into the next wall of water.

Reg smiled to himself as he thought 'Tha rest I caan mannage, but thaat were a difficult wan Vi un now mistake, en am pleased ta gaat shod ov em.'

He glanced at his compass before adding 'Latitude 40° 50'

north. Longitude 05° 12' west, shood bring as jus bove tha poor beggars un trouble, weth wan moore chaang ov coorse.'

Passing The Carracks rocks a mile on his Port side he altered course and set two of the crew to watch from the bow.

****

Vehicles were parked haphazardly along the road sides and in gateways. Anna had never seen so many in the village as she stepped out of the Morris, fifty yards from the Tinners Arms at ten past nine and struggled to open the back door of the car against the strong press of wind.

She saw men and women talking in huddled groups behind whatever wind barrier was close. Cars, lorries and tractors acted like buttresses and many who were unable to find immediate shelter were bent almost double like the old pine trees that lined up behind the pub.

Mabena Nancekivell saw Anna and waved frantically to her, her words lost on the wind. She was in the relative shelter of the entrance to the pub together with several others handing out mugs of tea.

Managing a smile, the wife of the pub landlord said 'Anna. Goodness me, woss a dreadful night tis bin, tis good ta see ee.'

Nodding, and umming an answer while grabbing a mug of hot sweet tea all in one she took a drink before saying 'In St Ives they seem to think the ship is a big one with lots of men onboard. The bus I was on had to stop by the parish church and turn around because of the heavy sea in the harbour and the waves breaking over the road. They're putting sand bags in front of the houses and shops as they think it could get worse at high tide.'

Anna continued, 'Everyone is worried about the lifeboat which was launched. There were a lot of wives and relatives waiting around the lifeboat house, so feeling pretty useless there I thought I may be of some use here, I begged a lift, so here I am.'

Shaking her head slowly before she spoke Mabena said 'Sum

ov tha men av gon ta coast gard station, Ter is down bay tha Chapel waiting weth Eli Bolitho an is tractur ta take tha cliff rescue gear down un case tha lifeboat caant get ta um.'

'Mabena, do you have any bandages or perhaps a bed sheet I can take and cut up?' Handing the jug of tea to a neighbour she took her through into the empty pub where she helped Anna gather supplies that could be used which were then put into a khaki haversack.

When Anna returned to the door of the pub two of the army land girls she had met earlier in the summer and in the bar since, were waiting for her. 'Ma'am, Mavis told me you were here, we've brought all the field dressings we have, can we help?'

Gratefully Anna replied, 'Yes please, and you both seem to be dressed for the weather, let's go down to the Methodist chapel and see what's going on.'

A dozen men were gathered in the shelter of the chapel hall surrounding a man sat on a pew with a cup of tea in his hand. Terry Nancekivell greeted Anna and the army land girls with a warm smile that quickly faded as he nodded in the direction of the puffing man who was the centre of attention before he said to them 'Dave Petherick run bake frum tha coastguard station close ta Zennur Ead. He saw tha ship on tha rocks, firm lik, an being battered lik hell bay tha sea summin terrible. Us is waiting for the coastguard men ta arrive frum Sennen with tha cliff rescue equipment an us ill use tha tractur to get ta Carnelloe Cliffs.'

Like many organisations since the outbreak of war the coastguard service was now part of the armed forces. From cliff top lookout posts around all the country they provided a constant lookout not only for ships in distress but for enemy aircraft, submarines and early warning of invasion, their pre-war blue outfits now replaced by khaki battledress and rifles when available.

The three women set off for the coastguard station with four men from the village. To Anna it was a familiar walk, past the Tinners Arms and the church through the cow pats of the dairy farm into the narrow lane leading to the coast a quarter of a mile away.

At first the high stone and earth hedges provided a thankful barrier to the walkers. The noise of the wind raging above meant they had to shout to each other to be heard but the ancient stone boundaries protected them from the power of the storm and they made quick progress. The protection stopped as the farmed land gave way to the open sweep of the coast.

The first flurry of sleet and rain hit the group with such a force it took their breath away and stopped them in their tracks before they scurried back to the shelter of the wall, the coastguard station was visible only thirty or so yards away. Anna decided to make a run for the station, leaving the others in the shelter of the hedges.

The wind came in gusts of sixty or seventy miles an hour, making her crouch and bend double until she reached the station hut that was surrounded by sandbags on all sides apart from the one facing the sea in front and the coastline spreading out to the West.

Screened from the direct flow of the storm on one side of the hut Anna stopped to get her breath and look down the coastline and the wreck. At first it seemed impossible that what she saw could have happened. Across Pendour Cove and Veor Cove a quarter of a mile away from her, a grey painted cargo ship, the size of a small liner, was laying across rocks that were partly submerged in the broiling, foaming sea.

Waves weighing hundreds of tons crashed down onto the decks and against the hull of the stranded ship sending a series of shattering metallic echoes across the water which could be heard clearly above the din of the screaming wind.

The rocks the ship had foundered on were the jagged fingers of a headland two hundred feet high that sloped gradually downwards towards the sea like a huge toothed wedge. Thousands of years of tides and storms had eroded the base of the promontory that jutted into the sea to form the trap the cargo ship had been blown onto.

Stuck firmly between the rocks the bow of the ship was a hundred feet from the land which was being pounded by the waves that passed over the stricken ship, sending white spray towards the brown remnants of the autumn heather and gorse bushes that covered the sloping headland.

The two army land girls bounced into the void between the sand bags and the hut next to Anna, looking at the ship one of them said 'My God, this is terrible, do you know what is going to happen, ma'am?'

Swapping places with them she shouted back 'No, but you both stay under cover and I'll try and find out.'

Inside the small building were two men in army greatcoats, two others in battledress, all staring towards Pendour Cove and the approaching sea. 'Excuse me' she said to the four khaki clad backs 'Could I speak to whoever is in charge.'

Glancing around briefly before returning to look out of the window through his binoculars one of the men said 'Andrews, Captain Andrews, how can I help?

Peering over the shoulder of the captain she said, 'I'm Sister Jack, Captain, from the QA's in Falmouth, I have two assistants outside; can we help in any way?'

Without turning and indicating with his elbow he said, 'Squeeze in here Sister, there's a spare pair of binoculars in front of you, look away from the ship about a hundred yards out to sea.'

Loud gusts of wind shook the wooden hut and through the rain and sleet that lashed the glass in front of them and ran down it like a waterfall Anna saw what the men were looking at.

Momentarily she stopped breathing in an effort to keep her body still and focus on the dancing shape of the St Ives lifeboat as it forced its way through the mountainous waves like a cork in a fast-moving stream, towards the cargo vessel and the crew of the ship.

******

Reg Barbary had no time to look anywhere other than at the vessel that lay in front of him, and at the rocks she was skewered on. He leaned his head towards Tom Jenkins as he shouted into his ear 'Dan an Fred av rigged up the rocket launcher to fire a line to the poor buggers when you want to

Reg.'

The Cox took a quick glance over the stern of the lifeboat at the following sea before returning his stare forward and answering his deputy 'Ay Tom, good. Us av less thaan an half hour ta get tha crew ovv fore tha tide turns. Aftur thet us wont av nuff watur. I'm goin inside tha tew rocks rite head, tell tha lads to bay reedy ta fire a line ta em when I says. Us ought ta av thray lines ta her iv us can, see how ee goes.'

The lifeboat motored under the stern of the stricken ship and the point between the rocks he was aiming for. The pummelling the ship was receiving from the sea was already breaking her back and visible cracks were appearing in the hull of the vessel that towered above the rescue boat.

Pushing the control throttle ahead the last half inch he reached the final capacity of power the diesel engines were able to produce, forcing the little craft between the rocks and into the lee of calmer water the crippled ship had made.

The cargo vessel now formed a barrier between the oncoming sea and the land. In the newly created lake violent surges of confused foaming water rose up to the level of the slanting deck like the tentacles of an octopus trying to reach the sheltering crew before dropping back thirty feet or more.

As waves smashed into the seaward side of the ship, mountains of sea water and spray flashed over the decks into the lake and onto the lifeboat itself. The pounding of the waves echoed through the ship like a hammer hitting an anvil.

With a nod from the Cox the bowmen fired the rocket lines towards the after deck of the ship. After five attempts only two of the lines had been retrieved and made secure. Reg Barbary now had another danger to contend with.

One of the large cargo handling derricks of the vessel had been torn off the deck of the ship and there were spars and wire rigging laying semi submerged under the water, close to the hull.

Time was now against the lifeboat. It seemed like early dawn as the grey overcast day refused to throw more light onto the scene but Reg looked at his watch. It was eleven in the morning and in ten minutes the tide would start to recede and the lifeboat would be trapped behind the wreck.

If that were to happen he knew that they would all perish. The water level would go down but that would not stop the raging wind from sending wave after wave towards the ship and the shoreline, the small boat would be swamped and driven onto the rocks below the cliffs.

There was no need for orders, the crew were ready at their stations and waiting now for their Coxswain to make the next move. Manoeuvring between the submerged and floating debris he waited for the next rush of water and moved full ahead with his engines towards the vessel, bringing her side onto the ship.

The surge of water lifted the boat towards the deck, thirty feet above, as a clean breach of sea water cascaded over the vessel. One error now would be their last but Reg held the lifeboat firm and as they got to within six feet of the deck level two of the waiting crew slid down the ropes and were met by the lifeboat men and quickly bundled onboard. Two others followed and another three, perhaps sensing how critical the time factor was, jumped from the leaning deck, crashing into the cockpit below.

Reg threw his engines into reverse for two or three seconds before going full ahead away from the ship. He circled the fallen debris and came back again to repeat the same manoeuvre. This time eight crew made the dash for safety but two of them misjudged the movement, leaving their jump too late. One landed on the rail of the lifeboat with his feet in the water and was quickly pulled aboard. The other man fell between the side of the ship and under the lifeboat, disappearing from view.

The Coxswain had no time to look for the man his only concern now was the falling level of the water between the rocks he had negotiated to get to the ship. Shouting at the top of his voice he said 'Laast time bout lads'.

He knew it was wrong, there should have been no last time, but he could see the milling crew still on the deck of the ship clinging to stanchions and anything that enabled them to brace themselves against the waves ripping over and around them, waiting.

He was now committed and as the lifeboat approached the

side of the ship he knew that he was going too fast, but speed was the only weapon he had left. His lifeboat hit the side of the ship hard, there was a dull thud of wood banging against the riveted metal plates of the ship, and a top section of the bow crumpled and splintered in a loud grinding sound as the tidal push lifted them upwards.

For the next few seconds Reg could do nothing. Close to the top of the lift more crew jumped and slid down the lines that had been fired to them by rocket. Nine saved this time and he could see more under the after deck shelter.

His mouth was dry and despite the intense cold he found himself sweating under the heavy oil skins. Pulling away from the ship he started to loop around the obstacles in front of him and bring his boat about to face the wind and in line with the two rocks that when he went through them earlier had been welcome collaborators in his battle, but had now changed sides and represented a formidable danger.

Aloud but unheard he shouted 'Vi, tis bleedy close maid, but I as ta go!' Judgment and his engine speed was all he had. He idled his engine against the wind and mushy water and waited.

A swirl of sea funnelled between the rocks whose sides had become clearly visible, it wasn't enough, and he knew it. To go now would mean the boat getting stuck in a valley of stone and the next wave that raced through would swamp them, the one after that would toss the boat and the men in it onto the sharp jagged faces of the rocks and into the broiling water.

A curl of white on top of a wave approaching the escape route made his eyes lighten 'Ere we is me ansum, cum on, cum on' he shouted into the screeching wind. There was no going back now.

The Coxswain pushed hard at the engine throttle to give him maximum power and the propellers bit into the cold seawater sending the boat towards the valley of rocks and the approaching wave.

The bow hit the bottom of solid rock like a train and sent a shudder through the keel and the hull. The men in the open cock pit were pitched violently forward by the impact but Reg had expected it, the last ounce of strength in his body given to riding the jolt and keeping the wheel in his hands tight and not yielding to one single movement. He saw the water hit the bow and he knew it was over.

He smiled and shouted into the driving sleet 'Us won Vi!, Us won ma darlin! We beat em!'

The boat struggled to keep its position in the valley with the sea racing past but his engines gained the upper hand and the boat rose higher on the water and inched its way between the two stone pinnacles and into the open sea.

Tom Jenkins struggled over to Reg Barbary and shouted 'Propur job Cox, rite propur job. Tis gawin ta bay a pint or two from me an tha boays later I can tel ee!'

Keeping his fixed stare ahead he shouted back 'Tel em if thay bys tha beer, I'l put tha rum un tha bar!'

******

The coastguard lookout hut erupted in shouts and hand claps as the onlookers to the battle that had been played out in front of them saw the lifeboat escape.

Private Jim Boyde, a part-time member of the coastguard between running a fish monger's business in Sennen shook his head saying 'That was one of the finest pieces of seamanship and bravery I have ever seen. To spot that broad of water on the lee ward side of the ship and get in and out so quickly was bloody magnificent.'

They all watched the dot of a boat push a steady path through the wind and waves that were now in front of them. Visible one moment, engulfed by water the next the lifeboat held it's rolling, dipping course for home.

'Will he be able to get back for the crew that are still onboard?' it was Anna who had asked the question.

The private replied 'No Sister, their job is over, the next high-water mark will be towards midnight tonight and if those unfortunate lads that are left are not off within the hours we have left of daylight, then I'm afraid they are finished.'

Captain Andrews picked up the field telephone that was in front of him and vigorously turned the small handle on the side of the machine and waited before speaking into it 'Andrews here, I need to speak to Major Pearce'. Waiting with the telephone in his hand he suddenly said 'Yes Sir, the lifeboat got away from the wreck safely but we believe with some damage and certainly some casualties on board. Yes Sir, I can see from here that the Sennen men have arrived above the vessel and are erecting a Breeches Buoy to try to get the rest of the crew off' after a pause he continued 'Not sure Sir, we think around twenty got into the lifeboat, one was lost trying to get on, and we think there are another ten to fifteen still onboard.'

As he put the field telephone down a bang was heard above the noise outside. One of the other lookouts said, 'They've fired a rocket line across to the ship, Sir.' Looking at the scene across the cove the captain in charge of the operation said to Anna 'I think your services could be very welcome sister in a short while.'

'What are they going to do, Sir?' Anna asked.

Handing her his binoculars the captain explained 'Take a look at the last outcrop of rock before the headland shears away almost vertically onto the rocks and into the sea below' picking up another pair of binoculars he carried on 'Can you see the group of men now, just back from the edge, struggling with the three lengths of timber a bit longer than they are? The first two lengths are now in position forming a triangle that faces the sea, here comes the next piece, and my God, it must be a struggle in the conditions, here it comes. Right, it looks as if they have it secured. Now you can see the three lengths form a simple pyramid shape.'

Another loud bang echoed across the cove above the sound of the storm as a second rocket shot into the air from the headland above the ship. A lookout reported 'They got that one Sir by the look of it.'

Without putting down the glasses the captain said 'Good, yes I see it. Sister if you look towards the after deck where the crew are taking cover, two of them are hauling on the light line that was sent over to them on the end of the rocket. At the end of it will be a Tail Block fastened to a length of much stronger rope which they will lash to the rail or mast. Here they go, there're tying it to the stern derrick mast'

'Through that block is a continuous loop of rope. On that loop you can see the chaps on the headland have attached a second very strong line which the crew are now pulling across.'

There was silence as the efforts and progress of the two crewmen were watched. They had been lucky with the first line, judging the speed of oncoming waves accurately and dodging between them.

This time they were caught in the open and both were lost to the observers under a wall of rushing white water. The fishmonger was first to speak 'Christ, one of the poor sods has been washed overboard.'

There was another silence as they watched two more crew clamber up onto the exposed after deck and run towards the mast. As they reached it another wave came crashing over them, but this time they had some shelter from the thick base of the derrick, and held on.

The three men untied the second line from the loop and lashed it higher up the mast before retreating to the bottom of the derrick. One of the men, who they later learnt was the captain of the vessel, took out a red ensign flag from a pocket, and raised it up and down with his hand three times as an affirmative signal to tell the rescuers they could now 'haul away'.

Turning to Anna the captain said 'Sister, I have a feeling your services may be needed soon. The Breeches Buoy will be attached to the loop now and hopefully we can start the painfully slow process of bringing as many men as possible over one at a time before nightfall and the tide turns'

'We have one stretcher and an assortment of field dressings that you can take and Jim will lead you from here, the wind has eased with the tide but is still gusting at sixty miles an hour plus, so be extra careful when you pass Horseback Zawn between here and the ship, and good luck.'

There was an army lorry parked back from the coastguard hut and a steady trickle of men, civilian as well as army, carrying ropes and ladders along the narrow path that skirted the cliffs around the coves.

The whole rescue apparatus had now been firmly secured to the ground and to nearby rocks by large metal rings and heavy metal stakes that had been driven into the unyielding surfaces by men with heavy sledge hammers.

From the pyramid of wooden posts rope lines now stretched to the mast on the stern of the trapped ship over fifty yards away and a hundred feet above the rocks and swirling sea.

From the shelter of a granite boulder only twenty feet away from the wood scaffold Anna watched as four of the rescuers started to pass the looped line through their hands with the Breeches Buoy that had been attached to the loop being sent over to the men on the ship for the first time. One of the rescue team she recognised as Simon Tremayne.
The Breeches Buoy had been attached to the loop and was being sent over to the men on the ship for the first time.

She was surprised by the simplicity of this man-made Angle of Mercy that glided silently towards the stricken crew members huddled under the cover of the after deck shelter.

Seen by most people on all ships, boats, around beaches and swimming pools a normal life saving ring painted white with three bands of bright red around it was suspended by four separate ropes, less than two yards long, from a block that was attached to the top line that stretched from the derrick mast of the ship through the pyramid scaffold to the headland. Passing through the same block was the continuous loop of rope that ran through the eye of the lower jackstay block the crew had fastened to the derrick mast.

Hanging below the life saving ring swung the template of a pair of men's breeches cut off at the knees, made from strong ships canvass. A separate steadying line was paid out by another man with a dozen others waiting behind him.

'These people are really well organised' Anna thought to herself as she watched the last means of escape for the crew move steadily towards the wrecked ship. It had almost reached the men when a big wave hit the bow of the vessel with a loud clanging bang.

In front of everyone on the headland the whole of the bow section front half of the ship seemed to open up as the back of the ship was finally broken and the forward half of the bow section skewed away from the main body leaving a gapping, jagged hole.

For a fraction of a second the men hauling the buoy towards the ship stopped as they looked through the driving sleet and rain at the ship that had now broken into two separate parts. Quickly the hauling continued with more vigour until the Breeches Buoy was grabbed by a crew member standing under the derrick mast.

The first of the twenty crewmen left onboard left the shelter of the bottom of the mast and pulled himself up between the two secured lines and eased himself into the centre of the life ring and was supported by the canvass breeches with his legs dangling under them.

With the vertical movement of the same red flag to signal their readiness the men on shore started to pull at the looped rope and bring the suspended seaman slowly across.

The Captain of the merchant ship had chosen the position of the link to the headland well and he was one of the three men under the mast directing his side of the rescue and as the first of his crew started his journey to safety, the space below the shelter of the mast was taken by another of the waiting sailors. Had he chosen the bow section for the rescue attempt most of the men would by now be dead.

Pulling the collar of her army greatcoat above level of her ears and the start of her hat, Anna scrambled over to the nearest of the two men who were controlling the rescue operations on the headland and above the roar of the wind that seemed louder the closer she got to the edge of the rocky platform she shouted to him that she was a nurse and asked if there was a doctor present.

It was not clear if a doctor was around or not but ambulances had been told to stand by and park at Zennor for any casualties. Back behind the shelter of the granite rock the nursing sister signalled with her arms to the two land army girls above her to follow her down. The girls came scrambling down the safety rope dragging a stretcher and their scant supplies.

It was difficult to count the number of people on the headland, but it seemed to be more than a hundred, with a balance of servicemen and local men and several women. Twenty or so of the volunteers would pull on the loop rope on the signal from the man stood under the wood scaffold. A slow, steady movement that quickened as the legs of the seaman came within reach of the rocky headland and the outstretched arms of two coastguards.

With practiced ease the two burly men plucked the crew member out of the buoy and onto the ground where another rescuer wrapped a grey blanket around the shoulders of the thankful seaman.

The breeches buoy was now on its way back to the ship as one of the rescue coordinators squat besides the first crewman ashore with his arm around his shoulders talking to him. Anna could see him nodding as the man spoke into his ear. Standing up his place was taken by two other men who eased the crewman up from the ground and started to lead him slowly towards the guide rope that led to the tractors. The exhaustion of the seaman was clear as his legs buckled and his helpers took the man's full weight by placing their arms under his.

The officer signalled to Anna for her to speak to him and she struggled over the rocks to the exposed platform. The cold sleet hurt as it hit her face and she was glad to be able to turn away from it when she reached him 'The man with the flag is the ship's captain. He told the first chap across to tell us that the next four men are all badly injured and will require treatment. There are now nineteen men to be brought across, I only hope we have time, the stern section is getting a tremendous battering and could shift at any time.'

She stood with the officer being buffeted by gusts of wind and watched as a wounded man was carried across the exposed deck of the ship. The tide was approaching its lowest point and the waves that were crashing into the hull sent spray and water over the top of the tilting rail towards the men but for the moment the crew were safe from the waves engulfing them on the deck.

Before going back to the shelter of the boulder Anna had asked for assistance in carrying the wounded back to the tractors. The officer instructed a team of soldiers and civilians to help her and for the tractor drivers to act as ambulances.

The rescued man was unconscious as they lifted him out of the harness and onto the stretcher. Anna looked at the seaman and felt for a pulse. There was none. Behind her wind break she took another look at him before telling the officer that he was dead.

The next three crew were all badly injured but alive. They were taken back up the hill and placed into the trailer of the tractor Anna had first noted. One of the men needed help in breathing and she cleared his airways while instructing the two land girls to assist the other casualties. The makeshift ambulance started the journey over the fields towards Zennor village.

There were two ambulances waiting next to the Methodist Chapel, each with a civilian nurse and a local doctor stood in the entrance, quick to look at the injured as they arrived.

The three men were carefully taken off the trailer and put into one ambulance while Anna spoke to the doctor about the condition of the men.

The familiar voice of Mabena said 'Anna, av sum hot tay, tha other maids av a cup, ee looks propur chilled.'

She took the thick mug and swallowed the warm, sweet liquid quickly before saying 'Nothing ever tasted so good Mabena, thank you! Can I have another cup before we go back?' her cup was full to the brim before she finished the sentence.

Climbing up onto the tractor's trailer the three women sat on bales of blankets and more stretchers that were needed at the headland. As the tractor moved away more sandwiches were pressed into their hands.

Moving closer to the two army land girls Anna shouted, 'I feel so much better after the tea and a bite to eat, are you both alright?'

Both of the young girls nodded a 'yes' as they munched a sandwich with one hand and held onto the rail of the trailer with the other, swaying as the tractor bounced its way over the ploughed fields, before it came to a halt by a gatepost, the engine idling noisily.

The driver looked back and shouted to Anna 'Thams cummin

up weth sum ov tha cru.' A tractor and trailer passed through the opening and past them. She counted seven men wrapped in blankets that covered the tops of their bodies and heads.

The violent buffeting of the wind started again as they left the last cultivated field and shelter of stone hedges for the open heath land of the headland.

Mavis, one of the land army girls, said to Anna 'When we were having a cup of tea our tractor driver told me he thought this was one of the worst storms he can remember. He believes that some of the crew will have to stay onboard overnight and wait to be rescued tomorrow.'

The leader of the rescue team had told Anna that low water time was at five twenty. Looking at her watch she thought 'Less than two hours before the tide starts its journey back.' Turning her head inside the high collar of her greatcoat and standing up slightly she could see down the headland and into Veor Cove without being hit in the face by the rain that came with the gusting wind.

A clear rim of rocks and stones was now visible in the cove with the rolling surf of each wave ending their journey in a foaming white mush on the grey black surface of boulders.

Anna could hear as well as see the pounding the ship was still getting. The hollow metallic thuds of each boring wave gave a cruel echo around the cove. It was like watching a person being beaten by a gang of thugs as their victim lay helpless on the ground.

Once the tractor had stopped Anna and the two helpers scrambled down the guide rope dragging two stretchers and blankets, back to the shelter of the granite boulder. Two more crew were being helped up the headland by soldiers and local men and another was half way across from the ship in the Breeches Buoy when the sound of a wave hitting the stern section was followed by shouting and the cries of the men hauling the man to safety.

The three women in the shelter of the boulder watched in horror as the whole stern section of the ship started to tilt towards them slackening the loop rope and plunging the man in the breeches buoy onto the rocks and swirling water below.

Men dashed from all directions to help pull on the loop rope and to take in the slack from the top line and reinstate the pulley system.

Standing back from the wood scaffold and the men pulling the on the Breeches Buoy Anna waited until the crew man was lifted out from the cork ring like a broken rag doll and laid carefully down on the ground.

There was nothing she could do apart from checking to find signs of life she knew had gone has soon as he had been dashed on the rocks and then covering him with a blanket.

Each battering wave now made the remains of the ship shift slightly with a grinding shudder that made the angle of the deck lean ever more towards the land. The Breeches Buoy was now back under the derrick mast.

The captain frantically waved the red ensign flag from side to side, indicating that he needed time before hauling restarted. The rescuers on the headland watched as two of the men left the mast base to be replaced by others, one of them lowering himself into the buoy before the captain moved the flag in an up and down movement and the buoy started its journey away from the ship and across the open expanse of rocks and sea.

The officer in charge of the operation guessed what was going through the minds of the remaining crew. He shouted instructions to a group of men away from the headland platform that were lost to Anna by the wind.

The men ran behind the rescue apparatus with their own coils of rope, metal stakes and sledge hammers. As they moved past her she caught a glimpse of a familiar face, most of it hidden under an oil skin hat that was tied under his neck. Simon Tremayne managed a quick glance in her direction and a smile as he rushed past and disappeared from view.

Moving outside of her wind barrier she saw the men hammering two metal stakes into the hard ground, one was dressed in oil skins the other in a khaki uniform covered by a greatcoat. Both sets of garments flapped like flags on a mast head as the wind beat against the materials.

As soon as the stakes were in place a coil of rope was secured to each of them and one end thrown the hundred feet down the face of the cliff onto the dull black rocks of the cove.

The nurse watched as four of the men, including Simon, turned their backs to the wind and let themselves down the cliff, passing the rope through their hands as they descended.

A third rope followed the men down. Attached to it was a metal rocket launcher and tripod. The first men on the ground untied the launcher and let the rope return to the top. Soon after two red rockets followed and finally two boxes of line.

It had been a shock to see him, and her shock turning to concern as she watched the four men erect the tripod out of reach of the breakers. Her attention was then diverted as one more crew man was being lifted out of the buoy and placed on the ground by his helpers, his legs unable to carry his own weight. He was a big, heavy man and it had taken three of the rescuers to lift him from the buoy.

The nursing sister looked into the face of the seaman sat crossed legged and now wearing a blanket around his head and shoulders. His face was covered in lines of white sea salt and his eyes ringed with red circles.

Smiling before shouting into his covered ear Anna said 'You're safe now, do you have any injuries?'

His hand caught hold of Anna's and he held it firmly, gently, saying nothing he looked straight ahead as tears cut lines through the salt on his face.

After a moment she said 'We'll get you into the warmth, everything will be alright you really are safe now.' She signalled to the men close to the guide line rope leading to the tractors who came over and eased the sailor to his feet before leading the silent survivor away.

Repeated sounds of grinding metal followed the pounding waves and as she watched the next crew member come to within twenty feet of the headland the whole of the stern section of the stranded vessel gave a mighty gasp and turned slowly on its side and collapse like a pack of stacked playing cards onto the rocks as the riveted metal plates of the hull gave way under the weight of tons of sea water.

The man in the breeches buoy was thrust into the side of the cliff but his rescuers were quickly able to haul him the few feet to the ledge of the rescue platform. Anna was close to the edge when he was dragged to safety and pulled out of the buoy harness. He had the same exhausted look of all the rescued men but managed a smile and a 'Thank you' to each person his eyes came into contact with.

Five crew were now left, all in extreme danger. After a hand signal from the officer to the men on the shore line they heard the loud sound of a rocket being fired, followed quickly by a second. More men and equipment now descended the cliff to the rocky beach below, including those in charge of the operation.

Those left at the top of the cliff could now do nothing but watch the final attempt to rescue the stranded crew. The constant wash of waves coming over the ship and surging through the gap that had appeared between the two halves of the merchant vessel, foamed wildly over the tops of sharp rocks and deep pools that lay between the crew and the tantalisingly close shoreline.

The wind still continued to blow in strong gusts and it carried the first rocket and line out of reach of the waiting crew, the second line was caught and they started to pull it across. There no time left for a top line. One loop line was all they would be able to use, and as soon as it was secured the men onshore started to send out the buoy.

Several cries of anguish left the group standing on the headland as they watched one of the crew climb down a rope he had thrown over the side and tread water until a wave went past. He struck out to swim the hundred feet towards the men on the shoreline. He was followed by a second man close behind.

'It must be tempting' Anna thought 'They can see the land and the rescue team on the water line and they look as though they are strong swimmers.' The sailor in the breeches buoy was being hauled from the ship his legs touching the sea below until he seemed to be dragged through it by the brute force of the men on shore.

He overtook the two swimming men and it was then that the observers on the headland could see that they were as good as dead. The drag of the outgoing tide was too strong and both men looked as though they were swimming up a fast flowing waterfall, getting nowhere.

A wave broke like a detonating bomb against the hull of the ship and they were submerged by the weight and mass of sea water as it travelled over the deck and on top of them.

Both men surfaced and tried again to swim to shore but another surge of foaming water overwhelmed and engulfed them. Anna and the other rescuers watched helplessly and in silence as the sailors were swept like corks in the racing water and thrown against a blackened ridge of rocks.

Another wall of water reached them as they tried desperately to escape the battering. The men were enveloped by the frenzied grasping white sea, and disappeared completely.

The young woman who had come to love the coast, and the sea that was part of it, gazed through tears past the crippled ship to the grey heaving water and said out loud 'I don't know you, you aren't the same sea that has given me so much pleasure, so much comfort, no, today you are cruel, unkind. You wanted your sacrifice and now you have it. Everything here is alien today, ugly, cold and alien, why don't you show some compassion. They were words which no one heard as the gale swept them away like the struggling sailors.

The next two crewmen were met half way by the rescue men up to their chests in the sea. With no top line attached the breeches buoy became unstable as the crew reached the water line and they were in danger of being washed out of the protective ring. Each rescuer worn a harness with a line attached to the back of it, and several times Anna watched as the men, which included Simon Tremayne, were overwhelmed by a wave and dragged under the sea. She held her breath each time as he disappeared from view but was expertly pulled to safety by the men on the shoreline.

In the fading light the last man to get into the breeches buoy from the merchant ship was its captain. Two of the rescue team reached for him in the water and Simon formed part of the line of men ashore that pulled the rope bringing the exhausted man onto the shore.

Rope ladders had been lowered over the cliff face and harnesses put around the captain and crew to help haul them up the vertical surface to the rocky platform of the headland.

Anna and the two land girls met the crew from the ship as they reached the top. As blankets were put around them in place of the harnesses Anna asked each if they were injured.

The master of the ship had a blood-soaked bandage tied around his hand and a gash above his right eye. The blood had mingled with white salt and had long ago congealed. 'Sir, it will be easier to help you when you get to the ambulances in the village, can you make it?'

After a flicker of a smile he said, 'Ah yes Sister, thank you' looking back towards his stricken ship he added 'After that, I should say we can manage just about anything.'

Before he left the headland with the help of two local men the captain sat in the shelter of the granite boulder and spoke to the last man to reach the top. Anna needed to apply a field dressing to an injury on the back of the crewman's head. Speaking to the captain she said 'He needs a stitch or two Sir, but I will patch him up and stay with him until we get to the village.'

After she had finished Anna let one of the land army girls put a blanket around the man and stay talking with him while she went towards the group of rescuers who had climbed up from the beach below and included Simon.

Like the ship's crew many of the rescuers were wrapped in dry blankets and several were making their way towards the path leading to the tractors above.

In the dim conditions Anna forced her way forward against the gale until she reached Simon. Using him as a wind break she looked up and said, 'Are you alright, do you have any injuries Simon?'

Rubbing both eyes, he blinked and replied, 'Banged my head on a rock, but apart from being really cold, I'm fine Anna.'

Bringing his head towards her she looked at the wound before saying 'You ought to see a doctor, the wound isn't too bad but it does need a stitch, but you could have concussion so you must get yourself checked out, promise?'

'Hot drink and then a doctor, I promise! I'll see you in the village afterwards Anna.'

The leader of the rescue operation interrupted the conversation as he shouted to Anna 'Thank you Sister. You and the two girls have been a great help, you must all be frozen and wet through, but thank you.'

Anna thanked the man for his words and watched him as he started the climb up the slope with Simon Tremayne.

The three women and the injured seaman sat in the trailer of the tractor as it started the last bumpy trip back to Zennor. It was only now that they all realised how cold and soaked through they actually were.

******

A blast of heat hit Anna when she pushed against the door of the Tinners and guided herself around the blackout curtain into the bar that was packed with more people than she had ever seen in the local pub before.

She was cold and the sudden warmth of the room made her feel light headed. Anna eased her way to the end fire that had space in front of it. The burning, crackling logs radiated a warmth that made her fingers ache in pain as the circulation came back to them and turning her back to the warmth she closed her eyes and let the heat penetrate the wet clothes she stood in.

Opening her eyes she knew she was not yet able to function normally and she nodded, while at the same time trying to form a smile, at some familiar faces through a fog of cigarette smoke. 'I'll be alright in a moment' she told herself. 'I just need a few moments by the fire.'

Sam Trembath, a mining supervisor who worked for the Tremayne family handed Anna a glass, saying 'Miss, I think you've earned this, and it will bring a bit of warmth to you.'

'Thank you' is what Anna wanted to say but she could only manage a nod in thanks before she took a sip from the glass, which was a mixture of port and brandy.

Her eyes began to focus around the room. She was relieved to see that her own bedraggled appearance was shared by most of the people in the pub.

She was soaked to her skin. Her clothes were made heavy by the weight of water soaked into them. She was exhausted, but feeling had come back to her hands and face, but her back and shoulders felt cold and she ached as she moved her body.

Anna had no idea how long she stood with her back to the fire until blinking her tired eyes, she found herself being spoken to by Simon Tremayne.

She knew he was close to her when he spoke, but he seemed far away as if he were at the end of a tunnel and it sounded as though he was shouting.

He looked wild with his face and hair a mixture of dried blood and lines of white salt from the sea, 'We should leave now, Anna' she heard Simon say. 'I'll take you back to the hospital.' As she put her glass down his hand cupped her elbow and he led her through an avenue of faces.

They walked the short distance to where Simon had parked his car. A return to the damp wind made Anna start to shiver as she sat in the front seat. The vehicle climbed the hill out of the village and Simon glanced quickly at Anna before saying 'I share my house with my sister, but she stays with our parents during the middle of the week. If you like you can have the spare room and use her clothes while yours dry, and I will take you back to Falmouth whenever you want to go.'

Anna had not uttered a single word since she had entered the pub. Now she turned to look at him before saying 'I think you made a mistake in the Tinners, Simon. A lot of your friends will get the wrong idea and I think my going to your house will make the mistake greater.'

Staring ahead into the dark while negotiating the twisting road he replied, 'No Anna, I made no mistake, of that I am absolutely sure' his voice had returned to normal, his breathing back to a regular rhythm and after a brief pause he added 'We saw men die today. I have never been close to death, never been as close as I was today to being killed myself. No Anna, no mistake.'

Two granite gate post marked the start of a gravel drive to Simon's house. The car was parked in his garage and after helping Anna out and closing the set of double garage doors, he guided her towards the house through the darkness.

After closing the front door and adjusting the blackout curtain Simon switched on a dim hall light. The switch was to the side of a wooden hat and coat stand which had a mirror at its centre.

He caught sight of his own reflection in the mirror and took a deep intake of air into his lungs before saying 'My God boy, you look terrible'

Looking at Anna he said, 'I had no idea of the state I was in, I must have looked a freighting sight when I walked into the pub.'

Smiling at him Anna just nodded agreement as she looked at the cut above his right eye. The blood had congealed, but before doing so had run into his hair and down the side of his face.

'How very fortunate that you should happen to invite a nurse into your home, Mr Tremayne. You should have had a couple of stitches, but I think we may be able to save you!'

He led Anna into the kitchen and quickly began to resuscitate the dampened fire of the kitchen range. Taking their outer coats he spread them on the backs of wooden chairs and then showed Anna the guest bedroom before giving her a selection of his sister's clothes.

On the way out of the room he said over his shoulder 'If you bring your wet things down to the kitchen we can spread them around and dry them off.'

Walking along the oak flooring of the landing to his own bedroom he threw his soaked cloths into a corner and put on a dry shirt and corduroy trousers before plunging his wet, cold feet into well worn slippers.

In the kitchen the fire had sprung to life as he opened the metal doors and the heat that came out quickly made the room warm and comfortable. Simon lit the five candles that sat on a shelf above the Cornish slab and switched off the main light leaving the room bathed in the yellow and red light.

He was across the hall in his office retrieving the bottle of whisky when he heard Anna open the door to the kitchen and he shouted 'Anna, you can hang your wet cloths on the drying rails above the range, I won't be a moment'.

By the time Simon came through the door of the kitchen Anna had spread her clothes out on the rails above the range and had settled herself in Christine's favourite chair, a yard from the red embers and crackling flames of the fire.

Simon thought that she was asleep as he pushed open the door but her head raised itself gently from her bridged hands as she turned it to face him before saying 'Simon, I've been thinking that my being here is going to cause you, and perhaps me, a lot of trouble, but I also have to say that perhaps you might just be right. We all live so close to death at the moment and the 'normal' suddenly isn't the 'normal' anymore. But please promise me no one will get hurt, because there's enough hurt around at the moment, and I don't want to be the cause of more.'

Kneeling down on the carpet in front of the fire Simon was almost level with her face before saying 'No hurt, just us two at this moment, and no more than that, I promise' He quietly added 'Would you like a whisky?' He was busy pouring a small measure before she answered 'Please.'

As he handed her the dimpled glass he chuckled when he noticed that she was wearing a skirt belonging to Christine, no shoes and an Arran sweater of his that would have given shelter to both Anna and his sister.

'I know' she said, as amused as he was 'it looks just too much, but inside here it's now dry and warm, thank you!'

She took a sip of whisky and let it warm her before taking another look at Simon, who was now sat on the floor with his back to the fire.

'Simon' she said looking at the cut on his forehead, 'I must have a look at that, do you have some hot water and some clean cloth that I can use to tidy you up?' After a quick search he brought back what was needed.

Anna patted the spot on the floor where she wanted her patient to sit and she sat on the edge of her chair which made her a little higher than Simon. Turning his head to one side with her hands she carefully examined the gash saying 'It's started to heal already, but I will have to clean the blood away and have another look, you had better take off your shirt'

She washed away the dried blood and sea water from his hair and face and gently cleaned his wound. In the absence of surgical spirit she dabbed a small amount of whisky into the cut which brought Simon's attention back from what Anna thought was a distant dream.

The 'Ouch' from Simon was followed by a smile and when Anna announced that he would mend well he said 'Thank you, Anna. That was very kind of you'

He took both her hands in his and brought them to his lips, and gently kissed them.

Never taking her eyes away from his Anna gently pulled her hands away and at the same time kissed him, a warm, long kiss.

Anna had made her decision. She crawled out of her borrowed clothes before kissing Simon again and they made love in the warmth and gently light of the fire.

Falmouth, 4th December 1941

Anna smiled to herself and felt good inside. She had honestly enjoyed their lovemaking of the night before. So much so that it was she who had clung to him this morning after he had gently woken her in the darkness.

The cold wind and drizzle was still blowing across Falmouth Bay and only the very palest of greys gave any hint that daylight was less than an hour away. Anna cupped his right ear in her left hand before kissing him on the cheek and whispering 'My next day off is Thursday, a week away, I'll be at the Tinner's, and Simon thank you for last night, after such a sad and horrible day it was lovely.'

The timing was bad. Sliding out of the front passenger seat and onto the narrow unlit pavement she almost fell onto her flat mate, Gail Moore.

Dressed in her own damp khaki trousers and the comfortable Arran sweater belonging to Simon, the rest of her belongings Anna had bundled up and were being carried under her arm.

Nursing Sister Gail Moore had just finished her stint of night duty. Even in the darkness before the dawn she was quick to notice the outline of the broad features of Simon and she was equally quick to propel Anna through the front door of the house where they both shared a flat.

Gail gave Anna a wry smile and said 'My God, Anna, for such a naughty girl you seem mighty pleased with yourself!

Like the proverbial cat that got the cream no less, will you please stop smiling, and while I take off my rather smelly uniform and you put your fresh one on, you must tell me all about it, and this time none of the prim and proper stuff I usually get from you, this time I've caught you out proper, and I want the rude and naughty bits!'

Glancing at her watch Anna replied, 'Gail I'm going to be late if I don't hurry on and I must get to work, but I will tell you tonight, I promise'

Adjusting her headdress in the mirror by the door of their flat Anna shouted to Gail 'I should be finished around six and I'll buy some fish and chips for both of us, and then we can talk, and talk, and talk, how does that sound?'

An unseen voice echoed back 'You ought to go to Confession you naughty girl, hold on though, do Jewish girls go to Confession?'

Anna just smiled and gently closed the door.

Smiling was something Anna did a lot as a nurse. She felt it important to the staff she was in charge of and certainly to the patients in her care, that her worries, depressions, or more recently her grief should not be transferred to them.

Today she felt especially happy and able to smile because she wanted to. 'Happy' she thought to herself, 'Now happy is something I have not been for a long time, in fact, not since I was with John in France, now that was happiness. A strong, fulfilling inner happiness. It really is a nice feeling to have back, even if perhaps, it is not going to last.'

The early grey sky of the morning stayed all day over the seaport but the violent gale force winds had subdued and now a fine cold rain fell as long as the murky daylight hours lasted, blown along by the south west winds that had swept in from the Atlantic and up past the Lizard point.

Anna had hardly noticed the weather conditions, and the day had flown past and no task had been too difficult or a problem. Today problems did not exist.

Mindful of times in the recent past when she had come home on Gail's day off to find her and Jan Thompson in various states of undress Anna now always made the simple operation of unlocking the door to their flat an exercise in loud noise and ample warning.

Tonight there was no need for such elaborate precautions, Gail Moore sat expectantly in the lounge on the sofa with an open bottle of sherry, one glass half full the other being filled as Anna entered the room to be greeted by the words 'I told Jan I had a frightful headache and got rid of him, come and sit down and have a drink, we can eat at the same time and you can tell me all about it.'

It had taken a little time for the two girls to trust each other, but over the past few months a trust had been cemented by both after careful testing. Despite her sometimes brash ways Gail had been a great comfort when Anna had come back from Plymouth after the blitz and news of Miriam's death.

Never able or willing to tell anyone the intimate details of their lovemaking Anna non-the-less kept Gail spellbound as she unfolded the story of their first meeting at the Tinners Arms, the subsequent meetings and of the extraordinary happenings of the cliff rescue and the events afterwards.

Shaking her head slowly from side to side Gail muttered 'Anna girl, you have got yourself into an almighty tangle here, if you don't mind my saying so. The Tremayne family is a powerful force to be reckoned with and the old battle axe of a mother is a formidable force on her own, so be careful'

Topping up her glass Gail held Anna's gaze, saying 'And, and, well come on, bloody hell Anna, what is he like in bed, I almost ripped Jan's cloths off this afternoon getting him between the sheets just thinking about what you two got up too last night, well?'

Breathing deeply, she said 'O Gail, I can't tell you everything that happen last night and this morning'

Interrupting immediately Gail said 'And this morning, you said, 'and this morning', bloody hell, go on, go on.'

Tutting out loud she continued 'Well he's, he's very gentle, very passionate, very warm, very, very….No Gail, I'm not saying any more, in fact I've said too much already, and you do know that I mean it, so please, no more.'

Blinking at Anna Gail said 'You said more than I thought you ever would and it all sounds wonderful, as well as rather dangerous to me, and besides, the chips are getting cold!'

A New Love

Zennor, 8th December 1941

It was gone four in the morning when Anna climbed into her bed. There had been two emergency operations at the hospital, both servicemen and both with complicated bullet and shrapnel wounds.

It was a well rehearsed contingency that started with a telephone call from a liaison officer of the SOE and the arrival of the wounded men together with several armed soldiers dressed in the camouflage suits. They would isolate the ward and operating theatre and stand guard outside them.

Anna had been looking forward to a day off, and after a few hours sleep and a walk back to the hospital, she would know if she was needed and her hopes would be realised or she would need to return to duty. Before seven in the morning she walked the short distance to the hospital in the continuing cold drizzle.

Returning to the flat an hour later she was pleased. Pleased because the men she seen operated on had both come through well and no other casualties had been brought in, and pleased because she could take the rest of the day off.

Lying on her bed with the narrow view of Falmouth Bay blanked out by the miserable rain, she fell asleep and waking at ten thirty Anna felt guilty and a little breathless from a dream she had had. Breathless because in her dream she had been sharing her bed with Simon Tremayne, guilty because less than two weeks ago her dreams had been totally occupied by John McCloud.

Her eyes went to the framed photograph of her and her fiancé taken in Pont-Aven that was on the small dressing table in front of her bed. Aloud she said 'Oh John, what am I going to do. I think I, well I don't really know, but I think I, I might just be in love with Simon'

'Mind you, I think you would approve' pausing for a moment she added, 'Perhaps you wouldn't, perhaps I, Oh shit, what have I got myself into. Damn it, I'm going to take a chance on the small amount of petrol I've got and see if I can get to the north coast on your motorbike John, and also take a chance on Simon being at the pub on a Monday.'

Within an hour she was heading North towards Zennor. Pulling her motorcycle back onto its stand Anna put her heavy leather gloves and the helmet and goggles into the pannier box but still wearing the long dark brown leather motorcycle coat she made her way towards the Tinners Arms door. It was quarter past one and she thought that the bar would be quiet at this time of year and on a Monday.

The sound of voices and noise grew as she approached the inn, it was louder than normal and she wondered why, before opening the door and stepping down onto the flag stoned floor of the bar.

She went in unnoticed because of the numbers of people there. Making her way to the bar Terry Nancekivell greeted her as warmly as always 'Morning Anna, unusual day ta see ee on maid, shandy?'

With a quiet 'Umm…..no thanks Terry, I've just got off my bike and I'm a bit cold, are you still out of whisky, if you are I'll have a gin and tonic, please.'

'Whisky rrived this morning, do ee want sum of Mabena's home made ginger ale in it?'

Nodding she said, 'That sounds good, how is she?'

Getting her drink and placing it in front of her he answered 'Ansum, she's upstairs but her'l be down dreckly.'

Putting the change from her one pound note on the counter he turned to serve the next customer before she could ask the reason for the full house.

The whisky and ginger was a real treat and tasted good. As she was taking her second sip she felt a hand clutch her elbow, without turning she knew it was Simon and smiled as turning her head she looked over her shoulder and up into his face.

'My God what a surprise to see you, have you heard the news

Anna?'

Shaking her head she said 'No, what's happened?'

Almost shouting he said, 'Come over to the window, I can't hear myself think here' Stood next to the table in the window opposite the bar he said 'That's a bit better! You haven't heard?' again shaking her head he continued 'The Japs bombed a naval base in Hawaii yesterday and sank several ships, killing thousands of sailors, so the Yanks are now officially in the war against Germany as well as Japan!'

Looking blankly at Simon she said, 'I think I need another whisky and ginger Simon.' While handing her the refilled glass he managed to touch Anna's fingers for just a second before stepping back slightly and starting to talk again.

'What on earth are you doing here on a Monday Anna, it was only Sam Trembath telling me about the Americans coming into the war that made work impossible without a lunch time pint for the both him and me that I'm here,' he finished by saying 'so I've had two bits of luck today, first the Yanks, second seeing you!'

She searched in her mind for the words, the right words, words that were supposed to be a little aloof, unimpassioned, lukewarm even. They never came, all she could think of saying without pause for breath was 'Well damn it Simon, I just wanted to see you, and I couldn't wait until Thursday, because you see so often these days Thursday's never come, and that's the plain fact, so there it is, and of course, so am I!'

They looked at each other silently until he swallowed and broke the silence with the question 'Can you come back to the house for a while?'

Finishing her drink before she spoke Anna said 'Only for a while, and only if I can have one more drink and then leave before you do. I want to drive up to Towednack Church for a few moments before coming back to your house when the coast is clear, that is if I don't run out of petrol first!'

She had been twice to Towednack Church in the summer months after Mabena had told her about it, saying 'Tis special Anna, built un a site whare tha ancients wurshipped, high up un they hills tis paceful lik. Paceful an special.'

Anna remembered that even at the height of the summer heat

the church still held a chill as she had sat in a pew, the carved wooden end depicting the man who donated it in 1633, and finding it very easy to think about the past and also to plan her future.

Now in the depths of winter her Ariel Red Hunter purred up the hill from Zennor into a thick wet blanket of rain, sleet and mist, with visibility of no more than fifty feet.

She was cold when she arrived at the gate to the South of the church. The wind had gone around to the North East, bringing gusts of freezing air and long flurries of snow. Before going through the gate Anna glanced up, running her eyes from the squat granite bell tower along the two roof lines that covered each gallery inside.

The flurries of snow had given way to a steady swirling fall that twisted around lichen covered grey and green head stones of graves; starting to pile against the weather side of border stones and between the cobbles marking the short path to the porch entrance.

Lifting the latch to the heavy oak door Anna stepped inside. This was no grand cardinal statement but a house made for refuge, a sanctuary from the outside world for people being carried along paths they did not want to tread, and during her first visits Anna felt like one of them, but not now, somehow her path seemed more defined, she knew what she had to do now and looked forward to doing it.

She looked first at the granite slab that formed the top of the alter before saying 'Hello again, I'm back. Just a quick visit, and oh my it really is cold in here today.' As on her previous visits the next thing she did was go to the open message book that rested on its own small table against one of the three pillars supporting the roof timbers.

Two people (two pilgrims in Anna's mind) had already been to the church earlier in the day. She read the first message that one of them had written, the neat capitals of each word stood out clearly in the dim light as she repeated it out loud 'Please pray for my only son, Richard, whose aircraft was shot down over the sea, three days ago. Please let him be a prisoner, please God let him be safe and well.'

The plea carried no name, and it was like hundreds more in

the thick book where most asked for help and prayers for sick friends or relatives, while others mourned those killed or missing because of the war.

The book offered a desperate plea from people. It lay like a beacon, ready to be lit by writing a call for help, and for others to share their grief, hopes or grateful thanks.

The last entry made Anna smile as she read it 'Thank you for your prayers and thoughts after I left a message here last month. I knew inside that I was being helped along and last week Shirley had a beautiful baby girl and the day after a letter arrived saying Robert was safe and a POW in Germany. Bless all of you'.

Putting six pennies in the church box Anna then lit three candles, placing them in the ornate iron pricket stand saying aloud 'Ladies first, so this one is for you Miriam, next is yours John and if Peter Adnans is with you, then the last is for him.'

Anna turned quickly in alarm as the church door creaked noisily open and she saw the outline of Simon Tremayne. Closing the door he said quietly 'I frightened you, I'm sorry, only I was concerned that you may have run out of petrol.'

'My God you did startled me Simon.'

Smiling he looked towards the altar of the church and back to her remarking 'Well I suppose this is as good a place as any to be startled by your God and even me! Why did you come here in such awful weather?'

She had to think before the answers came, not sure herself 'Umm, I think to say 'thank you', you see I was here twice in the summer and found the remoteness, the tranquillity soothing, it was almost as if I was being repaired inside by simply sitting on Matthew's pew, which I prefer to James's. Other churches always seem crowded somehow, but here there is something else, something I really can't describe, perhaps I'm not meant to.' Overtaken by a shiver she said, 'I really am icy cold, shall we go?'

Waiting for her by the door he said, 'Let's go back to my house, I will tell you all about the history of this church and at the same time you can enjoy the pleasure of a cup of tea and fresh saffron cakes from the village baker, that is after I top up your tank with some two-stroke petrol.'

In front of the black Cornish slab range in the kitchen Anna relaxed in the warmth, holding her mug of tea and cake while Simon excitedly explained the history of Towednack Church.

'It was built in the 13th century on the site of a Celtic hermitage, the tower being added later, in about 1500, I think. I know it was difficult to see your hand in front of your face today, but surrounding it are a dozen or so Celtic settlements some of them dating back to the Bronze age, five hundred years before Christianity was thought about!'

'Anna, you mustn't forget that the original religion of the ancient Cornish was of worship to the Earth Mother, a pure form of Paganism, Christianity to many would have been a religion forced on the people living where we are today'

'Now I have a theory……..' She watched as he took on a boyish manner, beaming and bursting with enthusiasm and at that moment she knew that sometimes he reminder her of John McCloud.

'Now wouldn't it have been a marvellous spoof Anna if the spiritual paths had been deliberately crossed,' clapping his hands in appreciation of his own joke he beamed with delight 'think about it, they were bright, intelligent people, excellent traders and entrepreneurs. I believe that under some pressure, they accepted a façade of Christianity because it suited them, but that in secret, and believe me to this day Anna, many Cornish and Celtic folk still pay homage to pagan images and idols!'

Thinking of Mabena Nancekivell and the superstitions so openly discussed at the Tinners Arms, and in fact everywhere in Cornwall, Anna was fully able to accept his theory. She told him of her experience with the hare and of the response to her drawing of it in the pub.

Finishing her tea she held the empty mug it had come in both hands and looked at it before speaking 'You really are a bit of a puzzle Simon, a lapsed Methodist who often visits quiet, lonely Anglican churches, who has a strong belief in pagan religions and if you don't mind my saying serves tea in the most wonderfully delicate china mugs that have a definite satanic look to them.'

She looked hard at him before continuing 'Don't look so

worried, I am only joking Simon' teasingly she added 'Or I think I am! This mug, it's jet black but has hints of red fire and even silver running through it, it's beautiful, and so delicate, the one you have is the same, they really are stunning.'

'Another passion of mine Anna. It's called Raku ware and these were made in a pottery in St Ives. It's a very special technique invented by our new enemies, the Japanese! I keep shaking my head Anna when I think back to just before the war started and I had such good fun and friendship from a German and a Japanese chap who were students at the same pottery that produced these mugs, the madness and waste of it all, it is so sad.'

The boyish manner had returned as he told her of his love of pottery and an equal love of collecting contemporary paintings from artist in the same town as the pottery was made, and from Newlyn, close to Penzance.

As he finished Anna stood up and put her back to kitchen range, grateful to feel the warmth before speaking 'Simon, I really must go, it's practically dark outside and I must be back at the hospital soon.'

He took both of her hands in his and said 'Stay, I'll get you back in the morning, like the last time, please stay.'

She put her arms around him and kissed him before stepping back saying 'And like the devil, you are a great tempter Mr Tremayne, but I have a staff shortage and there are a few things happening at the moment around the port that mean I have to keep in contact.'

She kissed him again with herself becoming the temptress she finished with 'Besides which, I am determined to get a whole day off this week, which could possibly include another night!'

Putting on the full length leather riding coat and the partly dried out cloves and hat, Anna followed Simon along the hallway past the hat and coat stand to the front door which seemed to explode inwards as he reached it, letting in a cold rush of air which was followed by a young woman wearing a long winter coat and a scarf pulled tightly around her head and tied under her chin.

Anna and the stranger stared at each other for a fraction of a second before Simon hurriedly introduced the women 'Chrissie, this is Anna. Anna this is my sister, Christine.'

They smiled at each other and started talking simultaneously before Anna held out her hand and uttered 'Hello, I'm Anna, your brother very kindly, but perhaps illegally, loaned me some petrol for my motorcycle, and then had the very good manners to warm me up with a cup of tea and a saffron cake, nice to meet you Christine, goodbye.'

Still a little wide eyed his sister replied 'Yes, well it was good to meet you, cheerio then.'

Outside, Simon escorted Anna to the garage where her motorcycle had been parked under cover. Without looking around or at Simon she said, 'You went as white as a ghost, but there, I suppose you have a lot to be guilty about!'

He was shaking his head at the same time as saying 'Don't tease, she just took me by surprise that's all, and anyway, she really is a sweetie, you'll like her a lot.'

Anna kissed Simon quickly and before leaving said, 'Hope to see you Thursday, and yes, I think I will like Christine!'

Simon watched Anna kick start the Red Hunter and leave through the round granite gatepost and disappear quickly into the swirling mist and rain, leaving behind only the fading sound of the machine as it roared up the hill on the St Ives road.

Before going back inside he thought to himself, 'How strange, I actually feel pleased they met, proud even!'

Going into the kitchen his sister just looked at him before she declared 'What a beautiful woman, so now I have at last met Anna, wow!'

Sitting down he tried desperately to maintain a casual air saying, 'We met in the Tinners and I let her have some of the two-stoke petrol we use for the lawn mower to get her back to the hospital in Falmouth.'

Still wide-eyed Chrissie shook her head slowly from side to side and saying at the same time, 'Oh, Simon, oh my dear, dear brother, what are you going to do?'

Unable to keep a straight face he smiled and said, 'Well now, I have absolutely no idea at this moment in time, but nothing this side of Christmas, except to go immediately find the new bottle of whisky I've hidden so that we can toast the arrival of our American cousins into this war!'

With a glass in each of their hands she declared 'To the Yanks, Anna, and the New Year. I really can't wait!'

Falmouth, Christmas Day, 1941

The Christmas decorations started at the entrance to the hospital with each ward making a big effort to push back the gloom of the dark and light greens of the interior of the building by putting up the paper chains, bunting and sprigs of holly that the local members of the Women's Institute had provided.

There had been no air raids or alerts in the town for three days and a festive holiday mood had settled on everyone as soon as the Falmouth Silver Band arrived at nine in the morning to sing carols in the corridors and wards of the hospital.

Commander Alex Read did not suit red, but his traditional role of Father Christmas went well during a hectic morning that he enjoyed as much as his staff and patients.

This was the third Christmas Day of the war and the doctors and nurses of the hospital that now admitted only military personnel played their festive roles, determined to ensure that their patients and themselves would enjoy the day.

Returning from his office and walking back into the main ward, the head of the hospital thought to himself 'The one thing you can be sure of in a war, is that you can never be sure of anything, but at least I had a good morning with the patients and staff before the blasted phone rang'

Finding Anna he said as quietly as possible 'Sister, sorry to break things up but I've had a call from the military at the docks, and they have another batch of men arriving from across the Channel and our services will be called for in about an hour'

'Usual routine, you will be in ops with me and if you can locate your other people on the duty roster I will organise my side of things and we will meet in twenty minutes, try and keep things quiet for the sake of the lads, oh, and bye the way, Happy Christmas!'

The small medical team slipped away from the wards as other doctors and nurses not on the emergency duty roster were busy serving a glass of sherry or a bottle of stout to the men in their beds or sat smoking and chatting in chairs in 'day rooms' off of the main wards.

It was growing dark when the first of the casualties arrived. Three stretchers were brought in and Alex Read, with the help of Anna and two other nurses quickly prepared them for an assessment of the condition of each after an initial examination.

Like most of the wounded men that had landed in Falmouth over the past months the medical team found that the facial features of the men rarely matched the clothing they wore, and this batch were no exception.

Wearing old and well worn mismatched outfits each had the vague appearance of French farmers or fishermen, but here in the bright lights of the pre-med room they looked like young men in hastily put together costumes ready for a local amateur theatrical production.

One of the injured had been given morphine recently. Oblivious to the goings on around him he just beamed intermittent smiles and uttered words and sentences that were impossible to interpret.

He was the most severely injure of the men brought in, with shrapnel wounds to his back and neck. Severe, but not critical was the judgement of the surgeon as he instructed Anna to prepare him for surgery before passing on to the next stretcher where two nurses had cut away the top layers of clothing of the big shouldered man who had been placed on his front with his forehead resting on his hands.

The man had similar shrapnel injuries to the first, but not as many. The surgeon gently praised apart the skin of one of the entrances where a piece of metal casing had penetrated, causing the patient to winched in pain and shout in a broad Australian accent 'Christ mate, that bloody hurts, but don't worry I'm so bloody pleased to be here just poke away, honest.'

Alex Read laughed and responded by saying 'Sorry about that young man. Well you have a couple of largish bits of iron stuck in your back, plus a few smaller surface pieces, but nothing that will stop you dancing in a few weeks time, are you army or air force?'

Turning his head on its side to get a view of the doctor he said, 'I'm a sergeant pilot in the Royal Australian Air Force, Sir, from Bathurst, New South Wales.'

While his nursing sister put a temporary dressing over his wounds the surgeon asked 'Your wounds are fairly fresh looking, how did you get them?'

'I was shot down over France about six months ago and I've been hidden and passed along a chain of resistance people from North of Paris to the coast, jeezes there must have been thirty or so blokes brought over the Channel while Jerry was having his Christmas sausage!'

'Well Sir, I'll tell you straight, when we walked into a patrol of Jerries a couple of nights ago we all thought that was it, too right we did. Fred and me copped a grenade one of the buggers threw. Next thing we remember was that the French lads are taking us down to the beach, and here we are, Christmas Day in good old England, Jesus, and whod've thought it, eh!'

'An ladies, please just keep talking, the sound of your voices has to be the best Christmas present ever!'

The cheery and grateful pilot was joined by a third casualty requiring minor surgery, the last four stretchers needed only stitches or fractures to be set. With all the operations complete by a little after ten in the evening the surgeon, anaesthetist and the nurses were able eat a belated Christmas dinner, which Alex Read augmented it with two bottles of red wine and a final glass of port with the Christmas pudding.

Sister Jack now wanted to get back to her flat, and there was a special reason. A parcel had been delivered by hand to the reception desk during the afternoon, wrapped in brown paper, but with a festive sprig of holly tied to it, and the word fragile appearing twice on the package. Also attached by thin string was a small envelope which she quickly opened.

Inside the envelope was a card with the words 'Merry Christmas Anna, love Simon'. Anna had taken the parcel into the empty staff room where she opened it, inside was a richly coloured almond shaped Raku dish.

It was eleven thirty when she walked out of the hospital entrance to face a cold driving wind that made her slip the hood on her cape over her headdress and start the short walk back to her flat holding onto the parcel tucked under her arm together with remains of a bottle of Port, courtesy of her boss.

She could hear voices on the opposite side of the road, two, three, possible four, in the total darkness of the blackout it was impossible to tell, but they were the friendly voices of Christmas revellers, and their laughter made her happy.

It also made her think of her parents in London, Simon Tremayne and Gail Moore who had got a three day leave pass and had travelled home to see her parents in Wales for the festivities.

Not far from her front door she was startled by a movement in front of her and a black shape getting out of a car 'Anna?' she quickly recognised the voice as Simon's and said 'What are you doing here on Christmas night, what a lovely surprise!'

After a quick kiss he said 'Anna, it's so good to see you, well almost see you in the dark, but listen, can you come back to my house? Oh, I forgot, Merry Christmas, or what's left of it!'

'Merry Christmas, and thank you for my present, it is so beautiful, but Simon, I can't come back to Zennor tonight, I have to start at six in the morning'

Without thinking she added 'Why don't you come in for a glass of Port, but please, please be very quiet as we have rules about everything, and especially about entertaining in our quarters late at night that are very boring but they are there.'

Anna pressed herself hard against Simon the moment they had tumbled into her bed with a series of kisses, and suppressed giggles.

From a loving embrace, she wrenched herself free before stretching over his chest and fumbling on her bed side table. Alarmed he said 'What's the problem?' resuming her limpet position alongside him she said 'Just checking the time, and we still have twelve minutes of Christmas Day left'

Kissing him on the lips before starting to run her hand slowly down his chest she added 'Merry Christmas Simon!'

Before Anna slipped into a blissful, exhausted and soothing sleep she recounted her third Christmas of the war with a smile.

She had been on her ward since seven in the morning, had attended to the seriously ill and wounded patients with the nurses on duty with her, had festooned her uniform with tinsel and played waitress to her patients as well as singing carols to them and with them, assisted in three surgical operations in theatre, had eaten Christmas dinner, and had made love to her new boyfriend.

The last thing she remembered was the word 'boyfriend', and it sounded good.

CHAPTER FOUR   1942

Back From The Dead

******

A Family at War

******

Goodbye to Cornwall

Back from the Dead

Truro, 1st January 1942

Robert Tremayne paced slowly in front of the open coal fire in the sitting room of his large house close to the Cathedral in Truro. He patiently waited as a maid placed an afternoon tea tray on a small table, before leaving the room.

When the door closed he was alone with his son and he shook his head slowly from side to side before speaking 'Simon, your mother is distraught, as indeed am I by what has happened. I've had Clare's father on the telephone twice now, he told me she is terribly upset. What on earth is going on, why have you suddenly decided to call off your engagement? She is such a nice girl, and from a very good and well connected family, so why?'

From the long settee where he sat Simon knew there was no going back and looked his father in the face as he said, 'Because I'm not sure that I love Clare, and also because there is a war on, and finally, because I have accepted a commission in the Royal Engineers and expect to be away fighting in this war very soon.'

His father gaped at him, and grew red with fury, and shouted 'Absolutely not young man, you are on an exemption list and you cannot be replaced. We would lose thousands of pounds in profits if you were not in charge of the mining interest, thousands! No, young man I will not allow you to go, and that's final.'

Knowing that if he got up from the settee the confrontation would spiral out of control he stayed seated and replied 'Dad, I've persuaded Sam Trembath to take over my role, he's certainly more than capable, and if he isn't acceptable to you I have been in contact with a recently retired mining engineer in

Wales who was one of my lecturers at Camborne. He would be happy to take the position until the war is over'

'Also, father I've been in touch with the reserved occupation board and told them of the men able to take my place and they have agreed to my request, mainly because the Army is desperate for qualified engineers.'

A silence gripped the room until the door handle turned and Simon's mother came in. Looking at her son her eyes narrowed as she said 'You have brought shame on this family Simon. Shame and dishonour, what they will say at the chapel I simply cannot imagine. I can hardly believe you are our son.'

His father spluttered 'There's worse to come Patricia, much worse; he's now announced that he's leaving the firm and joining the army. We will lose thousand of pounds, thousands of pounds I can assure you, its a complete disaster, a complete and utter disaster.'

Turning to Simon his mother said 'Is this true? Have you taken leave of your senses boy? You can't simply leave, you have a duty to your father, and to me and your brothers and sister, we won't allow it Simon, so there, we will simply not allow this to happen.'

He knew his mother would be the more difficult of the two parents's to argue with and also knew she would stop at nothing to keep him in line, so he had rehearsed his speech carefully.

'Now please, I don't want to quarrel with you, but you must see how important it is for me to do this. I cannot, will not, carry on seeing every one of my friends leaving their jobs and professions to do their 'bit' in uniform while I continue to keep my head down, living a life of comparative luxury and safety, when in my heart...... well in my heart I know only too well the mines could clearly be managed by someone else for the time being'

For the first time he got up from the settee and stood facing both of his parents before continuing 'There's a war on, our country needs engineers and I can play a significant and important role by becoming an officer, and think of it mother, your son receiving a King's Commission as a Captain,'

'I believe that everyone at the chapel will be proud of me and pleased for you both and I know that to be the truth'

'I am also clear in my own head that if I have to defy both of you for the sake of my country, then sadly, very sadly, I will.'

There was a silence that he had expected, rehearsed for, before his mother said, 'And given this sudden rush of patriotism Simon, why did you find it necessary to abandon Clare, surly in your new world a wife from such a good family would be a benefit, a true asset, so why then walk away from her as well as us?'

He knew from the start this would be the most difficult hurdle to jump, he knew that what he said next would determine the way the relationship with his family would develop in the future, or end in the room.

'We are none of us able to foresee the future, but what is clear is that with the Americans at last in, then the war will intensify over the next year or so, before it ends'

'My feelings towards Clare have changed I will acknowledge that, as to whether they have changed because of the war I cannot say, but I cannot live a lie where my feelings are concerned, that would not be fair to Clare or to me, and please remember that this is the way you both brought me up to behave, you see, I am merely being honest in the way you told me was so important.'

With his hand on the handle of one of the double doors that led to the hallway he turned to face his parents, saying 'I am truly sorry for upsetting you both and of course Clare and her family, but I am not sorry that I have made the decisions that I have, and honestly believe them to be the right ones, I just hope you will accept that, and that you will give me your support.'

The parents heard the front door close and putting a log onto the fire before speaking to his wife Robert Tremayne said 'This is going to cost us a lot of money Patricia, and more besides. Clare's parents will be very resentful of this, luckily he's recently retired from the planning committee of the council, which is fortunate, but the family are still something of a power in the area.'

Mrs Tremayne had said nothing since her son had left the room but had shared the same view of the fire as her husband before looking scornfully at him and saying 'Don't talk such rubbish Robert. We will survive Simon going and well you know it, but there is something else, or perhaps someone else behind all this and I have every intention of finding out the truth'

'The fact is we have absolutely no option but to give Simon our total support, and mark my words the community will race to fall in line to judge against both of us if we do not, and very obviously our son clearly knows this'

'No, we will go along with his decisions because we have no choice, but there is more to it, mark my words.'

Later that day Simon waited for Anna in a pub close to her hospital. He stood up when she came into the lounge bar and kissed her briefly before she sat on the wood settle next to him.

At ease and relaxed in his company Anna told him about her last stint at work but as she talked she noticed that he was edgy, fidgety and she said 'Simon, what is the problem, I know there is one, what is it?'

His laughing eyes returned as he said 'I am that transparent am I? Well, there have been a few problems, but now I am pleased to say, they have been sorted out. Anna, I have to tell you what I've done.............'. Simon told her everything that he had told his parents only hours before, and of his decision to become an officer.

After he had finished Anna looked at him, her eyes bored into his for several seconds before she said 'Simon, have you done all this because of me? I hope not, because you seemed a very settled person when I first met you, and when we first made love I told you I could not bear being responsible for other people getting hurt.'

Shaking his head he said 'No Anna, the war has changed me, not just meeting you. The damned war and the constant shadow it casts over everything and every action in life'

There was a hesitation before he continued by saying, 'I would be less than honest if I didn't say that because of the change that has happened within me I have taken a different view of where my life should go both now and after the war is over'

'It came as quite a shock to me when I realised that the whole of my life had been shaped by other people whose intentions were perfectly well meaning and honest, but who took no account of what I wanted from it'

'I was blind to it Anna. I knew something was missing. Gunther, the German potter I told you about, had a freedom in his head and body that I envied. His parents were wealthy industrialist, yet there he was working in St Ives, earning little or no money, living in the coldest room imaginable, but he was somehow richer than me in all ways, and I knew it'

'When we met at the Tinners for the first time and we shook hands to say goodbye, I looked at you. I knew right then. I'm not a silly man, or much of a romantic one, but Anna, all I can say is that at that moment I knew I loved you.'

Unable now to look at him she sat staring at the table in front of her before having the courage and getting her words together before looking at him and saying 'Simon, I need to tell you the truth, because you see I fell in love before. He was such a lovely chap and I loved him dearly. He was killed just after we became engaged and the moment he died, well, a small part of me died with him.'

'I have often looked back and thought that if I have any regret it is only that I stuck to the army rules too much when perhaps we should have been together more and having more fun, but then at that time Simon, the war was almost someone else's, a bit abstract and detached from us, and from our love'

'He was a surgeon, we worked together in France and we were in Belgium when the Germans invaded, so we both saw people being killed and dying in front of us every day, but the feeling was that it was never going to really touch us'

'Daft wasn't it, but that is the way we both felt without really saying anything to each other'

'Then of course the war did touch us, and the poor dear man was blown to pieces and he died in my arms' unable to carry on she said 'Simon, I'm so sorry, I have to leave, I am sorry.'

Pleased to be enveloped by the blackout regulations when they got outside of the pub the couple walked arm in arm, silently towards her flat. Knowing that Gail would be at home she did not want to invite him inside, so they sat silently in his car that was parked outside.

With her head on his shoulder they held hands, each deep into their own private thoughts. Both bruised by people and events around them. Both numb from the experiences.

It was Anna who spoke first and there was a slightly hard edge to her voice when he heard her say 'Simon, when will you be leaving Cornwall?'

'Not sure, but I think towards the end of the month, why?'

'Because, having been such a wonderful Florence Nightingale and worked tirelessly over the Christmas and New Year I have been awarded a five day leave pass and rail warrant to take me home, and I was wondering if we could spend a couple of days together in London'

'We could stay at a hotel, have some nice food, and I really want to see Noel Coward's 'Blithe Spirit' at the Piccadilly Theatre before I go on to my parents?'

To Simon her words were like an explosion that blew away any doubts or possible recriminations he had had. With an echo of child like excitement he almost shouted

'Brilliant idea Anna! As it happens, I have to go up to London to the Ministry of Mines to give them a report and briefing, so tell me when and I will be there!'

She tightened her grip of his hands and snuggled even closer before saying 'January 1st, 1942. My goodness what a way to start your new year Simon Tremayne! I'm not so sure you should have broken off your engagement, but I certainly am sure about your decision to join the army'

'The day I told my parents I was going to become an army nursing sister my father said that many people would share a guilt about not fighting Hitler and despite losing John and several other truly close friends I think he was right'

'All I can say Simon is that I really do admire what you have done when it would have been so easy to have done nothing.'

In the total black of the night Anna cupped her hands around the outline of his face and kissed him before saying 'Happy New Year Darling.'

Anna used her torch to give enough light to get through the entrance of the house and up the stairs to her flat. Using it again to look at her watch she saw it was eleven thirty and she was a little surprised to see light creeping from under the door.

As she opened it Gale came rushing over to her and said 'Anna, where the hell have you been, I've looked everywhere for you, here, there's a telegram for you.'

Telegrams in war time always brought with them a sense of dread, a foreboding of bad news wrapped in a small buff envelope. She eased open the gummed flap and took out the telegram.

The three thin lines of telex paper pasted to the inner sheet read 'Delighted to inform you Stop Major Peter Adnans safely back home Stop Regards Mary Atkins Stop.'

Throwing her arms around an anxious looking Gale she said 'How utterly, utterly wonderful. One of my friends is back from the dead, it's so wonderful!'

'Thank goodness for that, I hate telegrams they normally seem to bring only bad news, how would you like a glass of not so good, but perfectly drinkable Alicanti wine, it was apparently washed up from a wreck only a few miles from here, Tom Gibbs gave it to us as a New Year present!'

Gail poured the wine and gave her beaming flat mate a glass adding 'To your good news, cheers, and a happy new year to you Anna!'

London, 5th January 1942

The train pulled into Paddington station at two thirty-five, the engine giving out one finale belch of hissing white steam from under its front wheels before relaxing into a gentle panting while passengers hurried past.

Anna stood still and let the stream of passengers' rush past on each side of her when she reached the entrance to the station on her way to a taxi rank. She was shocked by the sight of the destruction and damage of the buildings that surrounded the station.

The day was a dismal one and added to the melancholy she felt. Tones of grey were made darker by a steady drizzle of fine rain, and a chilling wind completed the sad January feel.

Sat in the back of a taxi she saw that many of the buildings that had been familiar to her stood as piles of blackened rubble, while many of those still standing had sand bag columns on either side of their entrances and boarded up windows.

It was Anna who had insisted that they take separate trains and meet in the foyal of a small hotel in Kensington, the Cranborne which she had booked on the telephone.

From a seat in the reception area Simon put down the pre-war magazine he had been holding without reading and got up as he saw Anna come through the hotel doors. 'I've booked us in darling' he said after picking up her case and sweeping past the reception desk towards the stairs.

Their room was stiflingly hot and although clean it had a shabby feel and look to it. She felt guilty, saying 'Oh dear Simon, a bit grim isn't it, sorry darling but all the other places I know were either booked out or smouldering bomb sites.'

'Rubbish, Anna there's a war on and its fine. We have a toilet across the hall and the bed is so hard it will act as an excellent air raid shelter should we need it! Plus, the porter is in the process of organising tickets for us to see 'Blithe Spirit' this evening'

He ran his fingers through her hair and held her close to him before finishing by saying 'And most importantly we are here together, and frankly it seems like the most natural thing in the world to me, but you do seem a little tense darling, come on, please relax Anna.'

'Yes, you're right, it does seem very natural being here with you but relaxed I am certainly not, guilt does seem to hang around my neck these days.'

After shaking her head in silent anger and frustration she put her arms around his neck and said, 'Damn it, I'm sorry, I must stop this guilt thing Simon, in a few weeks you will be in the army and we will be miles from each other for God knows how long so let's enjoy ourselves while we can.'

Anna kissed him before adding 'In fact I think we should test the air raid capabilities of this bed after I've been to the loo!'

The show at the Piccadilly Theatre started at six and they arrived in time for a drink in the theatre bar before the performance started and ordered the same drinks for collection during the interval.

After the interval curtain came down they joined the rush of people to collect their order from the theatre bar. Anna felt lifted by the performance as she shouted above the noise of the crowd around her 'That was exactly what I needed to see Simon, a good Noel Coward comedy with lots to laugh about. Mum and dad brought me to the West End a lot before the war, oh Simon I had a really good laugh, such good fun!'

Crammed shoulder to shoulder with other theatre goers Simon shouted into her ear 'I read in *'The Times'* today that this evening we had a choice of going to see Handle's 'Messiah' at the Albert Hall, or Margot Fonteyn in the Sadler's Wells Ballet plus, and this has really surprised me, we could have gone to any one of twenty six plays or musicals. Twenty six Anna, and all within a taxi ride of our hotel.'

She thought for a moment before remarking 'I must admit I had no idea there was so much going on in between the air raids. I think Herr Hitler must be very disappointed, and pretty angry, that after the pummelling the blighter is giving London, the city simply refuses to lie down and die, but goes on and on!'

After the show Anna led the way through a steady drizzle of rain across two streets and through an ally way in the blackout with the occasional flash of her torch to pick out familiar landmarks. Whole sections of road were fenced off where sticks of bombs had fallen and the buildings had been damaged or demolished. Suddenly unsure of bearings she asked an ARP warden the way.

'Thank you' she said 'I would have wondered around for hours! Over here Simon'

A final flash of light from the torch at a what looked like a hastily painted sign above a long boarded window which simply read 'Restaurant' and she said 'Here we are, *'Baglioni's'*, now renamed with great imagination, and my mother and fathers favourite London restaurant.'

Inside it was crowded and the waitress said in a thick Italian accent 'No problem, two people, please wait a moment'. Another waitress took their coats before leading them to a table where they sat down and Simon looked around.

He was puzzled, the restaurant was clearly Italian at one time but now had French, American and Commonwealth flags vaguely hiding the original wall paintings of Naples, Florence and Rome.

Anna saw he was perplexed by the strange mixture of accents and bizarre décor so she explained 'The owners are two Italians who have been in London for the past fifteen years. Mum and dad know the families very well, but because Italy declared war on us they, and hundreds of other Italians, were automatically interned in a prison camp on the Isle of Man'

'Daddy and several others are trying to get them released. Senior Sanzeni and his brother are as anti fascist as we are, but there must be a small element of their countrymen living here that are not, so sadly they have been locked up until they can be vetted. In the meantime, the whole family not interned or released are here keeping the place going.'

At Anna's suggestion Simon was served with the restaurant's traditionally huge portion of Rozotto alla Milanese only a moment before her chicken tetrazzini appeared. Pouring red wine from the carafe on the table into two glass tumblers Simon raised his saying 'Cheers Anna, I feel really happy, and I like this place it's, it's….. Hell, how can I explain? I know, it reminds me of being on holiday abroad before the war started, sort of exotic, excepting the weather outside!'

After the meal he said 'I know you've told me a little about Peter Adnans, but what is he seriously like?'

Anna took her time to tell him everything about the slightly eccentric but brilliant surgeon and felt pleased to be able to do so. Pleased because although Peter would always remind her of most of her worst times he would also remind her of most of her best times. 'Well now, to look at he's tall, six foot four, give or take a bit, and big. Huge hands and broad shoulders, fair haired. In fact John used to rag him terribly, because he has German ancestors! But we both agreed that his mild, gentle manner never fitted in with his frame, he always seemed to try and make himself smaller somehow.'

Soon after receiving the telegram from Mary Atkins she had

contacted her and she had given Anna Peter Adnans's telephone number. They had already had a brief but cheerful talk, and she had arranged to meet him for lunch the next day at the Savoy, where he was staying, while Simon was at the Ministry.

With her head tilted slightly to one side she looked at Simon and raised her glass 'Here's to us! I'm pleased you like this place, and you are right it has that nice friendly feel to it'

A serious look went across her face as she said 'Simon, I have to admit that I'm feeling a wee bit nervous about meeting Peter tomorrow. So much has happened since Dunkirk. So much. Still, it must go both ways, so we shall see, cheers darling.'

London, 6th January 1942

'This is it, Miss. They've taken the 'Savoy' sign down 'cause of the bombing Miss, but here we are'. The driver of the black London taxi dropped her at the top of the cul-de-sac as instructed.

She needed the short walk to the entrance of the hotel and used the few steps to collect herself. She breathed deeply as she went past the elderly uniformed doorman, returning his salute with a gentle nod before walking past a protective wall of sandbags and through the revolving doors into the foyer.

Now inside the hotel Anna stopped and looked around. It was an odd combination of pre-war opulence and war time reality as she looked at the lavish art deco fittings and mirrors of the reception area and then at the red, white and blue painted steel girders put in place to support the ornate ceilings and walls.

There was also an odd combination of clients using the hotel and restaurants. An unusual balance of men in khaki uniforms and an equal number in dark pin striped suits looking incongruous with the familiar attachment of a square khaki box holding a gas mask, and a steel helmet slung over a shoulder or carried next to an attaché case.

A group of ten or more men with another three women

jostled together noisily, shouting at one another, their expensive, stylish looking clothes and wild antics at odds with the perfected calm of the environment surrounding them and the dowdiness of the world outside.

As she approached the polished dark mahogany and brass reception desk she was unable to hold back a smile while thinking to herself 'Americans! My goodness, why are they always so incredibly loud!'

At the reception Anna spoke to a smartly dressed man behind the desk 'Good morning, Major Adnans is expecting me, my name is Anna Jack.'

Well into his sixties the man straightened his back at the mention of the name, replying 'Yes Madam, Master Peter said to expect you, if you would care to follow James, he will take you to his suite.'

'This way madam.' Once inside the lift James closed the doors with a clang and selected the floor they were going to by turning a brass arrow next to the door of the lift to a sign that read 'Royal Suite' and saying shakily 'I've been taking Master Peter to this suite ma'am since he was a baby, yes, a small baby.'

He opened the doors of the lift and politely asked her to follow him. Knocking gently on a door which opened immediately he said, 'Master Peter, the lady you are expecting.'

Peter Adnans stood in the door frame, dressed in well pressed barafia army trousers a khaki shirt and tie, looking sun tanned, fit and well.

Grabbing Anna's hand with his and pulling her through the door, he said 'Thank you James. Anna, how wonderful to see you, please come in.'

'Peter, I can't believe it's really you!'

Frowning slightly, he laughed before he put his arm around her shoulders and guided her into the day room of his suite saying, 'Anna it's so good to see you, you are like a breath of fine Scottish air to me, now do sit down, it's sherry time and we have lots to talk about.'

Anna searched his face and studied his body movements while he poured out two glasses of sherry before handing her one and sitting down opposite.

He was different she thought, more confident with himself, more self assured, now I wonder what has happened to him over the past year and a half to cause that?

'Salou Anna, to you, and to absent friends.'

Raising her glass towards him Anna said, 'Salou Peter, it's so good to see you, now tell me all about it, what happened to you at Dunkirk and after, and how come you look so suntanned and very fit and healthy?'

Before replying he paused and looked away from her and quickly, very slightly, shook his head as if clearing his mind to concentrate on the present before he continued 'My goodness, so much happened after you took the men through the barrier and onto the pier towards the rescue vessels, so much'

'First of all I waited with the remaining chaps who were on stretchers, and frankly Anna, I was at a total loss about what to do with them'

'I watched in absolute horror as a German spotter plane pin pointed the pier you were on, knowing full well what would come next'

'As the German artillery were finding their ranges several salvos of shells fell behind where we were, but luckily we were sheltered by piles of fallen bricks from a house that had been hit and the lads were unhurt, and most of them were under sedation anyway, and not aware of what was going on'

'Finally, I decided that it was useless to stay. Two of the boys had deteriorated badly and the only thing I could think of was to try and get back to the hospital we started out from'

'It was a nightmare Anna, but finally I got hold of an army lorry before it was totally immobilised by it's driver and I managed to pile the lads onto the back of it and as the dawn light crept up I got them back to the hospital that had been taken over by French doctors and nurses. Sadly, the two boys I knew were very poorly had died by the time we got there, but the others were taken into the crowded building where at least they had some basic treatment'

'In truth, I actually have no idea of what happened next. I can't even remember getting back to the hospital. My next recollection is of waking up on the floor between two stretchers in a corridor of the hotel that had become the hospital and looking at the some of the men I had arrived with. A blanket had been put over me and a pillow placed under my head. Anna, I had been asleep for six hours! I saw that the lads had been as well cared for as possible, and eventually found a French doctor to talk to'

'The poor chap was exhausted and told me that there were another twenty or so British soldiers spread around the building, he did not speak English and he asked if I would be able to have a look at them. After a strong cup of coffee I went around and saw the other British casualties, and well Anna, after that I simply could not leave them, how could I, so I stayed until the Germans arrived.'

Anna leaned over and squeezed his right arm in a genuine bond of understanding to his predicament, saying 'Peter, I can't begin to understand how very unnerving it must have been to just stay and wait, not knowing what was going to happen. But what was it like when they did arrive?'

With a brighter look on his face he replied 'Peculiar Anna, quite peculiar. To begin with Maurice Pagnol, the senior French doctor, came to see me early in the evening the night before Jerry arrived, that was, let me see, the 3rd of June. He was armed with two glasses and a bottle of Armanac!'

'After pouring a measure in both glasses and handing me one he said, "Thank you for your help my friend, but alas I have been told that the Germans will be here in the morning, there is absolutely nothing else to be done".

'We toasted each other and he left to see to his own men leaving me with the promise to join him and his colleagues for a last dinner in the basement kitchens at ten that evening'

'I then supervised making our chaps as comfortable as possible before disposing of the blood soaked white coat I had been wearing for what seemed months and getting a jug of hot water so that I could have a refreshing, and desperately needed shave. After that I put on the cleanest uniform I could muster from the bits and pieces I could find and joined the group for dinner'

'By the time we all gathered together the extraordinary tiredness every one felt seemed to be pushed away Anna.

There was a surreal calmness with everyone, as though a heavy burden had been lifted from our shoulders and that our fate was now in someone else's hands so all we could do was wait. Simply wait and see what fate had in store for all of us, it was truly bizarre'

'The French were such a jolly lot, and absolutely determined not to let Jerry have the benefit of what was left in the cellars of the hotel that had become our hospital.' Animated now, and looking much more like the Peter Adnans she had known, he continued with the full description of the final night in Dunkirk.

'We started with Champagne, had white burgundy with a fish course of fillets of sole, my last bottle of Mouton Rothschild with duck and chateaux u'cme with desert. All of this was followed by cigars, coffee and brandy; it was an absolute feast on our last night of freedom Anna'

'Finally, each of us in turn stood up from the table and made a toast to our friends and families as well as to each other, before we shook each other by the hand and crawled into our beds'

'I suppose we all had about three hours sleep before getting up and doing the rounds to look at the chaps. It was about six thirty in the morning when an orderly came racing into the room where I was to announce that a group of German infantry had stopped outside the hospital, and an officer was approaching the entrance'

'I went outside to the top of the steps of the entrance and stood behind Maurice Pagnol as the young, tired looking invader climbed rather unsteadily up the steps of our make shift hospital, and stared into his eyes before saying in perfect French "Good morning doctor, I am Hauptmann Halder. I am very sorry to disturb you, but I have a number of seriously wounded men, do you think you could possibly assist them?".

'Maurice immediately sent a medical team from the hospital which followed a sergeant to where the wounded Germans were and the Frenchman invited the officer inside for a cup of coffee which he gladly accepted'

'I was then introduced to the infantry officer and to my amazement he spoke the most perfect English, telling me that he had often been in London before the war on business!'

'It was all quiet queer Anna, but after that, well things started to happen that will live with me forever.'

'A German field kitchen was set up in the grounds behind the hospital during the day and by evening each patient had received a bowl of soup, fresh bread and a solid meal. The much feared invading soldiers were handing out cigarettes, sitting by beds or stretchers showing photographs of wives, children or girlfriends and the wounded of both French and British armies were using Christian names when speaking to the same men that twenty four hours earlier they had been trying so desperately to kill!'

'During the day we were able to get much needed dressings and a limited amount of medicines and pain killers from a team of German doctors and nurses. Our main concern was for the burns cases that seemed to be almost mad through the pain and distress they were in'

'We were asked courteously by the same doctors to select the most critical cases that were stable enough to be moved back to proper hospitals the next day, and one could feel that a general sense of normality was returning, helped hugely by the proper nights sleep that followed, without the sound of bombs or shells screaming down.'

'The next morning Maurice Pagnol and I were having breakfast together in a small room overlooking a glistening blue English Channel with a clear, cloudless sky above it before doing our rounds of the men. Before we had finished we were joined by Gunther Halder the first German infantry officer we saw'

'It was impossible not to be amiable to the chap Anna, the first time we had met him he was as exhausted as we were, and his demeanour had not been triumphant or conquering, but seemingly simply relieved by his own survival, and he had a very definite sense of duty towards the well being and care of his men, especially the wounded'

'Well, Anna, the German Captain was talking calmly about the devastation of the town when the door of the room was pushed brusquely open and banged loudly as it hit against the wall behind it. The open-door frame then revealed another

German officer who spoke with some arrogance to Gunther, and I have to say it was an arrogance that was returned equally and only ended when both men went hurriedly outside of the room, closing the door with another loud slam'

'Maurice and I simply looked at each other incredulously until the door opened again and Captain Halder came back in. He stood red faced and clearly very angry before saying "That was Hauptsturmfuhrer Rein of the Waffen SS. I have been ordered to tell you that all of your patients will be moved out by mid morning, and will be accompanied by junior doctors and nursing staff only."

"All senior doctors will march with other captured officers and men to a camp in Belgium. I am sorry, but these are the orders I have been instructed to give you."

'Maurice was the next to turn red with anger as he stood up rigidly from the table and spoke to the clearly embarrassed infantry officer'

"Captain Halder, I must lodge a complaint. Many of these men need specialist care for the next twenty-four hours, and many will certainly die if they do not receive it, including some of your own men, this is madness."

'Before I could say another word the young German put his hands on the back of a chair and leaned on it heavily before saying to us'

"Gentlemen, you must listen to me very carefully. I am a Wehrmacht Infantry Officer. I fight for my country because it is at war, but I am not a political person"

"However, Captain Rein is a Waffen SS officer and a fanatical member of the Nazi Party, and in short whatever order he gives, then you must obey them, or he will have you shot"

"Believe me gentlemen, I do not like the man and he does not like me, but I have seen him shoot several people, German and others, for disobeying his orders, so please get your things together and be outside in one hour together with all of your senior staff."

'He was unable to look at either of us as he turned towards the door, saying 'Believe me gentlemen, I am sorry about this.'

Anna wanted to ask several questions but knew not to for the moment as Peter refilled their glasses before continuing by saying, 'We were both speechless. But at that very moment Maurice Pagnol and I both understood the full immensity and gravity of our situation'

'In that small room with a view of the sea and open skies we had become the prisoners of an invading force. We were captives'

'Our own wishes and thoughts had become irrelevant and totally unimportant. Others were now directing us, giving us orders that we had to obey. "Obey" or we would be killed, it was a chilling moment Anna'

'I have never felt so utterly miserable, so utterly defeated, and strangely cornered, like a wounded stag in the Highlands'

'Maurice sat down heavily and said "I feel thoroughly ashamed of myself Peter, and thoroughly ashamed of our countries. How could we have let this happen, how could we have let our own peoples down so badly."

'The poor chap put his hands up to cover his face and wept for a minute before sweeping one of them angrily across the table sending the coffee cups and saucers crashing onto the floor'

'He wiped the tears from his face before standing up and almost whispering "We have no choice Peter, I will go and tell my doctors and staff what is going to happen, and perhaps you should do the same for your patients."

She felt the surgeon was close to tears himself as he put a hand to his face and massaged his eyes for a second before continuing.

'Although I knew he was in the absolute depths of despair Anna, less than an hour later, Maurice walked down the steps of his makeshift hospital and turned around at the bottom one before looking back to his countrymen at the top, where he smiled broadly and shouted at the top of his voice "Take care mon amies, we will all be back very soon. Vive le France!"

'At first we walked in a small group of twenty or so men, guarded by a couple Germans but as soon as we got to Bray Dunnes the numbers swelled to several hundred soldiers from all the Allied countries'

'By early evening we had marched to the outskirts of Oostvieteren, back into Belgium once again Anna, and were directed, well I suppose I should say 'herded' through a gate and into the local football stadium'

'I have to say that my tummy turned over as we marched under the Swastika flag that had been hung over the entrance to the stadium, to spend a thoroughly miserable night in the open.'

'The next day as we moved off several local people lined the sides of the roads. No smiling ones, only sad looking individuals who handed us bread, water, wine and I even had a cup of coffee and a chocolate bar thrust into my hands.'

'There were no welcoming slaps of gratitude this time, only the occasional pat of sympathy, the sort of gently pat a mother would give to her child after waking from a bad dream, and goodness, bad dream it was,' his story was interrupted by a knock on the door and he said 'Anna, I've taken the liberty of arranging for a light cold buffet lunch to be served here, Oh, and I've booked a table for dinner this evening for us and this new friend of yours, Mr Tremayne isn't it, and yes, I am intrigued, young lady!'

With a glass of white wine in their hands and lunch in front of them Anna sat back and said 'Peter, the food looks delicious but I really can't wait for you to tell me what happened next!'

'Yes, well, from now on what happened is like a fairy tale, and in honesty Anna, like most fairy tales, the story has a lot of funny parts, some grim and grisly ones but almost all of it is too fantastic to believe!' He paused to take a long drink of his wine and wiped his lips on a clean white linen napkin before picking up a piece of cold American ham on a fork.

Impatiently Anna said 'Oh please, please don't stop Peter. Please, go on, I can't wait!'

'Well, by late afternoon we must have walked about twenty miles or so from Oostvieteren and the column of hundreds of soldiers started to creep through a town called Lichtervelde'

'For most of the day I had been walking besides Maurice Pagnol and trying to improve my miserably poor French vocabulary by chatting to him and several of his colleagues.'

'This time there seemed to be quite a large crowd of silent Belgians lining both sides of the road, and again the inhabitants of the town were handing out all sorts of treats and goodies, it was a very kind gesture'

'Our German guards were few and far between, and actually good eggs on the whole. Several times the sad procession came to a halt as well wishers put arms around us and offered words of encouragement as well as gifts of food and drink'

'Where the road entering the town narrowed, a sudden surge of people came forward into the walking ranks of men and I found myself surrounded by a group of young men and women'

'Before I could make any sense about what was happening the group seemed to envelop and separate me and Maurice Pagnol and lead us away from the line of marching prisoners and quickly through the open door of a butcher's shop'

'We were hurriedly ushered through the open gap of the butcher's counter and led through to a back room, which was out of sight of the main road'

'Waiting there was a huge man, six feet six plus Anna, dressed as a Catholic Priest and at his side an equally short woman dressed as a nun. Maurice and I were hastily told to put on the black trousers and coat that had been handed to us over our uniforms and told to follow them'

'The last item we were asked to add to the new set of clothes was a jet black wide brimmed felt hat that seemed far too large for me!'

Anna could only gently shake her head very slowly from side to side and sit slightly open mouthed in disbelief as the consultant surgeon continued.

'We walked about twenty yards or so towards a dusty looking Citroen where Maurice and I joined another individual dressed similarly to ourselves in the back of the car while the tall priest sat behind the steering wheel and the nun sat next to him'

'As the car started to gather speed and head out of the town the nun turned to the three of us in the back and said very calmly in English "Do any of you speak French?"

'She seemed rather relieved when Maurice spoke in his native tongue and myself and the other occupant told her that we both spoke the language to a small degree, but badly'

'Turning her head back towards the road ahead she then proceeded to tell us that we would be taken to a "safe house" in Brussels before making arrangements for getting us back to England over the next few months'

'On the back seat of the car we all seemed to turn our heads at the same time to verify with each other that what we had all heard was true "back to England" surely not?'

'The priest had no English and the nun translated his instructions that should we be stopped at a road block Maurice should say he was from Paris and us two from the Roscoff area of Brittany, hence our unusual French accent, and that we had lost all our belongings, including our papers in the upheaval of the past weeks; and we were going back to a Benedictine Monastery in Brussels'

'The man next to me was an English soldier, just twenty years old Anna, and from Birmingham. A nice lad, and at that time as shocked by the sudden turn of events as his older back seat companions!'

'What happened after is something I have been told not to talk about by the chappie that debriefed me but I will go completely mad if I don't tell someone, so this is for your ears only Anna'

'I can say that we spent a couple of weeks in a very pleasant house that clearly belonged to a rich family, on the outskirts of Brussels'

'Then the Gestapo began to establish their onerous links with the collaborators in Belgium and things became much more difficult for everyone, and we were split up for safety reasons'

'It was a very emotional time when Maurice was told that he would be first to leave the "three musketeers" as our helpers had started to call us'

'Will you go to England, or stay in France, I asked him?'

"Peter, I will go anywhere I can help with the final eviction of the monsters that now occupy my country, so we will see. Thank you for your help and support my friend, we will meet again, in happier times and under better conditions, au revoir!"

'I haven't met him yet, but I did speak to him on the telephone just two days ago Anna. He arrived at a place called Falmouth, which is in Cornwall, on Christmas day with twenty or so other escapees from France. Would you believe it!'

Of course, Anna did believe it as she remembered well the wounded Australian airman and the other men her team had treated at her hospital after the secret operation to bring him and the others out of France in the quiet of the Christmas festivities, but she decided not to divulge the activities that she had been party to, but instead said 'Were the priest and nun still around to help the both of you left together?'

'No Anna, they had melted away within an hour of our arrival at the house in Brussels, but I did meet her again,' he sat back into the plush arm chair of the hotel suite, lost for a fraction of time in his thoughts before saying 'but that part comes later on in the fairy story young lady, so you must be patient!'

'No, we seemed to have several organisers at this stage. Derek Watson, my fellow escapee, actually, the correct word, so I was told at my de-briefing is "evader". So, we "evaders" were moved to an apartment, almost in the centre of Brussels, and occupied the spare room of the two bedrooms belonging to a doctor and his wife, Edith and Pierre'

'Charming people Anna, quite charming, but sadly they are part of the grim side of the story. You see we received a visit from a woman who told us it was necessary for us to get proper papers and documents before we could proceed any further with our escape'

'We were told to call her Bridgette and the next morning she collected us after providing us with rather smart but ill-fitting business suits, shirts and ties, shoes and the three of us walked to a tram stop before going a mile or so through the city to a photographer's studio where we both had our pictures taken for the identity cards and other papers we would need'

'I have to say it was very unnerving walking past groups of German soldiers in broad daylight I can tell you, but our guide kept up a running conversation that made it seem as if we were all old friends out for a walk in the warm June sunshine'

'An hour later we were walking back to our hiding place but we were stopped as we entered the road the house was on by another woman who made gushing sounds of welcome to the three of us while at the same time shepherding us into a café at the corner of the street'

'Frankly, I thought we were in for a treat as the smell of fresh coffee hit us as we went through the entrance, but I quickly knew something was wrong, when for the second time in weeks we all scurried straight through the cafe and out of the back entrance to a waiting car which our new escort started and we all drove away in'

'The conversation was so hurried between the two women in the vehicle I concede that I understood practically nothing of it and could only sense that something tragic had happened, but knew then was not the time to ask what'

'After only ten minutes or so the car came to a stop in the drive way of a suburban house and we were led into a kitchen and quickly to a room in the attic, where we stayed for two days, under the watchful eye of Louise whose husband had been a General in the first world war, and had been killed at the battle of Mons.'

'She was an absolute hoot Anna. I suppose she must have been in her late seventies but she looked and most certainly acted twenty years younger. She had perfect English, and told us that she was dedicated to helping the new resistance movement that was growing around her each day to fight the Bosch'

'It was mid afternoon when Bridgette came to the house and told us we would be leaving the next morning and we were being split up again. She also told us that Edith and Pierre had been arrested and were being held by the Gestapo at a very grim prison in the city.'

'My goodness Anna, the poor thing looked so very pale and frightened as she told us that several German soldiers and Gestapo had raided the flat only twenty minutes before our return. The brutes had smashed down the front door before racing up the stairs of the building and forcing their way into the apartment'

'The young woman cried when she told us that Edith and

Pierre, both pensioners, were literally dragged down the stairs and pushed into an army truck, before being driven away. She added that she was going to the South of the country to keep out of the way for a while and that our new guides would arrive after breakfast, the next morning.'

'We were then given our forged papers and identity cards, so now Anna, I was M. Henri Charles Vallet, and my profession was as an optician with a special dispensation from military service because of a heart problem!'

'For the life of me Anna sleep simply would not come that night in the attic bedroom. It really was frightfully hot up there and so I went over and over in my mind, yet again, what had happened to all of us in so short a time, how were we defeated so soundly by the Germans, questions, questions, over and over.'

'The young lad across the room was fast asleep, but it was a troubled slumber he was enveloped by, and he would probably have been embarrassed if he had known I was privy to his low whispers for his mother and other friends, during our time together he had told me that he had celebrated his twentieth birthday the day before Belgium had been invaded'

'It was strange that as I lay wide awake in that small room for the first time in my life Anna, I felt old. Old and rather weary at the grand old age of twenty eight, quiet absurd, don't you think!'

Anna had grappled with the same long nights of recrimination, of trying to find someone to blame 'I think that perhaps we all became a bit older Peter. Too much happened in too short a time' she replied, before letting him continue.

'We fellow evaders shook hands after breakfast and before I could wish him 'good luck' he said rather sadly "I wish we could stay together Sir. I know that will not be possible, but I do wish it was, you see I feel a bit scared, to be honest with you".

'What on earth did you say, or perhaps what could you say?' Anna asked.

'Quite Anna. What was to be said? The best I could do was to tell the truth. In fact, and you will like this, I thought about our Mr John McCloud, and remembered how he used to tackle these tricky moments by being totally honest and rather brazen and brash with it, so I said "Derek, I am as frightened as you are, probably more so, if you don't mind my saying so, but look, if we get caught, then we will end up as POW's, so nothing ventured, nothing gained".'

"Now, let's put ourselves in the position of the people of the resistance movement who have been so good to us. Derek, if they get caught then the consequences for them could be very unpleasant, just how unpleasant we have yet to find out, but my feeling is that the Gestapo is a very nasty lot, without feeling and quite ruthless"

'Thankfully any further rather hopeless efforts at giving help and advice were brushed aside as the cheerful sound of our hostess bringing us coffee lightened up the darkish moment before our new guides arrived and both of us went our separate ways.'

'Unfortunately, I found out that the lad got as far as Poitieres last November before he and his helper were picked up. He is now in a POW camp in Austria and the Frenchman leading him was executed.'

'I began to realise Anna, that the shock of such a humiliating and quick defeat had been so devastating, so traumatic for most Belgians, that the initial response of doing anything to hit back, to wildly lash out at the Germans for taking away their freedom and way of life was in most cases clumsy and totally incompetent'

'They quickly learnt that the Germans had been preparing the invasion of their country for a long time, and that those preparations had been expertly and clinically put into place. It involved several thousands of their own countrymen and women with German connections and blood links who moved quickly to support the new people in power'

'The brutality of their conquerors was sadly quick to show itself Anna. My next guide was a middle aged man who drove a cattle truck that he had parked some way from the house. Walking beside him he told me that Edith and Pierre had been sent to a German concentration camp that had been erected at Natweiler, in Eastern France and that after being tortured for several days Pierre had been executed by a firing squad in the grounds of the prison, and Edith sent to Germany'

'Those poor souls Anna, she was now in some sort of prison and he was now dead, and all because they had tried to carry on a fight that their generals and leaders had so quickly run away from'

'I was hidden in between six large and absolutely disgusting pig swill bins in the back of the lorry. The smell was frightful Anna and for about six hours of stop and go we travelled along until we reached a farm a mile or so from a village called Limelette, in the Wallonia district of Belgium. It was a beautiful mixed farm with cattle and arable crops, owned by the Van Dam family, and it was also my home until the spring of 1941.'

Shifting around in her chair Anna frowned before saying 'I'm puzzled Peter, why was there a sudden hold put on the efforts to get you home, we are now January 1942, over eighteen months have gone by?'

Peter Adnans placed his glass onto a small table before sweeping his large hands away from himself like the gesture made by a vicar in a pulpit before addressing his congregation and starting his sermon 'It's what I said earlier Anna, the hasty and brave actions of the first weeks of occupation had played into the hands of the Germans. It was a case of the amateurs versus the seasoned and vicious professionals of war'

'The Nazis moved quickly to grind and crush any seeds of resistance. They were clever, of that there is absolutely no doubt. They were clever, clinical, extremely brutal and without any form of pity whatsoever'

'But like all bullies Anna, and I do so remember they were the same at my prep school, these Nazi bullies are simply not clever enough. They lack the flexibility of mind, lack that creative level of liberal thinking that reasoned people have'

'It is true that the Belgians and the French have had their physical movements restricted by invasion, but Hitler will never be able to stamp out the vision of freedom that remains in each of them, and I tell you, at every tick of the clock those people are scheming, planning and fighting for their eventual freedom'

'Where most of the military and political leaders failed the people of France and Belgium, so the people themselves have now formed the new resistance to occupation and the most squalid cloak of shame they are being forced to wear will soon be tossed away'

'These new people that have started to fill the vacuum of leadership are bright, intelligent, loyal and absolutely fearlessly. Fact is, Jerry doesn't stand a chance in the long term, and I can tell you Anna each member of the résistance I have met, men and women, has a rage inside them that is without compromise of any sort. Only unconditional freedom will be accepted, and they will win it.'

Anna was almost mesmerised by Peter's dancing hands as he waved them around with each sentence 'Now, where was I? Ah yes, the Van Dam's. With the hospitality of Roland Van Dam and his wife Nicol, whose family had worked the land for over two centuries, I stayed at the farm for six months or so, until March, last year'

'After a while I became doctor to resistance members in the area and had managed to accumulate a rather good pharmacy and built a basic but clean area where I even performed emergency operations, some rather complex'

'For the first time since university I had time to carry out some very interesting research into foot bone structure using the feet of dead dogs and other animals. Well, it was all rather jolly really, I had been told that I would be moving South towards Paris in a few weeks, and I was settled in the routine of helping around the farm and of being the emergency doctor, but then one night everything was turned topsy turvy'

'We were all having dinner together when we heard a huge kafalcul going on overhead. Everyone raced outside in the pitch dark and we saw a glowing trail of fire coming from the engine of a plane overhead'

'As it was lost to view over the ridge of a hill we waited stiffly until a flash of bright orange lit up the sky line and was followed by an ear shattering explosion. "It was a Wellington bomber, definitely British, not German" someone said in the dark, followed by "Maybe they baled out?"

'Roland, and two of the farm workers, Daniel, and Francoise

cycled off in the direction the plane had taken, with Daniel shouting over his shoulder "Peter, you had better get ready to move out quickly in case the Bosch send troops to search the area for survivors."

Peter Adnans was about to continue when a soft knock on the door of his suite made him get up and open it. Anna sat still and heard the voice of James, the porter say, 'Master Peter, would it be in order for me to clear away your lunch trays?'

They both walked to the window that overlooked the city while James put the lunch time dishes onto a trolley and they looked out over the war ravage city towards St. Paul's Cathedral, where smoke from a heavy raid on the capital two nights before still drifted from the charred remains of homes and office buildings gutted by bombs and incendiaries.

The surgeon spoke first as he rested his forehead on a hand that was pressed against the criss cross of gummed tape spread across the window. 'I do feel rather guilty Anna when I look at the bomb damage to London and knowing you went through some dreadful times in Plymouth. Fact is, while you were going through all the bombing I was having a rather spendid time really, mind you, I suppose I did rather make up for my good times when I tell you what happened next!'

Anna squeezed his arm, saying quietly 'Shall I give James a hand with the plates, he seems to be taking a long time to clear things away?'

Taking a deep breath Peter whispered, 'No Anna, leave it to me, but thank you.' before turning away from the window and going to help the elderly man put the remaining dishes onto a trolley.

As he helped pile the silver salvers and plates he said 'James, do you remember the quail Daddy and I used to bring down once or twice through the winter months from the estate in Scotland and have them cooked for us by the head chief, before the war?'

The old man beamed, his wait in the wings rewarded and he answered by saying 'Like yesterday, Master Peter, just like yesterday, such wonderful times, wonderful times!'

'Indeed, they were. Well James, I feasted on quail casseroled in brandy and red wine only two weeks ago in a log cabin on the edge of a pine forest close to a snow covered mountain top, and I have to tell you my first thoughts were of those days when the best chef in London, Monsieur Virlogeux, prepared and cooked them, and you had your waiters serve up the dish to our family and friends in the restaurant downstairs!'

Anna did not know whether the story of the quail was true or not, it really did not matter. What she did know was that to James the rich memory was as fresh as the birds had been, and very important to the loyal hotel employee, years past his retirement. As Peter held open the door to the suite he said, 'Thank everyone James, that was splendid.'

Patting his seat Anna almost shouted 'Come on, please sit down and finish!'

Looking slightly vague the surgeon clapped his hands and said 'Now, where was I? Oh yes. An hour or so later Francoise came back accompanied by an RAF flight sergeant, called Richard Castello, from Liverpool'

'Before Francoise had finished his ride across the court yard to the front of the farm house he was yelling "Peter, you have to leave, there are German troops everywhere."

'It all happened so quickly that afterwards, and now as we speak, I felt a great sense of sadness that I could not thank the people who had given me a home, and Anna it was like a home where I had become a member of the family.'

'Was there only one survivor from the aircraft?' Anna asked.

'No, Richard was sure that at least another three crew had baled out of the Wellington, but he could not be absolutely sure, but the three of us cycled to the village where we were hidden in the cellars of the local *estimate,* which was opposite the local police station, and told to wait'

'We were brought food and coffee during the day and also visited by two rather tough looking Belgians who clearly knew a lot about me, and of course absolutely nothing about Richard, who I thought was an extremely decent chap'

'Actually Anna, it was then that I realised things had changed from when I was rescued the previous year. One has to say my escape was like a University Rag Day prank, there was an aspect of the comic to it, and the brutal killing of Pierre was the sad result'

'Just after dark the two men came back to our cellar and gave Richard a set of farm labourer's cloths to put over his uniform before saying that because he had no ID papers he would be moved away first, and I would follow tomorrow'

'There was a coldness to the chaps that led him away and when Francoise came to visit me in the evening I told him about the men. He simply said "Peter, the resistance movement has suffered several setbacks. Two German Gestapo agents posed as RAF survivors and were able to expose a line of helpers before being found out. Three of our members had been tortured and then shot before we were able prove the agents' identities and we able to kill both of them, so Richard would have been questioned at length before being fed into the system of escape."

'I think that from a rather shaky start and with the sacrifice of many close colleagues, the amateurs had now become professionals Anna. I was moved to two more farms before leaving Belgium and going to Paris, not the nice part of the city that we all went too with John and the others, but a dreary, dirty area called Montparnasse and frankly I was pleased to leave.'

Anna listened intently while at the same time remembering her conversation with John McCloud almost two years ago to the day as they sat outside the Café Marque in Paris "The left bank Anna, that was a special time in my life. Our Lord Peter over there, bless him, would hate it, far too dirty, but I loved it. I'll take you there one day Anna if you like?"

She felt a gentle squeeze on her hand and heard Peter Adnans saying 'Anna, are you alright my dear?'

Shaking her head she focused her moist eyes on his and blinked several times before saying 'I'm sorry Peter. For a moment, I was quite lost in the past, I am sorry, what happened next, please go on.'

'I was moved to small flat where I met two more 'evaders'. Super chaps. One from New Zealand, one from Australia. I must say it was a real treat to have long chats in English. We waited for a couple of days and the forth member of our group arrived. He was a Polish lad called Stepan Paz. All three had been shot down on the way back from separate bombing missions over Germany'

'From then on Anna we were "packages" to be delivered to the French and Spanish border and the Pyrenees range of mountains that sat in between.'

Anna sat back for a moment before asking 'But why go all the way to the south when you were so close to the English Channel?'

'One of my very first questions, and apparently the Germans thought the same as me Anna because they quickly realised men were being smuggled to the channel ports and whisked back home so they instigated two tight demarcation zones around all the channel ports, each zone requiring different sets of papers to enter'

'They thought the likelihood of people being smuggled over a thousand miles through occupied country was minimal, so you see Anna, cracks in the thinking of the mighty war machine were becoming visible, the amateurs were learning fast!'

'Neither of the ANZAC chaps spoke French so Ben Shaw, the New Zealander was teamed with me and Dan Manning with Stepan Paz, the Polish man. We were together for three days and visited by the same elderly gentleman each day with food, fresh bread and horrid coffee made from acorns'

'We never had a name but he seemed very well informed about what we could expect and how we should work. He told us that our guide would stay with us the night before we left the flat to start our journey, when final instructions would be issued.'

Anna leaned back in the comfortable winged armchair before saying 'What time of year was it?'

'Oh, late September I suppose. The city had a definite autumnal feel about it and the nights were getting dark early, in fact it was almost dark outside when we heard footsteps coming up the stairs to our attic room accompanied by the whistling of 'Frere Jacque', which was the 'all clear' signal for us'

'The door opened slowly and a very attractive young woman came in and introduced herself as Madeleine. I knew I had seen her before but it was she who solved the mystery when after she introduced herself to the others by shaking their hands she came to me she and said, "Well now Monsieur I must say you look better in check shirt and grey trousers then you did in a Priest's vestment's!" My Nun had returned Anna!'

'We went through the next days plan in full and she was very definite about what she expected of all of us should we be caught. She would go with Dan and Stepan, we would follow a little way behind'

'We left the flat at seven in the morning to go to a railway station quite close. It was the height of the rush hour by the time we arrived outside and joined the queues that filed past the waiting ticket inspectors and the German police agents who lurked behind some of them'

'It was nerve racking stuff Anna, perhaps not so bad for me as my French had greatly improved, but for the other chaps it was very tense indeed'

'We got onto the train to Orleans and changed there for the final part of our first day's journey to Tours. After walking to a bar, we had a beer and left, following an older woman who had greeted Madeleine when she entered. That night and the following were spent in rather cramped conditions in the back room of a concierge's quarters while we waited for our guide to return'

'She returned later in the evening and told us to be ready the next morning to leave at seven. With breaks in safe houses we spent the next ten days travelling by train to Poitiers, Limoges, Perigueux and then finally to Bordeaux, where we were hidden under tarpaulins on the back of an empty timber lorry that had delivered a load of tree trunks to a local saw mill.'

'Our next quarters were woodcutters log cabins on the edge of a vast forest in the Landes region, about thirty miles north of Biarritz.'

Shaking his head slowly from side to side he closed his eyes and breathed deeply before continuing 'Imaging what a treat it was Anna to wake up that first morning to discover that the huts opened up onto the beaches of the Atlantic and the Bay of Biscay. To feel the fresh sea air of the Atlantic blowing against our faces was absolutely wonderful. We were all rather ladish I have to say, like lions suddenly let out of their gages!'

'The whole region is about the size of Wales and covered with dense pine forest speckled with small hamlets in between, and although the Germans were around in some numbers the large area simply swallowed the blighters up.'

'It was cold I have to admit, cold, but bracing and it certainly cemented in my mind what it feels like to be free, and to wonder as one pleased in our new wooded world.'

'Peter' Anna asked 'What had become of Madeleine?'

'Well she seemed to come and go like the tides. But when she was there we were able to walk through the forest for hours on our own and talk and talk Anna. My how we talked.' Anna watched as his animation of the scene faltered as he thought back to the time that clearly meant so much to him before finishing with: 'It was wonderful really, truly wonderful.'

Anna sensed something new in the man opposite. The way his voice lingered on certain words, how sentences that started in his usual quick and sharp way tailed off or became slower, and always when Madeleine was mentioned. She leaned across to him and put her hand on his arm before saying 'Peter, are you in love with Madeleine?'

He sat back for a moment, knowing he was unable to look at her, he could only tap his fingers on the arm of his chair for a moment before smiling and looking up and saying 'John always told me that you had a knack of reading his mind, and that at times it was at trifle annoying Anna!'

'I found her the most fascinating woman I have ever met, she was a true wonder. She intervened when we were stopped by the French police or Germans by telling the most outrageous lies or stories, and because she was so diminutive these tough chaps who towered over her all seemed totally mesmerised and believed every bit of twaddle she told them, she was absolutely fantastic Anna, a cat with the heart and strength of a lioness.'

'Us 'evaders' all thought that we were going to go over the border into Spain through St Jean-de-Luz but something had gone wrong. None of the resistance people would talk about it but we all had the feeling that the line had maybe been infiltrated by the Gestapo'

'Madeleine would only say that the original plan had been amended and that we would stay where we were for a while before going over the border a different way, and that was all she would say.'

'We stayed for another couple of weeks until we were told to expect to move again and the next day we were driven out of the forest hidden between newly cut tree trunks on a log carrier to a small wood foresters cabin a few miles out of Lescun, some hundred and fifty miles from our Atlantic haven overlooking the sand dunes to another area of forest, this time over six thousand feet above sea level!'

'The difference in climate was instant the moment we clambered out of our hideaway between the tree trunks and jumped onto the hard ground and gaze in utter amazement at the peaks of several mountains that were all part of the Pyrenees range, stretching from the Atlantic on one side and ending at the Mediterranean.'

'The lorry had dropped us off on a back road, or rather track, with forest ranging up on each side and a light dusting of snow on the ground. Smiling, Madeleine said to us, "Don't look so worried, we have not been abandoned, our new home is off the road a little way into the forest."

'We trudged into the wood about a hundred yards before finding the cabin, which I have to say was very warm and rather cosy. That night she told us that the trek over the mountains was not going to be easy. She had done it several times in summer and it had been a hard and physical trip but now, the first week in December it would be doubly difficult because of snow at the higher levels.'

Anna felt an involuntary shiver run through her body before she said, 'You surely couldn't walk along wearing a jacket and tie, how did you all manage?'

'It really was terribly well organised Anna. The very first thing we did was to change into a set of warm woodcutters clothing that was waiting for each of us. She told us that we would stay in the hut for two or three nights, possibly more, until our guide arrived.'

The big hands of the surgeon stopped waving around as they started a slow patting movement as the palm of his left hand tapped the back of his right that rested on his lap. He gazed for a moment past Anna towards St Paul's cathederal before turning back and starting again by saying, 'The next day was one of the most wonderful of my life Anna, and I really do not mind admitting so. We all had strict instructions not to stray onto the road that went past the cabin, but we were more or less free to roam around to the forest edge below the start of the mountain range'

'I asked Madeleine if she would like to walk with me and she and I, both wrapped up in our new winter garments, set off to the snow line that was just visible. We walked for an hour until we passed the cover of the trees and found a hollow of rocks where we could sit virtually unseen from above or below'

'With the sun beating down on our backs we sat and looked towards the west knowing that for me the mountains in the distance were the last barrier before I could at last breath the air as a free man again'

'The sun at midday was hot; we took off our outer jackets and simply soaked up the warmth of the sun. Madeleine was sat with a rock at her back looking at a high mountain ridge ahead of her when she excitedly handed me her binoculars and pointed to a jagged rock outcrop high above us, and still in the dark shadow of the west. I focused in on what she had pointed at and sat motionless before I said, "What are they?", I was puzzled, I know my birds of prey from countless highland walks in Scotland, but I had never seen anything like these'

'She took the binoculars from me and almost shouted "They're Lammergeiers Peter, the largest birds in Europe, aren't they just so beautiful." It was then Anna, right at that moment, looking at her with binoculars held to her eyes that, yes, I knew I was hopelessly in love with her'

'In fact, she put down the glasses and turned towards me and I think we both knew it, could not help it really, neither of us said anything, we just sort of became one person'

'In my mind, the rest of that day and the next two were like richly coloured mosaics. I think back to different times of our days together and I see the extraordinary colours of the Pyrences exploding in front of me they were so bright and clear'

'The deep greens of the meadow in front of us, the recent frost melted by the sun and the deep indigo blue of the cloudless sky was breathtaking. The snow capped peaks of the mountains seemed to reflect the brilliant sunshine into deep ravines and crevices, casting giant shadows and shapes that changed slowly as the sun travelled around our backs'

'Anna, the scene simply silenced speech, there seemed no subject on earth that could match what we were part of during those precious moments. The ugliness and dreadfulness of the war that was raging only an hour or so away was forgotten'

'For three days we talked, and talked, but no matter how hard I tried she would never, not once, talk about herself, her family or the past. You know what I'm like Anna, I need to talk, need to tell people who I am, what I do, what wines I like, that is me! But Madeleine was a closed book; she said it was too dangerous to tell me anything in case we were captured by the Germans, and so it was.'

The surgeon was quiet now. Elbows on knees while his flying hands acted as pillars to support his chin, his eyes held Ann's as he said 'Completely mad isn't it. You see "Falling in love" had always been something other chaps did, not me. I remember being rather irritated when John told me he loved you, I simply never knew what to expect, but there I was head over heels in love, and the sad irony Anna, is that to this day, I do not know her real name'

'Towards the end of our third day of bliss we were walking back to the cabin when Madeleine said that she thought it very likely that our guide would turn up that evening, and so he did Anna!'

'Almost as big as the mountains around us Jesus Sotelo could be heard coming through the forest as the light was fading singing at the top of his voice five minutes before his huge frame appeared'

'My first thoughts were of the German or French border patrols that may be in the area and when I mentioned this to Madeleine she was quick to say, laughing at the same time, I might add "No, no Peter, Suso would have spent the past hour of daylight high above us in the mountains carefully reconnoitring the area through an ancient brass spy glass he says with some pride, his grandfather took from an English naval officer he had killed at sea!"

Anna was pleased that the melancholy of the story had been lifted by the sudden appearance in it of the larger than life guide, and she felt more at ease as her old boss continued.

'Madeleine went to greet this massive man who was dressed in a huge dark brown fur coat with a rifle slung over his shoulder. Looking from behind she seemed almost to be swallowed up whole as he enveloped her with his coat, and they both disappeared inside it, amid wild shouts of welcome'

'The temperature outside had now plummeted and after a bone crushing hand shake and instruction to call him Suso, we went quickly into the warmth of the cabin, and as he was taking off his various layers of clothing so to came various items of food and drink from the 'poachers' pockets' that lined the inside of his garments'

'This absolute bear of a man Anna had a presence about him that was rather alarming to be honest. Madeleine, I think sensed my disquiet and whispered to me

"He really is the gentlest giant you will ever meet Peter."

'Out loud I asked her "Doesn't Suso mean Jesus in Spanish?" before she could answer he came over and said in a language that was neither Spanish or French

"Suso" followed by a slow shake from side to side of his large bearded head as he repeated "Non Jesus, Non Jesus, Iss Suso".

'She quickly explained to all of us that he was a committed communist with a reward on his head and fervently agnostic, while Suso pulled the cork out of a bottle and poured at least three fingers of amber spirit into glasses and cups before handing one to each of us and interrupting her by saying "Basque Wheeeskey, Iss verry good, Cheers!"

'After banging our mugs and glasses together we followed Suso's and Madeleine's example by downing the whole lot in one swig. I felt rather as though my tummy was about to explode until the liquid began to infiltrate other parts of my anatomy. Poor Dan Manning raced coughing and spluttering outside into the night with Madeleine and Suso doing nothing other than roar with laughter!'

'Madeleine told us that he was from the Basque region of Spain, and like the Catalans, they had a very separate sense of identity, language and culture to the rest of the country and were constantly pursued by Franco's fascist army.'

'While she explained all this Suso was noisily preparing a casserole for our dinner. The story I told Arthur earlier about the quail was true Anna, courtesy of our guide, as from somewhere inside his clothing he produced three recently caught quail that he plucked, gutted and after pouring in red wine and brandy, he swung the blackened pot over the fire and went outside to listen for signs of patrols'

'That evening, translating through Madeleine he told us of what to expect when we started our journey a couple of hours before dusk the next day'

'We were lucky because the snows were late and still high on the mountains, leaving most of our route open, but that we would be the last 'Evaders' he would lead through the mountain pass until the next Spring'

'What a night it was. By the warm light of a roaring log fire and with candles dotted around the single room that was dormitory, kitchen and dining room all in one, the six of us sat around the long table and drank the local red wine that had been left for us, together with Suso's wondrous casserole'

'After the stew we tucked into wedges of deliciously strong hard cheeses that are made in the area while the proud Basque told us the history of his country and it's people'

'Anna, it was while I was sat there with the others listening to this fascinating man that I was also able to study Madeleine's face which reminded me so much of a Rembrandt painting I had seen once in London'

'I remembered this one picture in particular because it was hard to believe that any painter could create such fire, warmth and beauty from an almost black canvass, but that night I understood completely the emotion that inspired him to create it'

'It was only Madeleine's face and a collar of white around

her neck that the flames and candle light danced on. Her dark woollen hat and the blackness of the rest of the room behind her left her seemingly suspended in air and gave her the same look that Rembrandt had given his model three hundred years earlier. She looked truly beautiful Anna. I was, should say am, completely lost to her in every way.'

Peter Adnans stopped, rubbing both of his eyes with a thumb and forefinger of one hand, using them finally to flatten out the moisture that would have formed his tears by softly dragging them from the bridge of his nose to the sides of his cheek bones before looking at Anna and saying, 'Sorry about that, soppy really I know, but I do find it upsetting at times, I know I shouldn't because I have so much to look forward too, but there we are.'

Anna almost copied her former boss as she knew she to was close to tears, instead she shook her head before saying 'Oh Peter, what a bloody horrible time we are all going through, it isn't fair, I don't know what else to say'

She paused for a second before adding 'Can I have another glass of wine, please.'

Smiling at her he said 'Jolly good idea! Anyway, my dear friend, to continue, the Basque was insistent that it would not be necessary to stand guard outside the hut and we all had such total faith in this man from the mountains that well into the night and hazy from wine we crawled onto our bunk beds that were scattered around the walls of the room while he put a final load of logs onto the fire and blew out each candle before heaving himself onto the slatted wood bunk and thin mattress, disappearing under his vast outer coat.

The bunks were arranged in two's, one lower, another above, and Madeleine slipped noiselessly into mine, and with the top of her head below my chin we watched the dancing flames of the fire and giggled at the loud snores from our neighbours before we to fell asleep in that lovely red and orange fire glow.'

'We set off in the afternoon the next day in brilliant winter sunshine, every footstep giving a crunching, grinding sound as we stepped on frozen blades of grass, twigs and through the top crust of a recent dusting of frozen snow'

'Suso in the lead, Madeleine and myself last in line we started our journey west towards Spain and freedom. It was strange, my fellow evaders in front of me were full of eagerness at the prospect reaching the border, but my feelings had changed'

'Instead, I had a sudden urge not to leave France. I know it sounds utterly ridiculous Anna, but it suddenly seemed to me that the one thing that I had never had in my life was right here besides me, and the closer we got to the border the quicker she would be gone from my life.'

Anna realised that Peter Adnans was talking as much to himself at this point as he was to her. It was as if reliving these precious moments was as important to him as it was to tell Anna about them 'Madeleine seemed to sense my feeling, gripping as my arm she said "Peter, look up at those mountain peaks with the late sun turning the white snow a bright golden red. We are so lucky to live in Europe, so lucky to have this on our doorsteps, and one day we will come back, you and me, and roam as we want, so please, please do not be sad."

'She was right, it was beautiful, my goodness me it was also cold, and as the forest gave way to open green pasture land in deep valley's, so the mountains started to tower over us on each side and looking up to find the peaks became impossible as the light faded and we worked our way slowly between them'

'We were about to leave the cover of a line of tall beech trees when Suso quickly raised a hand and we all crouched down before he motioned for us to gather around him. He pointed to a spot across the valley we were following and quietly he whispered "Iss beg bear, look!"

'Sure enough Anna, five brown bears, one massive one and four smaller were playing in a snow covered meadow, jumping around like children, it was wonderful to see, and they disappeared into other trees as soon as they saw us.'

'All night we walked along the scaly slippery tracks, stopping occasionally for a rest and swig of Suso's seemingly never ending bottle, and more than once to avoid herds of charging wild boar and frieghtened Ibex'

'Our guide wanted us to get to a point he knew where we

would be able to take cover in the forest and sleep while he looked at the road and river that marked the boundary between the two countries in the daylight'

'We arrived at the spot Suso had aimed for with four of hours of darkness left until dawn with the temperature well below freezing. For breakfast, we ate a little bread and cheese together with chorizo sausage plus several swigs of red wine before finding individual plots that had some degree of cover to put our sleeping bags. I lay in mine, exhausted, extremely cold and tired but unable to drift off'

'I felt as though I was sleeping in the bottom of a telescope with the tall straight pine trees of the forest acting like the walls holding the reflector at the top. I looked up in total awe at the brightest carpet of stars I have ever seen, until I felt two fingers on my lips and knew she was there'

'We struggled noiselessly into my bag and lay there together side by side watching the same stars listening to the distant haunting sound of packs of wild wolves baying until we fell asleep. Anna, I had never been so happy in all my life'

'When we woke Suso had gone. It wasn't until towards midday that he came silently back and told us that there was a lot of activity by both German and French patrols close to us and that on the other side of the border the Spanish police were being unusually alert. We would have to wait until nightfall to cross over and so we spent a rather tense day as on a couple of occasions we heard cars or lorries quite near, then when night fell we started off again'

'It was absolutely pitch black but Suso had a cat's instinct and this was most certainly his territory, his own back garden so to speak of and we simply followed the black shape that led us'

'After walking four or five hours we halted. I could hear water running and one by one we followed Suso down a bank and across a narrow stream. On the other side we set off again and began to follow him, this time with the squelching sound of cold mountain water in our boots, until he stopped after about half an hour'

'After he had spoken to Madeleine she spoke quietly to us as we gathered around her "Suso has told me to tell you that this is the most difficult and dangerous of moments for all of us, you must be very quiet, and wait", not knowing what to expect Anna we all obeyed his order to the full and stood motionless while he looked about and finally began walking and counting his paces at the same time until he suddenly stopped besides a rock and disappeared from view'

'He reappeared quickly and walked back signalling us to gather around him. Having looked around at the tense faces in front of him, lit now by silver moonlight, he threw back his cape and produced an open bottle of brandy which he passed to me first before saying in between peels of loud laughter "Bien Espania" - Welcome to Spain!'

'Madeleine had of course been in on the joke and told us that Suso always had a bottle of Spanish brandy hidden away on the escape routes he used that were at least three miles into Spanish territory, and safety'

'You can imagine the euphoric feeling we had. We were free men Anna. We still had to be careful because the neutral status of Spain that meant that any evaders found would be interned in camps, but we were free from the fear of persecution and worse from the Gestapo'

'Spanish brandy had never tasted so good as I took a long swig from that bottle Anna. I was free. Free. Since arriving home I've had time to think about the word. It's such a little one with so many meanings. Liberate, unbind, independent, unrestricted, expression. Take away "Free" and one can't use the others Anna'

'I've thought about it so many times since my escape. You see I have to admit that until my freedom had been stripped away from me I had never once, not once in my whole privileged life, appreciated what it was to be a person without the ability to act, think, argue, disagree as I thought fit'

'When Maurice Pagnol and I were ordered to be outside the hospital in Dunkirk in an hour or risk being shot, we both knew the dreadful truth of it. The truth that we had surrendered our freedom to become prisoners, and the same thing has happened to the people of Belgium, Holland, France, Poland'

Shaking his head from side to side a stern, hard look came

over the face of the surgeon as he turned to his friend and said 'Freedom was indeed a mighty gift and I know that. It was a gift that had been given back to us through the pain of others Anna, and I shall never forget that pain for the rest of my life.'

Moments later his expression eased, the severity had gone and the familiar lightness in his face and voice came back again as he continued 'As the first shades of dawn appeared, the terrain we had been tramping all night changed as we started to walk with ease along the old Roman road that followed the lush green Hecho Valley that opened up with the light'

'We said good bye to Suso close to a small Spanish village and after more bone crushing handshakes and bear hugs he left us hidden by the road side until a lorry arrived and with Madeleine and me in the front and the lads in the back we were driven to the outskirts of Bilbao and another 'safe house' and the luxury of a bath'

'I knew that that night would be our last together. I begged her to come back with me, but she would not hear of it, saying instead "Peter, we both have so much to do, you in England and me here, this terrible war will not last forever, and after it is won we will be together again, I promise you."

'I asked her how I would contact her, all she would say is that she would contact me. Repeatedly telling me that she could not give me her true identity in case I was ever captured and interrogated by the Gestapo and that would mean certain death for her family and comrades in the resistance'

'The next morning, I watched as she got into a car and waved to me through the window of it until it turned a corner and she disappeared from my view. I felt quite wretched Anna. Lost and empty'

'I know that Madeleine is not her real name. Sometimes at night, I try to imagine what it is, mad isn't it! The Right Honourable Peter Adnans, besotted by a woman whose name he doesn't know!'

'Actually, she did let a couple things out of the bag, her father for instance has something to do with the church, and I believe that she is a history teacher, but apart from that my dear Anna, the love of my life is an anonymous stranger!'

'The four of us were taken the next day to the British Consulate in Bilbao. From there we travelled in a Foreign Office car to Gibraltar and we were flown home in a Sunderland flying boat, and my dear friend Anna, here I am.'

His voice held a sad note as he finished before placing a hand on top of hers and saying 'Now young lady, I want to know all about you and your war and I really am looking forward to meeting this Mr Tremayne at dinner this evening but as I said earlier Anna, I have to meet daddy at the House of Lords this afternoon. Churchill has just appointed him as a liaison between our government and Americans for the job of finding room for the two million or so GI's expected here soon, it's all very exciting, isn't it, you know I feel Jerry is on the run already!'

Escorting Anna down to the foyer of the hotel and helping her into a taxi he waved a goodbye before stepping into the next taxi cab and heading towards the parliament buildings by the side of the River Thames.

North London, 7th January 1942

A jubilant David Jack embraced his daughter as soon as he had finished his rapid decent of the stairs shouting as he made the journey 'Merry Christmas, Happy New Year and lots more darling. Has Mummy told you the news Anna?'

Struggling to take off her heavy greatcoat while at the same time as saying 'No Daddy, what news.' she hung it up on oak hall stand and walked with her father into the kitchen carrying her khaki valise and a brown paper carrier bag.

'We had a letter yesterday from my brother Leonard. They are all safe in America, safe and well, Thank God, if there is one that is, which I doubt!'

Mary Jack motioned her husband in the direction of the drinks cupboard with the remark 'Enough David thank you, I know it's only five o'clock, but it must six somewhere!'

Sitting down at the kitchen table Mary put her hand on her daughters and said 'It really is such wonderful news Anna, daddy has been very worried. Sadly, there is still no word of his aunts and an uncle, but it is a truly good way to start the New Year to know that Len, Rita and the two girls are safe.'

Three glasses were placed on the table and Anna said cheekily 'Oh, no lemon or limes?'

David Jack only looked at his daughter, but not before she burst into laughter and at the same time reaching into her carrier bag and saying, 'Look what I have brought, courtesy of the Savoy if you please!'

As two lemons and two limes rolled there way towards her father he shook his head, saying 'You have the devil in you miss, always did have. And what's this I hear about you and this new boyfriend dining in style with the rich and supposedly famous or is this new chap of yours one of them?'

Mary caught the slight blush that swept across Anna's face as she rebuked her husband light heartedly 'David, you are such a terrible hypocrite at times. Only the week before last you were hob knobbing at the Reform Club with Lord Piers and Lord Alton, but at least Anna had the good sense to borrow some limes which is more than you did'

David Jack was returning from the kitchen with a knife and board to cut off a slice each of the precious limes when Mary asked Anna 'How is Mr Adnans darling? It must have been like daddy having the letter from his brother when you heard that he was safe and had got home.'

She took her glass in her hand before replying with 'Before I say anything else, cheers mummy, cheers daddy. Happy New Year! It's so nice to be home again'

They clinked their glasses and took a sip of their drinks before she continued 'Yes it was such a wonderful surprise, oh and by the way daddy, hold on a moment'

The two parents exchanged glances as their daughter disappeared again from view below the level of the table as she rummaged in her carrier bag. Sitting back in her chair she looked again at her father and said, 'Peter asked me to give this to you as a belated Christmas present daddy.'

The brown paper wrapping was peeled away to reveal a bottle of single malt whisky. Her father's look of genuine surprise ended when he exclaimed 'Always liked the family, never agreed with them, but they always had good taste, wouldn't be surprised if they have Jewish blood in them somewhere down the line! Only joking Anna, it really was a kind gesture and I hope we will be able to meet him soon.'

Mary Jack placed the heavy metal cooking pot in the centre of the table before taking her seat with her daughter and husband and saying, 'Pretty ghastly dinner I'm afraid but after Christmas and the New Year we are terribly short of ration coupons, so this evenings creation is a casserole with several layers of sliced potatoes, spread over with tomato puree and spam and finally covered with a white sauce and bread crumbs.'

During dinner, they caught up with news of family and friends until David Jack brought them back to the present with 'This is the first time we have been together since the Americans entered the war. Now we shall see something girls. The build up will be slow but at my meeting at the Reform Club all the talk was of nothing else. Hitler is on the run. The cracks are beginning to appear, but we still have a long, long way to go'

'I've heard that Peter Adnans's father has been given a role in organising some of the plans to house and train the Americans when they start to arrive in very large numbers over the next year, and in seriousness Anna, you know that I could never agree with their politics but I do not doubt Lord Roxenton's ability in this particular matter, he will do the job well, and indeed it is strange how this war is making people of all political persuasions pull in the same direction if only for the benefit of being able to argue and disagree with each other after the war is over!'

'So Anna, what is this new boyfriend of yours like?'
Mary Jack was quick to intercede with 'David, don't be so insensitive, leave the girl alone will you.'

'I don't mind mummy. Let me see now, Simon is very different from John, but at the same time they are very similar really. He's a very hard working and professional mining engineer, very kind, perhaps too kind, extremely artistic, he loves the modern painters and adores pottery'

'He's not as single minded as John but I think that's because his mother and father have always been in the background organising his life, and because until a couple of weeks ago his path seemed well and truly laid out for him. I think that becoming an officer in the Royal Engineers will be very good for him, I really do, and I also know that he will change because of it'

'He got on with Peter Adnans ever so well at dinner last night, we really had a super time. And Daddy, I took a menu from the Savoy Restaurant, so you could rant and rage!'

She passed her father the folded menu which he took and studied while the two women looked at each other with knowing smiles, while they waited for the predictable comments that began quickly with 'Good God alive, just look at this will you, Lobster with brandy sauce, fillet of beef, wild duck, veal, quail, grilled steak, a dozen different deserts, and all for five shillings, plus eight shillings for a half carafe of wine, my how the rich do fare in these times of rationing!'

'Now, if I had my way ladies………..' David Jack sentence was interrupted abruptly as the slow wailing sound of air raid sirens began to start outside and the two parents stood up quickly.

Mary Jack looked at her husband first, saying 'You go David, I will take care of things here. Anna and I will go to the shelter until the all clear. And David, please be careful.'

Anna saw her father in the hall way of the house as he struggled into his blue boiler suit before pulling on Wellington's, a well-worn duffle coat and tapping the top of his black tin hat with the white letters ARP painted at the front of it before turning at the blackout curtain behind the front door and shouting 'Hurry up girls, and get to the shelter. I'll see you later, after the all clear siren goes.'

Like most houses in the long terrace, each had there own Anderson shelter in the back garden. Anna and her mother made their way to the corrugated roofed structure and stepped down to the well-prepared shelter, dug into the garden.

'I thought Mr Hitler had gone on holiday Anna, it's been three nights without a raid, but here we go again!'

The two women talked for an hour and listened to the sound of bombs dropping some way from them. 'Sounds like they are going for the docks and the ships on the river again Anna.

With a bit of luck we should be alright this time.'

It was past three in the morning when the 'All Clear' was heard, David Jack came back and the three of them had a cup of tea in the kitchen before going to bed.

'We were lucky tonight Anna, it was the East End that had the worst of it. A lot of our firemen have raced over from here to help'

Rubbing his eyes he stretched and yawned before saying 'Another night in London. We need a victory of some sorts soon girls. Even my moral is sagging a bit.'

A Family at War

Falmouth, 20th January 1942

Rubbing her eyes before trying to focus them again on her alarm clock and talking directly to it Anna said, 'Umm, God, 10.15, who on earth is knocking on the door at this time, I've only been in bed a couple of hours, umm, get up, get up girl, it must be an emergency.'

Wrapping her dressing gown quickly around herself she passed the uniform she had hung over the back of a chair when she had finished her night duty and shouted at the door to her flat before she reached it to stop another bout of banging 'One moment, I'm coming.'

As she pulled opened the door Anna's mouth went dry, her cheeks hollowed as she swallowed hard before speaking to the well dressed middle aged woman in front of her, who she knew was Patricia Tremayne, Simon's mother.

Thinking that her anticipated emergency somehow involved Simon, Anna said softly 'Can I help you, is something wrong, is anyone hurt?'

The visitor took a step towards the entrance saying at the same time 'I'm Mrs Tremayne and I want to speak to you right now, young lady.'

Anna was now wide awake now. The dryness had gone from her mouth and throat completely, and her heart beat had slowed to its normal pace as her right arm touched the door frame and barred the visitor from entering.

Throughout the encounter neither woman had lost eye contact with each other and Anna's voice was calm and steady as she said 'Mrs Tremayne I have just finished an eighteen hour stint of duty on my ward and in the operating theatre, now would not be a good time for us to talk, although I would sincerely like to meet you another time, if that is possible?'

Patricia Tremayne went red with rage. She was not used to being spoken to in such a defiant way, and was not sure about how to cope with such impudence.

It was Anna who spoke next by saying 'Would it be possible for us to meet, please?'

The pause had given the older woman time to adjust before replying 'No it will not be possible, and I can say here on your doorstep what I would have said to you inside'

'I want you to leave my son alone from this moment onwards. You have caused a great deal of trouble to my family and I will not stand idly by and let that happen'

'I want you to understand that if you continue to see Simon, and he continues to see you, he will be disinherited completely, and will know longer be part of my family, is that abundantly clear to you?'

Anna's eyes bored deep into Simon's mothers when she said 'Mrs Tremayne, how dare you speak to me like that, you will kindly remember that you are addressing an Army nurse, on military premises and that I could have you arrested by the military police for trespassing, which is what I will do if you do not leave immediately.'

Mrs Tremayne's crimson face twitched in anger before stuttering a reply by saying

'I have many friends in high places young lady, and I will get my way. I will not have a son of mine involved with a beastly family of Jews, never.'

She thrust her hand into a pocket of her winter coat and produced a white envelope which she threw at Anna's feet, saying 'I found these at Simon's house he will have no need of them from now on.'

Anna felt drained as she watched the embittered woman turn and walk quickly towards the stairs that led down to the entrance of the nursing quarters and took her out of view.

She picked up the envelope as she closed the door and put it into her dressing gown pocket while she made herself a cup of tea and went back to bed. Propped up by cushions she took a sip of the hot liquid before opening the white envelope.

At first she was puzzled as dozens of small pieces of paper fell like snow flakes onto her bed. When she looked more closely Anna could only shake her head as she realised that they were torn up photographs of Simon and her taken in London.

Truro, 20th January 1942

Simon Tremayne was more relaxed as he opened the double doors to his parents lounge than he could ever remember being since his childhood. The last time he had confronted them he had been taught, nervous but today was different, today he felt that the burden of guilt had been lifted from his shoulders.

He closed the doors behind him and turned smiling as he approached his mother, saying 'Morning mother, morning dad. I've had a long and very good meeting with the men who will look after the land around the mine when I leave. Reg Trembath will liaise with them, and of course both of you almost daily on any matters arising from the mining interest.'

His effort to give his customary kiss to his mother was in vain as she raised her right arm and turned her head away from him saying at the same time 'Simon, I saw this woman you have been seeing this morning, and I told her in no uncertain terms that she was would not be welcome by me or my family, and never would be, no matter what the circumstances. I also told her that you would be totally disinherited…' Her vehement angry comments were interrupted by her husband who said 'Patricia, I must…'

Her open palm slammed onto the table in front of her making one of the empty china tea cups on it jump from the saucer it rested on and roll like a seesaw on the polished wood surface.

Angrier than he had ever seen her she shouted 'Be quiet Robert. Simon must be told of the consequences of his selfish and shameful actions.'

Simon straightened up and walked to the open fire that was burning away. Warming his hands quickly he turned and faced both of his parents before saying 'Mother, I don't really believe that you understand what is happening. You are presuming there will be something for me to come back too when this war is over, and I am telling you, and I want you both to listen for a change. If Germany invades this country and we lose the war, then we will have lost everything, we will all be disinherited. You, Daddy, Henry, David, Chrissie and me. We will have nothing'

'When I was in London I met a man who had been made a prisoner of war after Dunkirk. He managed to escape with the help of the Belgian and French resistance movements. Not trained soldiers, but ordinary people who risked their lives so that our men could get back to this country and continue the fight'

'Some of those ordinary people where taken out into the street where they lived by the Gestapo and shot like dogs for helping, just for helping, nothing else. I only hope we will be as brave if we are conquered and humiliated in the same way'

'So, I hope with all my heart that you will both accept what I am going to do with my life and also accept that there will be no meaningful life unless we beat these people'

'I also hope that over time you will change your mind about Anna; both of you. But the fact remains that Cornish mining engineers are welcome the world over and if I have to leave with her, I'm sorry, but I will'

'I love Anna, and I have to tell you both that I fully intend to marry her if she will have me, when the war is over. Until then both she and I have a lot of work to do and nothing will get in the way of that, everything comes second to winning the war'

'I sincerely hope you did not upset Anna mother, because she really doesn't deserve that. She has seen active and very bloody service in France, Belgium and here. She is highly thought of by her peers, and frankly deserves a great deal of respect, and absolutely nothing less'

'I will be leaving for London on the early train in two days. I'm not sure whether Henry and David will be able to get there, but Chrissie said she would love to, and it would make me very proud if you would come with us, but that must now be your decision'

Simon did not wait for a reply but on his way out of the room he looked towards Robert Tremayne and said 'Father, I see you have that old warehouse with the river landing facilities up for sale. Too cheap if you don't mind my saying, in fact between you me I would hang on to everything for a while. The odds are that the Americans will be using the whole area in very large numbers by the end of the year, or early next year'

'They will turn our Cornwall and indeed the country on its head Dad, no doubt about that. My feeling is that it could be a very valuable piece of property suddenly.'

Mother and father looked into the fire as their son closed the doors and left them alone. Robert was the first to speak 'I think the lad may be right you know, if these Yankees do come in numbers then property prices could soar like the Devil, Patricia!'

His wife had not altered the position she sat in but now looked away from the fire and stared through the windows of their house across the road towards the Cathedral that dominated the Cornish city.

'I have two wars on my hands' she said slowly and quietly 'Two wars; one against the Germans and another against this interloper. I can have little influence on the war against the Germans, but you will not win young lady, of that I am surer than anything else in my life.'

Not quite sure what is wife was talking about Robert Tremayne said 'Sorry darling, what were you saying? You know the more I think about what Simon said about property prices the more I like the sound of it……..,'

He never completed the sentence only shrugged his shoulders as he heard the doors slam loudly as his wife left the room and him on his own.

To the glowing fire he said 'Americans, I love the cars they make, and their refrigerators. And they are so rich. Simon could be right, in fact I have a good mind to buy the land next to the warehouses from that scallywag John Tonkin, yes I think I will, I won't let on it's me that's buying it as he will get suspicious but buy it I will'

'To make a tidy profit out of that old pirate right under his very nose would make it a double pleasure!'

Robert Tremayne wrapped up against the chill wind and left the house to call on his solicitor, quietly whistling a tune from an American cowboy film he had seen without telling his wife, who he knew would have disapproved, when he was last in Exeter on business.

Goodbye to Cornwall

Falmouth, 21st January 1942

Steering with one hand Simon Tremayne gripped Anna's right hand saying, 'Don't be a clot darling, you did what anyone would have, and I'm simply ashamed by my mother's dreadful behaviour.'

He looked rather pensive for a second and drew a big intake of air before continuing and shaking his head at the same time 'Although my dear Anna, I have to be honest and say I don't know anyone, and I mean anyone, male or female, who would have dared speak to my mother like that!'

Laughing out loud while still shaking his head in disbelief he double declutched the gear box into a low gear for the climb out of the town.

The couple were driving out of Falmouth, the wind battering the blue MG, the windscreen wipers struggling to clear away the pelting rain that was sweeping in from the South West across the peninsular.

She glanced several times at a smiling driver before saying 'You like this weather, don't you! You really are quite mad. Sort of Cornish mad, but very handsome Mr Tremayne, in fact I'm going to kiss you like mad when we stop!'

Simon braked hard and the car skidded to a halt and stalled in the middle of the steep road leading out of the town and he shouted 'Well, what are you waiting for?'

Anna leaned quickly across and kissed him before saying 'I mean when we stop properly, you wonderful mad Cornishman. Where are you taking me anyway?'

After the car sprang to life and started its steady climb again he said, 'As this is our last look around Cornwall together for a while I want to take you somewhere special before having a lunch time pint and pasty at a pub. It's a pity about the weather because this is one place that demands sunshine, but there we are, it is January after all'

The couple drove through Penzance and stopped briefly to look at Newlyn Harbour through the car windows 'My God Anna, I can't believe I didn't bring you here before. This harbour together with the fisherfolk that have worked on the quay have been painted by some of the best artist in Europe over the past hundred years. In the sunshine, the light is dazzling and the colours are as varied as the subjects'

Simon smiled broadly before adding 'There is so much to show you when I get back!'

After the short stop, they headed out and onto the Lands' End road. Now there was hardly a hundred yards between some form of army road block or fortification pointing out to sea or along the approach roads and into the sky.

Skirting Porthcurno she noticed some tough looking military police wearing rain soaked capes that covered machine guns as they hurriedly waved them through. 'Why is there so much military activity around here?' Anna asked.

Looking straight ahead and straining his eyes through the rain lashed windscreen he said 'You can't see it from the road, but out of sight over the cliff edge there is a very sensitive telegraph station set in the cliff face above Porthcurno Beach with lines coming in from all around the world, in fact a few of our miners have helped dig into the hillside to enlarge the galleries and the facilities'

'It certainly is well protected. The beach has been mined and I've even heard that they have put mustard gas and flame throwers on the levels above the high tide mark in case of a seaborne raid or landing, ah, we're almost there'

The car stopped on a grassy verge and Simon turned to Anna before he spoke 'The rain has eased away, it's a bit blowey but come on!'

From where they had parked all that she could see was a grassed bank that led to an outcrop of rocks in the distance, and beyond that a grey fog that clung to the sea below them.

Simon opened the door on the passenger's side and helped

pull Anna out of the bucket seat and into the teeth of a gusting force eight gale that they both had trouble standing upright in. 'It will be a bit more sheltered down here, come on.'

The couple forced their way along an ash covered path until reaching the line of rocks she had seen from the car. He stopped in the sudden shelter of the rock barrier and turned Anna around so that she was facing the sea with a headland in the distance.

At first when she looked down she blinked not quite believing what she saw 'Goodness, it looks like a Roman amphitheatre cut into the rock; is it?'

Shouting back he said, 'Almost right, spectacular isn't it. It is an amphitheatre but is being built by a lady called Rowena Cade, who is a close friend of mine. I came to the first production in 1932 of Shakespeare's "The Tempest". Can you ever imagine a better place to present the play! She's away at t moment otherwise we could have called on her. She called it the Minack Theatre, and after the war she wants to enlarge it, but that's all in the future'

Looking past the lines of shaped granite that formed seats for the audience onto the beach below the headland he said 'I've seen the sea wash over the sand down there and give off four different shades of bright sparkling green in the sunshine. Next time we'll come in summer, bring a picnic and swim all afternoon!'

Stepping out of the pub after the promised pasty and pint of bitter the couple headed towards Lands End between intervals of blustery wind and rain that shook the car like a cat shakes a mouse.

They took a road that by-passed the bottom tip of the country as Simon shouted above the noise of the engine 'Most of the area around Lands End is swamped in army installations to prevent any possible landings by parachute, but they get less and less as the natural defences of the high cliffs of the coastline start when we get past Sennen Cove, so we'll head there'

Driving through St Just they headed out of the village towards Cape Cornwall.The rain had stopped, but the wind was as strong as ever at the point where the Atlantic Ocean and Bristol Channel meet.

As they got out of the car spectacular shafts of sunshine broke through the low dark grey cloud that had hid them, illuminating Lands End and the rocks in the distance like searchlight beams. He put his arm around the shoulders of Anna 'It never ever ceases to thrill me when I see that, my goodness we are lucky people at times, living where we live, being so close to all this.'

Sensing a hint of sadness she replied, 'What will you miss most Simon, the sea and countryside, or the people?'

'Both I suppose, no wait a minute. The people and especially you Anna. I can carry pictures of the sea and sunsets in my head anywhere, but I will miss talking to you and that's a fact. Listen, can we go right back to 'Howlsedhes', we may just get a glimpse of the sunset if we hurry?'

Before he had finished talking a bank of clouds swept in front of them, hurling rain mixed with snow and sleet at the couple. Simon laughed as he added 'Good old Cornwall, four seasons in one day!'

Giving him a quick kiss she said, 'I have to be back at the hospital by midnight, so we have plenty of time to watch the sunset and I do love your house Simon.'

Going back into St Just and through the town square they quickly passed Geevor tin mine and a mile from it the Trewellard tin mine that Simon had managed for the family.

The squat grey granite houses of the miners reminded him of an appointment he had this evening as he said 'Before I take you back to the hospital would you come with me to the Tinners this evening. It seems the lads from the mine have a going away present for me and two of the miners who are volunteering for service in the navy. There will be some sandwiches and beer on the go; please?'

There was a hesitation before she answered the request 'Do you think it wise darling that I should be with you in public?'

Without taking his eyes away from the winding coastal road and the low stone walls either side of it he said 'Anna, I don't know where I shall be this time next week, so please make my last day here one neither of us will forget in a hurry, please.'

She said nothing, just gripped the hand that was on the gear stick and squeezed it gently.

 The balance of the year was now on the side of the approaching season as late January gave up hints of lighter evenings. At his home, they sat on cushions on the the wide wooden window sill that surrounded the inside of the bay window that faced Westwards from his bedroom, Anna with her raku mug full of tea, Simon with his.

 Looking towards the horizon the winter sun was painting bright red and orange edges to the metal grey clouds that were masking it, before a small rim of red eased itself slowly above them.

 As the two elements jostled for the final position in the daily battle of sunset, they watched as thick vertical lines of driving rain started to scurry quickly across the horizon like a giant grey curtain until the sun was once again captive behind them, and the sky darkened.

 He knew that the battle was never over until the last rays of light disappeared completely and as his arm pulled Anna closer to him so in the distance the curved edge of a watery red sun appeared on the horizon for the last moments of daylight before it dipped quickly out of sight.

 'Beautiful, just beautiful' Anna whispered.

 He kissed the top of her head and her black hair before saying 'Anna, I know you don't want to be committed to anyone at the moment, but would you consider marrying me after the war is finished?'

 She rested the back of her head under his chin and shuffled her bottom further into him before answering. 'Oh Simon, sat here it's so easy to think everything is normal, that the war is someone else's perhaps. But the reality is that it is still here and people are dying as we speak to each other'

 'Peace seems such a long way away Simon but of course I would, and if we did and it was ever possible, I would like us to get married at Towednack Church.'

 His frown was hidden as he said, 'I will make it possible Anna, I promise' kissing her again on the back of her head he chuckled before adding 'Not sure what the Methodist are going to think of me getting married in a protestant Church mind you!'

Anna stood up, took hold of his hand, and leading him towards his bed she said, 'Well darling I think they will sigh with deep relief knowing that at least they do not have to go to a Synagogue!'

By the light of an almost full Moon they could see the outline of several cars and small lorries parked on the two roads leading to the Tinners Arms as they arrived at seven o'clock, and heard the sound of noisy banter coming from inside.

Simon and Anna slipped through the double blackout curtains of the entrance to the pub to a hail of shouting and clapping from at least twenty or so men, all dressed in similar dark jackets, with a stiff white wing collar and matching tie.

The members of the male voice choir of Trewellard mine who were not working a shift stood with pint glasses in hand as each one welcomed their old boss to the gathering.

A pint of bitter was on the bar by the time they reached it for Simon, and Terry Nancekivell shouted to Anna 'Us have some decent whisky in do ee want some with ginger ale?'

Nodding an answer above the din of voices she took the drink and was about to take a sip when a hand touched hers and she turned to see Christine Tremayne behind her.

'Hello Anna, it's ever so good to see you, and of course that brother of mine, I suppose! Only kidding, the truth is I really am going to miss him.'

Anna felt difficult, ill at ease in the presence of Simon's sister who was such a direct and rather threatening link to his mother, and she was also slightly uneasy with the throng of loud male voices vibrating around her.

The young nursing sister who had dodged bullets, mortar shells and dive bomber attacks, had survived heavy bombing raids and artillery fire suddenly felt vulnerable, like an outsider in a small ancient settlement, a member of a different tribe, looking in on the customs of a new one.

Anna was searching for the right words but Christine started before she could speak. Grabbing her brother and turning him around she shouted, 'Listen dear brother, I have some tip top news for you two to hear'

Beaming from ear to ear she announced 'I received my call-up papers this morning, I'm going to join the WRAF's next week. The government are calling up all single women above twenty-one, isn't it simply tremendous!'

Simon embraced his sister with a Cornish wrestling hug, lifting her off her feet before saying 'Wow Chrissie, that is wonderful news, I'm so happy for you.'

Anna waited until Simon's sister turned towards her before putting both arms around her and saying 'Christine, I just know you will be credit to yourself, your parents and to the air force, well done, I think it's splendid news.'

Before she replied Christine looked at her brother before looking back at Anna and saying, 'Oh gosh, I suppose I will have to salute you in future, in fact both of you!'

Anna replied first 'I have I strong suspicion Christine that you will rise like a shooting star in the ranks, and we will end up saluting you!'

Shouting again in her ear Simon said, 'How on earth have mum and dad taken the news, you have told them I presume?'

'Actually, I had a piece of very good luck. When I went to find them and make the announcement they were with that old prig Mr Roach from the chapel. He couldn't wait to tell me that he was there to tell mum and dad how proud he was that his daughter Marjory, whom I never could stand, had received her call-up papers and she was going to join the WRAC's as a driver'

'I calmly told him my good news in front of mummy and daddy, well, after that they could hardly say 'no' now could they!'

The loud throng of voices came to a hesitant halt as Terry Nancekivell banged the wood bar in front of him with a large red ash tray. When quiet had been restored he announced to everyone in the bar 'Rite thaan, the men of the chior reckons them have enough moon light outside to give Simon an us a few songs before he puts on is uniform an sets of to them foreign parts, over the Tamar!'

'Tis also the last time for a bit that Dave an Paul Pinnick will be singing weth the choir as them's away an all to put on the Andrews uniform an puts to sea. Now, it be bleedy cold out there so wrap up, an remember, no bleedy lights, as I'll bay in deep trouble again!'

The audience from the bar and village stood on the road looking into the small courtyard that formed outside the pub entrance and where the choir had gathered facing Tom Spear, the choir master.

Simon stood arm in arm with Anna and his sister as the choir sang the traditional songs of the county. Songs that evoked pictures of the landscape, history, culture and people of the land they all shared, bringing tears to many of the onlookers as they thought of loved ones who were far away from Cornwall fighting, and of some who had been killed and would never return home.

Loud clapping and cheering followed the choir back inside the pub, followed by some of the audience. The heat from the fire made Anna's face tingle after the chill of the night air as she stood by the bar with Christine Tremayne as Simon and the two young men joining the navy were manoeuvred into the middle of the room and faced Reg Trembath.

The new manager of the mine cleared his throat before looking around the room and starting. 'Ladies and Gentlemen, I think you will all agree that the choir sang their hearts out tonight, and I also think that like me, it will be a long time before any of us forget it'

'Now the reason we are here this evening is to say goodbye to three local men who are off to join the forces. All three born and raised in Cornwall, all three going to do their bit by volunteering to fight on our behalf and going off to war'

'They will all be missed by their families, loved ones and work mates, and I hope they will carry the memory of the county they represent, and they can be sure that we are proud of each of them'

'Now Simon, David and Paul, kindly step forward, thank you'

As each man stood in the centre of the room Sam Trembath placed a silver Celtic cross attached to a silver chain around the heads of each of them before saying,   'These crosses were made from silver mined from the land you were all born in. They are a token of our gratitude to each of you, and at the same time something that we hope will remind all of you of your time with us here. Lads, we all wish you the very best of luck and a safe return home again.'

Christine and Anna caught each other's' watery gaze and Simon's sister whispered to her 'I really am so proud of him, I know I rag him terribly, but we have been very close and I hope he comes home safely'

'Anna, I want you to know I'm so pleased that he found you, he told me he loves you desperately, and despite mummy, well I know everything will work out for the best.'

On the slow journey, back to Falmouth and the hospital Anna rested her head on his shoulder and kept her right hand on Simon's left whenever he let go the steering wheel to change gear and drive the car along the winding country roads. They said little, happy to be close.

Before starting the drive down into the blacked out town, he pulled off the road and stopped the car. From where they were parked they could see out over Falmouth Bay with Pendennis Castle throwing strong black shadows over the docks as the moon crept behind it. The water in the bay was like a mill pond with occasional streaks of phosphorous glowing in the wake of a small naval patrol boat that hurried across it.

Simon was first to speak 'I know you have to be on duty soon, and we haven't got long Anna' He paused and looked out over the town and water in front of it, and sighed deeply before continuing 'All I can think of saying is that I love you very much, and also to thank you for the best few months of my life, you've been a good friend to me. Thank you.'

Before Anna spoke she brushed away the tears on her cheeks with her finger tips 'Simon, I don't think you understand how important it was to me when we met at the Spitfire dance. No stop, please don't laugh at me darling!'

'I know you were a bit tipsy, but when the band started to play the music for a Valetta and I saw you were my next partner to dance with I felt like a teenager! You gave me back a sparkle that I had lost in Belgium'

'Tomorrow I'll feel horrid. Empty and horrid. But I'll also feel happy deep down. Happy just knowing that when all this madness ends, and I know it will end darling, because someone who was also special told me so; we will be able to start again and build our lives in peace.'

Zennor, 13th February 1942

The worried, slightly cross expression on Mabena's face was one that Anna had never seen before. Hardly had she parked her motorcycle in the lane up from the Tinners Arms when Anna heard her voice shout 'Anna maid, us av got ta av a chat lik'

The two women hurried past the pub and church and started walking down the lane that ran alongside the dairy farm where Star lived. It was only then that the stout Cornish woman started talking.

'Anna, thus is a vury difficult theng fur I ta tel ee, an I feels rite shamed at tha saam time. Truth is ee as rally upset thet snotty mawthur ov Simon's, maid. Oh, sha bay a real witch thet wan, weth an evil tongue an hur an hur bin spreadin all sorts ov lies round bout yew, un no mistake'

'Her av got it un fur yew, an trouble is a lot ov folk round err listens, an listens harder ta tha sound ov hur money thet talks as loud as her lik. Problem is Anna, sometimes tha evil chat doos work'

'Twas during las war I remembur a book writer, Mr Lawrence he waas called, famous an aal, I av sin is books un tha library an mentioned un tha papers, not always sayin nice things either, cause is books was real naughty lik'

'Ee an is wife lived un tha cottage just below Simon's owse. Trouble waas is wife was a furriner, a German. Her waas nice as pie lik, but cause they waas a bit, well artiefied an Lunnon lik, an as I say weth her baying German an all, people sort ov ganged up on em propur'

'Twas shameful, an' me mum would av nothin to do we it, but twas egged on lik bay someone thaat didn't lik em ta start weth. Well in tha end tha poor souls waas pushed out, made ta leave lik, an they went back ta Lunnon so I waas told, twas nasty, really nasty'

'Now maid, a boay in tha village told me hur as got ta a couple ov men folk that comes inta tha pub ta bay difacult an nasty ta ee, an as they do both owe hur money then lik or not them will try things, so bay careful lik.'

Anna squeezed Mabena's thick arm as they walked slowly in the cold sunny early afternoon. They stopped at the first corner and leaning on the stone hedge both friends looked towards Zennor Head and the sea before Anna said 'Mabena, thank you. I know Mrs Tremayne dislikes me, hates me in fact, and if I'm honest I can understand why.'

With a look of surprise Mabena glanced quickly at her saying 'How's thaat than?'

'Well, before the war brought me here she had everything planned for Simon. His fiancé was approved of....'

Mabena interrupted Anna with 'Thaat miss iss a raal beagle, iv evur theere was wan!'

After a smile and a giggle Anna continued 'Simon was in a reserved occupation, and safe from being called up for military service, and the truth of it, is that he was safe from possibly being killed in action'

'Suddenly, everything has been turned on its head, and she can see only me as the reason for the change, she sadly cannot accept that the war is what brought about the real change in her son, not me'

'Personally, I believe Simon would have joined the forces, knowing me or not and Mabena I think I have come to love Simon as much as the only other man I have ever loved and who was killed in 1940. Maybe not love in the same way, but I really do love him.'

Without taking her eyes away from the view of Zennor Head Mabena said 'I always dud sense ee ad bin hurt badly Anna, twas always un yewr eyes whan us first met ee, but et faded as yew got ta know us, I'm am sorry maid'

'I ate this war, an weth all tha sufferin gwain un tis ard ta understand tha likes ov Missus Tremayne wanin ta cause more ov et, but tis a strange world'

As they turned back towards the pub the landlord's wife said 'Friday tha 13th today. I ate's et whan tha 13th falls un a Friday. Yew'm still gwain ta av ta watch owt Anna maid, thet bleedy woman won't stop cause Simon's gone way.'

Stopping in front of the swept over pine trees Anna said, 'Well she can't have a go at me if I'm not around, and

Mabena, please keep this to yourself, but the reason I'm here on a Friday at all is to say goodbye to you, I will be leaving Cornwall tomorrow, but please don't tell Terry for a few days, I'm not suppose to tell anyone really.'

Nodding before responding to Anna's statement she replied 'That well taake tha sting owt ov er meddlin iv yew be'ant round maid, that's fur sure! Now yew go an pack your gloves way un tha pannier ov yewr bike, an give me a few minutes fur yew cums unta tha pub lik'

Mabena walked into her domain and gently moved her husband to one side before setting her thick hands palm downwards on the bar counter and addressing the dozen or so regular drinkers standing in front of her.

'Now boays, I knaw that wan or tew ov ee hav it un mind ta bay a bit rude lik ta Simon Tremaynes lady friend when yew next sees her, an it so happens hur is cumin un fur a drink un a minute'

The landlord's wife paused before continuing and her voice went an octave lower as she said 'Now let ma warn ee. I waant allow et, an ee all knaw I means et, so that thum tha does will share a very special place un my ead fur a long, long time ta cum, an don't ee forget et.'

The area around the bar went deadly quiet for a second before Mabena herself broke the spell of silence by saying in her normal cheerful manner 'Caan I gat anyone anythin?'

Noticing Anna's arrival at the bar she said 'Aff a bittur shandy is in?' Her smile swept around the men and Mabena was pleased to hear her husbands welcome echoed by several 'Murnun Miss Anna' from the majority of the men who had become firm devotees of the likeable newcomer.

Anna sat in the window seat opposite the bar and talked at length to the men until it was time for her to leave. She hugged Terry before she and Mabena walked to her Red Hunter. Embracing her as a good friend she stood back and said 'Terry an me waant ee to hav this Anna'

The Cornish woman handed Anna a small silver Celtic cross saying 'Tis identical ta tha wan us did giv ta Simon an tha tew boays, not sure why I got em ta make fower, but prahaps I knew yew would need in.'

Anna took the gift and undoing the top of her coat put it around her neck before saying 'Thank you both. I will be back, but of course you already know that! Truth is I have a lot to come back for thanks to you. Bye for now Mabena.'

'Take care ov ee'self Anna. I've knaw doubts us is gwain ta meet gain, none at all, go un now maid, an bay careful lik, watch owt fur Pieskies, Knockers an rabbits that look lik Hares!'

CHAPTER FIVE 1943

The Tide of War Turns

******

Invasion of Britain

******

Whites Only - No Blacks

The Tide of War Turns

Wiltshire, 12th April 1943

Anna's room was in the eaves of Marlborough House and the heart of a two hundred acre estate, three miles from the town that the house and its lands was named after in Wiltshire.

The thin film of ice covering the lower panes of glass of the narrow sash window retreated as Anna placed her mug of hot tea on the wood sill under them, and she looked out.

It was cold, and overnight the last efforts of winter had left a half inch of snow on the lawns that swept from the hospital towards a lake in front of her.

From a cloudless blue sky the sun had started to shine directly onto the water of the lake and small clouds of fine mist drifted in swirls across it in the cold morning air.

She looked at her watch saying to herself, 'Eight twenty here, so…that would be I suppose, eleven thirty in Egypt, if of course that is where you are, and I bet it's a lot hotter than here. But even so, I bet it isn't so beautiful'.

Before the war the room that Anna occupied had belonged to one of the many men and women who ran the estate before it had been requisitioned and turned into a specialist unit where men from all of the services, but mainly from the RAF, suffering from extreme burn wounds were sent for pioneering treatment.

From Falmouth Anna had been posted to more than six different army and naval establishments around the country, training new nursing teams in the methods of treatment applied when casualty clearing stations were set up during battlefield conditions.

It was as she was getting settled into the routine of her last posting that she received a short note from Mary Atkins telling her that she had requested her transfer to the burns unit.

Her brief was to learn as much as possible about the treatment being given and the methods used to diagnose the seriousness of burn injuries in battlefield conditions, and at a later date to pass on her knowledge to other sisters and nursing staff in readiness for future Allied operations.

The night duty she had just finished had been an easy one and the letter in her hand from Simon was opened excitedly after she had finished pulling her warm dressing gown around her and propping herself up against her cushions in the narrow iron framed single bed. Comfortable, she started to read the letter that had taken six weeks to reach her:

"*My Darling Anna,*   2nd *March, 1943*

How I miss you darling and hope that you are keeping well at home in our lovely England, with spring around the corner. At last I can tell you what I have been up to since last November, as we have all seen every aspect of our endeavours boldly printed in the popular newspapers which we saw today.

After some hasty training near Glasgow last Autumn, I was seconded to an American Engineering Corps and got ready to take part in "Operation Torch", and the invasion of North Africa.

As you have no doubt read, the task force that landed on the North African coast was the largest ever assembled in any war. One hundred and twenty ships sailed across the Atlantic with over thirty-five thousand American troops and their equipment.

A further thirty-nine thousand Americans in one convoy, together with twenty-three thousand British, Commonwealth, Free French and Polish Forces in another convoy had sailed at different times from Scotland.

All three separate convoys got to their positions with unheard of secrecy off of the African Coast and the armada stretched from Safi, on the Atlantic coast of Morocco, to Algiers in the Mediterranean. Almost a thousand mile front which was defended by double our number of German, French and local North African troops. Most of the French soldiers were loyal to the Vichy Government of Marshall Petain in Franc, but not all of them Anna.

It was imperative that we establish a bridgehead on this coastline before going after our main objective, which was, and as I write, still is, Field Marshall Rommel and his Afrika Corps to the East in Tunisia.

I have to say that the Americans I have been with over the past months have been a super lot and very good to work with, but my goodness Anna, they were in for a terrible shock when the landings took place.

There was a well held feeling throughout the ship, that I have to say I found a little naive, that although they expected the French to be somewhat antagonistic towards us British, mainly because we had to destroy their naval fleet at Oran, and other historical differences, they would welcome the Americans with open arms, and as liberators!

Sadly, some fifteen hundred Americans were killed and over seven hundred of the defending French soldiers suffered the same fate before an armistice was concluded and we were able to secure the area against any form of German counter attack.

One of the reasons I was seconded to the Americans was my ability to speak French at a reasonable level, and during the landings on the beach I came into contact with a group of Free French forces who had overrun a position of Vichy French.

Anna, to see Frenchmen killing fellow Frenchmen was truly terrible. One can only hope that such terrible acts will not cause a civil war to break out between them and that someone will be able to bring the sides together.

Going back to the Americans. They are so refreshing to work with it has made my job much easier than I expected. They are excellent engineers. They all work hard and with great professionalism, bringing new ideas and a sense of urgency to each task they are given, and I must say we have all learnt a great deal from the last few months working together.

The social differences between our armies are stark indeed. The officers seem to be judged solely on how good they are at their job and little, in fact no respect is shown them by their men if it is judged that the work in hand is not up to scratch, or indeed on time!

Darling, I must close now. I will write as soon as I can with more news, and as always, I hope you are safe and well.

Your loving Simon"

Anna placed the light blue coloured aerogramme envelope in a drawer of a small desk together with others she had received from Simon. Sipping her tea she said aloud 'I knew inside that you were part of that operation. You're safe and well. Please stay so.'

Headquarters, London, 7th August 1943

Behind the main hospital were the headquarters, administration block and Mary Atkins office. The room was wide with a high ceiling surrounded on three sides by tall dark oak book shelves, stacked floor to ceiling with matching leather-bound volumes of medical books, glass fronted display cabinets full of medals attached to colourful ribbons, and piles of yellowing letters that belonged to past members of the all the medical regiments.

Each measured section was neatly spaced apart by ornately framed oil paintings and etched pictures of women dressed in nursing uniforms, with the backgrounds of desert, hills or trenches.

Standing and returning the salute Mary Atkins then offered Anna her hand which she shook warmly before accepting the seat opposite the colonel. 'Anna it's so good to see you again, please do take a seat. Have you heard from Simon?'

'Yes, I had a letter only a couple of days ago. He was in fine spirits. He's now been transferred back to his British regiment after the success of the North African campaign, and goodness only knows where he is now, but I suspect he was involved in the attack on Sicily, especially as he was careful to write about everything apart from that country and what he was really doing!'

Nodding almost wearily the veteran woman of two wars said 'I'm so pleased he is safe and well. It really has been a long haul in no mistake, but you know, I believe that the tide of the war has finally begun to turn in our favour Anna'

'The Russians have all but routed the Germans in many battles and even the war in Asia is beginning to slowly go our way. It is slow, and sadly we have a long way to travel, but we are starting to hit back.'

Anna asked 'Do you think the tide really started to turn after the invasion of North Africa at the end of last year?'

Mary Atkins was silent for a moment before she answered 'Yes Anna, I think you maybe right. As you will remember the newspapers on both sides of the Atlantic were full of the news of the Allied landings, but I think it will be many years before the whole truth behind the events in the region are brought into the public domain'

'What was well known at the time was that despite having titanic arguments with Charles de Gaulle, Winston Churchill held a singular loyalty to him, based on his view that he is the only man capable of providing the leadership to unite France and prevent a civil war after liberation of the country.'

With a puzzled frown Anna asked another question 'Why was Admiral Darlan's name banded about so much at the time as being the man to be in charge of France?'

'Ah, one of the first disagreements with our new American allies my dear! From what I've heard, Mr Roosevelt took an immediate dislike to de Gaulle when only two weeks after Pearl Harbour the French leader, without consulting Churchill or any of his Allies, sent a submarine and three corvettes of the Free French navy to the two tiny Vichy held Islands of St Pierre and Miquelon, off the coast of Newfoundland'

'You will remember the name of the submarine Anna from your Plymouth days. It was called the *'Surcouf'*, the vessel on which British and French sailors killed each other.'

'These small enclaves of French culture and law, so very close to Canadian territory, made them valuable propaganda tools for Petain's Nazi led France and de Gaulle was determined that they should be returned to Free French control. And after a brief engagement, so they were.'

'A colleague told me that when Winston heard the news he sipped his whisky and soda, despairingly hunched his shoulders and carried on with the business of the day. But President Roosevelt was enraged by the maverick operation, which he saw as further evidence that the General was an untrustworthy nuisance.'

'You see Roosevelt's plan was to cultivate secret links with the Vichy leaders in France, through diplomats and emissaries he had sent to the region. His governments choice of alternative leaders to Petain and de Gaulle were Admiral Darlan as head of a French government in exile, and General Henri Giraud as chief of the armed forces'

'The Americans believed that after the Allied invasion of North Africa the local forces would instantly accept both men's authority and switch sides to the Free French'

Shaking her head, she added sourly 'It was a total miscalculation Anna. Francois Darlan was seen in American political circles as the man the president could best use as a pawn, during the war and after because he was ardently anti communist. They forgot to find out he was also anti-Semitic, and an Anglophobe of the worst kind!'

'He was Petain's duputy, had talked to Hitler on many occasions and during a wireless broadcast to the French nation had openly declared "Germany is a far better friend than Britain could ever be", so it was little wonder that when Winston heard about the broadcast he declared "The man should be shot!"

'Winston saw Darlan as a Nazi collaborator and political opportunist and Giraud as a light weight of no significance and he flew into a vitriolic rage when he was told that the Americans had made a 'deal' with Darlan, making him high commissioner for French North Africa'

'Neither a seething Churchill or de Gaulle could ever accept the public face of so hated a collaborator being celebrated and honoured in the way the American President had directed, but for the sake of the ultimate goal of defeating Germany, Winston kept quiet'

'Only time will bring out the truth of what happened next of course Anna, but as we now know last Christmas eve Admiral

Darlan was assassinated by a young Frenchmen who the German propaganda machine say had been trained by British SOE secret agents, and even landed by one of our submarines'

'The admiral was shot twice in the stomach with bullets from a captured German Walther pistol and his last words on the hospital operating table were "I knew the British would kill me."

'What is fact is that within weeks Charles de Gaulle filled the political and military vacuum and has now assumed total command of all Free French Forces in North Africa and elsewhere'

'And another fact is that a fuming President Roosevelt had no option but to accept the Frenchman as the voice of France.'

Anna took advantage of her commanding officer stopping to drink her cup of tea to say 'Do you think we will invade France soon?'

Shaking her head slowly she replied, 'I am certainly not in any position to say officially 'Yes' or 'No' to that Anna. But I can speculate; and my personal feeling is that we will not be raising our glasses of wine and toasting each other in France until next year!'

'But in the meantime, we all have a lot of work to do in the way of preparation for the day when we do go back to France, and we have learnt a great deal from the sacrifices of the invasion of North Africa and Sicily.'

Looking at the young woman in front of her with the warmth of a knowing friend she continued 'I know you wanted to be involved in the campaign Anna and that you have felt perhaps a bit left out of things, but what you have been doing over the past months has been part of a planned strategy. The next part of that strategy is about to be put in place, which is why I wanted to have a chat to you'

'Anna, my orders prevent me from telling you exactly what we have in mind, but your next posting will form part of a larger jigsaw, a jigsaw that will be finished in the days when we finally land in France'

'I want you to go to an RAF station which uses the Dakota and other transport aircraft. You will act as the normal medical centre for the station but I also want you to start up a training programme for a new type of casualty clearing station that will use aircraft in the same way as we use ambulances'

'At this stage we think the RAF's own doctors and nurses will man what will become known officially as the Air Ambulance Unit, but it is vital we have a knowledge of this method of bringing back the wounded from the battlefield by the fastest means now available'

'Over the next few months you will receive a large number of fresh nurses and sisters. I want you to hone them into shape along the same lines and methods that we employed in France. I also want you to pass on your new-found knowledge of assessing and treating burns casualties'

'From past experience, we know our wounded will come through to us with the usual battlefield injuries. Now it will be very important to quickly assess if a casualty would have a better chance of survival by being flown back to Britain'

'Remember, you have the battlefield experience, you have the home front blitz experience. In short Anna, like it or not, you have joined the ranks of us "old timers!"'

'Part of the training for all of you will be to gain flying experience. At every opportunity, I want you and your new gals to fly with the RAF as passengers. Again, from past experience I have found that to many men at the top of RAF command our efforts will not be seen as important'

'So, Anna, expect the usual male obstructions and ridicule - something we are both well used to!'

'The station commander will have direct orders from his superior to assist you, but you and I know that will not stop the usual childish forms of obstruction from the Brycream Boys'

'Now, to carry out this new task Anna, as soon as you leave the burns unit hospital I want you to take a few days home leave prior to going to the new posting. Before that happens, I am going to promote you to the rank of Matron, which will give you at least a bit more clout with the men in charge of the base.'

Sat as though frozen to her chair, she had followed her commanding officer's rapid verbal instructions, and the picture she had in her head of the task that she been assigned to was clear. It was the last thing Mary Atkins had said that made her speechless.

Anna found herself staring up into the smiling face of her former Matron to hear her say 'Congratulations Matron Jack!'

Invasion of Britain

RAF Portlan, Cornwall, 19th October 1943

The tapping on the open door of her office made Anna raise her eyes from the file on her desk and smile at the man in a blue uniform who stood in the entrance.

'Matron, I couldn't help over hearing what you said to aircraftsman Thomas, but if it's of any help I have to pick up an engine part from RAF St Eval tomorrow morning. I could easily drop you off in St Ives by taking a slight detour, but it will mean leaving here at seven and of course getting back could be a problem ma'am.'

Narrowing her eyes at the man she replied 'Uumm, now that is tempting Sergeant Philips, very tempting. I feel like a day away from the base and close to the sea. I'll make a couple of enquiries about the return bit and let you know before you go off duty, and thank you.'

'A day of greys!' Anna said aloud as the Austin 10 utility truck turned the corner at the top of Trelyon Avenue and St Ives bay rolled out in front of her.

'Sorry ma'am, I didn't quite catch that.'

'Oh, nothing important, I was just saying what a dull old day it was, but the cloud is beginning to break over to the West, so perhaps we will have a bit of sunshine later'

'Now you have to drop me off in a moment, don't you, so that you can take the left-hand fork in the road and head out of the town, and I can walk down the hill, past the station and onto the sea front.'

'Are you sure that will be alright Matron, it's a bit of a walk, and being a Sunday before eight I doubt you will get a cuppa anywhere.'

'Don't worry Sergeant Philips, just drop me here and I will enjoy the walk, and thank you for the lift.'

At first glance the town seemed deserted until looking towards the bay from above the railway station. Then Anna saw khaki clad figures in the distance milling around the closest of the two pill boxes that protected the harbour entrance. In the car park of the railway station, the sound of the soldiers' laughter came drifting towards her and cut through the silence of the Sunday morning.

Walking slowly down Treggenna Hill Anna thought, 'I know it would look better in sunshine but my goodness how dull and war weary everything seems.'

Many of the shops had closed and were boarded up, the rest had little to sell and the displays in their windows had a shabby, sad look about them that matched the greyness of the autumn morning.

As she walked to the end of High Street there was a sudden hubbub of voices as the Parish Church came into view and where a dozen or so mainly elderly men and women stood outside the entrance to the church, talking intently to the vicar.

Walking past the parishioners who had attended the early Sunday service Anna smiled and returned their greetings as she walked around Island House and turned the corner to give her a view of the West Pier and the lifeboat house.

The peace of the early Sunday was shattered by the loud squawking of the bickering seagulls squabbling on the beach as she made her way across the cobbled road and the sea front.

The tide was at its lowest point, exposing the beach in front of her and revealing a tangle of mooring lines that small fishing boats were tied to, waiting for the water to return.

Occupying a slatted wood seat in front of the harbour wall railings Anna sat looking at the ribbed patterns in the sand that the outgoing tide had made, trapping pools of seawater in the sallow hollows that reflected the clouds as they scudded overhead and the glimmer of soft sun light that was hidden by them.

Dragging in long deep breaths of sea air she felt relaxed and pleased to be away from the camp for a few hours, and of the time to think back over the past weeks since her promotion to matron, and the posting back again to her Cornwall.

After settling into a routine at the RAF base she was able to surprise Terry and Mabena Nancekivell by walking into the bar of the Tinners Arms just after opening time on a Saturday evening.

That night in particular Anna felt an unfamiliar sense of belonging, of community, something she had not experienced away from the London neighbourhood she grew up in.

Terry Nancekivell raced from behind the bar counter to give her a tight hug before shouting up the stairs to tell Mabena and his daughter that she was in the bar. Each one of the locals at the bar had shaken her hand vigorously, and Mabena's embrace was equal to the one she had received from her mother, back in London.

Whispering to no one she said 'I need to visit The Tinners and see my friends. I don't want to be alone today, normally I don't mind my own company but today I wish one of you boys were here. Simon, or if not you John.'

She smiled, and then chuckled to herself before adding out loud 'What a terrible Jezebel I am, sorry boys!'

She was lost in her own deep thoughts until a voice broke through the momentary dream 'Tis un tha way baack Muss, an midduy should sha a bit ov sunshine, witch us el all bay pleased ta sha. Av ee bin ere bafore Muss?'

Anna quickly gathered her thoughts together before speaking, 'Oh yes, many times, but I've been away for the past eighteen months, so it's a real treat to sit here and remember some nice times.'

She looked at the elderly but sprightly and fit looking man who wore a dark blue knitted Guernsey jumper, under a thick Pea jacket the same colour. Across the front of the oiled wool she saw the word "Coxswain" embroidered in white cotton cross stitches.

Beneath his black fishing cap she saw grey blue eyes set into a lined face that had been wind blown into a deep mahogany colour after his years at sea, his wispy grey beard and hair highlighting the trade mark.

Offering her hand to shake his she said, 'I'm Anna Jack by the way, are you the Coxswain of the lifeboat here?'

He finished the handshake, turned slowly away from her and put both of his big hands on the railing in front of them before looking in the direction of the turning tide and with a one-sided smile said, 'Yah Muss, name bay Reg Barbary, an rite nuff, for ma sins, I bay Coxswain!'

So, this was the man who she had watched from the cliff tops as he steered his lifeboat between the rocks to rescue crew members from the wrecked merchant ship.

'Mr Barbary, it really is a pleasure to meet you. I was the nursing sister with the cliff rescue team when you saved most of the crew from the ship that ran aground at Veor Cove, almost two years ago.'

He took a deep intake of air into his lungs and puffed out his weather-beaten cheeks before exhaling and saying 'Muss, thaat wur a fearsum day, fearsum as any thin I recollects long tha coast' pausing he looked hard at Anna before continuing 'I caant stand heights Muss, et mus tav bin sum wind up where ee was that day, ee was very brave an all, iv ee don mind I sayun.'

Anna could vividly remember, and would never forget the terrible weather, and the tragedy of the men who drowned that day, but she looked hard into the eyes of the man opposite her before making her next comment without any doubt in her mind. 'No Mr Barbary, it was you, you and your crew who were the brave ones.'

And on a lighter note she added 'But I will say I have never been so cold in all my life! O my goodness I was cold, and to even think about it now makes me shiver!'

The old seaman smiled broadly, causing fan tails of wrinkles to form at the corners of his eyes before taking an ancient looking briar pipe out of a trouser pocket which he proceeded to bang noisily against the iron railings in front of him before saying 'I'm un ma way ta tha lifeboat owse, wood yew lik ah cup ah tay Muss?'

Hardly pausing she replied, 'That would be lovely, thank you, and please call me Anna!'

Reg could not answer. He was busy sucking air through the black briar pipe, which was held and sheltered by one cupped hand while the other gripped a petrol lighter.

With practiced expertise he had quickly scratched out the bowl of the pipe with his pen knife and with another bang on the iron railing scattered the dark contents between the cobbles on the pavement before putting in a fresh plug of tobacco from a leather pouch.

Letting out a stream of blue smoke before he replied he said, 'Rite than Muss Anna, thenk us awt ta gat kettle un.'

Reg unlocked the sliding doors and slowly pulled them a couple of feet along the metal runners before switching on the electric lights above the lifeboat. The boat rested on top of its cradle, ready to be hitched up to the tractor and pulled onto the beach as soon as any distress signal was issued.

There was no more that a foot gap between the lifeboat and the walls of the house. Reg automatically turned sideways and edged his way past the cork fenders that hung over the side towards the wood stairs that led to a platform overlooking the bow of the vessel.

In his wake Anna followed, her eyes stinging from the powerful odours of the machinery, lifesaving equipment and fog of smoke from his recently packed and lit pipe.

Handing Anna a tin mug of tea he said 'Fraid us is owt ov sugur, bloomin ration-en!'

'This is just right, thank you.' Anna replied.

The lifeboat man was about to speak when the sliding doors at the entrance gave a sharp grinding sound as they were wrenched back quickly and the sound of a loud and excited voice shouted 'Reg! Reg bay ee thair?'

The Coxswain stood up and shouted back 'Aye Dick, aven ah dish ov tay wa a frend lik, waats up?'

The voice shouted even louder 'Reg ee nevur sin tha bleedy lik. I meens et, nevur sin tha lik afore, get up ta tha war memorial bleedy quick Reg.'

A frown crossed his already lined face as he faced Anna 'Think us ad best sha whaat ee's gappin un bout.'

From outside the boathouse they looked up the hill towards the church and the commotion emanating from the area around it. They were unable to see anything over the line of local people who had magically appeared and stretched across the road in front of them.

Both being drawn by the sound Anna's first comment was 'Reg, where on earth have all these people come from, is it some sort of carnival?'

'B'aint no carnival Muss Anna, an I'm jiggered iv I's nows what's dragged tha beggurs owt ov a Sunday bed, but us ad bettur av a look, maid.'

Walking up the road they joined the solid lines of jostling men, women and children who stood cheering and clapping with some waving small paper Union Jack flags. Over the shoulders of the onlookers Anna peered between a man wearing a black fisherman's cap above his working garb and a woman with a dull green and blue head scarf that had been hastily wrapped over a head full of bulging hair curlers.

For several moments Anna stood speechless with her mouth slightly open and blinked her eyes in disbelief at the sight in front of her before turning her head sideways and catching the eye of the lifeboat Coxswain. She shouted loudly and excitedly, 'Good God Reg, the Yanks are here!'

Anna stared up along High Street and back past the war memorial into St Andrews Street which skirted the Parish Church. In both directions the road was full of several hundred American soldiers in full battledress, complete with steel helmets, kit bags, backpacks and with each man carrying a rifle or machine gun over their shoulder.

The quiet Sunday morning had been transformed by the arrival of the Americans and word had spread fast through the small town; as it does when the lifeboat is called out and people race to lend a helping hand.

Looking at some of the faces of the cheering, shouting and laughing crowd Anna could do no more than smile and laugh with them as the lost infection of laughter spread.

Suddenly it seemed there were flashes and sparkles of hope again. An air of optimism had returned with the young brash Americans that more than three years of bloody and tough war had almost extinguished.

Although through Anna's eyes her fellow country men and

women looked sadly poor and dowdy against the well dressed, fresh newcomers it still seemed to her that the grey of the day had been lifted by the arrival of these young men and that a much needed celebration had started. And hope had been restored.

Standing by the war memorial three American soldiers stood in front of a group of their officers. One was holding an unfurled Stars and Strips flag that did it's best to catch the passing breeze and display its bright reds and vivid white stars on dark blue. Each side of him soldiers held smaller banners, one showing a golden eagle on a purple background the other one had large gold numbers against green.

British officers joined their American counterparts. Each one of them quickly contaminated by the new infection of laughter. At intervals groups of soldiers headed by a corporal or sergeant were handed a piece of white paper by one of the British officers and directed away from the main line of men towards the middle or upper parts of the town.

The soldiers seemed to walk casually rather than march, as if they were out for a Sunday stroll with their heavy cumbersome loads. There was a lot of laughter and chat amongst them which gained in level as they heard the clapping and shouts of welcome that was coming from the crowd of local people watching them.

The lady in scarf and hair rollers next to Anna shouted to her neighbour 'Daphne, don't they all look healthy an sort of, well sort of clean. Some of em is proper hansum as well!'

After receiving a friendly nudge of rebuke, together with a quiet laugh from Daphne she finished by adding 'Well they is Daf, tis just a pity us isn't twenty years younger girl!'

Anna had to agree with the woman's comments, or at least some of them, because the young men were exactly as she had described them. Not dashing or grand, nothing Teutonic or strutting in these chaps, they seemed friendly, open and most certainly very self-confident and at ease with themselves.

As she watched, the corporal who led the group passing in front of her suddenly left his men and came over towards them and bent down to the height of the children at the front, and she heard him say 'Hi there! It's real good to see you, my name is Charlie. Would you like some candy!'

The soldier could hardly get up under the weight of the friendly hands that were patting him on the back and the cries of 'Welcome to Cornwall Yank, it's good to see you!'

More men broke their own ranks to hand out chewing gum and candy to the children and some of the adults. All ages equally happy to accept the gifts of sweets - that almost forgotten luxury, after years of war time rationing.

The scene reminded Anna of the tale of the Pied Piper of Hamblin as many of the people and children in the crowd followed in the ranks of soldiers as they walked along the streets and narrow lanes of the town to find the accommodation they had been billeted to in houses and hotels.

'Muss Anna, would ee lik ah nothur cup ov tay?'

Turning away from the dwindling numbers of newly arrived Americans the two new friends began to walk towards the West pier and the boathouse when she looked at her watch and said 'Reg, I would like one but I was going to walk to Zennor to see friends of mine but it's almost eleven and I have to be there before one'ish, I won't have time now will I?'

With a slight shake of his head he said 'Not nuff time ta walk in, but theere is a buz leaven bout wan frum Porthmoer Beach.'

Thinking for a second she said 'Umm, I think it will all be a bit rushed, so I'll put off going to Zennor today, which means I would love another cup of tea, and perhaps this time we will be able to finish it!'

'Now tell me, what do you think of our new Allies, what a surprise, hey!'

'Ay undeed t'was a surprise un now mustake. Not easy ta keep thengs quiet round ere I can tell ee!'

'Ah had a word weth Dick Reynolds, he drives tha tractur fur us boat, ee saays ole train load ov em cam un an nother tew will bay followun un nex few daays'

'Us wondured why a lot ov tha coast an cliff tops up frum Porthmeor waas fenced ovv lik, only lass waak, now ee seems they es gwain ta bay used bey tha Yanks fur trainin. An whaat doos I think'em?'

The old seaman narrowed his eyes and frowned before

replying 'T'will nevur bay saame gwain Muss Anna, mark ma, twil nevur bay tha same gwain'

The twinkle in the seaman's eyes made Anna smile as he finished by saying

'I saw tha look un sum ov they maids, an I means tha married wans, well as tha youngins an tis lik Chrestmas is yer, early lik!'

Setting down her haversack on her desk and hanging her coat on the tottering coat stand in the corner of her office, she looked at the duty roster suspended on the green painted wall.

'Good!' She said aloud after looking at the clock on the wall which read six forty five. Picking up a telephone Anna asked the operator to put her through to the duty sister, and waiting for a reply. 'Sister Moore here.'

Quietly Anna said 'Gail, it's me are you busy?'

Clearing her throat Sister Gail Moore replied crisply 'No Matron, everything is under control here.'

Continuing in hushed tones Anna said 'Gail, tell your senior nurse that I need you for an hour and pop over to my office, I have some amazing news!'

Gail Moore knocked on the door of her matron's office and went in when she heard a 'Come' spoken from inside.

'Close the door quickly Gail and come over here. Coffee, tea, opps sorry, no coffee, tea?' The nursing sister accepted tea and sat down while Anna took the top off of a red and gold coloured tin tea caddy and put two teaspoons of tea into a white china pot, poured boiling water over black leaves before slotting the lid into place and leaving the pot to brew before quickly sitting down opposite Gail.

Leaning slightly forward over her desk Anna said, 'I went to St Ives this morning, and you will never guess in a million years what happened!'

Searching her friend's face Gail said 'O my God, don't say you bumped into Simon's fire snorting dragon of a mother?'

Tutting twice and shaking her head, Anna said 'No, of course not, silly. It was really early when sergeant Phillips dropped me off and it was as quiet as the grave in the town, well I was having a cup of tea with the Coxswain of the lifeboat when all hell broke out, I can tell you'

'I walked up to where the commotion was coming from and low and behold Gail, you will never believe this, but the whole town was full, and I do mean full, of spanking and sparkling new American soldiers, literally hundreds of them marching along chewing gum, laughing and shouting to the locals, it was like some sort of movie at the cinema! And on the way back I saw hundreds and hundreds more from the bus I was on.'

The eyes of the nursing sister widened in amazement as Anna got up from her desk and poured the tea through a strainer into two cups, added milk and placed both back on the flat surface before taking her seat again and looking at the woman opposite, waiting for a response.

Narrowing her eyes before speaking Gail said 'You haven't been drinking that scrumpy, no of course you haven't. Actually Anna, suddenly what one of the orderlies said earlier today now makes a bit of sense. She told me that on her way back from Bodmin in an ambulance she saw that three or four big fields that were empty only last week were now covered in row after row of tents'

'I know the Yanks have been arriving in droves over the past year, but they all seemed to stationed in the midlands and around London, so why here, and why now?'

Anna told her what Reg Barbary had told her about large areas of the coasts and beaches being closed off to the public for use as training areas.

Still baffled she asked, 'But training for what?'

Wide eyed Anna simply replied with 'The same as us Gail, the return to France next year!'

Drinking the tea Gail could only think of adding 'What did they look like? What I mean is, are they any different?' Laughing out loud she added 'Actually, I don't know what I mean!'

Sharing her laughter Anna said 'Well now, I have to say they all looked very, very clean and well dressed. Not exactly dashing, or grand, but smart and tidy. And there were certainly some rather dishy ones amongst them, I can tell you!'

'There was something else about them as well, they certainly did brighten up a rather drab looking St Ives, the locals greeted them like heroes, in fact it was all very gay, and there was a sudden carnival atmosphere to the place.'

The two friends talked until Gail got up, saying 'I had best be getting back. Such excitement in boring old Cornwall! Sadly though, not for ladies who are practically engaged to be married. But certainly for us single gals!'

Looking at the clock she added 'Only four hours to the end of my duty, then Matron, I am going to wash every piece of underwear I have!'

******

For the quiet rural counties of Devon and Cornwall the following weeks were like nothing that had ever happened in their history as thousands and thousands of young American troops and their equipment poured into the towns and villages.

For the past three years of the war both communities had seen it's young men and a lot of young women march out of the counties into the armed forces and to work in armament factories in the industrial centres of the country.

Suddenly the whole of Cornwall and Devon started to resonate with the sound of the accents of Texan's, New Yorkers and all of the different States that made up the vast country across the Atlantic.

In Cornwall not a single backwater of the ancient land was not going to be affected by the friendly, and at times, not so friendly invasion. From May 1943, an average number of over one hundred thousand American troops each month would land on the Island of Britain until close to two million American men and women lived here, in prefabricated Quonset or Nissan huts, under tents, in requisitioned stately homes, asylums, schools, or with small families.

Truro, 31st October 1943

Simon Tremayne's parents were in their bedroom getting ready to attend the Sunday morning service at the chapel when

Robert said, 'Let us hope we get through the service without the air raid siren going off again like it did last week, and we had to spend an hour or so in that dreadful community shelter close to the chapel.'

Clearing his throat nervously he approached the subject he knew could send his wife into a furious tantrum, but by broaching the subject before the Sunday service he knew any tirade would at least be over by the time they faced the other members of their chapel.

'Patricia, darling. I do beg you, please, try to keep an open mind about this woman. Simon is no fool my dear. My goodness he was certainly right about the property next to Falmouth docks, the whole area has trebled in value since the Americans arrived!'

'Old John Tonkin has only recently found out that it was us that bought the wharfs he was selling, and he is hopping mad, crossed the street yesterday rather than pass the time of day with me, ahh, ahh, wonderful'

'Yes, but besides that darling one has to say some of these Jewish families are very nice, and also very well connected. At least stop chastising the boy in your letters for getting involved with her. From what I've read in the newspapers that lad has been through a great deal in North Africa and now possibly Sicily'

'I would hate to give him cause for worry, in fact in my notes to him I only ever mention good things, things about Christine getting promoted to corporal and how she seems to thrive on what ever it is she cannot talk about, but which gives her so much satisfaction. He really is a good lad Patricia, and I have to say I am jolly proud of him.'

Patricia Tremayne looked at the reflection of her face in the mirror in front of her while a fine cloud of face powder drifted up as she patted her nose and cheeks.

Putting the soft pad back into the round powder compact she snapped the lid shut and got up from the dressing table saying 'Robert, you will remember that we have four American soldiers coming to tea, following my letter to the commander of the camp close to town, won't you. And perhaps I forgot to tell you that I especially wanted him to note that I did not want any Jewish people amonst them.'

Nodding, he muttered a soft 'Yes darling, I do remember. We had better be going or we shall be late for the service.'

Carlean US Army Camp, Cornwall, 6*th* November 1943

The hastily erected army camp now occupied both sides of the narrow road that led away from Bodmin moor. Behind the high hedgerows there were now over three hundred tents and ten prefabricated huts occupying the fifty acres of land that been requisitioned from local farmers.

The tents and buildings would be a temporary home to the twelve hundred infantry troops together with their support teams of engineers, nursing and medical staff, mess facilities, bath houses, cinema and PX store.

Colonel Jeffery J. Strauss Jnr. stood at the entrance to one of the smaller Nissan huts that stood each side of the larger Qonset hut that was the officers' mess to the men and senior nursing staff of the 43rd Infantry Company.

The American introduced himself first to Wing Commander Donaldson before leading him into the interior of the half moon shaped building made from corrugated metal sheets laid over a wood and ply-wood skeleton.

There were raised eye brows from the twenty three British men and women as they followed their welcoming America host through the plain wooden door and into the mess hall. The inside of the bleak looking hut had been decorated and furnished to the standard the visitors had long since forgotten.

Plush easy chairs rested on best quality carpet, paintings and framed photographs on the walls showed spectacular images of landscapes and city sky scrapers. A long table boasted food not seen or tasted since before the war. The buffet had platters of meat, salmon, fresh vegetables and a fruit bowl that had at its centre a pineapple surrounded by oranges and apples. None of the Islanders had seen such a display since war had started.

As each visitor was introduced to the American commander his adjutant would ask what each would like to drink from the bar and a waiter would appear magically with the requested beverage, which in the case of gin and tonic came complete with mounds of ice and fresh slices of lemon.

Other American officers were introduced. Well groomed and good mannered they all oozed self confidence and well being. Anna and her fellow countrymen and women all felt more than a bit shabby, dour, after the long haul of four long and weary years of war.

One young Lieutenant from Florida politely introduced himself to Anna and Kathleen Winter. 'Good evening ladies, my name is Al Quarterman, and it sure is nice to meet you, and to be here at last.' After shaking each woman's hand and without any hint of a smile he continued by saying 'But eh, does it ever stop raining here?'

Kathleen was smiling as Anna replied, 'It will stop raining Lieutenant, and when it does your eyes will be dazzled by the greens of the fields and blues of the sea. Now tell us, how did you all get to England?'

'One heck of a journey ma'am. We boarded the Queen Mary in New York. Sailed up to Halifax in Canada and then came straight across the Atlantic without any escort ships travelling at thirty-five knots all the way, and landed in the city of Liverpool.'

'My goodness ladies, now that city has been bombed! Bombed like we saw on the Pathe Newsreels at the cinema back home, terrible, real terrible.'

Sensing that the young man was about to stop to draw breath Anna said 'I'm afraid Al that you will be seeing a lot of cities and small towns that have been and are still being bombed each and every day and night, we had a bombing raid over Falmouth only two days ago which killed several civilians and service men. But tell me, did you say that the Queen Mary went across the Atlantic on her own, and not as part of a convoy?'

'No escorts ma'am, straight across, well zigzagged across, still doing top speed though, tell ya, when we Americans build ships, we build em well, like we did the Queen Mary, and ma'am, no need for you to worry anymore, we've arrived here to win this war for you!'

Anna needed time. She knew she could not reply quickly so

instead said 'Oh really, how interesting, tell me Lieutenant, could I possibly have another 'G 'an T'?'

The young man from Florida looked blankly and in puzzlement at Anna before saying 'G an what ma'am?'

Swallowing hard Anna said slowly 'Ah, I see, right then. Gin and Tonic, for both of us, please.' Now able to acknowledge the request the officer replied, 'Certainly ma'am, coming up!'

Looking at Kathleen the matron quietly, and scornfully said 'Bloody cheek of it, first the Queen Mary is built in America and then we have no need to worry about the Germans any longer because that pimply moron has arrived. I am bloody fuming Kathleen, I had better talk to someone else in case I cause a rift between us and our new bloody saviours!'

Easing herself through the crowd of uniforms Anna joined Gail Moore who was talking to two of the infantry officers 'Matron, please meet Captain Jesse Garvey and Captain Billy Roberts, both of these gentlemen are from Louisiana, in the southern part of America.'

Shaking each by the hand while the two men confirmed their names and where they came from in the drawling tones of the deep South Anna managed to say without the slightest hint of cynicism 'How nice to meet you both' and looking her colleague squarely in the eyes added 'And Sister Moore you seem to have picked up an invaluable knowledge of the geography of America very quickly which I'm sure will prove very useful in the future!'

Before anyone could comment a fresh accent caught her ear, and one with a very slight hint of an Irish brogue attached to it. She accepted the hand that was placed in front of her as the man it belonged to said, 'Now Matron, I can't let these southern boys have all the limelight, I'm Patrick Flynn, from Boston.'

Taking a step back she replied, 'Hello Patrick, welcome to Cornwall. And how are you coping with the weather?'

Laughing before he replied he said, 'I know we Americans can stretch a line or two but there ain't no way I could convince you or myself that Boston is in any of the sunshine States, and my wife wrote to me yesterday to say she had had the first really bad frost of the winter. Mind you, even I have gotta say is does rain like the very devil here!'

Instantly liking the man and his impish way she asked, 'Is this your first visit to Britian?'

'I guess you could say that. I only hesitate because I did land very briefly in Scotland, literally only for a couple of hours last October. I was in a convoy that had sailed from the States and we mustered off Scotland before going to Morocco, at the start of the North African campaign. I've only just joined this outfit from Sicily, Italy.'

Unsure of how to say what she wanted to diplomatically Anna asked, 'I thought that maybe you had spent some time in Ireland as you have just the hint of an Irish accent.'

'You're not the first British person to pose the same question which was a puzzle to me at first. You see back home in Boston over half of the population of the city are descendants of Irish immigrants, my own grandfather came from a place called Skibbereen, in County Cork, and he never ever stopped talking about the wild beauty of the place, and how he missed it'

Patrick Flynn had the most piercing green eyes Anna had ever seen and they bored into hers as he finished talking by saying 'Of course that was before he was chased out of his own country by the English at the turn of the century, so I kind of feel deep down that I know what those poor old Frenchies went through when they were invaded and occupied by the Germans.'

There wasn't a hint of malice in his look or the tone of voice. His eyes seemed to laugh at the slight embarrassment and guilt Anna knew she felt, and at her total inability to offer any form of defence to the burden of history.

It was the commander of the camp that provided an escape for the matron as his adjutant cleared his throat loudly and announce to the gathering 'Ladies and Gentlemen, Colonel Strauss would like to say a few words.'

The Colonel stood under a wood carving of the American Eagle and between the flag of his country and one of the Union Jack as he started his speech: 'I would first of all like to thank you ladies and gentlemen for being our welcome guests this evening. It is for me a very humbling experience to be here in England and among the people that alone have kept the light of freedom burning for so long, and have paid such a terrible price in terms of human suffering in the process'

'The welcome the British people have extended to us has been almost beyond words. Now it is our turn. The long years of isolation ended the day the Japs bombed us as the Nazis have bombed you. We are here to train for the invasion and liberation of Europe. We know it won't be easy, but together we will kick Hitler and his cronies out of France and out of this World!'

'I would ask you in advance to sometimes take into consideration how young, homesick and inexperienced a lot of the troops under my command are. Ladies and gentlemen, the majority of these men have never been out of the State they were born in, let alone out of the country'

'Their knowledge of other countries and cultures is limited, but their determination to succeed in the defence of freedom is at the core of their upbringing and the Constitution that has surrounded it'

The West Point Colonel and veteran of the first war, twenty years before paused and smiled before looking around the room and saying 'Now our visitors may have noticed a certain trait that us Americans have for boasting! To the average GI everything in and from America is bigger and better. I know you will find this tendency irritating and darn right annoying'

'Please be patient with us, please be a little tolerant, because I assure you that at heart these are good men, mostly very young, and they are a long, long way from their homes, families and loved ones'

'Oh, just one final thing, which is an apology from me. Something I overheard as I was passing a group of you earlier needs to be clarified. I will personally pin a notice on the officer's mess notice board to the effect that the liner we travelled across the Atlantic on, the *Queen Mary,* was definitely built in Scotland, not the USA!'

Whites Only, No Blacks

RAF Portlan, 9th November 1943

   Nurse Simmons placed the buff coloured files on her Matron's desk. She had just finished speaking Kathleen Winter's name when the telephone in front of Anna rang and the sister herself spoke 'Matron, we've just received six or seven American soldiers who have been injured in a road accident, with more on the way, at least two of them are critical.'

  'Is the duty doctor there or on his way?' Nodding in silence while she listened, Anna then replied 'Good, right Sister, I'll come over with Nurse Simmons.'

 On the way out of her office building she called out to Sergeant Philips as she rushed past him 'We have a number of emergencies that will need to go to Truro for surgery will you organised three ambulances please.'

    The patient and casualty reception tent had ten beds in it and Anna saw it was almost full as she entered. Gail Moore and two nurses had arrived seconds before them still dressed in their flying overalls from a training flight.

  Many of the men were in severe shock and pain. The duty doctor was an experienced medical man, and together with the nursing team they dealt calmly with the thrashing arms of some and the screams of others with a detached and clinical manner, while at the same time providing words of comfort.

  Anna went to the last stretcher that was being carried in. Together with a nurse they eased the big framed man off the stretcher onto a bed with the same practiced gentleness that a mother puts a child into a cot.

The Lieutenant was unconscious and had difficulty in breathing. With closed eyes he would gasp for a breath, and struggle until he secured the next, the effort bringing spasms of pain that cut through his unconscious state and ended in a moan of pain.

Captain Parkin finished giving the soldier he was treating an injection before looking at Anna and saying, 'This young chap is fine internally but will need an op. on both legs, you can see the lower fibular has been crushed'

Pointing at two beds he said 'Those two need to be operated on immediately and we need to get them away to the base hospital straight away if you can. What's the state of play with the rest Matron?'

Out of the corner of her eye she saw that Sergeant Philips and the stretcher bearers were waiting inside the tent for orders. She called him over and gave instructions for the first of the injured to be ferried away, before looking back at the doctor and saying, 'Beds three, six, seven, ten and twelve seem to have internal injuries, with ten and seven the most critical Sir'.

'Right Matron, let's have a look shall we.'

This was the first real test of the casualty clearing station acting as a unit, and Anna was pleased. By early evening all of the injured had been taken away from the RAF base to hospitals for operations or the sort of longer term care they were unable to give.

The medical officer was the first to say, 'Matron that was like old times, quite exciting, and for your younger novices, the first taste of the battle front, and what to expect in the future!'

Turning to the sisters, nurses and orderlies who were still in the tent he said 'Well done all of you. You managed that with speed and calm, well done.'

The Matron added her own praise to her team, finishing by saying 'Girls, today is what we are all about. If you ever needed a glimpse of what to expect when we go into action, then today you got it. Now I want you to think about this.....imagine the last few hours multiplied by two and then by three or more days, not hours, but days, and that is what you have to look forward too when we reach France and the action starts!'

Kathleen Winter had gone straight to bed to grab a few hours sleep before her duty began at midnight. Sat in front of Anna's desk Alison Forbes and Gail Moore both said 'Yes please!' to Anna's invitation of a glass of sherry.

The Matron raised her glass to the women 'That was good, and by being good we certainly saved the life of one of those men, if not more. Salut!'

'You know, it wasn't until we had sorted them out that it suddenly dawned on me that each of those chaps was black, everyone. Which camp were they from?'

Gail Moore looked first at Kathleen and then back to Anna before saying 'They were from Colonel Strauss's camp, Matron.'

Anna looked rather vaguely at the two women in front of her before replying 'Strange, I don't remember seeing any black soldiers at the camp or officers at the reception we went too?'

The awkward silence in the room was broken by Alison Forbes as she said, 'That was most welcome Matron, thank you, now I had better be going back to make sure everything is ship shape before the next shift takes over.'

As the door closed Anna said 'Gail, I feel rather silly, what have I missed? What is going on?'

'I honestly had not realised that you didn't know' Gail Moore replied.

'Gail, this is becoming irritating, know what?'

'Anna, we didn't see any black officers or soldiers at the reception party because they are segregated from the white people and live in a separate area of the camp. An area that was put up for them only. They are not allowed to mix with any white person because of the American colour bar.'

The matron refilled their small sherry glasses and sat back in her wooden Captain's chair saying nothing, only staring into the amber coloured drink in her hand.

It was Gail who broke the silence 'I'm sorry Anna, I just assumed you knew.'

Shaking her head she said 'It's hardly your fault Gail, I must seem rather stupid. I certainly feel it. I also feel really bloody angry. Angry at myself for not knowing'

'Only three miles away we have hundreds of black Indian soldiers, I've seen the men in our casualty area and their officers at the mess, and damn it, there are West Indian pilots flying the aircraft from this station, are you telling me they are not allowed into the American base because the colour of their skin is black?'

With honesty Gail answered her 'I simply don't know. But I do know that the two groups, the whites and the blacks are kept well apart from each other at the camp and elsewhere.'

Thinking back to the nursing sister from Jamaica who had taken her down Union Street in Plymouth, Anna said softly, 'Well Miriam, what would you have made of this I wonder? It makes me feel sick to my stomach.'

When Gail closed the office door and left Anna alone she realised for the first time how isolated the position of Matron had made her.

RAF Portlan, 3rd December 1943

Through her sleep Anna heard the knock and saw her small room lose its darkness as the door opened and the silhouette of a male orderly appeared with the light from the corridor behind him. 'Matron, sorry to disturb you, but Sister Moore has had a bit of an accident, nothing critical, but she's in a bit of a state, and she refused to let any of us call the duty MO. We've put her in the isolation tent, away from the other patients, and Sister Forbes thought you would like to know, ma'am.'

Anna was awake instantly and replied 'Thank you Ian, I'll be right behind you.'
She dressed quickly, taking a look at her noisy round bedside clock which showed twelve fifteen.

At first glance the Matron thought that Gail had been in a car accident. Her face was a mass of red welts with dark blue bruises around her eyes and cheek bones.

She stood above the bed and said to the sister 'What on earth happened, were you in an accident or something?'

Through swollen lips she mumbled quietly 'Can I talk to you alone please Matron?'

The matron looked at Alison Forbes, who was the duty night Sister, and without any questions she left the side of the bed and the tent with the male orderly, leaving the two women alone.

Reaching for a chair Anna sat besides the nursing Sister. She took a hand and gently squeezed it before saying 'Now Gail, everyone has left, so what happened to you?'

Looking straight ahead at the foot of the bed Gail whispered 'They beat me Anna. They punched me, slapped me, tore my uniform, ripped open my shirt and tore at my bra and between my legs. They called me such horrible names, horrible'

'I was so afraid, I thought I was going to die. I really thought they were going to kill me Anna.'

Gail's sobbing stopped her from saying any more. Her tears ran from her swollen eyes and down her scratched red cheeks. She drew deep faltering gasps of air into her lungs that made her whole body shake and tremble.

Anna got up from the chair and sat on the bed. She put her arms around the distraught nurse, and friend, before gently pulling her head into her own body and hugged her like a baby, patting her back, and saying 'Your safe now Gail, I'm here and so are your friends. Everything will be alright, I promise everything will be alright, just try and rest, please.'

Gail Moore fell into an exhausted sleep and Anna laid her down before she pulled a white sheet up to her neck and left the tent. She asked a duty nurse to stay with the Sister and Anna went to the main reception area of the centre.

Talking to Alison Forbes at the reception desk was a tall black American officer who she vaguely remembered. His smart uniform had patches of mud on it and a trousers leg had been torn. Approaching them both she said 'Sorry to disturb you but I need to talk to you urgently Sister Forbes.'

The sister turned around quickly saying 'Yes Matron, oh this is Lieutenant Dulles. He brought Sister Moore in.'

Looking towards the American she said, 'We won't be a moment, could I have a word with you after, please

Lieutenant.'

Without waiting for a reply she guided the duty Sister out of the room before saying quietly 'Gail is asleep, but she is in a dreadful state. Did you examine her fully when you undressed her?'

Nodding she answered 'She's badly bruised, but apart from that there were no signs of anything broken or major contusions around the head or neck and no dislocations'

Stopping for a moment she leaned forward to make sure no one else heard her next sentence 'Matron, Gail's brassiere and her pants were almost torn to shreds, I've put them in a safe place, but the fact is I'm not sure what she went through. What I mean is whether or not she had been raped.'

Anna thought for a moment before saying 'Alison, could you go and fetch Commander Donaldson, this is getting too ugly, I have to ignore Gail's wishes, and also get the MO to see her.'

'You say the American at reception brought Gail into the camp, I seem to know his face, was he with the group of injured men from the road accident?'

The duty Sister nodded as she said 'Yes, he had broken ribs as far as I can remember. He's only been out of the main hospital a week and he carried Gail in as though she were a baby, which must have hurt like heck.'

'I'll go and see him if you can take care of the rest Alison.'

Going back into the reception area Anna took a sharp intake of air and quickly ran forward when she saw that the American officer had collapsed on the floor, with a bright red patch of blood growing slowly on the ground beside his still body.

A nurse and Anna put the soldier on a stretcher and then into a ward bed. The duty MO was David Holmes and Anna explained that the young officer was now the priority before looking at Gail. Before he went to look at Gail he said 'Pretty sure that chap will be alright. I'd like you to X-Ray him to be on the safe side, but I believe he's only torn the outer suchers. The surgeon that operated on him will ring me later.'

Going through into the isolation ward where Gail had been put the doctor stood by her bed with Anna at his side 'Now then, what do we have here Matron?'

After looking at Gail Moore the doctor spoke to Anna and Wing Commander Donaldson in the station leader's office. 'She really is in deep shock, and frankly I'm hardly surprised Commander. She has been brutally beaten, quite shocking to be honest'

'She has minor concussion due to a bang on the head and I would like her to be X-Rayed but there is no major damage that I can see. She has cuts and bruises that are quite vicious, whoever did it was extremely brutal'

'Oh, and by the way, she told me that she had not been raped and the only reason she was not raped and killed by the two men that did this to her was because that young man in the emergency tent intervened and beat them off.'

When the MO left his office the base commander looked at Anna before saying 'Matron, I think it would be a wise precaution to have someone sit with Sister Moore until she wakes up, and in the mean time I am going to telephone Colonel Strauss and tell him about the incident.'

Without a moment's thought Anna replied, 'Yes Sir, I'll sit with her.'

Sitting on a seat next to the bed with a large mug of cocoa she said softly 'Oh Gail, what have you been up too, you silly thing.'

For the second time that night the male orderly had been charged with the job of waking up his Matron which he did by gently shaking her shoulder and saying 'Matron, Sister Forbes is having a spot of trouble with some Yank 'Snowdrops' at the emergency tent and needs your help.'

Rubbing her eyes briefly before looking at Gail and making a mental note that it was almost four in the morning, and that she seemed stable she said 'Snowdrops, what do you mean Ian?'

'American military police matron. They have white helmets, which is where the nick name comes from.'

As Anna neared the tent she heard Alison Forbes say, 'I'm sorry Sergeant, I can not let you or your men into that area until I've spoken to my Matron.'

Protesting loudly, she heard the policemen almost shout 'Now look here, I've been ordered by my CO to bring Dulles back to our camp immediately.'

Coming in from the reception area the Matron said 'Sister Forbes is there a problem?'

Without answering directly she said, 'Could I have a word please Matron'

Inside the emergency tent and away from the four Americans that Anna had counted the duty Sister said 'Matron, what a bloody cheek that nasty man had. I found all of the MP's inside the tent before anyone could stop them with a stretcher and two bearers just about to detached the American from his drip and take him away without so much as a word!'

'I'm sorry Matron, but I told him to get out immediately or I'd call our own security guards.'

'Well done, I think you did absolutely right Alison'

Taking the black officer's hand in hers she took his pulse before saying 'The lad is in no condition to be moved anywhere at the moment, and I will go and tell the Sergeant that right now'

Pausing she added quietly 'Alison, go out through the emergency exit and get the duty guard officer and a couple of men here quickly, just to be on the safe side.'

Clearing her voice before speaking Anna said in a matter of fact way 'Sorry Sergeant, your man is far too ill to be moved at present, and he will have to stay where he is.'

The Sergeant looked hard at Anna before brushing her aside with his hand and saying in a southern drawl 'Mam, that nigger in there is dangerous. We understand that he attacked one of your people. I have my orders to take him back, and I will take responsibility for him from now on.'

Anna was about to shout at the man as he passed her but her sentence was interrupted by the loud voice of the officer of the watch 'Stay exactly where you are sergeant or my men will have you all disarmed, arrested and thrown in the guard room behind bars.'

The officer, together with six armed Royal Airforce Regiment guards quickly swarmed around the Americans. Anna could sense that by the look on the faces of the men a showdown would have been welcome, and it was a feeling that the American sergeant was quick to acknowledge as he said 'I'm only carrying out my orders Sir. The man in there is dangerous and I have been told to bring him back to our camp under escort.'

The British officer leaned forward as he spoke 'Thank you sergeant for your truly invaluable warning. I will now post my men in his tent to protect all of us, and in the mean time I want you and your men off this camp, immediately.'

After a quick pause he added 'Ah, one moment. That is Sergeant, if Matron Jack does not want me to arrest you first for disobeying the orders of a senior officer, Her orders sergeant, a very serious offence in this country!'

Looking towards Anna he said 'Matron, what would you like me to do with this chap?'

Turning her back on the American she replied, 'Please get him out of my sight and away from here Lieutenant and make sure he does not come back.'

'Our great pleasure Matron, I can assure you!'

At six o'clock in the morning the day duty staff were taking over when Gail started to wake. Anna waited until she had been washed and her dressings changed before handing her a cup of tea and asking the nurses present to leave. 'How are you feeling?' she asked.

'Terrible. Physically better, but angry Anna, bloody angry. If Spence hadn't barged in God knows what would have happened. They were brutes. Nasty brutes and real animals.'

Interrupting the injured sister Anna said 'Gail, Lieutenant Dulles is in the next tent. He's alright, but some of his stitches burst and he lost a lot of blood after he brought you here'

'The Americans told us that he was the one who attacked you. They came here last night and tried to arrest him. We managed to stop them, but he will have to go back to his unit today Gail.'

For the first time she stared directly at Anna and held the look as she said 'If you let him go back to his unit Anna the two men that attacked me will find him, castrate him and then kill him before sending me his testicles'

'The reason I know this will happen is because as the men were beating me and tearing at my clothes they told me that is what they intended to do because they don't allow 'niggers' as they kept saying, to go out with white women back in Louisiana.'

Trying to force a smile Anna said, 'Surely not Gail, you're exaggerating, they would never go that far.'

Gail took a sip of her tea before continuing 'Can I tell you the whole story?'
Nodding a yes Anna sat back and listened.

'Some time after the lorry crash when we received the black GI's here I was in the 'Fox and Hounds' pub with several others when Spencer came up to me to say thank you. We had a few drinks and since then we've been out several times together. He's a single chap, a wonderful dancer and really good fun'

'Last week I arranged to meet him at the pub. I was early and because I was on my own I waited in the 'snug', the bar between the lounge and public ones. While I was sat there Captain Garvey, who we both met at the American reception, came in and asked if I would go to a movie with him. He was in the lounge bar with Captain Roberts, who we also met'

'When I said I was waiting for Spence he stepped back in absolute shock and horror and almost screamed "Back home we would tar and feather any white woman for going out with a nigger. I reckon it's 'bout time we started to do it here, to kick some fucking sense into you stupid limeys".

'He was very drunk and very aggressive and although he did frighten me I didn't take it too seriously until I told Spencer what had happened'

'He did take it seriously Anna. Deadly serious. He told me that most of the white officers were no problem but nearly all of the ones from the south hated the black soldiers and especially hated black officers'

'The stories I heard about the black GI's being falsely accused of crimes they had not committed and the cruel beatings and even the murder of men because of the colour of their skin, shocked me to my core.'

'He told me that seventy five percent of all black people in America lived in the south and that for them segregation and racism was written into the law and was part of everyday life.'

'Coloured people are not allowed onto buses reserved for

whites, or to go into cinemas, bars, theatres, even churches and sit side by side with white people. I could hardly believe what he was telling me Anna'

'Spencer's father is a church minister and has been constantly threatened and was once severely beaten for trying to protect negroes in his parish. The stories I've heard Anna are terrible, almost like going back to the last century and slavery, we honestly have no idea about the conditions that most of the black people are forced to live in in America.'

'Spence has told me that the more he meets English people the more he is disgusted with his fellow Americans and that he and thousands like him will not tolerate being second class citizens in their own country after the war is finished'

'From what he told me it's his political views as well as the colour of his skin that Captain Garvey and Captain Roberts openly detest about him, coupled with the fact that he has done so well and he is liked by a lot of white officers and especially by Colonel Strauss, oh and do you remember Captain Flynn, well he's a good friend of Spencer.'

Gail took both of Anna's hands in her before pleading 'Anna, Spencer is a really nice, kind person and he doesn't deserve to end up dead because of me.'

The sister paused to finish her mug of tea and the interruption gave Anna the chance to ask 'How can you be sure it was these two captains that beat you?'

'I was supposed to meet Spencer at the Fox last night but he must have been held up at the camp and so when it was closing time I started to walk back here in the blackout on my own. I noticed that Captain Garvey and Roberts were in the pub and they were both very drunk and loud'

'It was those two who attacked me in the dark last night, but I will never to able to prove that. It was pitch black and they waited in the bushes not far from the pub and one of them grabbed me from behind while the other started to tear at my uniform and hit and slap me'

'I started to shout and scream and the one who was beating me said "Gag the bitch Jes".

'I don't know for sure but I suspect that Spencer must have been going to the Fox to see if I was still there when he heard me scream before I was choked and passed out.'

'Then I guess he must have beat them off and he saved me from God only knows what, but that won't matter Anna, because the minute Spencer leaves here, he is as good as dead, and not even Colonel Strauss will be able to help.'

Gail paused for a second before adding 'But Anna, you can help save him. In fact, Anna, you are his and my only hope.'

Anna left Gail and went to the ward where Spencer Dulles was lying. He was still asleep. She took his pulse which was steady and was about to take his temperature when a nurse entered the tent and said 'Matron, there is a Captain Flynn at the reception who would like to speak to you.'

The station commander had rang and told her to expect the American. Anna suggested they look at the injured black officer before they walked through the steady drizzle to her office. There, she took his raincoat and hat and hung them on her coat stand before showing him a seat and saying, 'I could offer you coffee, but you will probably hate it, so would you rather have tea?'

He looked quickly over her shoulder, through the office window and across the grey tarmac of the runways and hangers in the distance before smiling and saying 'Yeh, I guess you're probably right, I'll be safer with sweet tea, thank you Matron especially on such a lousy early morning. You know I wonder at times if it will ever stop raining for more than a couple of hours!'

Smiling as she replaced the telephone after ordering two cups of tea she replied, 'It will stop, and you do know by now that when it does, and the sun shines it's well worth waiting for Captain.'

Returning her smile he said 'Well I godda say that some of the scenery around the cliffs is spectacular. Now tell me Matron, I'm happy enough about Lieutenant Dulles so how is your nursing sister doing, and do you think she will be able to identify her attacker?'

Anna looked quizzically at the American before saying 'She knows exactly the identity of the two men who attacked her. But surely, from what your sergeant told us in the early hours of this morning when he came to take the Lieutenant away under guard, General Strauss had made up his mind that he was the attacker?'

The Captain paused for several moments before he answered Anna 'General Strauss was told by your station commander that it was Spencer Dulles who brought your nurse into the hospital and that in the process had injured himself'

'I can assure General Strauss neither knew nor sanctioned Spencer's arrest. Perhaps you could fill me in on what happened Matron.'

Paul Flynn arrived back at the air base at two in the afternoon. He looked sullen, almost sheepish Anna thought later. He had just left a meeting with the station commander and was now sat in the same chair he had occupied earlier that morning.

Instinctively he looked over her shoulder at the view of the aerodrome through the rain that had increased as the day had progressed, before saying 'Matron, fact is I should not be here in your office, and every lesson I was taught as a lawyer tells me I should put on my hat and coat, get back into my jeep and let my driver take me back to base and a decent cup of coffee.'

Looking now at Anna with a cold and unsmiling face he continued 'At any future Court Marshall hearing Matron I will deny anything about what I am going to tell you, and I can assure you that as a prosecuting attorney for the Department of Justice in my state, I am as good in court as you are in the operating theatre.'

With a deep sigh the American sat back on his chair heavily, his arms crossed over his stomach, his weight tilting the chair back on two legs as he rocked it slowly back and forth while he closed his eyes, saying nothing.

At first Anna was puzzled by his action. He seemed to be asleep as the chair moved to and fro until he exuded another deep sigh fluttered his eye lids and looked coldly at Anna before saying 'Sorry about that, I always think better with my eyes closed. Matron. I have just come from Wing Commander Donaldson's office. The ball game has changed big time since we met this morning'

'In short, my Colonel Strauss has been put under pressure from someone very high up in military headquarters in

London to get Spencer Dulles back to our camp immediately'

'At my meeting with commander Donaldson we agreed that he would be moved out of here by six this evening, despite a plea from your medical officer that he should be left here until tomorrow morning.'

Anna fidgeted with her fountain pen that lay on her desk in front of her, pushing it at one end so that it revolved around like a weather vain. As the pen stopped with the covered nib pointing towards the captain she looked at him hard and said 'It seems to me we are dealing with some very nasty people Captain. Off the record, just how nasty are they?'

The Irish American sighed wearily before replying 'The two officers you mentioned are the most bigoted and unpleasant I have personally ever met. Both are active Ku Klux Klan members and clearly they have a fellow member of the organisation amongst the top generals at supreme headquarters, in London'

'An order from London is as high as you can get in this country and Colonel Strauss has absolutely no option other than to insist the Lieutenant is handed over.'

As he started to set his chair in motion again Anna asked, 'Does your Colonel know that Sister Moore has made an official statement accusing the two white officers of attacking and wounding her?'

With his eyes closed he shook his head and answered her 'Yes he does Matron. Colonel Strauss is from Texas, but he is not a segregationalist and personally likes Spencer. He also knows the power some of these people have, and the fact is he cannot match it'

'As I told you, I was an attorney before the war, a barrister is what you would call me in this country. At a Court Marshall hearing your Sister's case would not last a morning'

'It was pitch black, there is only one witness, a Negro, and she has admitted having sex with the guy. It would be over by mid morning! Colonel Strauss and the two accused officers know this for a fact.'

The anger in Anna had returned and she knew she was out of order when she said: 'But that is grossly unfair, not to say unjust. What on earth sort of system do you people live under, especially when you personally could not help pointing out some of the shamefully unfair pages of this county's history in Ireland.'

'Toucha Matron, toucha, and I don't blame you for drawing parallels but would you mind if I gave you a brief history lesson about my country?'

'Please do Captain.'

'There are still people alive as we speak that remember the American civil war which ended less than sixty years ago in 1885. The Civil War was fought over slavery and the rights of all people, black or white to enjoy democracy and freedom on an equal basis, and six hundred thousand Americans died to win that right. Six hundred thousand Matron'

'The Southern Confederates were bound to lose and did, but they never got over the humiliation of defeat, and still haven't to this day. Out of a music hall character of the period called Jim Crow, who always played to the audience as being subservient to the white people, grew the fawning appeasement of the black people as a simple way of survival for the individual and his family'

'Matron it's an appeasement which last to this day, or rather I should say until the day the Japanese bombed Pearl Harbour and war came to the door step of the United States of America'

'Spencer Dulles is typical of a new movement. These young men and women are educated and committed to bring about the abolition of the race laws. They only have America as a homeland and they will fight for it in Europe and in the Pacific, knowing that the consequences of defeat will kick them back down the ladder for another hundred years'

'The big difference now is that by sending thousands of young black soldiers here and to Europe they have had a taste of living without the colour bar that exist in America'

'You English have accepted black Americans as equals, here to fight a common enemy. Many people now believe that if the black Americans of our country are not given equality after the Germans and Japanese are defeated then a second Civil War in America will be unavoidable'

'When they go home they will not slip back into the old

ways, and the absolute fact is Matron, the minority, and I do stress minority of white people in America are frightened to death by the prospect of black men and women enjoying the same wonderful freedom and prosperity they have'

'There will be desperate struggles and battles ahead in our country but at this moment we have got to defeat the enemy across the channel so that those struggles can happen'

'This is part of Colonel Strauss's problem, and certainly with regards to how we can help Lieutenant Dulles.'

The American looked as tired as Anna felt and despairingly she asked, 'What will happen to him Captain?'

'There is one all black regiment fighting in Sicily at the moment. As soon as he is better I will get him posted to it, my only fear is that he will be got at whilst in hospital or while waiting for the paperwork to go through.'

Angrily Anna said 'And what about the two monsters that almost killed my Sister? Will they be allowed to roam around my country free?'

She saw that the American was at a loss for words as he stared past her. Suddenly, the awful truth of what was going to happen to Spencer Dulles was clear to Anna.

Anna started to speak again, calmly and clinically, 'So Captain Flynn, in your legal jargon, 'to sum up', we have two brutal men who will go completely free; one black man who may, but only may escape being mutilated and murdered by his own countrymen, and we are left with a nursing sister who will be mentally scarred for life. Scarred Captain Flynn because Gail Moore will blame herself for his murder.'

Picking up her fountain pen she tapped the top of her desk with it gently and shook her head slowly from side to side before adding gravely 'Next month will be the fifth Christmas of the war for me and my countrymen and women. The fifth. We are tired Captain Flynn, my nation is so tired and so worn out by it all you cannot even begin to image what it has been like'

'We are tired, and yet,' she stumbled with the words 'And yet, I have to say that to sit opposite you and listen to the way you treat your own men and to have such little regard for my nurse,' she paused, her words lost, lost in memories that flashed through her mind of dead friends, lost love, her feelings suddenly replaced by an overwhelming sense of disappointment.

Anna stood up and faced the American and said 'Captain, for me this is just about the most dispiriting moment of the war, and I am utterly disgusted.'

The irritation and niggling annoyance of the visit of Captain Flynn was still with Anna after the American had left her office and she was glad when the telephone started to ring and she picked up the handset with her customary 'Matron.'

The operator's distant voice said, 'I've a Major Adnans on the line for you Matron, shall I put him through?'

'Thank you, yes.'

The sound of Peter Adnans voice was as welcome as sunshine as she heard him say 'Anna, hello, it's Peter here, Peter Adnans. Anna, are you there?'

She was about to answer when something made her turn around quickly, and as she did she saw a shadow, a familier dark outline against the wall close to her that sent a shiver running through her. Anna reached out and touched the shape that had now faded, before breaking into a broad smile while in her head the voice of John McCloud said, 'No Anna, No, No, No, do not accept it, fight it lass, fight it with any weapon you can!'

Anna knew she would.

RAF Portlan, 5th December 1943

Overnight the South Westerly wind that had brought Cornwall driving rain and grey skies for the past week shifted to the South East and a high-pressure ridge had formed to give an almost cloudless blue sky and the first heavy frost of the winter.

Anna looked out of the small office window towards the three runways and the half moon shaped Blister hangers that housed the Dakota's and other aircraft that used the aerodrome, before putting her back towards the window and sitting at her desk.

Her telephone rang loudly the duty switch board operator saying, 'There is a Captain Flynn to see you Matron, can you see him?'

'Yes, send him in please.'

Anna answered the knock on her office door with a soft 'Come in' and rose from her chair behind her desk as the nursing orderly opened it and announced, 'Captain Flynn for you Matron.'

Standing she said, 'Good morning Captain, I see we've managed to organise the sunshine you wanted so badly!'

Sitting down in front of her he replied, 'Yes Matron and it would seem that you organised the sun and a whole lot more, if I may say so!'

With a serious face she said 'Really? I can't imagine what you mean Captain.'

The American officer continued, 'Well I don't suppose I will ever get to the truth of what went on Matron, and having so much Irish blood running through my veins I don't suppose that I will ever figure out the ways of the English and how you people make things work, but from the bottom of my heart I want to thank you for what you did for Spencer Dulles'

'And before you start to deny you did anything, I can just tell you that I personally put Captain Garvey and Captain Roberts into a staff car that took them both to an airfield near Birmingham and they are flying back to the US as we speak'

'After that I went to the American base hospital in Falmouth and had a long chat to Spencer. As soon as he is fit he will fly from a base around here to North Africa, and then onto Sicily, where he will join a regiment of the 92nd Buffalo Division'

'The choice was his Matron. He could have gone back to America, but choose the option of Italy, and I can't say as I blame the guy, either!'

Anna had been studying the Americans face and listening to his accent while he gave her his version of the events of last night. The Irish lilt had become even more pronounced as he become animated in the story, and his eyes seemed just a shade or two greener then yesterday.

'Captain, I am so pleased.' In a more relaxed tone she added 'Some time ago now a dear friend of mine told me that out of the madness of war comes moments of true humanity. I'm really pleased that we were both able to witness one of those moments.'

'Matron, how is Sister Moore? Only it was the last thing that Spence asked me.'

Smiling she answered 'She is much better, and I've ordered her to take a weeks leave with her parents in Wales. At the same time, I also suggested that she goes to your hospital in Falmouth to visit Spencer before she catches the train at Truro.'

'That's a swell idea Matron, and thanks.'

Standing up in front of her he offered his hand saying 'Thank you again. As I said I won't pry too deeply into how you did what you did, but we know it was a senior British war cabinet minister called Lord Roxenton who put the fear of Christ into our generals, have you met the guy?'

In total honesty Anna was able to say, 'I've heard lots about the gentleman, but have never met him!'

CHAPTER SIX 1944

A Silent Fear

******

Return to France

A Silent Fear

Headquarters London, 14th January 1944

The screeching and scrapping of over two hundred chairs being pushed and pulled across polished wood parquet flooring was deafening as the senior nurses and medical officers stood to attention and Matron-in-Chief Mary Atkins entered the hall, walking down the centre of the room between the rows of seats and standing people.

Acting as both gymnasium and lecture hall Mary Atkins stood on the raised stage where she opened the first page of her notes that were laid out on a lectern in front of her. She broke the sudden silence by saying 'Good morning ladies and gentlemen, at ease, and please be seated.'

The veteran nurse paused while the men and women sat down, and she used the moment to look quickly around the hall, scanning the rows of faces as she went, recognising many.

She had a smile on her face when she started to speak, almost shouting, '1944'and then pausing until she said, 'I know it's been a long, long wait, but ladies and gentlemen at last, this is the year,1944, when we will finally go back to France!'

A murmur of voices with a ripple of excited hand claps echoed through the hall and only stopped when the Colonel continued: 'By which route or direction we will learn later, but our time has come again'

Placing both hands firmly on the lectern she leaned forward towards her audience 'Almost four years ago, in May 1940, along with some of you in the hall this morning, we were forced to retreat through France and Belgium with the German army and air force in full flight after us'

'For all of the British, French and Belgian forces in those dark and grim days of defeat it will be remembered as shameful and humiliating'

'For me I will always remember them as days when our casualty clearing stations, and the doctors, nurses and orderlies that manned them, responded with dedication, professionalism and extraordinary bravery'

'But please make no mistake, it was not by chance or luck that the stations responded so well, and we were able to treat the wounded of all countries involved. It was because of the hours and hours, weeks and weeks of hard, dedicated training and exercises that were put in before the battles started'

Mary Atkins stopped for a moment her eyes resting on Anna Jack briefly before looking back at her audience and saying, 'Ladies and gentlemen, a true testament to the devotion to duty and to the bravery of all those involved is the sad and brutal fact that buried in France and Belgium are seven doctors, nurses and orderlies, from my unit who gave their young lives in the cause of their profession, and the war they were fighting'

'All of you are busy at this time in some sort of military exercise for what will happen this year. At times, I know it is, and will be both tedious and tiring, but just remember this. When the Allies open up the second front and France is invaded, each of you will hold the lives of the wounded in your dedicated hands as they start to arrive at our casualty stations in their hundreds'

'Be prepared, be ready, none of us know when exactly we will be called to action, it could be next week, it could be October, but from this moment on I would ask each of you to think that it could be tomorrow, and be ready!'

Zennor, 18th January 1944

Following Mabena up the stairs and into her small sitting room at the back of the Tinners Arms Anna handed the landlady her cap and heavy greatcoat without thought or question, the automatic action of friends meeting in familiar surroundings, before sitting in a well used winged arm chair in front of a smouldering peat fire, where herbs hung from hooks and in pots on the hearth, sharing the fire's heat as they dried.

'Tis lovely to see ee Anna, a real surprise lik. Ee hav just mussed Terry, ees gan ta St Ives ta tha bank, an run a few errins'

'Now than maid fore I gets ee a dish ov tay let's look at ee'

The Cornish woman scrutinised Anna's cold face, still damp from the rain outside before saying 'Well now, ee looks ah damn site bettur than ee dud a month back maid, propur fitty lik. I said ta Terry I waas propur worried bout ee bayfor Chrestmas, now yum happier' narrowing her eyes as she looked at the nursing officer she added, 'Naw what's cause ov thaat than. How cums ee is suddenly appy lik?'

Laughing Anna replied, 'Mabena, you should be in the secret service running after spies and fifth columnists, they would not stand a chance!'

'You are right, I feel better for all sorts of reasons. Mainly it's knowing that this year we will start to really hit back at Hitler, and finally get this blasted war over and that makes the training and day to day routine more bearable, and it also makes my daily battles with the men in high positions much easier to take in my stride'

'But enough about me O Cornish wise one, how are you and your family, and how is Terry coping with the quietness of January in the pub?'

From the kitchen Anna heard her friend shout 'Bay naw good changin tha subject lik an thinkin I don't know summats up maid! But Lowina is fine an us hav heard frum tha boays an them is safe an well, which is a rite blessin.'

Handing Anna a cup and saucer of tea Mabena sat opposite her before saying 'But Anna, us av bin hellish busy lik, sance Chrestmas. Them Yanks av bin comin un droves an spendin lik ell. Nevur sin Terry so bleedy appy un January fore'

'That Yank officur yew naw an told im bout us as bin eer a lot lik weth other folk from tha saam camp. Propur gent. Sounden more Irish than Irish. Ee waas real surprised whan I told em ee'd bin eer fore un a previous life. An twas true Anna. I dos reckon he was eer, maybay through is grandfathur praps un tha boats or summin.'

Thinking for a moment Anna then said 'Have you had any of the black soldiers in? I only ask because I've heard there has been a bit of trouble around.'

Nodding and sighing at the same time she answered 'Yah, geet strappin boays an as good as gold. Real hansum sum ov em is. Us 'av ad no problems eer, or un St Ives, but tis bin bad un sum pubs close ta Truro an Falmouth'

'Problem is tween them own white boay's an them own black ones. Tis so bad un sum places lik Penryn that each lot as their own nights un tha pubs round tha town, so tis tha white Yank boay's wan nite an tha black Yank boay's un nex''

'Anna, course there is good an bad un both lots, but tis such a terrible shame ta sha tha nastiness. An tha fact is when ee talks to em separately tham all as nice as pie an so helpful an polite tis a treat'

'But I tell ee they do av wan thing un common, they is all scared as ell. Scared bout being killed, scared bout bein badly wounded when tha fightin starts'

'They is so young, an most of 'em is lonely. They'm way frum they's omes an families, an they can't cope weth tha bleedy rain all time, it gets em down propur'

'But tha main thin is thaat they is scared stiff bout what they is goin ta hav ta go through, tis such a shame Anna'

'An they is sow generous. Little Tommy Molland run past las wake holdin tha first orange tha lad ad ever ad. There's no age un im, just on siz but he didn't naw what twas, ee thought twas an orange rubbur ball!'

'All tha kids lov um, cause them is so lively an friendly lik, an we av sort ov furgot how ta be appy, an tha shortage ov food an new cloths I reckon as made us a bit dowdy an shabby so tha Yanks as put back a bit ov fun un people's lives'

'But I dud ere Simon's mothur, Mussus Tremayne dud ave

sum truble Anna.'

Looking surprised Anna replied 'What! How on earth did she manage to have trouble with black soldiers, quickly, tell me.'

'Hur writ ta tha American officer un charge ov tha camp close ta Truro inviting sum soldiers ta tay but asken him not ta send any Jewish boay's, but tha commandur wes Jewish esself, so ee sends along zix of the beggest black boay's un tha camp!'

Putting both hands to her face Anna laughed through closed fingers until she was forced to use them to wipe away the tears running down her face before saying 'Oh my goodness, what a sad war that poor woman is having.'

Nodding in agreement Mabena continued 'Course, our own boay's stirs thengs up a bit cause them can't stand any ov 'em, darkies or white uns!'

'I eard jus laast weak woss them gats payed, an tha Yanks gats fi-ve times moor then our boays, fi-ve times moor Anna, an them gats ovv weth our maids easy lik!
Well tis no wondur there's trouble.'

Shaking her head Anna said 'This is *de ja vu* Mabena. I remember that back in early 1940 I was told that the French troops were openly hostile and nasty to our boys because they were being paid a pittance compared to ours, and that they fiercely objected to being humiliated by the British running off with their women!'

Looking around the tiny room to make sure there were no witnesses Mabena added 'Don't nos anythin bout daiseyvous but baytween yew an me lik, aftur this is all ovur an our men folk cum ome there bay goin ta bay sum bleedy ructions, I can tel ee'

'Cornwall as bin turned un is ead Anna since tha Yanks arrived. Twill nevur bay tha same agan, an that's tha truth ov it, an mind you when they is gone I will miss they dough-nuts covered in sugur. but a lot ov tha women folk round will miss a lot more than dough-nuts, I tell 'ee!'

RAF Portlan, 29*th* February 1944

'You look well enough Gail, so what is this huge problem we have to talk about?'
Sister Moore looked at her Matron and good friend quickly before plunging her face into her hands and starting to cry.

Anna Jack got up from her desk and went around to her before saying 'Gail, what is the matter, please tell me.'

With both elbows on her knees Gail's chin rested on the bridge her hands formed, her mournful look made complete as more tears welled up in her eyes and started to slip down her face as she said, 'I'm pregnant Anna, three months pregnant to be precise. I'm surprised nobody has noticed, my tits are like barrage balloons, I look like a whale in the bath, I feel sick after a fag or a drink and even a bit of toast comes right back up.'

Pulling a chair close, so that she could sit beside Gail, Anna picked up her hands in both of hers before saying, 'But Gail, that is truly wonderful, wonderful news, why are you crying for goodness sake, you silly thing!'

Gail took a breath before replying, 'I only wish I could tell you Anna. Fact is I'm pleased! Never in a hundred bloody years thought that I would be, but yes I am actually happy inside'

'Happier than I have ever been in my whole life to be perfectly honest, but I can not stop the bloody water works for love nor money, daft isn't it'

Looking at her friend and boss squarely in the face, she continued: 'The baby will be black, or rather a bit of both which will annoy the hell out of some people, but to hell with them, I couldn't give a damn about what other people think'

Squeezing both of her friend's hands before smiling for the first time since she had entered the office Gail added 'And Anna, I honestly can't wait to see him, or her of course, I really can't wait!'

Anna noticed an instant change come over the extrovert woman as she stopped crying and said with vigour 'I have every intention of keeping the baby Anna. I know a lot of pressure will be put on me to have it adopted, in fact I know a girl from the village next to ours who has just had a child and was persuaded, or more like forced, to give it up immediately it was born. But I can assure you, as I sit here, I will not'

'I will not let this sweet little brat down, I want this baby but the truth is I feel that the only person I will have let down is you Anna. This is such an important time but I don't feel I will be able carry on much longer without being found out, and I know that would put you under pressure, so I will make it official this week.'

Patting the back of her hand Anna said 'Gail, you are a dopey thing at times. Dopey, but wonderful at the same time. You are such a natural nurse, which is why you are so good at it, and you are right, I will miss your input desperately, but I can assure you my good friend, that you can bow out with head held very high indeed as far as I am concerned'

'You have helped train dozens of nurses over the past months, and they will look back and thank you for the disciplines you taught them'

'Now you have another duty, Sister Moore, not to me or to the team here, but to that little thing growing like mad inside you. I am so happy for you Gail, give me a hug for pity sake!'

Finishing the gentle embrace Anna went to a dark green steel locker in the corner of her office and opened one of the double doors before pouring two glasses of sherry from the bottle that stood beside a half bottle of whisky and two bottles of Guinness.

Handing Gail a glass Anna went back to her own chair and sat down before raising her hand and saying 'Cheers Gail and congratulations to you, to your baby and to the baby's father, who I presume is Spencer?'

Smiling again the new mother to be put down the cigarette she had lit, raised her glass and clicked it against Anna's saying, 'Of course the daddy is Spence, I'll have you know I've been a very good girl recently!'

Looking down at her middle and patting her slight bulge she smiled as she added 'Clearly, not that good I suppose! But Anna, I just want you to know that I think you've been a true friend throughout this beastly war and at times I know I've been a selfish cow to you, so thank you for your support, especially when I was attacked'

'I don't know how I would have coped without you to be honest, and if Spence had been forced to go back to his camp and those mean monsters, well, I think I would have died.'

The Matron lifted her glass again 'Come on Gail, let's just drink to the future. With so much death surrounding us, you at least will provide some new life for us all to look forward to. And tell me, what does the father think of it all?'

'At first I wasn't sure about what I should do, even whether to tell Spence or not. But I have written to him today and told him that he is going to be a father and asked him at the same time if he would marry me'

'You see Anna, it is the 29th of February today, a leap year, so I am perfectly entitled to ask any man I want, so there we are!'

Anna fell silent for several moments before she drained her glass and took Gail's before filling each up again.

She looked at the calendar on the wall before saying 'You're right. The 29th of February, another leap year, bloody hell, where have the years gone'

'Gail, four years ago today, the 29th February, 1940, I was sat in an *estaminet* in France, a small café come bar, with a table of nursing sisters drinking the local wine when one of them looked straight at me and asked if I was going to propose to "someone in particular" that day. She took me completely off guard, I went crimson with embarrassment and sprayed her with red wine as I choked!'

Gail smiled with her friend as she said, 'Well Anna, and did you pop the question to "someone in particular" as you were asked?'

Looking sadly at her friend she wrinkled her nose and answered 'No Gail, no I didn't. And the fact is I should have done'

'So, after four long years of war, death and misery, we have another leap year. My God Gail no one ever thought it would go on this long, certainly not me. Another toast. To you, your new baby and the peace we all hope is around the corner.'

'I'll drink to that Matron Jack, but seriously, do you think it will be over this year Anna?'

Anna looked at the calendar again rather than at Gail before saying 'According to an American I spoke to recently he told me that 'those on high' expect that fighting our way across Europe will be a long and bitter campaign that will go into next year, unless Hitler sees the writing on the wall, and surrenders, or his people force him to do so.'

Waiting until she caught her friend's eyes Gail said 'Let's hope 'those on high' are wrong Anna, cheers!'

Zennor, 20th April 1944

'Las time ee wes err twas end ov February maid. Twas maze than, now tis propur maze!' Mabena and Anna had walked from the Tinners Arms, past St Senara's Church and had stopped to watch a herd of Guernsey cows graze quietly in the early spring sunshine.

Before Anna could make any comment Mabena continued 'Us il gaat as close ta Zennor Head as us can, but as I told 'ee frum tha 1st ov April all tha coastline round Cornwall as bin made unta what they calls 'Protected Zones' an ee hav gat tu hav a special Pass tu get unta em'

'Us hav got bleedy hundreds ov police, troops an thum detectives everywhur. Tis they detectives I think is creepy, an I dant lik em. Th'em not frum Cornwall an they is un tha pub all tha time, snoopin round an asking bout any strangers an tha lik'

'Fred Foot says ee an Joe Trevissick wes bleedy shot at, well, over them eads lik, when them got lost near tha coast close ta Falmouth only las wek. Bleedy red caps, they military police wes what shot at em fore them wes questioned lik. Mind yew tis a pity theys want bettur shots as them be both rascals, an wes no doubt up ta now good!

'Come on then' Anna said grabbing Mabena's arm 'Let's see how far we can get without being shot at!'

As they rounded the first bend in the lane that led to the sea Anna's face broke into a broad grin before she shouted 'Look Mabena, its Star coming to greet us!'

Racing towards them the golden retriever that belonged to

the dairy farm was barking furiously while he closed the distance to the two women. Panting and jumping up at Anna, Star greeted her as the old and trusted friend she was.

'Before I'm told off Star I will use your real Cornish name, so how are you Sterenn? I must say you look very fit and healthy, now come on and join us for a walk to the coast'

Stopping to look at a patch of violet colour in the hedge row Anna asked, 'What flower is that Mabena?'

'Them's Periwinkles. Eaten togethur bey lovurs twill cause a bump un err belly sure nuff! Them's pretty, a rite favourite ov mine'

Seeing Anna bend down she added 'An fore yew ask thems Cow Parsley, us used ta make pea-shooters out ov tha thick holla stems wen I wes a young'n'

As the trio started to head towards the sea again Mabena said 'Tis such a bootiful time ov yer Anna. Tha hedges up eer fore them gives way tu tha granite walls is so full ov colur. Red Campions, Dog Violets, Cow Thistle, Ladies Smock, jus bootiful I'm plaised ee could get ovur ta see us maid'

Mabena turned her head towards her friend saying in a serious tone 'Is ee gwain way agan, or can'ee say ort?'

With Anna's arm already looped around hers she simply squeezed the landlady's tighter and kept her head looking towards the sea in the distance and stayed silent.

'Wen ee squish me arm lik that un tha past tis as good as a 'Yes', far as I knaw'

'Anna, tis clear summat big is bout ta appen. Tha boays, soldiers an tha lik, is scared stiff Anna, tis plain on them's faces, an sad as ell'

'Tis why them gets drunk when evur them can, an goes a bit daft an crazy lik, an who can blame tha poor devils'

'Terry, ee gaats mad we'em un tha pub but I told um ta think a bit an only hope that our boays hav someone them can chat to, wareever them is, even if them is a bit drunk!'

'Tha Vickur up at St Senara's Church saays he gets our boay's, Yanks, Frenchies, an folk frum every place them Nazis hav takun, gwain unta is church for a bit ov comfurt lik. Ee told me that tis as iv them wants ta bey at peace weth themselves fore gwain unta battle'

'Tis lik tha atmosphere round us is buildin up fur an enormous thunder storm. There be a real fear bout Anna'

'No beggur saays anythin but tha pain that them boay's is feelin is un them eyes, an as a mothur it hurts ma ta see it'

'A couple of me cousins that lives near Falmouth hav told me that durin tha darkness soldiers an police keeps em all undoors, bey force iv them as tow, while lorries an tanks is rumbling long all night long'

'Cornwall is lik won bleedy big army camp Anna.'

They walked on in silence with Anna occasionally shielding her eyes from the sun as she followed the comic antics of pairs of birds as they swooped low above the hedges and fields collecting material for their nests, and seeming to argue and fight for the right to a strand of cow hair or tiny ball of wool from a sheep's fleece caught on gorse.

Another reason for Anna's silence was that she knew that the next bend was one of her favourites, and without thinking she quickened their pace to reach it.

As they rounded the corner so the whole of Anna's head was filled by the rich blue colour of the sea as it seemed to leap up to greet her.

The hedges had given way to low granite walls, and the two women sat either side of the stone style that marked the boundary between the cultivated farm land and the rough ledge of moorland that ran down to the edge of the high rugged cliffs. The coastguard station was fifty feet away; with its ring of sand bags a reminder of the war.

For a minute or so they sat on the stone until Mabena said 'Let ma see who bey un duty, an iv us can get ta Zennor Head'

Following a wave from Mabena, Anna and Sterenn got up and headed towards the headland. 'Twas Jim Rogers on duty, an he bey a regular at tha pub, says us hav at least an hour, so cum on!'

Sat on the rocks around Zennor Head both women shared the view of the coastline as it stretched out in front of them towards Cape Cornwall and Land's End. In places the cliff tops rose three hundred feet from the sea. For millions of years the constant pounding and grinding waves had created a confusion of tiny inlets next to broader bays with each one separated by pillars of jagged vertical rock formations.

'What a beautiful, beautiful afternoon Mabena. This is Cornwall at its best, and I do love it so'

'One of the things I will never get over is how the sun affects the colours of the water. Look down there Mabena, just past Horseback Zawn, the colour of the water turns from dark blue to light blue, and then a bright, bright emerald green! It's beautiful!'

Looking past Horseback Zawn towards Carneloe Long Rock she added 'And of course, I also remember Cornwall at it's cruellest and most dangerous when I look across the bay and the remains of the merchant ship broken and stranded on the rocks under the cliffs. My God, that was so awful.'

'Anna, tis important ta remembur tha good ov summat, as them keeps ee goin lik. So when ees away an tha war gets ee down keep tha blues an tha sparkling greens ov tha sha un ees ead, an breath slowly so that tha smell of tha tors mingles weth tha fresh smell ov tha flowers ee past bey today'

Mabena studied the side of Anna's face for a moment as she sat quietly facing west until she said 'Yum a funny maid Anna. I keeps forgettin how young ee is. Twenty eight means ee is only tew yers older than Mathew, me eldest. You av seen tow much for a youngen, an tis a shame really'

'Anna, if ee looks back t'wards village, Simon's house is looking back at ee? Hav ee heard frum im?'

Anna kept her head facing the sea and cliffs ahead. The fingers of her left hand scratched circles through the green moss that covered the rock she was sat on. She breathed deeply and turned slowly towards the Cornish woman.

She was about to speak when a series of loud and violent explosions ripped through the air and bounced off the sheer cliff faces opposite in deafening echoes, causing thousands of nesting seagulls to add their squawking cries to the continuing sounds of explosions and machine gun fire.

'The war is back Mabena, our peace destroyed for the moment, and look at poor Sterenn, he's already over the granite style! We had better head back in case we get caught up in the army exercise which is heading our way by the sound of it'

Smiling she added 'From the experience of this twenty seven year old, not twenty eight, thank you, I can only hear Bren Guns firing and the minute I hear an MG42 open up is the time when you and I will start running, but just in case, let's get moving!'

Return to France

Southampton Transit Camp, 29th May, 1944

The senior nursing sisters, surgeons and anaesthetist crammed into the large tent and stood to attention as the recently promoted Lieutenant Colonel Peter Adnans entered and took his place behind a wood trestle table together with his adjutant, Captain Mallory.

'Please stand easy and be seated' he said to the thirty three men and women in front of him. Moving in front of the table he looked around the large tent unsmiling and seriously before saying 'Ladies and Gentlemen the months and months of training, hard work and planning that we have all been part of are over'

'Within the next few days we will form part of the largest invasion force ever gathered together to start the liberation France and the whole of occupied Europe.'

The surgeon waited for the buzz of murmured excitement that rippled around the tent to stop before looking at his watch 'The time is now 07.30 hours. At a briefing, a short while ago I was informed that at five o'clock this morning the camp commander opened top secret orders. These orders confirmed both the time and place where the Allied invasion forces will land'

'Secrecy and security about the planned landing points is of vital importance to the operation ahead of us which has been given the code name "Overlord". The camp commander has told me that as from this moment, the whole camp, along the many hundreds more around the country, will be sealed off from the outside world and no movement, in or out of it will be allowed without a signed authority from me, which will be countersigned by my adjutant Captain Mallory'

'At the same time, no outward or inward telephone calls will be permitted under any circumstances whatsoever to anyone, except in the line of official duty, and only then in the presence of a senior officer'

'Now just so we are left in no doubt about the seriousness of the security clampdown, when you leave here you will see that coils of barbed wire now encircle us and that armed guards have been placed outside the camp perimeter and they will start patrolling twenty four hours a day to prevent personnel, that is officers as well as NCO's and other ranks from coming in or going out without authority. These guards have direct orders to shoot anyone who is seen to openly disobey those orders'

Peter Adnans paused as he again looked around the tent at the young faces in front of him. He kept his grim facial expression intact as he continued 'I have been told categorically that if any of us, no matter what his or her rank, is found breaking the high level of security in place, the individual will be arrested immediately and handed over to the military police and court marshalled at a later date. In short ladies and gentlemen, we must take these orders very seriously indeed.'

After a brief exchange of words with his adjutant, the awkward looking surgeon, who had been appointed head of two casualty clearing stations, moved to an easel that supported an oblong board, six feet long by four feet and covered by two grey blankets.

Releasing the blankets, he stepped to the side and for the first time the medical personal saw a large coloured map showing the landing points for the invasion of France through the beaches and towns of Normandy.

With a pointer, the commanding officer tapped the map, saying 'The initial D-Day landings will take place on the beaches of Normandy that stretch from St Vaast-la-Hougue here, to Ouistreham, here'

'Two invasions forces will take part. The Western Task Force and the Eastern Task Force. The beaches the Western Task Force will land on have been given the code names Utah and Omaha, and the troops attacking the German defences at these points will be mainly American'

'The Eastern force will attack the beaches code named Gold, Juno and Sword. The forces given the task of breaking through the defending positions on these beaches will be British, Canadian and a mixture of Dominion, Free French and Polish.'

Moving in front of the detailed map he pointed his stick and let it rest on one spot before turning to face the men and women in front of him.

Smiling now, Anna recognised the boyish way that still lingered beneath the forced seriousness of the army exterior as he said 'Juno Beach. This is where each one of us in this tent will take our first step on French soil after so many years away'

'Our two casualty clearing stations will be part of the much larger Royal Canadian Army Medical Corps contingent and we will all of us follow in the wake of the Canadian 3rd infantry division as it storms ashore onto the Normandy beaches on D-Day and the days that follow. Once we are all in France we will stay with the division until we reach the city of Caen'

'I will be on the second wave of landing craft in our group that carries troops together with three male orderlies. A further six doctors and twenty orderlies from our unit will follow in successive boats and establish basic facilities at the beach head as it is established. The same pattern will be followed by the Canadian medical units across the whole of the attack front which spans a half mile across'

'During the first hour of our initial attack the Canadians will put ashore over two thousand five hundred men and seventy tanks and other vehicles. The Germans are expected to put up a fierce and determined defence, but we have one crucial advantage, and that is surprise!'

'We know for sure that the German's believe that the invasion from this country will start from the Dover area, being the shortest distance between us and the mainland, and that most of their armoured and infantry reserves are stationed there, some two hundred miles from the actual landings'

'We have played along with this belief and have gone as far as to stage an elaborate and massive plan of deception in that area that has included the positioning hundreds of dummy tanks, aircraft, ships and guns and a colossal surge in radio message traffic designed to cement in the German's mind that the Pas de Calias is to be our destination'

'Over one hundred and thirty thousand Allied troops will land on the Normandy beaches during the first hours of the assault, and equal numbers will land over the days that follow'

'The complete CCC's, and all of you will be brought over on D-Day + 4 when we hope to be able to start to function as we have planned and prepared for'

Peter Adnans put down his pointer and took a sip from a glass of water before looking up smiling broadly and continuing 'Personally, I would have favoured landing along the Loire Valley so we could have stocked up with wine, but as it stands Calvados is the main bottled harvest of Normandy so at least we have something to look forward too!'

Taking a serious stance again he faced his audience before saying 'Now, one last thing. I'm sure you will all remember the basic rules of deer stalking?'

'Yes! That's right. Keep silent, keep down wind, keep your head down, keep your eyes open, pray for good weather and finally a huge measure of good luck!'

Anna put a hand to her face to hide the smile from her neighbours as she thought 'Deer stalking indeed! Yes Peter, you sweet man, all of us are so very familiar with the rules!'

Southampton Transit Camp, 6th June 1944

'So here we go again Anna, another day you will never forget, like the morning of the 10th of May 1940 in Saint-Remy-du-Nord when Belgium was invaded!'

Mary Atkins and Anna looked up at the sky from outside their tents as wave after wave of bomber aircraft flew over them in the direction of the English Channel. The ground they stood on trembled as the engine noise from over a thousand aircraft thundered above them.

The senior officer had arrived at the transit camp the night before, holding talks with the members of the medical units that had not left three days before to go aboard troop ships and landing craft, before crossing the channel with the invasion force to the Normandy beaches.

'D-Day Anna. D-Day and at long last a return to France! Come on, these Canadians love their coffee, lets see if we can grab a cup in the mess.'

The two medical women walked through the rows of hundreds of carefully camouflaged tents and vehicles in the early light of dawn towards the smell of freshly baked bread and coffee.

Sat opposite each other at one end of a long wooden table in the officer's mess tent they sipped their coffee before Mary Atkins looked at her watch and said quietly, 'It's 06.00 hours Anna, from now on it's all or nothing, there is no going back. I can tell you that Allied parachute troops started landing several hours ago behind the beaches and into the countryside to secure the bridges, knock-out gun installations and cut off the roads to prevent the Germans from deploying their reserve tanks and men rapidly'

'In the meantime the air forces of all the Allies have been carpet bombing railway lines, roads, ammunition dumps and communication centres, while the French resistance forces have moved into open offensive against individual areas of the rail and road system following a signal that was broadcasts over the BBC wireless last evening'

Anxiously started to wring her hands together before speaking again, she said 'The next ten days are going to be vital ones Anna, and certainly ones that are causing a lot of concern amongst the planners from Eisenhower and Montgomery down'

'They all realise that once the Germans know that Normandy is the main point of our landings they will throw everything into the battle to try and push our boys back into the sea, and don't forget, they have had over four years to prepare for this moment and a million soldiers to call on. The whole operation will be on a knife edge until we can get our troops, and most importantly, our tanks across the channel and onto French soil'

'But first we will have to secure our bridgehead and I fear that Peter Adnans and the medical teams are going to have a rough time as they follow the infantry ashore in about an hour's time. I do so hope that luck is on their side Anna.'

Juno Beach, Normandy, 10th June, 1944 - D-Day +4

Anna muttered quietly 'Christ, I will be so pleased to get off this bloody rocking tub.' With both hands, she pushed up the iron lever that kept the steel waterproof door closed against a rush of sea water. With the lever now swinging loosely she was able to put her shoulder to the heavy metal door and open it outwards onto the top deck of the troop transport ship.

The sight in front of Anna made her pause before going out onto the deck. Rolling in the swell of the sea a vast armada of hundreds of grey or camouflaged ships of different shapes and sizes stretched as far as she could see in front of the beaches and landing points that the invasion force had used during the initial battles four days earlier on D-Day, the sixth of June.

In the early grey daylight, she lead her group of medical carers across the tilting and heaving deck to the disembarkation point she had been shown by a naval load master. She and her team paused before taking a long and careful look at the invasion fleet around them.

The beach that only days ago gave the first toe hold for the D-Day landings lay a mile in front of the troop ship. At the centre of their landing point was the village of Bernieres-sur-Mer, now a tangle of shattered, burning and smouldering buildings with dense smoke bellowed in thick black coils across the promenade and once golden sand in the stiff breeze.

Squeezed onto a narrow band of sea shore Anna saw a solid jumble of military vehicles, tanks, men, wood crates, twisted and blacked metal beach defences, and bomb craters, while wrecked landing craft rose and fell slowly with the incoming waves.

Two similar sized troop ships were positioned next to theirs and the nursing team watched as a steady steam of troops clambered down the sides of both of them on wide rope nets before jumping into landing craft and being ferried to the shore.

Matron Jack looked over the side of the vessel and into the

sea that seemed to thrust itself towards her up the side of the ship in a powerful waveless surge, before stopping half way up the side of the hull and falling backwards.

From the top of the deck where Anna stood to sea level was the height of two houses and as she looked again she saw a flotilla of landing craft slowly edge their way close to the side of their ship. Above the din she caught the sound of the naval load master on the deck above her shouting into his megaphone.

They had rehearsed this moment only in the confines of a tent. Now the moment had come, the reality frightened her as vivid memories came back of getting onto a destroyer across a narrow gangplank at Dunkirk flashed painfully through her mind.

Passing silently in front of the waiting nurses the Canadian infantry men started to climb over the rails of the troop ship and down the rope ladders that had been unrolled like a collection of vast carpets of open linked rope squares spiralling fifty feet down the side of the ship and ending above the surging water below.

Two sailors stood at the gap in the rail close to the members of the casualty clearing station. At the order from their load master on the megaphone one of them shouted 'Time for your group ma'am, tides gone out a wee bit so it looks like you may get a bit wet when you reach the beach, but at least no machine guns will be firing at you ma'am.'

Anna turned her back to the sea and grasped the first rung of the rope net and started to climb down it, not daring to look any where other than at the rusting plates and rivets of the hull of the ship. She took her time to find each foothold and start her journey.

Halfway down the lattice work of rope squares the ship started to roll and she, together with the other nurses and sisters, found themselves hanging vertically in mid air two yards from the hull of the ship, dangling helplessly above the sea.

As quickly as the vessel rolled one way it went back to its original upright position which caused the climbers to smash back against the steel hull plates with a jolting thud.

Looking down she saw that their landing craft was coming up towards them on the top of a surge in the water. Shouting as loud as she could Anna said, 'Come on girls, lets get off this bloody thing!'

Four sailors stood in the packed landing craft and waiting for the right moment for it to reach the nurses one of them shouted 'Now! Jump, come on. Quickly!'

With blind faith Anna did just that. Her foot caught the top of the landing craft rail and a practiced helping hand from a sailor allowed her to jump into the packed space and slot into between the men and their kit.

She watched three other nurses' jump safely into the boat before it started to go into the trough of the wave and leave the remaining women clinging from the cargo net twenty or more feet above her.

The bosun steered the landing craft with the skill of an aeroplane pilot and throttled the engines to give him space away from the towering hull above until the wave surged back upwards and he nudged his way towards the women until they were all roughly bundled abroad and the flat-bottomed craft began heading towards the beach.

Most of the Canadians around her looked as ill as Anna felt as the square fronted boat punched, bounced and crashed its way forward through the water. The walls of the landing craft where higher than any of the nurses going ashore and her only view was of the sky above, the men in front, and the vertical ramp at the bow of the vessel that reminded her of a castle draw bridge ready to be lowered.

A change in the sound of the engine noise made the tightly packed occupants stiffen with expectancy, with fingers adjusting the straps of the heavy packs they all carried on their backs, and the shouted final orders and instructions from the men in charge.

With a scrapping, grinding sound the metal flat bottomed boat stopped moving forward as the engines were thrust into reverse and the bosun fought to keep it steady in the rolling surf, and outgoing tide.

As Anna watched, the clanging chains of the ramp started to pay out and the imagined draw bridge eased itself down into the water. More shouting started and she watched as the infantry men filed out of the boat and up to their waist in the surf that foamed around them.

The medical team stayed until the last of the soldiers had stepped onto the ramp and then Anna looked around before saying 'Time for a bit of a swim girls, okay then, France here we come!'

****

'Matron Jack, Ladies, Ladies, Ladies. What a wonderful and welcome sight you all are!' Below a yellowing surgical mask and blood splattered apron the face of Peter Adnans was one of exhaustion and fatigue, with his anaesthetist and male nursing orderly sharing the same look.

All three were gathered around two packing cases topped with planks of wood and covered in a blood-stained sheets that formed the operating table of their emergency theatre. The medical venue was situated inside the grenade blackened interior of a former gun emplacement that had been overrun by the Canadians in the first two hours of the landings.

Pieces of the equipment from the machine gun emplacement and scorched items of uniform left by the former German occupiers lay scattered across the floor, and in heaps by the narrow gun slits of the low building with it's uninterrupted view across the beach, and the sea in front of it.

On the operating table Peter Adnans continued to probe into the man's abdomen as the orderly changed a bag of plasma until he shouted, 'Got it!' and they saw the blood covered piece of jagged metal on the end of his tweezers. He looked up and was about to speak, but before he could Anna said 'Sir, would you like Sister James and a nurse to finish off?'

The eyes above the dirty surgical mask connected with the exhausted looking anaesthetist and orderly as he said 'Gentlemen, Florence Nightingale has truly arrived! Please stand down, and thank you both. Matron, we have all lost any sense of time since the landings, in fact none of us has had more than a few of hours sleep in the past four days, so thank you.'

Before she could answer a series of explosions sent vibrations rolling through the solid concrete mass, making the nurses duck and look anxiously outside before their commanding officer said 'Terrible nuisance that. Jerry has his long-range artillery sited a few miles inland and every twenty minutes or so he sends a couple of salvos of shells whistling over and they land rather haphazardly along the beach and out to sea. If I'm not mistaken Matron their gift will be returned within in the next few seconds or so.'

With his sentence hardly finished the guns from one of the cruisers lying off shore verified Peter Adnans prediction as they fired back three shells, and five tons of high explosive hurtled towards the unseen enemy entrenched in the Normandy countryside.

At last Anna was able to look at her boss and speak 'Sir, you all look exhausted. Shall I organise putting up our equipment while you all rest for a couple of hours?'

Nodding he replied 'I think so Matron, capital idea. The chaps waiting will be well enough for a little while and if you could stabilise any new arrivals we will get some sleep, and thank you again.'

Walking outside the squat concrete pill box Anna found their quartermaster had already started to organise the men to locate their vehicles, tents and equipment amongst the vast amounts of supplies that were being brought ashore from the hundreds of transport vessels anchored off shore.

By the time Peter Adnans woke, part of the casualty clearing station had sprung to life in the shadow of the battle scared gun emplacement. Three tents had been erected, two lorries with medical and other equipment had been unloaded, two large Red Cross banners staked into the sand dunes, and the first of their ambulances had arrived.

His exhausted sleep had taken him through six artillery attacks, with the shells landing as close as fifty yards away, a Messerschmitt 109 had crashed landed in the surf after being hit by a barrage of ack ack fire, and the steady bombardment of enemy positions inland continued from the naval ships off shore, the noise lost to his fatigue.

At the end of almost four hours sleep on a stretcher in the gun emplacement he woke up stiff and aching. Leaning onto one elbow his surroundings came into focus, while at the same time a familiar voice said 'Sir, got a mug of tea, some nice hot water and clean clothes ready for you in a tent next door. Oh, an Sir, Matron says to tell you that the second CCS unit has passed through from the beach landing zone and we've had orders to stand easy for the mo Sir.'

Anna called into the tent where her commanding officer had washed and changed into clean clothes 'Sir, it's Matron here, can I come in?'

'Please do, I am clean and presentable at last!'

As she stooped down to get inside the tent, she found him sat behind a folding table writing a letter. Looking up the surgeon said, 'Grab a supply box and make yourself comfortable. Sadly, I've just finished writing two very difficult letters to the parents of Captain Williams and Private Thomas who were killed during the initial landings. I should have found time before, but it simply has not been there'

With a deep sigh he shook his head while saying, 'Private Thomas was a good nursing orderly and was only nineteen Anna. A young teenager, and Nigel Williams was just twenty-nine. I remember him telling me rather proudly when I first met him that he had become a GP in a small Dorset village before enlisting, and he couldn't wait to get back'

'I've said all the right things that are expected, but honestly, I do wonder what help those words will be to the grieving mothers and fathers.'

'Sir, I simply must disagree' Anna replied. 'It's right that you wrote about the men under your command, men you knew and spent time with, and I believe the parents will be lifted by your words and personal thoughtfulness in contacting them.'

'Perhaps' He replied, and after another despondent sigh the surgeon added 'In fact, yes you are right, and thank you. With such a small number of men under my wing I suppose I can count my blessings in some ways that I have had only two fatalities, whereas I heard that the Americans that landed on Omaha beach suffered huge losses, poor devils. So, there will be hundreds of mourning wives, parents and sweethearts across the Atlantic as well as here'

Looking sternly at her he added 'Now Miss Anna Jack, please drop this Sir thing when there is no one around, at the moment I am in need of good friends around me, not army types!'

She gave a final 'Yes Sir!' while at the same time thinking about Patrick Flynn, and wondering if his infantry company had been involved in the landings on Omaha beach, and if he was safe.

'And more seriously Miss Jack, I am desperate for a drink but I've lost my blasted flask Anna. A lovely little silver Georgian one that mummy gave me some years ago, alas gone, along with every other item in my shoulder pouches, buried in the sand somewhere, down there on the beach!'

Anna reached down and picked up her khaki haversack before she pushed up the brass end of the narrow webbed strap and guided each one through the metal buckle, pulling open the flap and reaching in.

With a flourish, she fished out two bottles while at the same time saying 'Your very wish is my command, Sir! I managed to buy a litre of very ordinary van rouge, and was actually given this bottle of Calvados, both of which may help digest the indigestible tinned stew that I know is on it's way to us!'

'Given a bottle of Calvados, how on earth did you manage that?'

Handing the bottles to her commanding officer she then produced two thick dimpled glass tumblers which she placed with a hint of pride on the folding table that separated them before saying, 'And two extra gifts, courtesy of the same charming lady who lives in one of the houses on the outskirts of the village towards the crossroads'

'And how did I get it? As a matter of fact, it was all very strange really. I walked up past the burnt-out houses and hotels on the sea front trying to find out what was around. There are thousands and thousands of troops everywhere Peter, so I felt quite happy and safe, having already gotten used to the occasional shells whistling overhead and landing on the beach'

'I have to admit that despite the terrible damage to the village, and the fact that I was walking through the rubble and remains of people's homes, I felt shamefully pleased to be back in France'

'I started talking to a nurse from the Canadian army at a cross roads when a German sniper opened up and caused absolute mayhem and panic with people scurrying every where. No one was hurt but a soldier told us to take cover for a while until they flushed him out'

'We both took shelter in the door way of a house we thought had been abandoned as most of the windows had been smashed, and part of the roof destroyed, but the next thing that happened was that the door opened gently, and an elderly lady begged us to come in'

'The Canadian nurse was from Quebec so, to the surprise and delight of the lady we had a wonderful conversation in French for twenty minutes until after a great deal of rifle and machine gun fire from our lads, I was told that the sniper had been cleared away'

'On the way out she insisted we take a bottle Calvados each, and she told me where I might find wine, so here we are!'

The surgeon's batman and nursing orderly, Corporal Jarvis, coughed loudly outside the tent before lifting the entrance flap and saying 'Some dinner of sorts here for you both Sir.'

Two steaming oblong aluminium mess tins where brought in, held in the same hand by the long hinged handles of each and placed on the table. 'Managed to get some bread from a local chap as well, Sir.'

Thanking Peter Adnans' batman as he left the tent Anna leaned back on the supply box she was sat on and accepted a glass of the red wine which she raised towards the surgeon, saying 'Cheers, Peter, it's so good to see you. We were all very worried.'

After eating the stew Anna took their glasses outside the tent and rinsed them in cold water before returning and putting a large measure of Calvados into each, handing one glass back to her commanding officer before sitting back on her makeshift seat and saying, 'Were the landings really dreadful Peter, or would you rather not talk about it?'

Looking at the woman he had known for over four years he nodded his head slowly, saying quietly at the same time 'On the contrary Anna, I simply must talk about it to be honest. You mentioned the word 'Dreadful' and oh yes, the landings certainly were'

'In fact, all the things that your John told me about the beastliness of the civil war in Spain went through my head a hundred times Anna from the moment the ramp of the landing craft went down and those brave young, oh so young, Canadians charged out'

'We were in the second wave of landing craft to reach the beach ten minutes after the first. The noise level was extraordinary and quite, quite deafening'

'Honestly, my head still aches, still pounds from the noise and utter pandemonium. The loud throbbing of the engine, the sharp pinging sound as bullets started to ricochet off the metal sides and ramp of our landing craft, a menacing whizzing sound, as more bullets passed just inches above our heads together with the constant banging and crashing as the boat gouged through the water, it was all simply numbing'

'It was the very instant that the ramp went down that the madness really started. I think that the German 88's had got the range of the landing craft of the second wave and the moment the ramp crashed into the surf on the beach two successive high explosive shells exploded no more than twenty feet in front of our boat'

'The explosions simply decimated ten or more men at the front of the craft by the landing ramp. Arms, legs and blood were blown in all directions.'

'To my shame it was Corporal Jarvis who frankly got a grip of the situation Anna. He shouted, screamed actually, at us to get off the boat quickly or we would all be killed, and of course he was absolutely right'

'We leapt into the surf up to our waists and started wading to the beach past lifeless bodies in the water that had turned red from their blood, and past those who had been killed and had become draped quite grotesquely from the metal beach defences the Germans had driven into the sand.'

He drained the last dregs of Calvados from his glass and

poured himself another measure before starting again 'I simply can't get the sight out of my mind Anna. Each time I close my eyes I see the same scene. Men, young men, killed by sweeping machine gun fire or exploding mortar shells as they landed, their bodies floating in the water, lapping the edge of the beach or drifting onto the barbed wire that the concrete beach defences were covered in'

Anna knew that only silence was important, no comment, no helpful words of well meaning, no pat on the back of reassurance, only silence. She also thought back to John McCloud and remembered him saying "Perhaps the guilt never goes away".

It was as though the surgeon was reliving the horrors of the landings on his own and she wasn't present. Then she saw him take a deep breath of air, and blinking his eyes several times he looked at her before saying, 'I'm sorry Anna, truly sorry, but it was so dreadful, so horrid'

She now wanted to say the right thing but found herself unable to and the silence continued until he said 'Jarvis was magnificent Anna. Brave beyond words. We both carried the usual supply of dressings and morphia phials together with ten bags of blood plasma each and we started to treat men as soon as we reached the beachhead'

'Wounds from bullets and shrapnel from the mortars were the principal culprits. I remember one chap whose leg had been taken off just above the knee. He was losing blood rapidly and would have bleed to death in minutes if we hadn't had the plasma with us. I never had to say a word. Jarvis inserted a tube into the boy's arm and held the bag of plasma above his own head while I cut away his trousers, found his artery which I tide off'

'We were giving treatment just below a ridge of sand which provided some cover from the MG42's that were raking the whole beach with continuous arcs of fire that seemed to catch small groups of men who just fell to the ground like puppets whose strings had been cut by scissors'

'All the time I could hear the whiz and crack of bullets passing inches above our heads or the thudding sound as they landed all around us making the sand spurt violently upwards, but Jarvis never flinched, he held the bag of plasma above the soldier and never moved an inch.'

'Looking back, I simply do not know how we were not hit by the machine gun fire or shrapnel as we dodged from one wounded man to the next while all the time more and more men arrived on the beach from the ships out to sea, and inch by bloody inch the Canadians clawed their way forward until the next phase of the landings started, and the noise level became even more unbearable with the arrival of the tanks which started firing on the German positions immediately'

'Following the confusion, muddle and bloody carnage of the first assault as the day progressed the organisation on the landing zones got better and better until gradually we started to inch our way up the beach until the infantry finally overran the Germans and they started to surrender in absolute droves'

'By elevenish the beaches had been cleared of the main defences, with all of the machine guns and heavy guns being knocked out. We still had to contend with incoming artillery and mortar fire, and a rare attack from the Luftwaffe but the general level of noise had reduced, and gradually Anna, out of the chaos around us came a sense of order as the Royal Naval beachmasters took control and we were then able to start work on the scores of wounded from both armies'

'I do have another lasting memory of kneeling over a German chap who had a punctured lung and other wounds. I was busy trying desperately to help the chap when a voice with a very strong and chirpy cockney accent said "Cup of hot sweet tea, Sir? Got a spot of rum in it too, Sir!"

'I turned around and there were two Royal Navy sailors carrying a large metal tea urn across the scene of death and carnage and for the first time in days I laughed out loud, in fact I could not stop laughing at the absurdity and simple pleasure of hearing such wonderfully reassuring words amongst the chaos and death.'

He yawned loudly before saying 'Oh dear Anna, my eyes lids are dropping as I speak, but I would rather enjoy a last small nip of Calvados before I take advantage of our stand down and enjoy a long nap, before we pick up all our equipment, and gingerly move forward through the French countryside tomorrow, and return to the war.'

******

High up in the Bergohf headquarters of Hitler in Germany the Nazi leader stubbornly refused his generals the permission they clamoured for, to release the reserve panzers and to proceed to Normandy. He still believed that the action was a rouse and that the main attack would come from Dover and be aimed at the Pas de Calais.

Hitler and his generals had always been in strong agreement over one issue. They all knew that for any invasion to succeed the Allies would have to capture one of the major ports along the French coast in order to put ashore the thousands of men and the large amounts of equipment and fuel needed to sustain a rapid campaign.

Like the Germans, Winston Churchill and the senior Allied generals also knew that they would need a port larger than Dover to provide the key to winning the battle for Normandy, and of France itself.

In a stroke of outrageous and brilliant ingenuity the British and in particular Winston Churchill decided to have two complete ports constructed in Britain and transport them across the channel in what was one of the most astonishing engineering feats of modern history.

The Mulberry docks were designed and built in sections at different locations around the British Isles, without the builders knowing what it was they had just completed. It took less than a year from the initial designs to completion.

On D-Day + 3 hundreds of sections of the harbour and outer sea defences were towed across the channel and positioned off the beaches of Arromanches and St Laurent.

Over four hundred concrete units were made with the largest of the caissons weighing 6000 tons and standing 60 feet high. When in position these were flooded with sea water and pontoon bridges were attached, which rose and fell with the tide and created roadways and piers where the tanks and lorries could be off loaded from the ships arriving from Britain and direct from America.

By D-Day + 13 the two docks were fully operational and the full might of the invasion force unleashed to enable the unstoppable build-up of the Allied forces of liberation.

On D-Day + 4 the first metal beachhead airstrips were laid down by engineers over fields and sand dunes of several Normandy beaches. Squadrons of fighter aircraft piloted by Allied airmen pounded the German lines of communication from sunrise to sundown.

By contrast to the thousands of aircraft available to the Allies, the Germans had only one hundred and forty serviceable fighters to defend the whole coastline of France, Belgium and Holland.

On D-Day + 7 the first Dakota's started to evacuate severely injured men back to base hospitals around Britain. Those with serious burns and head injuries were considered the priority cases and many were undergoing operations in the theatres of permanent hospitals back across the channel, eight hours after the injuries had been inflicted on the battlefield.

The training that Anna and other senior nurses had been given to recognise the severity of burns cases would now help prioritise the men to be air lifted. Once in the Dakota RAF nursing sisters would continue the care of the men until they reached England.

A special core of nurses sprang into being. These RAF women earned the title of the 'Flying Nightingales' and saw action in all of the battles that raged across Europe until the end of the war.

The Dakota's would leave England full of cans of fuel, boxes of ammunition or firearms for the battle front. Following the rules of the Geneva Convention the aircraft were not allowed to display red cross markings on the wings or fuselage, and were treated as potential kills to enemy fighters.

Once the cargo had been taken off the aircraft beds that were strapped to the interior of the fuselage would be lowered and twenty-four lying patients and four sitting could be airlifted to hospitals.

By the end of November 1944, over 47,000 wounded had

been flown out of the battle grounds to hospitals all over the United Kingdom.

870,000 soldiers together with tanks and transport were landed in Normandy by the end of June, and the bridgehead had been firmly established. Despite ferocious counterattacks by the Germans the brilliance of the Allied planning and might of industrial America doomed every effort that the Nazi leadership made to push the invasion force back into the sea. Every tank, every soldier or aircraft the Allies lost in battle was quickly replaced as the reserves thundered ashore or landed on new air fields established in Normandy.

For the German generals in the field of battle, they knew that every tank or soldier that was committed to any counter attack and was lost, no such reserves now existed. Gradually, and with stubborn resistance, the occupiers were pushed back across the country they had so brutally conquered in the same humiliating way that the British and French armies had retreated in 1940.

Harassed by the complete dominance in the sky by the Allies, and by battle hardened troops, the beleaguered German army staggered back across the Riene and into Germany.

It was the beginning of the end, but the end was still a year away. Peter Adnans and Anna would follow the liberating army through France, back into Belgium and finally into Germany itself.

CHAPTER SEVEN 1945

White Rose of Munich

******

Return to Cornwall

White Rose of Munich

General Dietrich von Choltitz had received his chilling orders directly from Hitler: "Defend Paris brick by brick, stone by stone". The German general in charge of the city had over 20,000 garrison troops and SS units based in the capital, which since the invasion in Normandy had seen wide spread disruption and anarchy as the railway workers went on strike, followed by other commercial sectors and the police force.

On the 19th of August, sporadic fighting broke out throughout the city with open and vicious battles being fought between the German army of occupation and resistance members and the city police.

The Swedish consul, Raoul Nordling intervened and brokered a truce to stop the bloodshed. Imploring the general to realise that future history books would lay the blame for the destruction of the city on his shoulders, he persuaded von Choltitz that as a European and a Christian he should disobey Hitler's orders and spare the city.

On the 24th of August 1944, French and American forces entered Paris and the city finally regained its freedom the next day. Despite von Choltitz signing a surrender order, the battle for the capital cost the lives of over two thousand French soldiers and civilians, two hundred Americans, and three thousand Germans, but the fabric of the city remained intact.

******

Paris, 30*th* May 1945

Ignoring the cat calls and whistles of the soldiers Anna edged past the seats she remembered and headed for the group of tables under the cover of the glass and metal awning of the Café Marque, where most of the regular customers were hidden by the open pages of *'La Monde'* or *'La Figaro'* and the aroma of freshly ground coffee wafted to her on the light morning airs.

'Perfect!' she thought as she pulled the heavy wrought iron seat and green cushion under her and sat at the empty table, before ordering a coffee from the waiter who had appeared, the top of his knee length white apron and white shirt covered by a black waistcoat, and bow tie.

Smiling at the serious looking man as he placed her coffee on the table top in front of her, she apologetically asked, 'Monsieur, I am so sorry, but do you think I could have a Cognac, also?' He looked at her quickly and turned without comment, wearing the same deep furrowed frown.

Returning to her table minutes later the waiter leaned down towards Anna with a glass of Cognac on a tray. This time he held eye contact with her, the furrows remained but a smile flicked across his face as he said 'Mademoiselle, please forgive me, the past years have taught me not to look above the collar of any uniform. The Cognac is the best that we have left in our cellar!'

Sprinkling a small spoonful of sugar into the cup of coffee Anna drank a little before returning it to the saucer and then raising the small bulbous glass of Cognac to her nose and breathing in the fragrance trapped inside, which for the moment was all she wanted.

Finally taking a gentle sip she sat back and looked across the pavement café to the tables now occupied mostly by American soldiers, where she had sat at with John McCloud, Peter Adnans and the band of young nursing sisters, over four years ago, drinking champagne in the chill of a late January afternoon.

'It's not only the season that has changed since my last visit' Anna thought. 'Then the horse chestnut trees were leafless, today they are thick with green leaves, but the war has been here, I can feel the shadow that still hangs around like a bad smell'

Looking down the avenue she saw that four of the metal cages that protected the base of the trees had been crushed or torn apart, and the trees had been snapped off at different heights, leaving only jagged stumps in the pavement.

Two of the tall narrow buildings in the terrace had the blackened fronts of fire damage, and deep pits in the plaster and stonework of their façades. Pits that hid buried bullet heads from rifle and machine gun.

Remembering the devastation of London, Caen and the dozens of small French towns and villages the casualty clearing station had travelled through since the return to Europe, she raised her glass and pointing to the buildings opposite she said softly 'I never thought I would raise my glass to a Nazi, but thank you General von Choltitz for disobeying Hitler's orders to destroy Paris!'

As she tilted the glass back fond memories came flying back to her, quickly followed by another sense of pleasure, as through the distorted sides of her raised brandy goblet she saw the twisted and smiling face of Peter Adnans and heard him say, 'Good morning Anna, may I join you?'

She excitedly embraced her friend before they sat opposite each other and looking at her glass she said 'Shall I order you the same?

Nodding he replied 'Absolutely, please. I am in great need of'

Looking across at the swelling number of soldiers, and a sudden number of young women, he said 'Gosh, what a noisy lot. Still they have a lot to be happy and noisy about I suppose, after all, they have survived the war and will be on their way home soon.'

Peter watched Anna as the waiter returned with his coffee and cognac which he placed in front of him, before leaving them together. 'Sorry I'm so late' Peter said, 'I got your message from the hotel reception when I arrived just over an hour ago. Is your room alright Anna?'

'Wonderful Peter, and thank you. I arrived last night and had the most utterly fantastic bath. It was sheer luxury, as was dinner afterwards. Your letter was delivered to me yesterday morning, together with the leave pass and rail warrant'

'I have to tell you that after the past five weeks the timing was perfect. I needed to be returned to civilisation Peter, Buchenwald concentration camp was simply the most horrific thing I have been witness to.'

Unable to look at her he said 'I read your report about the place Anna, that is after Mary Atkins had finished it. It was at her suggestion that I issued the pass.'

Smiling, he added 'But my idea that the rail warrant be issued for Paris instead of London, and booking the rooms for you and me, courtesy of daddy, at the Regina Hotel, which I have to say has not changed in the least since I stayed there with the family in 1937! I just hope I wasn't too presumptuous?'

'Most certainly not Peter, I'm not ready, actually, not able to look my parents in the face yet, so thank you, it was very kind. I have spoken to mum and dad on a very bad telephone line, but after being in the camp I need a bit of time to come to terms with what I've seen and shake off the dirty feeling that clings me.'

After looking around at the people and surroundings she finished by saying 'Does it make any sense if I say that I also don't think I can talk about it here, only because this café has such good memories for me. Does that sound ridiculous?'

Her commanding officer placed his hand over hers and gently squeezed it before saying 'I think it perfectly laudable, and may I suggest having lunch here while remembering some good times before perhaps walking through the Trocadero gardens around the Eiffel Tower and chatting about the unpleasant ones.'

The two colleagues and friends sat on a wooden park bench facing the unique symbol of Paris after walking from the Café Marque in the warmth of the sun. He looked away from the steel structure towards Anna saying, 'We don't have to talk about the past weeks you know, I am honestly quite happy just being here.'

She quickly shook her head before replying, 'No Peter, I want to tell you, in fact I need to tell someone, and I would like that someone to be you'

'When I reported to Mary Atkins at headquarters she explained that we had to quickly provide a medical team to help with the people that had been freed from the concentration camps, and that the horrors being uncovered were much worse, and far more gruesome than anyone had ever imagined'

'She showed me two eye witness reports that had been circulated among senior staff from the first British and American army officers to enter Belson and Buchenwald. The reports were truly dreadful in it's description of the thousands, upon thousands of decaying bodies that lay heaped in piles around the camp, and the awfulness of the condition of the survivors, so I thought I was prepared for what was to come, Peter'

'We were flown to an airstrip close to Buchenwald, six miles from Weimar, by Dakota, three days after the first troops had crashed their tanks through the gates and barbed wire fences. I had been told that the camp was for Jews, POW's and also German political prisoners'

'What I hadn't been told was that from the vast numbers inside the camp the fittest of the military and civilian prisoners had been made slave workers. I can hardly believe I say that so calmly without screaming out loud. Slaves'

'Peter, these were ordinary people, these were doctors, plumbers, dentist, soldiers, airmen, teachers, priests. Ordinary, many very well-educated people, who for a variety of reasons had become slaves of Nazi Germany and forced to work in the armament factories and quarries close to the camp or be exterminated'

Turning her head slowly from side to side in a gesture of

shame and despair Anna continued, 'Each day these desperate people from France, Russia, Holland, Poland, Norway and of course Germany itself were forced marched out of the camp gates by guards armed with whips, dogs, guns, and into factories or quarries where they were subjected to the most brutal and bestial treatment imaginable'

'Just ordinary people Peter, just like you, just like me' Taking hold of both of his hands Anna stared hard at the man besides her before she said 'This is the awfulness you see, because given a different set of circumstances, it could have been you. Think about it. You have all the potential attributes that would have made you, Peter Adnans, the next Lord of Roxenton, a slave worker in a Nazi dominated England.'

She saw the perplexed look on his face and the questioning eyes as she continued, 'You would have been high on Hitler's list of enemies and considered a definite "Risk to the State and Fuhrer". The son of a Lord, therefore a threat, you mixed with known left-wing agitators who fought against fascism in Spain and of course you are a well known practicing Christian. Oh yes Peter, you would not have lasted long in Nazi Germany, or Nazi Great Britain if Hitler had conquered our country. No, you would have found yourself thrown into prison pretty quickly, stripped and made to wear filthy striped pyjamas, before being kicked and beaten by mindless thugs as you went into your factory'

'And me? Even with an English mother, I would have been a Jew in the eyes of a member of the Gestapo or SS. Well, I would have been stripped naked, my hair shaved off and then dragged, kicking and screaming into a gas chamber, built perhaps somewhere outside of London, along with my father and a hundred other Jews, Methodist or people not sympathetic to their rulers and slowly choked to death by inhaling poison gas pumped through the ceiling.'

Turning around to face the Eiffel Tower again, and the cloudless sky that surrounded it she added 'We were lucky Peter, simply lucky. The survivors of the camp that the girls and I have been treating for the last five weeks had no such luck. Their luck ran out the moment Hitler took control of Germany.'

Anna stopped, putting the palms of both hands over her face she shivered as she took a deep breath. Peter drew closer to her and put a hand on shoulder before saying 'Anna, don't go on, this is so upsetting it is hardly believable that any part of the human race could be part of such cruelty, please stop.'

Rubbing the tears from her eyes with her hands she replied, 'No Peter, No. I feel that I have to talk about it, but at times the sheer dreadfulness overcomes me, but I do want to carry on'

'It's strange that looking at the well manicured gardens in front of us or even back at the café having lunch, one's mind seems to try and blot out the beastliness, as though a limit has been reached, and to cope with the reality the brain shuts off for a moment,' there was a deep frown across her head as she finished saying 'It must be like a safety valve I suppose, but I must tell you everything Peter'

'The SS guards murdered men, women and little children by medical experiments and thousands and thousands of our fellow human beings were butchered like cattle by any means at their disposal, a bullet in the head, hanging, beatings, lethal injections'

'The Jews of all the nations were singled out for a special sort of cruelty by these cowardly brutes, as were the political prisoners of Germany itself'

'Directives from Berlin made a special note that thousands of outspoken German Catholics, Jehovah's Witness, communists, trade unionist, intellectuals and homosexuals were to be murdered should there be the slightest possibility of the camps being overrun and liberated.'

'Only two weeks before the Americans entered the camp, caged inside the barbed wire were over one hundred thousands wretched starving inmates. Sensing defeat as the distant sounds of allied shelling got closer the Nazi's did two things. Those fit enough to be forcibly marched along the roads further into Germany were made to do so, while those to weak to move were left for the camp guards to deal with'

She paused as if to gather strength from deep within herself before starting again 'I was told that the SS men and women subjected those left behind to levels of brutality too loathsome for me to repeat. They obeyed their orders from Berlin and went on a killing spree that defies any one's imagination. Thousands and thousands were butchered like cattle by any means at their disposal'

Smacking the back of one hand into her other Anna angrily said, 'How obscenely cruel it must have been for those poor people Peter, to hear the sound of freedom approaching after perhaps years of imprisonment and torture, only to see their freedom and dignity snatched away at the last moment by their barbarous guards.'

'Before setting off I had warned all of my girls what to expect, but clearly it was much, much worse than could ever be described on a few pieces of paper. As we entered through the camp gates we saw mounds of bodies, some as high as houses, being bulldozed like building rubble into mass graves fifty yards long. The smell was simply extraordinary. We saw battle hardened American troops who had fought across Europe openly crying, while others could do nothing other than vomit at the sight of what they had become witnesses too.'

Peter had not said a word during her story, but sat with his head bent forward, deep into his chest and his eyes fixed into a stare at the ground in front of them. Keeping the same position, he asked 'How Anna? How on earth could such a proud, cultured nation like Germany, a nation that produced Nietzsche, Goethe, Bach. How could they have let this shameful thing happen without trying to stop it?'

'Peter, I am part German. For the sake of my father and his family, as well as myself I had a special reason for wanting to find some good in a nation that had gone so utterly rotten.'

Anna paused for a second, knowing that this part of her story was as important to her as it was to the man she sat next to before saying 'Peter, I believe I succeeded, I believe I found out how, and perhaps why, it happened.'

Anna looked up from the bench seat and at the mass of steel of the Eiffel tower before she took a deep breath and continued her story. 'One of our very sick patients was a German protestant pastor from Munich, called Martin. He was thrown into the camp because he had spoken out against the

Nazi's in a Sunday sermon. One of his own church members had denounced him to the Gestapo, and he was then arrested'

'This chap is as proud and patriotic a German as we are British. During the First World War he was a national hero who had been awarded the country's highest award for gallantry by the Kaiser when he commanded a submarine, and suddenly, twenty years on, only twenty years, the man was an enemy of the German State – a traitor!'

'For the last month of his captivity, he had been hidden by fellow inmates of all nationalities at the camp after a prisoner, working as a clerk in the prison guards' office, had seen a list of Germen men and women that Berlin wanted executed immediately rather than that they should have any chance of being liberated by the advancing Allies.'

'As he became physically stronger we would chat in the evenings. He had no English and was always delighted to be able to talk in German about his experiences and of his hopes for the future'

'One evening I asked him "Martin, how was Hitler and his thugs allowed to stamp out the freedom the Germans had enjoyed. How did you come to love a dictator?"'

Peter Adnans raised his eyebrows as he said, 'What on earth did he say Anna?'

Calmly Anna continued, 'He gave me a brief history of the events in Germany since the end of the First War, and one has to say Peter, they are all horribly linked. He told me that he had entered the church in 1923, which was the same year that Hitler had tried to seize power by force with his Stormtroopers in Munich. A plan that failed and which resulted in him being put on trial and imprisoned'

'It was while in prison that Hitler wrote his book *"Mein Kampf"*, and it was also where he realised that the control of Germany could not be seized by brute force without going through a bloody and long civil war, the result of which would always be in doubt'

'In his prison cell Adolf Hitler perfected his plan to take complete control of Germany legitimately, through the ballot box'

'He also told me that Hitler had help from some unexpected

corners, for instance, I had no idea that the terms of the Treaty of Versailles at the end of the first world war had been so humiliating and had left such a bitter taste to Germans at all levels of society'

'The unsustainable burden of compensation and the loss of substantial areas of land and cities full of German people was a gift to Hitler, and the seeds of fascism were planted, and they grew very quickly'

'The French government in particular wanted the treaty and the financial reparations that were written into it, to weaken the German economy so much that there would be no chance of it ever being able to afford to re-equip their armed forces and attack France ever again'

'When the Germans defaulted on repayments the French and Belgian army, quite legitimately, under the terms of the treaty of Versailles, marched into the Ruhr, the industrial heartland of the Germany, and it wasn't until the Americans arranged a massive loan that reparations could be started again and the French and Belgian troops left the area and returned to their own borders.'

Anna stared at Peter before saying 'Imagine Britain losing a war and Kent being taken over by foreign troops until all the outstanding debts were repaid, one has to say that attitudes would harden and national pride would quickly rally to the person that offered an honourable way forward after such humiliation before the world'

'Another gift to the Nazi's was the Wall Street Crash and the following "Depression" of the early thirties which saw massive unemployment throughout the world, and more especially in Germany. A breeding ground for recruits to the cause of National Socialism had been quickly spotted, and cynically manipulated by very, very clever propaganda.'

Peter shaded his eyes with a hand from the sun that had shifted around Anna before saying 'But hold on Anna, what on earth does all this have to do with the terrible things you saw in one of Hitler's concentration camps?'

'Probably everything Peter, you see past events and decisions created the platform needed to gain total power, and I mean absolute power over the nation. In the elections of 1932 there was something for everyone. Hitler offered the German people full employment, more profits for business, an end to the threat of the communist, the Jewish money lenders and all left-wing parties, but probably the most important promise to the voters was that he would make Germany great again in the eyes of themselves, and of the world. His promises were very seductive, and all sections of society were lured into the trap, until it finally closed'

'Before the elections in speech after speech he said to the people, vote for me and I will rid Germany of every other opposition party. It was then that Martin, and people like him, realised the potential of the monster that had become head of the largest democratically elected party in Germany'

Shaking her head from side to side Anna quietly added 'But it was too late Peter, the grip had tightened, resistance or argument meant beatings, loss of jobs, imprisonment or death.'

'When I first saw Gertrude Kirst I thought she was about forty years old,' she hesitated for a second, recalling the moment when she found out the truth 'in fact she was only twenty two, and had been a prisoner for almost two years after the Gestapo had found leaflets in her room at a university in Munich, urging Germans to resist the Nazi's. Her crime had been distributing the leaflets for a group of young students called the *"The White Rose"*.'

'The group were the children of professional people, and the leaders were a brother, sister and their friend. All three had enthusiastically joined Hitler Youth groups in the early thirties, and all three grew to hate and detest the regime, as they witnessed the cruel brutality of the mindless thugs who had taken over the party'

'Their conscience led them to print leaflets warning the people that Germany would be forever dishonoured unless the youth of the nation rose up and spoke out'

'Their leaflets were pasted to walls, posted to other students and left in prominent buildings. Sadly Peter they were caught by the Gestapo, interrogated and the three of them were beheaded in a prison in Munich.'

'The same woman introduced me to a thirteen year old boy

called Christoph. A boy who sadly died from the effects of starvation the week before I left the prison. He belonged to a loosely organised but large group called *"The Edalweiss Pirates"*

'They were mainly from working class backgrounds, and the group started in Cologne. As the war raged on Cologne itself became the target of almost daily air raids by the Allied air forces. The group took advantage of the chaos around them to hide Jews, German political prisoners and deserters.

'In one cruel reprisal, the Gestapo rounded up dozens of people, some activists, some not, and as an example to the ordinary citizens of the city, they erected a long scaffold in a busy street. With great ceremony, the Gestapo hung thirteen men, women and children, six of them teenage boys. German teenage boys.'

Anna sighed deeply and continued 'A year after John was killed I remember that on my first walk along the cliffs from St Ives to Zennor I thought what a cruel irony it was that I was able to enjoy the beauty of the plants and flowers around me, and I marvelled at their ability to grow, to survive the onslaught of the ferocious storms of the winter'

'It was a strange coincidence that both of those resistance groups choose the white rose and the edelweiss, such hardy, dogged plants, as symbols of their refusal to lie down and be trampled on, to defy the brutish behaviour of the Gestapo thugs and cling on, to survive until the sun started to shine again.'

They both sat back on the park bench, looking over the gardens, silent for a moment, until Peter said 'To be honest Anna, my belief is that too many Germans remained silent, to many looked the other way. I have to say that I do not believe for one moment that we in Britain would have allowed the same dreadful crimes to have been committed against other human beings.'

Anna's hands lay on her lap, and she nervously twiddle with her thumbs as she thought about his statement, while at the same time thinking back over the past five weeks at Buchenwald. Five weeks that had been the most disturbing of her young life.   Several minutes went by until she finally said, 'I only wish I could be so sure Peter.'

Taking a deep breath followed by a long and sad sigh, she continued, 'I'm a bit muddled up inside my head at the moment Peter, and I don't seem able to make any sensible comment. What I can say is that what I was witness to in the camp is a classic symptom of every nasty fascist regime that takes over people's lives'

'What happened in Germany is the very reason that John McCloud and so many others went to Spain in 1936. They travelled in their thousands from around the world to fight against fascism and to try and stop the sort of brutish behaviour my girls and I saw at Buckenwald, and you were faced with when the Nazi officer ordered you and the other French doctor to march out of Dunkirk, or be shot.'

After another few moments of silence Anna smiled for the first time during their conversation and added, 'Peter, perhaps you are right. Perhaps in Britain, or any country where freedom of speech is part of the fabric of it's history, men like John, my father, you, and women like my Cornish friend Mabena, Gail Moore, and just perhaps me, well we would certainly make it bloody hard for a Nazi party, or anything similar to gain a foothold. Well, I most certainly hope so.'

Anna looped her arm through his as she said 'You have been a truly good friend to me through all this nightmare Peter, and I know you understand when I say that I still ache inside at the thought that John is not here with us. The funny thing is I honestly thought his memory would fade away with the years, but the fact is he still seems larger than life itself to me.'

They sat for some time saying nothing until Peter Adnans nudged her gently and said, 'What do you say to trying to find that gloriously rowdy bistro that John took us to, back in 1940?'

The brightest of smiles spread over Anna's face as she blurted out wildly 'Yes! Brilliant Peter, Bistro Corsaire!' Her features went from joy to puzzlement as she screwed up her eyes before suddenly shouting 'Tino Sablon! Tino Sablon, that was the chap that owned it, yes Peter, what a wonderful idea, thank you!'

In that moment, as he looked at Anna, he thought about the

surgeon he had come to admire and like so much, before he was killed. With a smile, he remembered John almost shouting to him 'It's her eyes Peter, bloody hell man, have you ever seen such passion and sparkle, such strength in a lass?'

He hadn't seen the sparkle for some time, but it was back, and he was pleased with himself that his suggestion had been the trigger that had caused it.

Standing up, and still arm in arm, they started to walk back to their hotel as Anna said 'So you're going to Brussels tomorrow?'

'Yes Anna. I've a meeting in the morning and in the afternoon I am going to start my search for Madeline, and I must say I have a terrible case of the tummy wobbles!'

'Oh, and I have one last piece of information Matron Jack, which I do believe will come as quiet a shock to you. Now then my dear, our good Mary Atkins has told me that on our return to England we will both be discharged from the army!'

Anna stopped dead in her tracks and stared open mouthed before saying, 'Discharged from the army? Oh my God Peter, civilians again. Civilians! So, at long last our war is really over. Peter, I can't believe it!'

They carried on walking for a few steps before she stopped again and added 'Bloody hell Peter, so what next?'

Return to Cornwall

Zennor, 20th September 1945

'Simon nevur cums un til tha evenins, nevur thease daays. Praps un a Sundaay, bet not durin tha waak.'

Anna stood with her back to the sea, and the window rocks of Zennor Head; looking towards St Ives along the coast, and at the rich autumn purples of the heather that carpeted the cliffs in front of her.

'Ee's changed Anna.Tis not tha same Simon Tremayne thet us dud gnaw fore tha war. Is mothur want speak ta um, bet I gnaw tha oald rascal ov a fathur doos snake ta ess owse, Howlsedhes just ta get es advice lik!'

'All ee doos es paint. Strange paintins ov tha sea, coast an ills. Them's strange, bet I likes em. Them calls it modun paintins, bet I dun think tis. I think tis as oald as them what dragged tha stones ta Chysauster, cause when I waas a yun chield I crawled unta a room them made thousands of yers back an saw paintins un tha rocks zackly lik ee doos'

Mabena fell silent as she studied Anna's back and thought 'Yum sufferin maid, sufferin inside so that I caan feel your pain frum ere.'

Turning to face a sea that was pounding the coast below Anna said softly, 'I've spoken to Simon on the telephone.You are right, he has changed, and I do like the change. He's a stronger person. He had a tough war Mabena, and it's the war that made him stronger,' smiling, and with raised eyebrows she added 'his mother still blames everything on me of course!'

The smile evaporated as she sat down and gently gripped Mabena's forearm with a hand before patting it and saying 'I know I've hurt Simon, and I will never forgive myself for that, but it was during the weeks that I spent nursing the prisoners at Buckenwald that I knew for sure I couldn't marry him. Him or marry anyone else in this world for that matter. So, I wrote to him at his home from the camp and explained to him why.'

Frowning, the Cornish woman looked hard at her before saying 'Anna, seems ta me tha tis tu final lik. Simon's not a bad man, an I think un truth, ee did gave up a lot fur ee maid, an do ee not think tis ta quick, ta quick ta decide lik, aftur all ee as both bin through?'

Anna began to reply but both women fell silent, their attention taken by the sound of a thunderous wave as it crashed into Pendour Cove and echoed off of Horseback Zawn below. They watched the wild froth of water fall back, dragging tons of smooth pebbles that had once been part of the cliff face, noisily back into the sea.

After the wave had subsided Anna started again 'Just a moment ago you said, "in truth" Mabena. Well the absolute truth for me is that I made a terrible mistake in thinking that I could love Simon when in truth,' Anna hesitated for a moment, unsure, but quickly certain as she continued 'in truth I never loved him, what I tried to do was to filter Simon through my head, while I tried to make him John McCloud, and that is the sad, sad truth.'

Looking at Mabena she smiled, shook her head and chuckled before saying 'I can remember the moment so clearly when the doubts began inside me. Doubts that meant I could never marry Simon. It was in my office at the airbase and after Gail Moore had told me about the white American officers that were going to kill Spencer'

'Sat alone, I was so enraged, but felt so utterly useless until….' Anna stopped and looked deep into the eyes of the Cornish woman before starting again 'Well, it was as though John suddenly came to life again. It's true Mabena. I felt a sudden inner strength and his presence'

'It wasn't frightening or sinister, it wasn't miraculous or earth shattering, no shinning shafts of light from the sky, but I suddenly felt that his crusades had become my crusades and his conscience mine'

'I felt suddenly stronger and absolutely determined to use every possible avenue to help Spencer, who's only crimes were that he had a black skin and a gentle, caring heart.'

Throughout the conversation neither woman had turned away from each other and when Mabena asked her 'Did ee tell Simon thaat?'

Anna looked away and silently shook her head, before saying 'No. No, I couldn't. It would have hurt him too much. I told him that there was no other man involved and that the prospect of peace had become as frightening as the prospect of war had been in 1939, in fact more so'

'When I telephoned him I also told him from my heart how important he had been to me, and also from my heart I told him that I could not be the wife he wanted, and that my future would take me away from England for several years.'

A look of surprise came to Mabena and it was her turn to put a hand on her friend's arm as she said 'So yum gwain way agin. Tis strange' There was a halting struggle for the words until she started again, 'Tis strange, cause I feels I hav gnawed ee forevur lik Anna, an I just see ee ere, livin your life un Cornwall, not sum bleedy foreign place.'

Nodding, Anna spoke quietly, in the same hesitant way as her friend 'I know, and perhaps, no, not perhaps, "Yes", I did think that I would finish the war and settle down here, but I simple can't. Honestly Mabena, not now, not yet, I seem to have another road to go down before I come back'

'Something, someone is taking me down a path that inside I know I have to go along. I only wish I knew for what reason or for how long and frankly, I don't, but I'm not afraid or unhappy by that.'

'I've often mentioned Peter Adnans to you, and especially when I found out that he was alive, when everyone thought that he had been killed in France.'

'Thaat's tha son ov tha Lord ov summat un Scotland?'

'Yes, that right,' Anna said, 'well the poor dear man fell hopelessly in love with a young Belgian girl who helped him to escape from France and into Spain over several months during 1942'

'It was a love shared by both, but the saddest thing about this love story is that only one of the lovers knew the real name of the other! The bizarre and terribly cruel circumstances that surrounded their brief relationship meant that he knew her only by the false name of Madeleine Guimard, a charade played out in case he was ever captured and tortured by the Gestapo, and forced into disclosing her real identity.'

'When Peter and I met in Paris, three, no four months ago, he told me that he was going to Brussels to find his Madeleine Guimard. It took him over a month before he found both of her parents and sadly the awful truth emerged that she been captured by the French Vichy police in 1944 and handed over to the Gestapo'

'One can guess how the poor girl must have suffered, but she never betrayed any of her friends in the resistance and she was eventually sent to Ravensbruck concentration camp.'

'Her parents told Peter that Dominique, her real name of course, had been murdered at the camp early this year, only months before the end of the war,' Anna saw that Mabena had turned away from her and was sitting with a hand hiding her eyes while tears rolled down her cheeks, and in a lighter tone she added 'I saw Peter at my parent's home only a couple of weeks ago and to my complete surprise not only was he was positively enthusiastic about the future, he was looking forward to it'

'My mother and I had been a little apprehensive after Peter had accepted an invitation to have dinner with us because of my dad's politics, but they hit it off famously, possibly aided by a couple of large gins, mind you!'

'It was amazing, that without any prompting, Peter told us that he had become close friends with Charles and Yves Besson, Dominique's parents and that a number of letters had been handed to them by a German girl who had been a prisoner with their daughter in Ravensbruck. Among the letters was one addressed to Peter.'

'The next day, in Paris, he told me that in it she had written of her love for him and her certain knowledge of his love for her. A love that had given her special strength when she needed it, and that although she doubted that they would meet again, she hoped he would remember the days when they walked in the sand dunes of the Atlantic coast and watched the Lammergeier's flying high above them in the Pyrenean mountains.'

'You see the letter was the link. It was the bridge between dream and reality. For me it was a set of photographs of John and myself at Pont-Aven, in Brittany. Peter had been given a picture of Dominique by her parents. For him it was the letter that was all he needed to keep alive the brief period of happiness that will never fade, and never be forgotten.'

Anna put her arm around Mabena's shoulders 'Come on, please. No more tears. There have had too many over the years. Both Peter and I have our memories, Simon has his, and we all have years, and years in front of us.'

Smiling, Mabena wiped the tears from her eyes and said, 'Terry an me hav bin lucky, our boays came through tha war an thems still live, thank goodness, an yah I gnaw ee still as yewr lives un front ov ee, bet wur will ee bey gwain aftur Zennor?'

Standing up Anna nodded in the direction of the sea saying 'Across the ocean Mabena, just like thousands, and thousands of Cornish men and women have been doing for thousands and thousands of years. Across the ocean and to who knows where or what, well?'

Sitting next to her friend again she added 'Dominique's father and mother help run a missionary school in the Belgian Congo. Peter told me that he could not possibly settle into life as a surgeon or consultant here immediately, and after being asked by the Bessons, he has agreed to go to the Congo and set up a new hospital for them, and I have agreed to go with him as his assistant, which is quite an exciting prospect.'

Shaking her head slowly from side to side and smiling broadly Mabena said 'I doos envy ee Anna, an yum bin lik a breath ov fresh air un my life, un no mistake.'

It was Anna's turn to shake her head and smile in the same

way as she said 'For me its been this place, where we are standing now and along the coast, this has been my breath of fresh air Mabena, and the truth is, it was you that helped me to understand it, and take it all in, thank you.'

Stepping over the granite style that marked the start of the lane to Zennor and past the coast guard hut, the two friends walked and talked about the past and the future until Anna stopped still, and cocking her head to one side, saying 'Now that's a familiar sound!'

The sound got louder until around the corner raced Sterenn, barking and moving as though the Hare was chasing him. The dog slid to an excited halt in front of Anna who at the same time as patting his bouncing head shouted above the noise of his barking 'Sterenn, I wondered if you would turn up!'

Together they wondered up the gradual incline of the lane with Anna stopping to look into the hedgerows and pastures of autumn landscape. 'Wild Thyme, Rock Samphire, Travellers Joy, Teasel, Sneezewort' Laughing as she finished she added 'Thanks to a wonderful teacher I am a walking encyclopaedia of Cornish plant life!'

With a faint hint of a smile the plant guru replied 'Tis a sad month Septembur, ee can see tha countryside crying ta get ta sleep, fore they winds an rain starts rollin in an winter settles.'

Mabena stopped by a wooden five-barred gate and motioned with her hand to Anna to stand next to her before saying, 'Err Anna, now look there un that mudded ditch. I ant sin them fur yeers, them bey Pennyroyals. I loves they lilac flowers, an twill cure most ails.'

'Another plant to be added to my encyclopaedia!', and then looking at her watch Anna said, 'It's almost two o'clock, I suppose Terry will have closed the pub by the time we get back?'

As they set off on the final stretch of lane before it opened up and the village appeared Mabena replied, 'He'll av closed haf our baack. Tis propur funny Anna, an I smiles bout 'em. Cornwall has gone rite back ta how twas fur war started! Tis as quiet as ell, thank God!'

'Wel, not how twas, tha people has changed, bet tha season's ant. No more Yanks, no more ov our own soldiers an sailors, maid. Cornwall is back tu ees age awld struggle agaain!'

Anna stopped before asking 'What was it like here before the D-Day landings Mabena?'

'Propur maze maid, propur maze. Ee could sense summat were up lik twards middle ov May. All tha boays cummin unta pub waas nervous, bet gentle as well. All tha regulars, Yanks an our own boays, seemed ta make wen last visit, sensing them waas close to gwain, lik.'

'That lovely chap, friend ov yours, tha Irishman frum America, ee came un an Anna, as he waas gwain out tha pub ee suddenly took hold oa me hand an said "Goodbye Mabena, thanks fur your kindness". Twas tha look un is eyes that said it waas final lik'

'I do gnaw that tha American boays had a terrible time when them landed un France, an a lot ov em waas killed. I often wondurs what happened ta em, ee ad such lovely green eyes?'

Grabbing her friends arm Anna started walking forward and at the same time saying, 'Well I have some very good news for you, in fact two bits of very good news! The first is that Patrick Flynn and his men landed on Utah beach and despite a great many of the boys being killed, he got through without being hurt and I did meet him at my casualty clearing centre after Caen fell, in fact we had a glass of wine together in a bar'

'And the other piece of good news is that I have been in touch with him by letter only a few weeks ago, because he, his wife and myself are the God parents to Gail and Spencer's bouncing baby boy!'

Stood by the steps leading to St Senara's Church, the Cornish woman smiled broadly before saying 'Ansum, propur ansum Anna. Terry will bey plaised as punch when I tells em'

'Twas a strange wen when they all left like Anna. I think twas tha laast week un May, fore tha landings. Us ad just ad tha dray un weth tha beer frum St Austell brewers whan Arthur Wilky rang frum St Ives, an all ee could say waas "Mabena maid, them all bleedy gone, just bleedy gone!". I said ta em "What bee talkin bout Arthur?"

'All ee could saay waas "They Yanks, an all our boays av gone, disappeared, place is bleedy deserted maid". An twas rite nuff Anna,' nodding at the Church she added 'them ad gone, all of em, twas bleedy quiet as that graveyard.'

'Course us did'nt gnaw what waas happenin, did us. As days went un rumours went round bout they ships an tha lik un Falmouth harbour an hidin long they rivur banks, but was'nt til tha 6th ov June that us did ear un tha wireless bout tha landins.'

'Anna I'm propur pleased bout Gail an they tew American boays, an ov course tha new babe. Whaat's em called tha boay?'

Walking the final yards across the cobbled courtyard to the closed door of the Tinners Arms, Anna looked at Mabena and laughing said 'John, of course, you see, I'm surrounded by them!'

Before going inside the pub Anna bent down and ruffled Sterenn's thick coat of fur around his neck before saying 'Bye, bye for a while Star. Thank you for your company!'

In the peaty and herb smell of Mabena's sitting room above the bar of the pub Anna sat in her usual chair while her friend put a plate of saffron cakes in front of her, and poured tea into her cup.'I'm sorry I won't see Terry or Lowena, before I go, but I have left a present for Lowena.'

'Why don't ee stay tha night maid?'

'You know I would like too, but I really don't want to bump into Simon, it just wouldn't be fair, so I've booked myself into a guest house in St Ives, and in a minute, I want to go down to Cape Cornwall before the light goes.'

On the lane above the Tinners the two friends gave each other a farewell hug before Anna started the motorcycle and Mabena shouted above the engine noise,

'Yew av a lot ov friends err Anna, now don ee go forgettin thaat, an yew take care now, I'm gona miss ee maid, an that bay tha truth.'

Pulling the collar of her long leather riding coat apart, Anna put two fingers down the neck of her cotton blouse and pulled up a silver chain with the Celtic cross attached to it that Mabena had given her two years before. Dangling the gift in front of her friend she shouted back, 'I'm going to miss you to, but look, I've worn this through mortar attacks, bombings, shelling and sniper fire and I have every intention of wearing it the next time I ask Terry for a drink! Give him my love, and you take care as well!'

With a last wave, she let out the clutch of the Ariel and set off with a roar towards the toe of the Cornwall. Following the narrow road that led up the hill and out of the village, Anna stopped at the top of it and turned around on the seat of the motorcycle to look back at Mabena, returning her farewell wave and at the same time looking at the village that had come to mean so much to her.

The 500cc motorcycle purred along the narrow road with its unforgiving granite boulder hedge rows and sudden sharp corners, that took Anna and her motorcycle through the middle of farms where chickens, pigs and sheep wondered casually in front of her, with the confidence of ownership, until the houses of St Just appeared in the distance.

Going through the square of the village she took the turning that took her out towards the headland and Cape Cornwall where she stopped the machine and sat looking towards Sennen Cove and the rocks offshore of Land's End for ten minutes before saying aloud 'Beautiful, absolutely beautiful! Now then, one more thing I would like to do, before the light goes.'

Towednack Church, 20th September 1945

Despite every effort to drop the metal latch quietly the heavy oak door seemed designed to punish latecomers as it closed noisily and echoes from her entrance bounced around the unlit shadowy interior, and timber rafters of the old church, causing the new visitor to feel uneasy for a second until her own voice joined the echoes as she reassuringly said loudly, 'Good evening church, I'm ever so pleased your door is always open.'

Anna went in and turned towards the main alter where she sat down in Matthew's pew and continued speaking 'Well now, as you can see I am back again! Yes, I survived the war, and I am pleased about that now, even though in some ways I feel guilty because I did.'

She looked around the empty church. Outside the sun had gone below the hills that surrounded the ancient building and only the last minutes of dusk remained, giving little light to the grey stone walls and oak wood work of the darkening interior.

Getting up, she walked to the black iron pricket stand, at the back of the building and put money into the collecting box, before picking up a bundle of candles, pushing each one onto a spike on the lower circular iron wheel. Anna then light a match, and holding it to the wick of a candle she then used it as a taper for the rest.

Folding her arms in front of herself she stepped back from the warm glow of the bees wax candles and looked around the church again before saying, 'That's better, everything looks brighter, warmer, less scary, and they do smell so nice.'

Looking at the dancing flames her thoughts went back over the past years for a moment before she sighed deeply and quietly uttered 'Oh dear, what a horrible time we all had. What I should do is dedicate each candle to a particular person or group, and I will try.'

Anna turned a candle in the pricket stand saying, 'I don't know what his name was but this one is for the little boy who was killed on the road side in Belgium and his mother, I still have bad dreams about you little one, and it's also for all the other refugees that died'

'I'm going to dedicate two candles for my friends and colleagues that died when the Châteaux near Ganappe was shelled and for all the other nurses killed in action'

'Another two for all the men and women in the navy, the army and airforces who will not be going home to family or friends'

'Oh, two more, a single candle for the young girl who was burnt to death in the Plymouth blitz, the other for all the people and children who were killed in their homes and in shelters.'

Anna stopped and turned around before she spoke directly to the brass cross above the granite alter, 'I still don't think I believe in the person this house was built for. But I'm so very pleased your church is here to listen to me again, you see when I came here the first time I was so full of sadness I really did not want to survive, now I'm thankful that I did. Thankful I am able to do this.'

Turning the wheel of burning candles she touched one and started to talk again, 'You are for the sad, sad people in the concentration camps, my own relations, murdered only because of their religion, I want one on it's own for the Germans who's conscience turned them against Hitler, and they were killed because of it, and another for Dominique, Peter's love, and other members of the resistance movements.'

'And I can't forget the people that survived can I, perhaps you even had a hand in helping them! My wonderful mum and dad and Mary Atkins. Louise Bridoux who wrote to me, happy that her husband had survived the war and was now home with her and their children and that she was pregnant again!'

'Gail, Spencer and their new baby, John. Tino Sablon. He owns a bistro in Paris and was a great friend of John's. He's a huge man, but when I told him that John had been killed he was completely overcome with grief, and wept uncontrollably like a baby, the poor man.'

She stopped turning the wheel for a moment and took out three candles from the lower wheel and put them onto the top one of the carousel, before saying, 'These are my own special people, people I think about each and every day. Miriam, whose smile still makes me smile! John, whose face I see each morning I wake up, and the last one is for our baby.'

Walking the few steps back to the front pew Anna sat down again, before leaning forward and resting her elbows on the prayer book rail 'I'm not praying to you, don't think that. I just want to talk'

'Six years is a long time you know to be at war. I was twenty-three when it started and next year I will be thirty.' She sat back and wiped her tears away before getting quickly up and returning to the wheels of burning candles.

'I want to put another candle up here on the top wheel, and it's for Simon.' Going back to her seat she paused for a moment before saying, 'I had to light a candle for Simon. You see he and I were going to get married here in your church, but I simply couldn't go ahead with it'

'I know that I can't, but not completely sure of the reasons why if I'm honest, and the guilt I feel because of the hurt I know I have caused him will never leave me. If you can please look after him, I do know he visits you here.'

Sitting silently for a while Anna then got up and walked slowly up the aisle to the open message book, resting as usual against a supporting roof pillar on its oak table.

She turned back several pages. Most of the hand-written comments were of glad tidings, mother's, lovers, wives, all giving thanks to their anonymous helpers for their prayers and support, happy to announce that loved one's had returned home safely.

Some were less happy, as the hope of reunion that had burnt like bright candle flames, had been extinguished by impersonal buff coloured envelopes that confirmed a death, and the truth of separation for ever.

Standing above the book Anna looked towards the granite alter and said aloud 'Even the sad messages thanked the strangers that had supported them, their loss made lighter by the strength of others,' she shook her head twice before finishing 'You really are a puzzle. A puzzle, but without question or doubt, a comfort.'

Walking up the aisle on the ancient flag stones until she reached the door of the church Anna turned around before saying 'Thank you for listening to me over the past few years, I will be back, not sure when, but I will be back.'

Smiling, she added 'And of course I know you will still be here!'

Anna closed the heavy oak door and listened as the sound of the iron handle slipping into the latch echoed inside the church, before she turned and walked towards the south gate.

Starting the motorcycle, she sat on the leather seat and took one last look at the place of worship and shelter, now silhouetted against a clear night sky, with the warm yellow light of the candles she had lit shining through the stained glass windows.

She felt somehow more contented with herself, and pleased

she had been able to visit her moorland sanctuary.

St Ives, 20*th* September 1945

In the dimpsey twilight Anna stopped at the top of Trelyon Avenue as the view of St Ives Bay opened up to her. She turned off the engine of her motorcycle and pulled the machine back onto its stand before walking to a wall, and looking down onto the North Cornish town.

The blackout regulations had been lifted and for the first time she saw the town with electric lights burning in homes, hotels, shops, and lighting the roads and pavements.

As always, the freshness of the sea air she breathed in excited Anna and despite an uneasiness that travelled with her she smiled as she re-started the bike and headed to the Carrick guest house on Back Road West, behind Porthmeor Beach.

Mrs Watkiss, the owner of the guest house greeted her warmly, and showed Anna her room at the top of the terraced house, before giving her a front door key, and leaving her to walk into the town to a fish and chip shop.

It was dark as she headed down the cobbled streets, lit in yellowed patches by lamps fastened half way up the side of a house, or on top of an ornate grey iron lamppost.

Walking past the Sloop Inn Anna stopped and looked in through the window that overlooked the harbour. She could see that the bar was full mostly of men, some playing darts while others sat around two tables playing euchre. One of the men sat down was Reg Barbary, the smoke from his pipe adding to the think fog of cigarettes and other pipe smokers.

Anna walked on, pleased that the lifeboat coxswain was still part of the jig saw puzzle of her life, and she smiled as she remembered being with him the day the Americans arrived to shatter the quiet of a Sunday, and of Cornwall for ever.

Ordering cod and chips, she watched both being put into separate pans of boiling lard and waited with others in the heat of the chip shop until nodding at the woman behind the hot frying range when asked if she wanted salt and vinegar before her order was scooped onto a sheet of greaseproof paper and wrapped in old pages of the *"St Ives Times"*.

Walking up Bunkers Hill with a bag of fish and chips she walked into Porthmeor Square where she heard the reassuring sound of waves breaking ahead. Anna quickened her pace until she reached the sea wall above the Porthmeor beach. Letting the gentle breeze flow past her, she stood still for a minute peering into the sea, letting her eyes adjust to the darkness.

Leaning against the sea wall, Anna rested her dinner on it, before unwrapping the newspaper cover and starting to eat the meal with her fingers.

The tide was on the way out, the lines of frothy surf leaving wide streaks of white in broad bands along the edge of the sand as it tumbled backwards into the black water.

She was tired. 'It's been a long day, a long but good day' she thought to herself as she returned to her room, falling asleep instantly as her head touched the white linen pillow case.

St Ives, 21st September 1945

Anna lay motionless in her bed, listening, hardly daring to move, hardly daring to breathe even in case the sound attracted other human noises, and the tranquillity of the moment would be lost.

On the slate roof above her bedroom she heard the squawking and sliding of seagulls, but the noise that she did not want to lose to other people was of the gentle surf breaking and reaching onto Porthmeor Beach.

The sound of the waves rushing up the beach was like the gentle breathing of a sleeping giant as the water rushed towards the land and then fell back to the sea again, dragging sand and pebbles with it.

She smiled as she realised that her own breathing was now in sync with the rise and fall of water. She breathed in as it started the journey up the beach until her lungs were full and she held the air inside until the dragging sound allowed her to expel the air gently and noiselessly.

Cosy, under a white cotton sheet and two woollen blankets,

Anna's eyes were closed, and her hands were intertwined, laying flat over her naval. After a last deep breath, she smiled before somewhere in the house a door slammed, and the magic moments were stolen.

Glancing at her watch she said softly 'Right Miss Jack time to get out of your pit, as Gail Moore would say, it's nearly seven. A quick piece of toast, a cup of tea and away girl!'

Stepping into the morning sunshine Anna fastened her bag to the black metal carrier that rested over the rear mudguard. She wanted to leave now. Leave St Ives, leave Cornwall, leave England. There were many things she wanted to do, suddenly she was impatient to do them.

She pulled the wooden toggles through the web loops on her leather riding coat, adjusted the flying helmet she always wore, after tucking in her black hair, and put her motorcycle goggles over the peak of the helmet, before pulling on the thick leather gloves and bringing the machine to a noisy start.

Waving goodbye to Mrs Watkiss who watched her from a window, she let out the clutch and followed the shadow of the terrace of houses until the sudden deep blue colour of the sea pounced on her as she rounded the corner and Porthmeor beach came into full view.

Anna stopped at the same spot where the night before she had dined off the sea wall table, and pulled the motorbike back onto its stand, letting the engine idle.

Putting her elbows on the wall she rested her chin on her hands as she looked out to sea, knowing she would not be back for a long time.

There was a gentle breeze and the tide was high, leaving a narrow band of sand around the bay for the waves to finish their dash for the land, and the beach seemed empty of people as she looked from Carrick rocks, back towards St Nicholas Chapel on the island.

As she was about to finish her sweep of the beach with her eyes she noticed just one person sat on a wooden folding chair, the legs piling into the soft sand, giving the solitary man a lop sided, uneven look as he faced the rising sea.

In front of him was a small canvas locked onto an easel and he was adding colour to the bleach white surface from a pallet, carefully balanced on a leg.

Anna knew immediately that the man was Simon. She felt the colour drain from her face, she stared speechless, unable to move, deep in thought until tears moved slowly down her cheeks.

Simon frowned, it was the sound of the engine that made him take his eyes away from the canvas, and the sea. A familiar noise, rising above the sound of the waves in front of him. He stood up, pallet in one hand, brush in the other, and turned around towards the town cemetery and Barnoon chapel, overlooking the sea.

The frown disappeared as he smiled to himself and turning back to the sea again he settled back onto the folding wood chair that sank another half inch into the soft sand as he sat down.

The smile continued as he looked at the blue and green water in front of him and he tenderly remembered Anna, while he listened to the Ariel Red Hunter thunder up Porthmeor Hill, hidden by the high churchyard wall.

THE END

Epilogue

Munich, May 1947

A young German student looked hard at the lecturer that stood in front of him
before asking his question 'Sir, How did it happen?'

The student's question to Martin Niemoeller, who Anna Jack had met in Buchenwald, had been asked many times before since his return to the University in 1945, after years in the concentration camps as a German political prisoner.

Each time he answered it with the same feeling of guilt and doubt. Looking past the student he gazed out of the open window, onto the green lawns and trees of the University before saying, 'I would like to quote you something that I wrote for a church sermon in1942'

'First they came for the communists, but I was not a Communist, so I did not
speak out.
Then they came for the Socialists and the Trade Unionist, but I was neither, so I
did not speak out.
Then they came for the Jews, but I was not a Jew so I did not speak out.
And when they came for me; there was no one left to speak out for me.'

Printed in Germany
by Amazon Distribution
GmbH, Leipzig